PRAISE FOR THE FIRST LIGHT SERIES

The Boat House Café
First Place, 20th-Century Fiction
Goethe Award for Historical Fiction

"**A triumphant tale of love, family and courage**....In this beautiful, lyrical novel, Linda Cardillo creates a fierce, strong-willed heroine, unafraid of hard work, solitude, or the judgment of her fellow islanders." – Judith Arnold, *USA Today* Bestselling Author

"Ultimately, this **beautifully written, passionate, page-turning adventure** of a blended family history and a **romance of grand proportions** will have readers yearning to continue the series with *The Uneven Road* and *Island Legacy*." – Chanticleer Book Reviews

"*The Boat House Café* ...is a compelling opening in a series, **a novel with powerful themes, a gripping narrative style, and an ingenious plot structure that makes it a work of great entertainment.**" – Ruffina Oserio, *Readers' Favorite*

The Uneven Road
2018 The BookLife Prize
Semi-Finalist

"**A measured, riveting tale**, written in a confident, impassioned voice." – *Kirkus Reviews*

"*The Uneven Road* is a **sophisticated coming-of-age novel...written with verve and intelligence.** Cardillo carefully constructs *The Uneven Road* with rich characterizations, diverging and interlocking plot elements, and fine attention to detail that explores family dynamics and the search for individual identity." – Chanticleer Book Reviews

Island Legacy
"**A tender, spirited family tale** to complete a warm, earnest series."
– *Kirkus Reviews*

"Cardillo's poignant novel is **a winding, intriguing story of relatable suffering**–the sorrow of losing loved ones, traversing long distances to visit those dear to us, and the pain (and growth) that arises through profound life changes." – The BookLife Prize

"...**a beautiful riveting journey of love, yesteryear, intrigue, disaster and redemption**...written in a lyrical tone with exquisite descriptions of Martha's Vineyard." – Chick Lit Café

"... **a profound connection** to nature and the land, a melding of cultures, the grief of loss, reconciling the past, and the power of love in its many forms." – Amazon 5-star review

A Place of Refuge

ALSO BY LINDA CARDILLO

Fiction

Love That Moves the Sun

The Boat House Café

The Uneven Road

Island Legacy

Catriona's Vow

Dancing on Sunday Afternoons

Across the Table

Italian Tales

A Mother's Heart

The Smallest Christmas Tree

Cookbook

Come Sit at My Table

A Place of Refuge

Book Four of First Light

Linda Cardillo

Bellastoria Press

BELLASTORIA PRESS
www.bellastoriapress.com
P.O. Box 60341
Longmeadow, Massachusetts 01116

For Daisy

PROLOGUE

SEPTEMBER 19, 1970

S he remembers nothing about the accident. Not the rain-slicked road that sent the oncoming car into a skid. Not *The Boston Globe* delivery truck driver who pulled her from the wreckage. Not the nurse on her way to work who stayed with her until the ambulance came.

She only remembers dying.

1971

IZZY

CHAPTER ONE

FEBRUARY 15

Caleb's birth pushed her over the edge.

It had been an occasion of great joy for her family—the first grandchild—after a year of both challenge and hope. First, the recurrence of her mother's lung cancer, the search for a bone marrow donor that resulted in a match with Josiah and a successful transplant, and then Izzy's accident.

She had been back on Chappaquiddick Island at her parents' home in Cove Meadow for nearly three months, her spirit crushed as thoroughly as the mangled roof of the Mustang that had fractured her skull. Izzy was dismayed that she could not share in the happiness filling the house. She felt a profound isolation that with shame she also recognized as selfishness. She envied her brother, Josiah, and his wife, Grace, and their experience of becoming parents. She believed that parenthood would now be something she'd never know.

The depression that had engulfed her since waking to life after the accident had been tolerable until Caleb's birth. But now she found herself in almost physical pain whenever she spent time in the presence of the baby. She was afraid to hold him. She spent her days walking the beach when the weather was anything less than a gale. Even in the rain or snow, she paced up and down below the house, thrusting her cane into the hard-packed sand at the water's edge.

In the past, of course, winter weather would have found her holed up by the stove, a thick pair of socks covering her always frozen feet, a mug of hot chocolate in her hand, and a book in her lap.

But she hadn't picked up a book since the day in the hospital when Jo had brought her a stack of nineteenth-century novels to read. She had reached for them eagerly and opened the first one, Melville's *Typee*. But within minutes, she realized that she couldn't remember the sentence she'd just read.

At first she thought it was fatigue. After all, she'd fractured her skull; she had constant headaches. Reading had always soothed her, taken her away. But not anymore.

She tried to ignore her fears, to deny them. But it soon became apparent that it wasn't only the words she read that she couldn't remember.

It was Josiah who had noticed the change in her first: the blank expression, the confusion, the dismay that even a brief conversation was beyond her ability to remember.

The neurologist had explained it succinctly. When she had died, however briefly after the accident, a part of her brain had died as well.

There was no point in returning to Harvard to finish the doctorate she had begun with such promise the year before. She couldn't even manage the paperwork to withdraw and had to depend on Josiah to fill out the form for her.

She was released from the hospital after a week, and Josiah and her father brought her home to Cove Meadow, where her mother was recuperating from the bone marrow transplant. Izzy spent the next three months reaching what she thought was a reluctant acceptance of her limitations—until Caleb had been born, just before Christmas.

Now, she recognized how fragile her acceptance had been and how she'd worn it as a mask, trying not to inflict the rest of the family with her despair.

It was while on one of her solitary walks below the Wampanoag Burial Ground that she was interrupted by a whirlwind in a sheepskin coat with dark curls flying around her face in the wind. Maria Belli, her college and then grad school roommate, was calling her name as she approached along the shore. Maria had been out of the country since August, doing a semester in Germany at the Bundestag as part of her masters in government at Harvard's JFK School of Government. She hadn't seen Izzy since before the accident, although she'd sent first a telegram and then postcards every week. Izzy hadn't answered any of them.

Izzy stood frozen, unable to move toward Maria and afraid of what Maria would see as soon as she got close. The scar on Izzy's forehead was no longer raw and covered almost entirely by her own curls. That had been one of the things that had bonded Izzy and Maria when they'd been freshmen at Smith, their naturally curly, impossible-to-control hair. But it wasn't the scar that Izzy wanted to hide. It was the emptiness. The sense of not being Izzy anymore that pervaded her.

Maria reached her with open arms and embraced her. Izzy stiffened, unable to hug Maria back. Maria took a step away and looked at her.

"I'm here, Izzy. I'm not letting go, and I'm not going to be pushed away. Now, we can walk some more on the beach or we can go into Edgartown for some coffee, but I want to know what's going on."

Izzy finally found her voice. "Did my parents ask you to come?"

Maria tucked her arm into Izzy's and started to walk.

"I'd like to tell you that it was the ability I inherited from my *Strega Nonna*—my great-grandmother, the witch—that enlightened me about your need for me. But, in fact, it was Grace."

"I've been trying so hard not to burden them with my sadness, but I guess I've failed."

"They don't see you as a burden, Izzy. They love you, but they don't know how to help you. I don't know how to help you either, but I can listen. And you know how opinionated I can be. If I think you are wallowing in self-pity, I have no qualms about reading you the riot act."

A small smile crossed Izzy's lips. "Oh, yes, I'm well aware that you'll tell me exactly what you think. My family has been tiptoeing around me."

"That's not what you need, Izzy. You can't spend the rest of your life hiding in your parents' house. I will not allow you to become another Emily Dickinson."

"At least Emily wrote poems. I can only write lists, to remind me of what I cannot hold onto in my memory. I don't know what to do, Maria. I don't know who I am anymore. All the dreams I had of earning my doctorate, of teaching, and of ultimately writing the Great American

Novel—they all disappeared that morning on the road when I died."

"But you came back, Izzy. *You came back.* There's a reason you came back."

"If there is, I don't know it."

"You simply haven't discovered it yet. And you're not going to discover it hiding on Chappy."

"I'm not capable of being anywhere else. I'm brain-damaged, Maria. As much as you would like to wave your nonna's magic wand—or whatever Italian godmothers used—I can't remember. How can I take care of myself away from here?"

"Well, since you asked, I have a suggestion. You need to get away, but you need to go somewhere safe, somewhere you won't be entirely on your own but you also won't be smothered by your family's worries."

"And where might this mythical place be?"

"My grandfather's farm."

"Your grandfather Raffaello? The dapper Italian archaeologist who always took us out to dinner at Anthony's Pier 4 when he was in Boston? The same farm outside Siena where you and I spent spring break, how many years ago?" Izzy's brain was still able to retrieve some, although not all, of her old memories.

"He's the only grandfather I have, so yes, Raffaello, and yes, his same farm, Portarello."

"You want me to go to the farm? What would I do there?"

"The farm still brings in students as interns to learn and work on the land and in the hotel my cousin Linda established in the old villa. You can work in the garden, you can cook, you can explore Tuscany. And my family will watch over you but from a distance. It's easier when it's not *your* mother or *your* sister. What do you think?"

"I think it sounds like a fairy tale, not reality."

"I think you're afraid."

"I don't want to talk about it, Maria."

"I'm not going away until we do talk about it. I agree, you are not the Izzy I know and love. But not because you've lost your short-term memory. The person I know is curious and passionate and open to new experiences. What I see before me is someone who has closed herself off to life, who is numb and unwilling to risk the possibility of failure or pain, when she knows that is the only way to rediscover who she is."

"Stop it, Maria! You have no idea how much I have lost and how much it hurts."

"No, you're right. I don't. But I do know that you have the capacity to imagine a new Izzy, even if you can't remember."

"What if I don't want to reinvent myself?"

"I don't believe you, Izzy. I don't believe that you are willing to accept this half-life. I don't believe you want to remain in this limbo of an existence."

Izzy pulled away from Maria and paced closer to the water's edge. She stood for a while looking at the bay.

"You know, there have been moments when I have longed for the peace I experienced in those moments when I died. Coming back has meant nothing but pain and the chaos of my brain. You're right. I don't want to stay like this."

"Then take the risk. Go to my grandfather's farm. At least give it the summer."

Izzy turned away from the water.

"Let me think about it. I can talk to Jo. I think he'll understand."

Together, they trudged back up the beach to the house.

Later that day, Izzy found Josiah at the construction site where the house he and Grace were building was starting to take shape.

"Can you spare a few minutes to talk?"

He put down his hammer. "What is it, Bird, in addition to the state of unrelieved sadness that seems to have overtaken you since the accident?" Josiah still called her by the shortened version of the nickname her father had given her, Hummingbird, because of how she had flitted from one absorption to another, drinking in the world around her.

"I'm thinking of leaving the island. My sadness, my despair, are hurting everyone. Especially Mom. Here she is, in the midst of the miracle your bone marrow offered her, and I'm like another cancer, stealing breath from her."

Josiah was silent. He didn't offer platitudes or deny the truth of what Izzy had described.

"Where will you go?"

Izzy was grateful that he hadn't immediately tried to dissuade her. She had turned to Josiah because he was no stranger to the need to leave. His reasons for going ten years earlier had been different, but he had also set out to redefine himself, much as she was hoping to do. They were biracial, the children of a Wampanoag sachem and an Irish-American, bound to the ancestral land of

Chappaquiddick, where the tribe had originated, but driven to understand what lay beyond the water.

"Maria's grandfather has a farm. I can work there for room and board. One doesn't need a lot of brain power to hoe vegetables and muck out pig pens."

"It sounds like you've got it all figured out."

She winced. "As much as this unfamiliar brain of mine can. I've started writing everything down to hold onto important stuff." She slapped the back pocket of her jeans, where the top of a small spiral-bound notebook protruded.

"Have you told Mom and Dad?"

"Not yet. There's more. The farm is in Italy."

He stopped. "They'll worry."

"Not any more than they worry now. I see how it's affecting Mom. At least if I'm away, she won't be confronted every day with my bleakness. I'm dragging you all down. If I go to the farm, I'll be with people who don't know who I was before, who won't be lamenting how much I've lost."

"You'll know."

"Maybe I'll forget *that* too."

"What can I do to help you? You didn't come out here just to give me advance notice."

"I wanted to gauge your reaction and ask you for advice. You left without their approval. I guess I'm looking for some of your courage."

"I not only left without their approval, I left without their knowledge. And I wasn't courageous. I was a sullen, smoldering teenager who was pissed at his parents and resentful of you. I'm the last person you should choose as a role model."

"But you faced their pain—and my sense of abandonment—and held fast to what you needed to do."

"And caused a lot of agony in the process. I'm not proud of that episode in my life."

"Do you think I'm being selfish?"

"Bird, I can't imagine what you are going through right now. But I can understand your feeling that if you stay, you'll drift into some limbo where you'll neither regain your former self nor find another Izzy who is different but whole. You're not selfish. You're actually showing signs of rejoining the living. You've been in some space inaccessible to the rest of us—halfway between the girl who died that day on Route 2 and us. Making the decision to go is a first step back to whoever is waiting inside you."

She gently punched his arm. "Thanks, big brother. That's exactly what I needed."

In the evening at the dinner table with everyone present, Izzy decided to announce her plans. She was afraid that if she waited, she'd waver in her decision and retreat back into her isolation.

Tobias glowered. Mae stiffened. Grace, nursing Caleb, turned to Josiah with raised eyebrows, silently questioning if he knew. Maria held her hand under the table and squeezed.

"Oh, Izzy. Italy? It's wonderful that you feel well enough to try something new. But so far away! What if ...?"

"Why can't you work on a farm here on the island? I'm sure if I asked around we'd find someone who needs an extra hand."

"Thanks, Dad. But if I stay on the island, stay here with you, I'm afraid I'll slip into complacency and accept this limited and constrained existence."

"Have we ever limited you in the past?"

Izzy had contracted polio as a child. Throughout her early years, especially during multiple corrective surgeries, her parents had encouraged her not to be limited by the disease.

"Of course not! You taught me ways to see my crippled leg as a challenge, not an impediment. Why can't you understand that I now need to find a way out of my crippled brain?"

Izzy knew it was going to take more than one dinner table conversation, but she had reached the limit of her own ability to argue. She tossed her napkin on the table and left the house, afraid that if she stayed they would hammer away at her fragile courage. She shook her head when Maria got up to join her. She needed to be alone.

Mae found her on the dock and slipped down beside her. She had had more than one important conversation with her children sitting in this spot, legs dangling over the side and the Milky Way overhead.

"Hummingbird, please forgive my initial reaction to your plan. I've almost lost you twice now, and I'll admit I'm afraid for you and for me. But I was more afraid of losing you in these last few months than at any other time, as you receded further and further away—not only from us but from yourself."

"I know, Mom. I sense how worried you are, how much my withdrawal is hurting you. I don't know any other way to remove that pain except to go away. We all seem trapped by my state of nonexistence. I can't bear dragging you all down with me. It's like a weight. Not the weight of a child carried with love and anticipation but the burden of my own fears. If I don't go, I'm afraid I'll never cast them off."

"I know that you need to go. I understand it not only with my head but with my heart. Remember, I left my own family when I was even younger than you are. The circumstances were very different. I was more like Josiah in running away without a word."

"I'm not running away!"

"No. But like my own mother, I want to keep you safe, pull you back from the wave I see gathering strength behind you. If you are in Italy, I am powerless to protect you."

"Mom, when I was only as far as Shear Pen Pond, you couldn't protect me. You can't protect me even now, under your roof, sitting at your table every day. I'm the only one who can do battle with the monster that stole my memory."

"When will you go?" The words were said with resignation, sadness, acceptance.

Six weeks later, after exchanging letters with Maria's grandfather and obtaining her passport, Izzy left Cove Meadow.

CHAPTER TWO

APRIL 1

After Marcantonio Ferri, Portarello's farm manager, met her at the bus station, Izzy collapsed, jet-lagged and on the edge of tears, and watched from the cramped passenger seat as his tiny Fiat climbed the mountain outside Siena, its windows covered with the dust that churned up from the serpentine road winding its way to the Portarello farm.

Despite her previous visit with Maria, she had seriously overestimated her ability to make the trip alone, even with a detailed itinerary and an Italian phrasebook clutched in her hand. From the moment she had bid her parents farewell at the gate in Logan Airport, she'd been engulfed with doubt. What had she been thinking, to step off the edge of the world when her entire being was already a stranger to her?

Each leg of the trip, rather than reassuring her she was another step closer to her destination, only increased her sense of disconnection and separation from the safety she'd left at Cove Meadow.

After she had contracted polio, she came to understand her own vulnerability. Her vaccine had failed, so why place confidence in the promises of protection? It was ultimately what had driven her away this time, seeking to save herself from the smothering, false security of home.

Her back stuck to the fake leather seat of the car. Although it was only the beginning of April, the temperature was unseasonably warm, and she felt the moisture in the air slithering through her scalp and wrapping itself around each strand of her hair. Despite the braid she'd rewoven in the airport ladies' room in Milan after a sleepless night on the plane from Boston, wisps were escaping and forming damp corkscrews around her face. As a teenager, she'd fought a mostly losing battle against her frizzy, tightly curled hair. She had finally given up her desire for the long, straight, smooth tresses that adorned every model and actress staring out at her from magazine covers and movie screens. She hadn't exactly embraced her curls, but she'd accepted them with resignation. She'd adopted a strategy of containment, a single braid down her back (just like her mother, she had reluctantly admitted) or a French twist held in place with a hundred bobby pins when she needed to look like a grownup. The last time she'd swept her hair up was probably when she'd interviewed for the doctoral program at Harvard. By that time, she'd recognized she was too engrossed as a literary scholar to indulge in any more high maintenance and totally futile attempts to change her hair. She was no longer a scholar, but she'd become accustomed to the simplicity of her hairstyle. Except that in this unexpected Tuscan heat and humidity, her hair had definitely escaped its simplicity and containment.

She pushed back the damp curls. Any hope she had of arriving at the farm looking like she had her life, not just her hair, under control, had evaporated somewhere between Florence and Siena on a bus with its windows stuck closed.

She hunted in her knapsack for a bandana to blot away the sweat trickling down her forehead. Her fingers unconsciously traced the scar tissue at the edge of her hairline. At a certain angle, with the light hitting it right, you could see the faint outline of the fracture that had altered her identity. The gesture reminded her to put on the floppy-brimmed straw hat she'd picked up at a kiosk in the Milan train station.

She was enmeshed in her wandering thoughts—an all-too-common pattern now, as her inability to focus was one of the constant reminders of her injury—when the voice of Marcantonio interrupted her.

"*Ecco!*" He was pointing out his open window and brought the car to a standstill so she could lean over and take in the view.

Across the valley, rising up out of the treetops, was the crenellated tower of the villa, the farm's main building, as solid and imposing as it had been when its stones were first laid in the thirteenth century. In spite of her fatigue and her loss of confidence in her decision, Izzy couldn't stop herself from smiling.

"*Sì*," she acknowledged Marcantonio's obvious pride. "*É bellissimo. Quasi in Paradiso.*" (It's beautiful. Almost in heaven.)

She startled herself at the Italian that had emerged from her lips. She hadn't thought the phrase in English and then translated it. It must have been a description Maria had uttered in the past, before the accident. A description Izzy might have found charming and poetic. Maybe she'd even written it down in a notebook. Whatever the reason, it had bubbled to the surface of memory when prompted by the breathtaking panorama before them.

Marcantonio released the clutch and resumed the climb up the mountain. But instead of leaving her to her aimless reverie, he launched into a stream of chatter in Italian, apparently convinced by that one utterance that she was fluent in his language.

She held up her hand to interrupt him and spoke a phrase she *had* written down in preparation for her journey. "*Mi dispiace. Non capito. Non parlo Italiano.*"

Marcantonio raised his eyebrows and pointed back to the vista they had just left. "*Ma ...?*"

Izzy shrugged. She had no explanation for her sudden outburst, let alone a reason she could give in Italian.

Marcantonio shook his head and resumed driving in silence. To Izzy's relief, they arrived at the villa ten minutes later. Marcantonio pulled the Fiat into the rear courtyard, got out of the car, and called up to an open window.

"*Linda, siamo arrivati!*"

"*Vengo subito,*" a woman's voice answered, and then in English, "I'll be right down."

Izzy slid out of the passenger seat and pulled her wet shirt away from her back. By the time she had retrieved her suitcase from the trunk, Linda had arrived.

"*Benvenuta,* Izzy!" She kissed Izzy on both cheeks, put one arm around her, and with the other picked up her luggage.

"Come, I'll show you first to your room so you can have a bath and get comfortable. This heat! It's drained the energy from all of us, even the rambunctious piglets. I can only imagine what it must feel like after a long day of travel."

Linda was Maria's cousin, also American, and Izzy was grateful that it was Linda, a familiar face, who had greeted her. She was equally grateful for Linda's understanding of her exhaustion.

The room was simply furnished, with white-washed walls and a faded woven rug on the stone floor. Izzy went straight to the window and opened the shutters that had kept the intense heat of the sun at bay during the day. She had a compelling need for light and air after the hours she'd spent in a succession of confining spaces. She leaned over the windowsill and was not disappointed. A cluster of cypress trees stood sentinel at the edge of a lawn that sloped away from the villa. Below a stone wall behind the trees, Izzy could see the orderly rows of a vegetable garden with variegated greens of early arugula, butter lettuce, and spinach. She lifted her eyes to the landscape on the far side of the garden. A sliver of gravel road cut through vineyards that were just beginning to leaf. Beyond the vineyards, the hills began, rising one after the other and shimmering in the haze.

She took a deep breath and turned back to Linda.

"I didn't realize how much I've missed the expansiveness of that view." She was struck by the sense of peace she felt at the window. It was a fragmentary parting of a veil, offering her a glimpse of another peace—far more profound—that had engulfed her in the aftermath of the accident.

"I never tire of it myself," Linda assured her. "I'll leave you to your settling in. If you remember, we gather for wine on the terrace at six o'clock. Most of our interns arrived two weeks ago. It will be a chance for you to meet everyone. After dinner we'll have our usual gathering in the library. We've got an archeological team

from Boston University arriving in two weeks and a few
bed-and-breakfast guests coming a few days later, so I'll
be briefing everyone on their assignments to give our
hospitality manager a hand in getting ready."

Linda closed the door quietly behind her as she left.
Izzy sank down onto the bed and flopped back against the
pillow. The linens were cool against her cheek and redolent
of lavender. The fragrance was a comfort, a reminder of
Cove Meadow and Granny Naomi's bundles of dried
herbs hanging from the rafters in her pantry. She closed
her eyes. ...

A knock on her door and an unfamiliar voice calling her
name roused her from the depths of sleep. The darkened
room, the strange voice, and her own profound fatigue
disoriented her as she first jolted up at the disruption.
Where was she? Who was waking her in the middle of
the night? Was she in the hospital? Her hands explored
her arms for an IV tube, her chest for an EKG sensor; she
listened for the whirr and click of machinery; she searched
the room for the green glow of a monitor screen. Nothing.
No cues to place her in this room.

The voice called her name again.

She rolled over to raise herself and caught a whiff
of lavender. Lavender. Her mind riffled through the
connection between lavender and location. She knew she
wasn't in Cove Meadow. She wasn't in her own bed, of
that she was sure. And then the association with lavender
tumbled into recognition in her brain. The villa. She was
at the villa.

She rubbed her face and answered the voice.

"Yes, come in."

A sliver of light from the corridor outlined the shape of a woman who appeared to be a few years younger than Izzy, and it gave Izzy enough illumination to find the chain on the lamp beside her bed. She blinked as its 30 watts offered a meager glow, giving shape to her surroundings.

"Linda thought you might have fallen asleep. I'm Pam McGrath, another intern. You've missed the wine hour, but we're about to sit down to dinner. Are you going to be able to join us?" Pam stayed by the threshold.

Izzy groaned inwardly. Not even here a few hours and she'd already messed up.

"I'm sorry. I should never have put my head down on the pillow. I just need to wash my face and I'll be ready. Would you mind waiting for me? It's been a while since I've been at Portarello." Despite her earlier visit with Maria, Izzy had no confidence in her ability to navigate the villa.

Pam agreed to wait and moved back into the passage. "I'll just be down hall in the library. Do you know where that is?"

"I think so. Give me five. Thanks for waking me up."

Izzy burrowed through her suitcase for a fresh shirt, grabbed one of the towels folded on a rack by the dresser, and escaped to the bathroom in the hall.

When she pressed on the light, she found herself staring into the bowl of a toilet that could have been a ceramic pasta dish. Burgundy, yellow, and pale-blue flowers encircled the bottom of the bowl, and delicate buds graced the rim. It felt positively sacrilegious to pee on them, but sinking onto the wooden seat, she pondered the thoughts of the artist who had created such a remarkably beautiful piece of plumbing. She would definitely have to add this to her notebook—not as a prompt to memory but as a record of discovery. She had promised herself when embarking on this journey that she would embrace it as if she were a sixteenth-century explorer, recording with wonder everything she encountered. She shook off the discouragement of her exhausting trip, washed her face, smoothed the tangles her nap had exacerbated, and headed off to find Pam and the library.

As she moved down the corridor she realized that her nose and her ears could have led her to dinner. The aromas of garlic, thyme, and roasting meat wafted toward her; and beneath the rattle of crockery, the faint hum of conversation rose up the stairwell. Through the open door of the library, Izzy saw Pam bent over a large wooden table, turning the pages of a thick book.

Izzy tapped lightly on the door, not wanting to startle Pam, whose back was to her.

"I hope I haven't kept you waiting long."

"No problem. I wasn't sure I was going to be able to wake you. I was pretty much in the same condition on my first day."

Izzy followed Pam down the curved, stone staircase.

"Watch out for the third step. It's loose. I've got responsibility for the house this month, and I've just given a punch list to Marcantonio for repairs before the spring and summer onslaught."

"How long have you been here?"

"I'm one of the handful of winter interns. I got here in February and I'll be leaving at the end of May."

"Where are you from?"

"Atlanta. Linda said you're from Martha's Vineyard. What brought you here?"

Izzy should have expected the question. Portarello offered serious professional training in organic farming, hotel management, conference planning, and archeological curating. She was here not to hone her skills but to reinvent herself. And, if she were truly honest, to hide. To reveal any of this to Pam, who exuded confidence with her punch list and her easy familiarity with the villa and its inhabitants, would obliterate any possibility of refuge.

"I'm here for the farming," Izzy answered with the least challenging assignment. It was all she felt capable of handling.

"How did you hear about us?"

"Through Maria Belli. We went to college together and I spent spring break here with her several years ago."

"And fell in love with it, right? Portarello grabs hold of you and doesn't let go."

They had reached the dining room, which resembled a convent refectory, with long wooden tables set up in a U-shape along three walls. Only one table was occupied, with Linda at the head.

She waved Izzy and Pam over and tapped her knife against her wine glass.

"Everyone, allow me to introduce our newest member of Portarello's illustrious cohort of interns. This is Izzy Monroe, of Martha's Vineyard in the U.S."

Izzy forced a smile on her face and curled her hands into fists at her side to keep them away from smoothing her hair.

Murmurs of welcome greeted her as Linda directed her to an empty seat. "I put you in the middle, so you'll have a chance to chat with everyone."

Izzy slipped into a cane chair next to Pam. A hand extended across the narrow table. "I'm Bennet, from New Zealand. I believe it's a bit bigger than your island, but it's an island nevertheless." At his initiative other voices offered their names and origins. Izzy realized she'd left her notebook on the bedside table. She'd never remember all the information bombarding her, and she fought the desire to tune out what was, in her panic, starting to sound like a cacophony. She knew they were all speaking English, but it might as well have been Swahili for any meaning she was taking in.

It was Pam who came to her rescue.

"Hey, guys, give her a chance to eat and take a breath. She's been travelling for a million hours in this enervating heat and hasn't yet assimilated our Portarello vibe."

With that pronouncement, the clamor died down, platters of mozzarella and marinated eggplant were passed down the table, and the antipasto course commenced. The rest of the meal—saffron risotto, followed by pork in an orange sauce with coffee gelato for dessert—passed in a haze of flavors that awakened Izzy from the fog that had surrounded her since leaving Chappy.

After the meal, Linda reminded everyone about the weekly meeting in the library to go over updates and plans.

The main topic was the arrival of the group of BU archaeologists who would be spending the summer on a dig on Portarello land.

"They'll be here in two weeks, a team of six graduate students and their professor."

With the organizational skill of a general deploying her troops for battle, Linda began issuing orders: Pam to form a team to air out rooms, dust, sweep, scrub bathrooms, and make beds; the kitchen crew to plan hearty menus on a two-week rotation that would feed a group of men engaging in rigorous physical work; the gardeners to ensure a steady supply of vegetables.

"This is their first visit to Portarello, and I don't want it to be their last. If their experience is a good one, we're hoping to establish an ongoing relationship with the program. Dottore Richetelli has been working with the university for months to negotiate this visit. He has been excavating a site here at Portarello for the last three years that he hopes may prove important to Etruscan scholarship. He's reached a point where sharing the treasures of Portarello with an experienced and knowledgeable team is part of his vision for the future of the farm. *Tocca ferro!*"

Izzy looked at Pam and mouthed, "What did she mean?"

Pam smiled. "It's like the English expression 'knock wood.' It literally means 'touch iron,' and you'll hear it a lot around here. She doesn't want to invite bad luck to mar something that is so clearly important to her grandfather."

"I've met Dr. Richetelli. When he was in Boston he took Maria and me on a tour of the Etruscan wing at the Museum of Fine Arts. His knowledge of the Etruscan civilization and his passion for it were compelling. I can understand why this dig is going to be so important."

Before she left the library, Linda asked Izzy to stop by her office in the morning to get her own assignment. As the meeting broke up, the interns drifted to their evening pursuits. Izzy overheard mention of going down to the village for drinks, an idea she would have once upon a time eagerly embraced. But she turned quickly away from the group to avoid an invitation to join them, knowing she was both too tired and too fragile to participate. In all her months of recuperation on Chappy, she hadn't once ventured across the water to Oak Bluffs to have a drink, even with people she knew well. She couldn't imagine doing it now with strangers. No matter how welcoming they were.

As tired as she was, she managed to find her way back to her room, despite a few false turns. In the morning, she'd map out routes to the main rooms in the villa.

CHAPTER THREE

APRIL 2

The next morning, a shaft of sunlight, roosters crowing, and the murmur of voices drifting up from the kitchen roused Izzy from an uneasy sleep. The unusual heat of the day before had barely dissipated during the night, and she had tossed restlessly in the unfamiliar bed.

She lay still for a few minutes, no longer as disoriented as she'd been the evening before when awakened in the dark by Pam's knock on the door. She knew where she was. Stretching to loosen the cramping of the leg afflicted by her childhood bout with polio, she steeled herself for a full day of this new world she had chosen to escape to.

As she dressed she was careful to place her notebook in the back pocket of her jeans. She braided her hair, made the bed, and took a deep breath as she headed for the dining room and breakfast.

The aroma of coffee drew her to a sideboard filled with bread, fruit, yoghurt, and soft-boiled eggs. No hearty bacon and eggs or pancakes that were the usual fare in her mother's Cove Meadow kitchen. No sugary cereal either. She reminded herself that she had come to Portarello to start anew, and if that included forgoing the comforts of her mother's breakfasts, she needed to suck it up and fill her plate with a slice of whole-wheat bread and some quince jelly.

The dining table was empty, and Izzy wondered if she had overslept, missing the other interns who were probably already at work. Another misstep. But then she heard voices outside and glanced out the window at a covered patio filled with long tables and wrought-iron chairs.

A few of the people she'd met the night before were gathered at one end of a table. She hesitated, contemplating staying inside, when one of the interns came bounding in from the patio, empty coffee cup in hand.

"Izzy! Good morning. Come join us outside."

Balancing her cup and plate, she pushed open the door to the patio with her shoulder and took a seat among the others, all of whom murmured some form of hello and resumed their conversations. She glanced around the table as she munched on her bread, wishing she had recorded even fragments of the previous evening. A few of the faces were familiar, but names, origins, or anything else they had shared were hovering in some irretrievable portion of her brain.

Why had she assumed that Portarello would be a hiding place for her? She felt totally exposed in the midst of these confident, chattering people. When she had visited with Maria in the spring five years earlier, the internship program was just getting started and operated only in the summer, so only the family had been around the table. She had possessed a fully functioning brain then, soaking up her first trip abroad with wonder and total absorption in every new experience. She'd been an obsessive note taker even then, before her ability to navigate the world depended on it.

She was abruptly pulled from her isolation by the girl who had awakened her for dinner the evening before. At least she knew her face and her voice, but her name eluded Izzy.

"Izzy, has Linda given you your assignment yet?"

Pam! The name slipped onto Izzy's tongue unsummoned.

"She asked me to stop by her office this morning, Pam. Would you mind showing me where that is?"

"Sure. She's usually in her office by this time. I can take you there before I head up to the pigs. We had a sow deliver six days ago and I want to check on them before my duties here in the house consume me. I was responsible for the pigs up until last week and was with the sow when she gave birth."

"We just have chickens at my parents' place. I've never worked with mammals before."

"Don't worry. You'll learn! I knew nothing about raising animals before I came here. If you've finished your coffee, I can guide you to the office."

Izzy dropped her dishes in the pass-through between the dining room and the kitchen and watched as the hands of the kitchen crew scooped them up. Beneath the sound of water rinsing the dishes she heard a cheerful voice trilling a lengthy Italian monologue. It may have simply been a grocery list for the week's meals, but it sounded like an enchanting fairytale to Izzy.

She followed Pam through the labyrinthine corridors of the villa to a wooden door marked "Ufficio." Pam knocked and waited until Linda's voice answered. Opening the door, Pam leaned in and announced Izzy.

"Izzy, reporting for duty." She turned to Izzy before she left. "I'll see you at lunch." And then she was gone.

Izzy stepped into the office.

"Is this a good time?"

"Of course! How did you sleep? Do you need anything in your room?"

"I'm fine, thanks. I'm here for my assignment."

"Before I place you, I'd like to know more about you, what you hope to learn here. It's my responsibility to make our internships productive for you as well as for the farm. I remember you from your visit with my cousin Maria, but both of you were just kids then. What interests have you developed in the intervening years?"

Izzy hesitated. She briefly considered omitting her year at Harvard, unable to explain why someone working on a doctorate in American Literature would be seeking an internship on a Tuscan farm, but she suspected Maria or her grandfather would have shared that piece of her history already. Realizing that Linda was probably well aware of her academic past, Izzy attempted to justify her unusual decision to seek work on a farm.

"I went to grad school immediately after I got my bachelor's degree at Smith. After all those years of intense scholarly work, I realized that I needed a break from the academic world. I knew that some of my happiest times as a child had been working alongside my grandmother in her vegetable garden. Maria knew how depleted I was and suggested coming here. I'm here to work, I want to assure you."

"Oh, I know that! Nonno Raffaello wouldn't have agreed to your coming if you weren't prepared to get your hands dirty!"

"I love getting dirt under my fingernails and collapsing exhausted in bed at the end of a day of working outside."

"Oh, wonderful! My original thought was to start you out in the vegetable garden, so I think we'll stick with that. Adelina is the head gardener and can show you what needs to be done. I'm afraid I'm waiting for an important phone call and can't leave the office right now to introduce you, but she is expecting you. Do you know the way?"

"I saw the garden from my window. I think I can find it."

"The gate is to the right of the chestnut tree. Just make sure you latch it again after you pass through."

Izzy made her way out of the building and across the grass to the chestnut tree. She was relieved that Linda hadn't pressed her. She was so determined to start fresh, without the baggage of her past. In her less-than-astute thinking, Izzy hadn't anticipated how curious these new people in her life would be about who she was. She resolved that morning to have some answers at the ready to deflect from her painful truth. Answers that she'd have to practice, over and over. Not only to remember them but to make herself over with a new history.

She shook off her fear of discovery as she descended to the garden to find Adelina and bury her past in the fertile soil of Portarello.

Adelina was kneeling at the edge of a row of radicchio, vigorously thinning the red leaves with nimble fingers. She looked up at Izzy's approach and shielded her eyes from the morning sun. A stocky, middle-aged woman with her hair in a tight bun covered by a faded kerchief, she reminded Izzy of the sturdy, competent Wampanoag tribeswomen who would gather at her grandmother Naomi's house in late summer to can the bounty of their gardens. Izzy's mother, Mae, had been welcomed into that circle by Naomi but had also remained separate from it. Her fair Irish skin and honey-colored hair were a constant reminder to some of the tribe that, despite being the wife of the sachem, she did not truly belong. Izzy and her brother, Josiah, had inherited not only the DNA that whispered of their mixed heritage but also that sense of separateness. Izzy's awareness of being "different" had been further complicated by her bout with polio as a child, although her parents had taught her not to be defined by her disease. She'd discovered the power of books during her long convalescence from surgeries, and that had driven her beyond the boundaries of her island home. Her education had widened the gulf between her and her generation in the tribe. At Smith, she'd been one of only two Wampanoag girls, and her brother had wound up marrying the other one. Her sister-in-law, Grace, had been the force behind alienated Jo's reconciliation with his parents and his Wampanoag heritage.

Adelina was as sun-browned as Izzy's Wampanoag aunties and watched her with the same skepticism Izzy had encountered when she'd left the island to study. Izzy could only imagine what was going through Adelina's head when she saw Izzy—another book-trained intellectual who didn't know asparagus from artichokes and neither of those from a weed.

"*Buon giorno,*" Izzy extended her hand. "*Mi chiamo Isabella, la nueva ragazza.*" She had scribbled the phrase on the inside of her wrist. Adelina looked at the inked

words and shrugged. Apparently believing that words
would be futile, Adelina rose from the row and beckoned
Izzy to follow her to a basket of tools.

"*Vieni qui.*"

When she had equipped Izzy, she handed her an empty
basket and led her to a row of leeks and demonstrated what
she wanted Izzy to do, dig up ten of the sturdy plants. She
held up her splayed hands. "*Dieci,*" she said.

"*Dieci,*" Izzy repeated and nodded her head. She knelt to
her task, silently repeating ten, ten, over and over so that
she wouldn't forget the simple instruction and harvest too
many.

The temperature was as stifling as the day before, and
Izzy had left her straw hat, of course, back in her room.
Harvesting the leeks wasn't difficult, but she worked
slowly, careful not to damage the deeply rooted bulbs and
shaking off the crumbling dirt before depositing them
in the basket. She was intent and focused on her task,
undistracted by the anxiety that had muffled her like a
dense fog since the accident, cutting her off from what
had once been joy in her experience of the world. Her
immersion in this physical task—the heat of the sun, the
pungent fragrance of the leeks as she released them from
the earth, the texture of the soil as it gave way beneath her
fingers—all served to release *her,* if only briefly, from the
prison of her damaged brain.

She was unaware that Adelina had come to her side.

"*Bene,*" she uttered. Then she spoke a string of
instructions, aided by hand motions. The key words that
Izzy was able to recognize were "*cucina*" and "*subito.*" Izzy
smiled in recognition.

"You want me to take these to the kitchen right away!" Izzy motioned toward the villa.

"*Si, si. Ma ritorno.*"

Return. Come back. She wasn't being dismissed! With relief, Izzy climbed up the hill, basket securely cradled in her arms.

When she returned to the garden, it was with her hat on her head and her pocket phrase book tucked behind her notebook. Adelina gestured for her to join her at a row of artichokes and demonstrated the weeds that needed to be removed. Izzy nodded in understanding and worked side by side with the older woman in companionable silence. They broke only at the sound of the bell calling them to the midday meal.

When Izzy took her place at the table with the other interns, she was pleased to see the leeks she'd harvested as the centerpiece of an aromatic risotto rich with butter and cheese.

She remained quiet during the meal, however. The solitude and healing power of the morning were quickly dissipated by the multiple conversations swirling around her among people who had already been working together for weeks. She slipped back into silence, convincing herself that she needed to be an observer in these early days. But in truth, she was afraid—afraid that some careless remark of hers would reveal her memory lapses. She panicked that not only could she not remember the names of the people surrounding her, she also grasped futilely for the conversation from the night before, fragments like wisps of stratus clouds or the disappearing contrail of a jet plane.

She was saved from her silence by the arrival of Linda as slivers of almond cake were handed around the table for dessert. Linda pulled a chair up next to her and smiled. "I've heard already from Adelina that you learn quickly. All is well from your perspective too?"

"Absolutely! The garden is amazing, and I can't believe we're eating what I picked only a few hours ago."

"That's part of the magic of Portarello. I'm glad you've had a good start. Enjoy the rest of the day." And then she was gone.

Izzy smiled, some of her anxiety eased. She could do this.

CHAPTER FOUR

APRIL 15

The first two weeks had been a challenge and a balm as Izzy tried to find her way, both literally and figuratively, around the farm. The sun, Adelina's gruff approval, and the satisfying work in the garden all reassured her. And some of the physical aspects of Portarello were still familiar, recognized from her visit with Maria five years before. But anything that involved interacting with the other interns, where her new memory loss might be revealed, led her to retreat into solitude. She had yet to join them on their excursions to the local bar and preferred to spend her evenings in her room. Pam seemed to recognize Izzy's reluctance, and, although she didn't push her, she continued to take Izzy under her wing as she had on her first day. But the comfortable pace that had marked these initial weeks was about to change with the imminent arrival of the archaeologists as Linda called them together the morning of their anticipated arrival.

"I've heard from the archaeology team. They've landed at the airport in Milan, so we can expect them as scheduled late this afternoon. It's time to put the final touches on our preparations."

Linda waved her arms at the group to get them moving, bodies dispersing in all directions to carry out her orders. Izzy, despite her status as a newcomer, felt a part of something. Her first task was to gather the produce for the evening meal. She worked quickly in the garden, filling baskets with butter lettuce and radicchio that would form the basis for the salad. Next on her list were peas, hanging delicately from their stalks, and Izzy followed Adelina's demonstration of picking them carefully.

Her baskets brimming, she climbed back up to the villa, deposited her bounty, and slipped into a bathroom to scrub the dirt from her hands. She glanced at herself in the slightly speckled mirror above the sink. The smudges under her eyes couldn't be washed away, evidence of the sleeplessness that continued to plague her, despite her rigorous work outdoors. She splashed her face with cold water, smoothed the stray wisps of her braid, and set off to find the housekeepers, the next task on the list she had jotted down when Linda had met with everyone earlier.

She located Pam on the upper level, her arms weighted down with linens and a key ring dangling from her hand.

"Izzy! You've finished in the garden? Thank goodness! Can you grab these sheets and start distributing them to the rooms in this corridor? Lori, Meg, and Tristan have dusted and swept, and those beds are ready to be made. Once all the rooms have their linens, please start making up the beds. I'll send Kate to help you as soon as I find her."

Izzy relieved Pam of the lavender-scented, crisply pressed sheets and started placing sets on each bed. The task gave her a chance to explore a side of the villa that was new to her. Each guest room was different, furnished with beds, dressers, and chairs that appeared mismatched. The kind of furniture one might find in the home of an elderly aunt. The fragrance of lemon oil triggered another Naomi moment for Izzy. The power of her sense of smell evoked not only her recollection of Naomi's home, with its worn but well-cared-for furniture, but an emotional response to her memory of the time she spent in her grandmother's home.

Izzy realized that she had experienced several of these moments of revelation since her arrival at Portarello, all sparked by a fragrance. In fact, her senses seemed heightened—the way the light saturated the landscape, or the insects droned in the lush vegetation, or the heat seeped into her bones. Perhaps because she was less engaged with people, the natural world rose in her consciousness, flooding her brain and sparking fleeting bits of new memories. She didn't want to raise her hopes that her brain was recovering. She'd had too many setbacks in her health throughout her life to place any confidence in her sense of smell or sight or touch to restore her to her former self.

Nevertheless, these fragments excited her in the moments when they occurred.

"Izzy? Izzy, are you OK?"

Izzy jumped at the voice beside her.

"You've been staring at the wall with the sheets in your hand and looking like you were somewhere else. I thought maybe you'd gotten sunstroke when you were down in the garden. Do you need to sit down?"

Izzy read the look on the girl's face as concern rather than criticism or resentment. But she must have thought Izzy was slacking off when everyone else was scrambling to get the villa ready.

Izzy shook her head. "I'm fine. Sorry to worry you. I just got distracted for a moment. This room reminds me of my grandmother's place."

"I know what you mean. My gran's living room looked like it had been frozen in time. Pam sent me to help you make the beds, so I'm here to give you a hand."

Izzy hoped her wandering brain wouldn't be the topic of conversation after hours when the interns gathered to relax. The girl helping her had seemed to accept Izzy's feeble explanation, but Izzy wasn't secure enough in her status as the newest member of the staff to believe that her behavior would be accepted as "normal."

She threw herself into the bed making.

They developed a rhythm, one on each side of the bed, shaking out the folded sheets and floating them down to the mattress. Tucking in corners, filling pillowcases, and fluffing up duvets, they marched down the corridor, dispatching the task quickly.

But Kate kept up a running monolog, peppering her conversation with a barrage of questions for Izzy about her background.

"I hope you don't mind my curiosity. I'm a journalism major, and I'm keeping a journal of my experience here for an article I hope to get published in the fall."

Izzy did mind, but she hadn't developed the ability to divert even small talk, let alone a journalist looking for a story. She mumbled a few safe answers about the Vineyard but shut down when Kate started probing about her limp.

"I prefer not to talk about my health. I learned even as a child that it doesn't define me."

Kate must have been used to evasive answers because she simply switched topics.

"Why did you come here?"

This time, Izzy was prepared. Her friendship with Maria, her previous visit to Portarello, and her wish to take a break from studying all rolled off her tongue in answer to Kate's question. She wasn't able to gauge Kate's willingness to accept her reasons and worried that her answer had sounded too practiced. Which, of course, it was. Izzy waited for the next probing question, but they were interrupted by Pam carrying a wooden crate filled with vases.

"Hey, when you finish with the beds, we need a few flowers in every room. Here are the vases. Bennet left a bucket of irises on the landing. I think we have enough for three or four blooms in every vase."

Izzy offered to take on the task, happy to break the cycle of Kate's interrogation. She lifted the crate from Pam's hands and escaped to find the irises. When she got to the landing, she sank down on the floor, realizing she was trembling and rattling the glass in the crate. What had just happened? She was reacting to Kate's questions as if it really had been an interrogation. Sweat had broken out on her forehead as if she'd been under a hot spotlight, with listeners in the shadows ready to denounce her memorized answers as lies.

She wiped her face with the edge of her shirt and took a deep breath.

Come on, Izzy. She's an ambitious journalism major, not some undercover cop ready to break you and accuse you of being a fraud. Izzy attempted to calm herself. Tears mingled with the drops of sweat trickling down her cheeks. She pressed her palms against her eyes. What the hell was she doing here? Wasn't it supposed to get better with each new day? Every time she thought she had mastered a challenge, another popped up. *Stop it! Stop overthinking things! Put the damn irises in the vases. At least that doesn't need much intelligence.*

Izzy grabbed three stems and thrust them into the first vase in the crate. But the futility of taking out her frustration and despair on the delicate blooms stopped her before she picked up the next bunch.

The wildflowers of Innisfree had been her playthings as a child. She and her best friend, Susan Hammond, had a secret hiding place under a bush of beach roses, where they brewed "perfume" and wove daisy chains. She still had her "old" memories, stored in a part of her brain that hadn't been damaged. The irises, like the aromas that had triggered responses since her arrival, pulled her out of her fear of being discovered.

With care, she plucked the next three flowers from the bucket, deliberately slowing herself down to calm the shaking that had overtaken her.

She almost heard Adelina whispering in her ear, "*Bene*," as she arranged the remainder of the blooms.

One by one she filled the vases with water and placed them in each room. By the time she finished, the bell chimed. After splashing some cold water on her face in the hall lavatory, she hurried to the refectory for lunch. She didn't want to be the last person to arrive.

Pam caught up with her.

"Thanks for all the help this morning. We got it done. Apparently, they made their train in Milan and should be here in time for dinner."

"Do you need me to help get them sorted out into their rooms when they arrive?"

"No, you're free until dinner. Go crash, or better yet, visit the pigs. Just be back and cleaned up for wine on the terrace at seven o'clock. Linda will want us all there to charm the weary travelers."

Pam's words were a gift. She considered the idea of a nap, but she wasn't sure she'd wake up in time for the command performance Linda was apparently expecting, and she couldn't depend on Pam to be her wake-up call again. Relishing her solitude, after lunch she set off for the path up to the pigs.

CHAPTER FIVE

APRIL 15 – 16

The distance to the pigs was farther than Izzy anticipated. The path was steep and rocky and harder on her legs than she was accustomed to, and her cane was in the bottom of her armoire, where it had lain since her arrival. She stopped to catch her breath and remove a pebble that had become lodged in her sandal. Spying a long branch lying just off the path, she lifted it out of the weeds. It was a good length and sturdy enough to support her if she stumbled.

Taking her discovery as a positive omen, she decided to press ahead and entered a small wooded area that offered some welcome shade in the afternoon heat.

Grateful for her walking stick, she continued trudging through the woods, ignoring twinges in her leg she knew would escalate into pain and rigidity. She'd come this far and didn't want to turn back. But after nearly thirty minutes of walking with no pigs in sight, she realized she must have taken the wrong trail.

She was exhausted, sweaty, and covered in a layer of dirt from her bare toes to the frizzed strands of her hair. If there had been a pond, she'd have jumped in. Somehow she managed to retrace her steps back to the villa. The vision of a bath and the sight of the villa's tower relieved her.

When she reached the villa, she entered the interns' wing from the back and climbed the stone steps to her room. The sun was about to slip behind the hills, so she flung open her shutters to let in some cooler evening air. That is when she heard the tinkling of glasses and the murmur of voices from the terrace.

The archeologists had arrived and the wine hour was in full swing. *Shit! Shit!* She was supposed to be down there, offering a charming welcome to disgruntled travelers.

She had one of her sandals in her hand and threw it across the room. How could she be so stupid and forget, once again, what she was supposed to be doing?

She looked at herself in the mirror and saw the bedraggled, filthy state she was in. Not only did she look a mess, but she could smell the result of her labors and her strenuous walk without lifting her arms. She had to clean up before she ventured down to the terrace. Under the shower, which at this hour was a trickle of lukewarm water, she let flow the tears she'd bottled up all day.

Out of the shower, she twisted her hair into a knot, pulled a cotton sundress over her head, wiped off her dusty sandals, and moved as quickly as she could to join the guests. Her leg throbbed, and she knew it wasn't only the physical exertion of the day but her skyrocketing stress levels that were hampering her.

She emerged through the French doors onto the stone terrace that served as the villa's entertaining space. Barely anyone paused in the midst of the ongoing conversations to notice her arrival. On the ledge sat a tray of glasses; bottles of water and last year's vintage red, white, and rosé; and a platter of prosciutto and salame, the bounty of the previous year's culling of the pigs. Doubting that she could handle even a watered glass of rosé, Izzy poured herself some sparkling water just to have something in her hand. She was relieved to have made it to the terrace before the bell for dinner but stood isolated in the midst of the laughter and small talk. She looked around for a way to ease herself into a group and settled on two sunburned young men. She was fairly certain she hadn't seen them before and so felt safe approaching them.

"Hi," she ventured, offering the hand without the glass. "I'm Izzy." *Please*, she prayed, *let them be archeologists and not interns.*

"Hi. I'm Frank, and this is Aaron."

Izzy tried to mask her relief. "Are you guys part of the archeology team?"

"Yeah. We're the guys who like to dig in the dirt."

"Well, you've come to the right place."

"We can't wait to get started. Dr. Richetelli has extolled this place for months."

"What we've seen so far, just on the ride up the mountain, has been amazing. How long have you been here?"

"Oh, I'm a newcomer. I'm only two weeks ahead of you, but it feels like a lot longer."

"Is that bad or good?"

"Oh, good, definitely! It's just that I've experienced a lot in a short time."

"Are you also here on a study program?"

"I work here. I'm not a guest. What about your group? How long will you stay?"

"That depends on what happens on the dig and Dr. Richetelli. Wherever he leads, we follow. But more than likely, that means we'll be here for the summer."

Izzy refrained from offering her own experience of working under a demanding, famous professor. She'd only trip up if even a glimmer of her studies at Harvard were to make its way into the conversation.

"What made you choose archaeology?" She looked at both of them. Safer ground to keep them talking.

The one she thought was Aaron shrugged. "I liked to muck around in the woods as a kid. Our corner of New England was rife with arrow heads. They were my show-and-tell project in fourth grade. I was lucky enough to have a teacher who saw the gleam in my eye and steered me out of boredom and troublemaking into an activity that led to this career."

"I don't have quite such a story of discovery and redemption," the other one interjected. "My father was an archaeologist and started taking me on digs when I was just a toddler. Whether I followed in his footsteps because of nature or nurture is still a topic of debate in my family."

"What do you do here?" Aaron asked.

"The garden," Izzy responded quickly and without embellishment. She didn't want them to ask her what she had asked them—why did you choose this?

At that moment one of the servers appeared in the doorway and invited everyone to move down the steps to dinner on the patio under the pergola.

Izzy joined the stream of people, relieved that she'd made it to the terrace ahead of dinner. She hadn't noticed if Linda had seen her late arrival.

Dinner was Portarello at its best, and the groans of pleasure echoing up and down the long tables attested to the success of the effort everyone had made to accommodate the archeologists.

As the guests drifted around the grounds or back to their rooms after dinner, word spread among the interns that Linda had called a brief meeting in the library.

"I just want to thank you all for rising to the occasion and pulling off such a great welcome." She went around the room to thank each of them for their contributions. "We're now ahead of being ready for the season. Now, go on, all of you. Celebrate a job well done! I'll see you all tomorrow."

As the group dispersed, Izzy could hear scattered comments about gathering down in the village for drinks. No one asked her to join the impromptu party, but she shrugged it off. She was, after all, the only new member of the cohort. Besides, she admitted to herself, she didn't have any energy left to sustain her façade. Greeting the archaeologists and entertaining them through dinner had exhausted her.

She slipped back to her room, shed her dress, and curled up with her notebook, determined to record as much as she could dredge up of names and details. She was also relieved that Linda hadn't commented on her late arrival to the wine reception. The debacle of getting lost in the woods and then not only losing her sense of time, but also completely blanking on her responsibility to welcome the new guests, appalled her.

What next, she thought. Will I sleep till noon tomorrow and forget my work in the garden? Was Dad right that I'm not ready to manage on my own? Am I always going to be dependent on someone "minding" me, telling me where I'm supposed to be and what I'm supposed to be doing?

She felt like ripping up her useless notebook. Instead, she stopped writing, unconvinced that the effort she was making to remember and record the day's events had any purpose. She was done, in so many ways, and doused the bedside lamp.

In the darkness her hearing was enhanced and she heard raucous voices below her window on the lawn. The archaeologists, she surmised. She didn't remember seeing a single woman among the group. She wanted to shut the window to block the disturbance, but the air was too stifling in her room. She turned away from the window with her pillow over her head and tried unsuccessfully to fall asleep.

Clouds that had obscured the moon earlier in the evening dispersed, and a sharp, bright slash of moonlight fell across her bed. She grappled for her watch on the night table and saw that it was three in the morning. The revelers on the lawn were gone. She must have slept for a few hours, but she despaired of finding her way back to sleep. She tossed uncomfortably for the next two hours and then rose at five. If no one was about in the kitchen with a fresh pot of coffee, she'd go for a walk.

The kitchen was dark. She unhooked the door of the dining room out to the pergola and left the still-sleeping building. She headed in the direction of the main gate, in the opposite direction from her failed excursion to find the pigs the afternoon before. She couldn't afford to get lost this morning. She'd keep to the road, walk for half an hour and then turn back. This time, she'd brought along her cane.

The morning air revived her, and her gait evened out with barely a trace of a limp. Gratitude for small graces, she smiled. A favorite lesson of Naomi's that Izzy had taken as her mantra over the years. Instead of allowing her anxiety of the night before to shadow this new day, she tried to focus on the present moment. She was surrounded by beauty and bird song. Water spilled down the hillside from a small stream, the wet rocks glistening in the early-morning sun. Izzy noted a variety of plants that were unfamiliar to her and wished she had her camera with her. She wanted to snap them and send them to her mother and Naomi. Instead, she pulled her notebook from her pocket, sat down on one of the stone walls that lined the road, and sketched the delicate stems and blooms.

Capturing what she saw forced her mind away from the past night's restlessness and self-doubt. It was a brief respite, as she sought to record the unfamiliar plants with a few spare lines. Her concentration was broken by the sound of a motor climbing the hill. She looked up from her perch on the wall to see a dairy truck chugging along in the rumble of second gear. The driver, a middle-aged woman with hands that looked as if they had kneaded a lot of mozzarella, waved to Izzy and proceeded on up to the Portarello gate. Izzy closed her notebook and followed her growling stomach to the kitchen, where she hoped breakfast would finally be set out.

Izzy would spend the rest of the day working with Adelina in the garden, weeding and thinning out lettuce and spinach and then transplanting tomato and pepper seedlings from the greenhouse at the bottom of the garden to a freshly prepared plot higher up.

At a brief break for lunch, Izzy noticed with relief that the archeologists were missing. No need to make gracious chitchat or remember what she'd heard from them the night before. She made herself a sandwich of mozzarella and roasted peppers, grabbed an apple, and took her meal to a shady corner on the lawn in the shadow of one of the cypress trees that stood sentinel above the vegetable garden. Wiping olive oil sliding down her chin with one of the handkerchiefs Naomi had sewn for her and insisted she take with her, she retrieved her notebook and flipped through it.

She didn't notice Linda at the window of the office overlooking the lawn.

After lunch, Izzy resumed her work, deftly tapping the tomato plants into the soil as Adelina nodded her approval. The absence of conversation between them was a gift that allowed Izzy to apply her mind to the physical task. Like the sense memories she was experiencing, learning with her hands, using her body rather than her brain, seemed to be creating new pathways that weren't disappearing the way words did. It didn't seem to matter whether it was work that required vigorous exertion or delicate hands; she knew she was retaining what Adelina was teaching her. Digging the trench for the tomato plants gave her an opportunity to put her whole body into the task, thrusting the shovel into the earth, working it in deep with her foot, and then throwing the strength of her back into lifting the friable soil. It was not just a newly discovered ability but an exercise in meditation. The rhythmic, repetitive work was like practicing scales on a piano. The phrase "mindless repetition" popped into her head and she smiled.

Just what I need and all that I can manage, she thought. Mindless work for the mindless. Despite her cynicism, she could look with satisfaction on the rows of newly planted tomatoes. Her academic work had never offered her such physical evidence of her efforts, unless one could equate a stack of paper that represented her analysis of *Moby Dick* with the thriving green evidence of her day's work.

Aching and with blisters on her hands from the shovel, she was shooed from the garden by Adelina, who wore no watch but knew by the position of the sun when it was time to stop.

Izzy climbed slowly up to the villa. Without the steady rhythm of digging to keep her muscles firing, she was suddenly aware of the fatigue in her limited leg. She tried not to drag it as she emerged from the garden gate to the lawn. Anyone at a window in the villa would notice the pronounced difference in her gait. She felt thrust back to adolescence, when her physical differences had loomed so large. She had wanted to dance, not hobble, with her useless limb. She steadied herself at the chestnut tree and then walked with as regular a stride as she could manage, gritting her teeth till she reached the door of the interns' quarters. Once inside, she caught her breath in the dim coolness of the passage. *Please don't let me meet anyone on my way to my room. Isn't my mindlessness enough of a burden? Do I now have to hide my physical limitations as well?*

When she reached her room, she stripped off her earth-stained clothes and collapsed on the bed. What she needed was a soak in a hot bath and a leg massage. Her sister-in-law, Grace, a nurse, had always been able to ease the sporadic flare-ups that had plagued Izzy, and the distance between her and Grace at this moment hit Izzy with unexpected force. She had wanted so desperately to free herself from the hovering of her family, but the price she was paying for her freedom kept mounting with each day that had passed since her departure.

She willed herself not to cry. It's getting old, Izzy, she castigated herself. Get yourself off the bed and find a damn bathtub. There must be one in this vast labyrinth. She pulled on her terry bathrobe, grabbed a towel, and set off in search of a tub.

One floor down and a few turns in a corridor later she found a large, tiled room with a claw-footed tub. Keeping her fingers crossed that there'd be enough hot water at this time of day, she opened the tap and waited as water gurgled up out of the pipes and began to fill the tub. When the level had reached enough to cover her outstretched legs, she eased herself in, keeping the tap open enough to allow a trickle. Leaning back, she closed her eyes and let the warmth seep into her aching, rigid muscles. She should have known better than to push her physical limits. Was lack of judgment just another side effect of her brain injury?

When the water turned tepid she scrubbed off the remnants of the garden she had carried away on her body. The dirt embedded under her nails had soaked away from her now-wrinkled fingers. With as much energy as she could muster, she massaged her calf. The next time she had an opportunity to catch a ride down to the village, she'd have to buy a rolling pin. It had been Grace's ingenious solution years ago, an effective tool for loosening up the rigidity that hampered her movements. Reluctantly, she pulled herself out of the water, rinsed out the grime that ringed the tub, and started to make her way back to her room. Wishing she'd left a trail of breadcrumbs, she finally found the staircase she'd descended earlier and saw the familiar hallway that led to her room. A frosted window that opened onto an inner courtyard offered a bit of natural light. It was the basket of dried flowers perched on the windowsill that was Izzy's mnemonic. Her therapist after the accident had suggested that she look for nonverbal cues to help her remember, and Izzy had seized on the flower basket when she first arrived. She hoped no one would remove it in a frenzy of decluttering. It looked as if it had been there for ages, faded from the filtered light and never dusted. Izzy offered a whispered thanks to the basket and gently touched one of the petals as if it were a talisman.

Inside the room she gathered up the dirty clothes she'd left where they had fallen. She supposed Portarello had a washing machine. At some point she'd need one but not today. Instead, she shoved the shirt and jeans into the bottom of the ancient wardrobe that served as her closet and pulled out a cotton dress for dinner. In the mirror she noted how brown she'd become after her two weeks in the garden. Her hair had lightened, too. She knew the Italian sun was strong but hadn't expected it to have such a profound effect so quickly. If only these outward signs of change had a counterpart inwardly.

When she arrived on the terrace she was surprised to find it empty except for Pam, who was setting out a tray of wine glasses. With relief, Izzy realized that for a change she wasn't late for the wine hour but actually early.

"Anything I can do to help?"

"Hey, Izzy! You look great, by the way. The Portarello vibe must be getting to you. As a matter of fact, you *can* help. Can you grab the three wine bottles on the sideboard in the small dining room? A corkscrew should be with them."

Izzy brought out the wine and set to uncorking the bottles.

"Where are the archaeologists?"

"As far as I know, they've made it back from the dig. At least, the kitchen has planned on feeding them tonight.

"How are you doing, two weeks in?"

"I'm good. A little sore from turning over a new plot for the tomatoes but otherwise OK."

If she said it out loud, perhaps she'd believe it herself.

"I know what you mean! When I first arrived I was determined to prove I could do anything the boys could do—drive the tractor, inoculate a pig, you name it. I think I soaked my aching body for hours the first couple of weeks. I found a great Italian version of BENGAY, by the way, that I can recommend."

"Thanks. I'll take you up on it. I'm hoping tomorrow all I'll have to do is water my newly planted seedlings, but somehow I don't think that's what Adelina will have in mind."

"Did you get a chance to see the piglets?"

"Not yet." Izzy wasn't going to admit her failed attempt to find them. Maybe a map of the farm existed that she could get a copy of. Pictures instead of words. That was what she needed to rely on.

By her third week, Izzy was feeling more secure in her daily routine and her knowledge of the layout of the villa and its immediate surroundings. She still wasn't sleeping well, although the physical exhaustion from her work in the garden at least allowed her to fall asleep. But invariably, something disturbed her almost every night—voices below her window, creaking pipes when someone took a late-night shower, weather rolling in over the hills.

Her early-morning walks were her antidote to her restless nights. Notebook and pencil tucked into her back pocket, she wandered a little farther each day and sketched whatever drew her eye. But she never left the road, still needing the certainty that she could find her way back to the villa.

Despite developing comfort with her surroundings, Izzy's interactions with the people of Portarello remained stilted and remote. After dinner, she withdrew from any communal activity, finding the partying that took place after hours problematic. Alcohol was always present, and Izzy feared the havoc a drink or two could wreak on her already muddled brain. She could pass on wine during dinner without anyone remarking on her abstinence, but she doubted she could refuse a drink or a passed joint and not have it become at least a question among the others, especially investigative journalist Kate.

She told herself that she wasn't joining in the revelry because the other interns were younger than she was. College kids with whom she had little in common. But in truth, she wasn't that much older than they were.

Pam was the only intern she felt safe with. She never questioned or even raised an eyebrow if Izzy slipped up on something she should have remembered. But she was leaving in a few days, her internship coming to an end. Kate, on the other hand, remained an irritant. Too inquisitive, too judgmental when Izzy made a mistake. More than once Izzy had come upon Kate conversing with someone and abruptly stop when she saw Izzy.

Izzy would have preferred to shrug off behavior she hadn't experienced since middle school, but Kate's rudeness gnawed on Izzy in her already fragile emotional state. Her only recourse was to avoid Kate as much as possible. Whatever Kate's assignment, it was far from the garden, for which Izzy was grateful. And on Izzy's early-morning walks, she never encountered another member of the Portarello community. The dairy driver, however, greeted her daily now with a big wave and a warm "Buon giorno."

Izzy wished the driver would stop long enough for her to capture her face and those amazing, strong hands in a sketch. But she was usually tearing up the gravel as she rushed to get her cheese and cream to the villa in the still oppressive heat.

CHAPTER SIX

MAY 1

One afternoon after her work in the garden, Izzy took refuge in the villa's library. She ran her fingers along the spines of the books. Since the accident she'd barely been able to read a comic strip, let alone a book. Once upon a time—in that other life when she'd had a fully functioning brain—books had been her lodestar, her companions, her salvation. She was torturing herself as she circumnavigated the room, its towering walls lined floor to ceiling with bookcases.

But she wasn't simply wandering aimlessly, using the room as a hideout because she'd rarely seen anyone in here, especially during the day. She had a purpose as she scanned the titles embossed on the spines. Somewhere in the library of an archeologist whose life's work was the Etruscans there ought to be at least one book on Etruscan civilization. One would think.

She was about to give up when she crouched down to a low shelf near the floor. A slim volume, bound in red leather, bore the word Etruscan on the spine and cover. She reached for the volume and flipped it open. The author was Raffaello Richetelli, Maria's grandfather. The book appeared to be a bound copy of his doctoral dissertation. With dismay, Izzy saw that it was written in Italian. Despite her lack of facility in the language, she lowered herself to sit cross-legged on the floor and began to turn the pages, stopping at the illustrations. She was lost in her concentration and unaware that someone else had entered the library until his voice interrupted her.

"You'll find more recent scholarship on the Etruscans on the bookcase to the left of the fireplace. Those books in front of you are close to the floor for a reason."

Izzy turned, startled, recognizing the voice.

"Professor Richetelli!" She scrambled to her feet.

"I didn't know you were interested in the Etruscans."

"It's hard to avoid the Etruscans this summer, with the work on the dig."

"What would you like to know?" He settled his long frame into one of the deep upholstered chairs flanking the mammoth hearth.

Izzy threw up her hands. "Everything! But for a start, I'd like to understand who they were, what they believed."

"We don't know much, I'm afraid. But the excavation may reveal some elements we haven't seen before."

"Both Maria and Linda have told me how important this dig is to you."

"It is the culmination of my life's work. If we find what I am hoping for, its significance will be immensely satisfying, not only for what it will add to our understanding of this ancient hidden culture, but also for what it means to me personally.

"I know I haven't had time even to greet you since your arrival at Portarello. I apologize for my preoccupation. My granddaughter reminded me—chided me—that I hadn't welcomed you personally. Please forgive me. That is why

I sought you out today. Linda told me I would find you here. It was a delightful surprise to come upon you with my book in your hand."

"I wish my Italian were stronger."

"If you would like to indulge an old man, I'd be happy to take you through the Etruscan gallery in the old granary. Most of the objects on display there were unearthed here at Portarello, and I discuss them in my dissertation."

"I'd like that very much. I know so little about the Etruscans, and I'm eager to learn."

"Then it's settled. I'll be your personal guide. I remember what an inquisitive, extraordinary mind you had when you spent your holiday here with Maria. That must have been about five years ago, yes? Even then I could see you were a scholar. We're very fortunate to have you here this summer, of all summers. I think you young people are very brave to take some time off from academia. In my day, we didn't dare take a breath between earning our degree and securing a university post. Ah, but you don't need to listen to the grumbling observations of an old man. An old man who has to get back to work at the dig.

"I have a busy week ahead, but after that I will have time to show you the gallery. Shall we say next Sunday morning early at the granary?"

Raffaello stood up, stretching to his full, lean height, and extended his hand.

Izzy took it and murmured her thanks for the invitation. She watched him leave and then sank down into the chair he had vacated.

She'd never imagined that he would remember her with such clarity from her first visit to Portarello. A scholar with an extraordinary mind, he had described her. Was he yet another person who would look upon her with pity, aghast at the loss? She had believed that by starting her life over at Portarello she could escape the disappointment and dismay of those who had once known the brilliant young girl on the verge of unlimited possibilities.

Her plan to reinvent herself among strangers was unraveling, especially as Raffaello was about to discover that the mind he had enjoyed so much in the past no longer existed.

She put the red bound dissertation back on the shelf. Feeling a strong need to flee the confines not only of the library but of the villa itself, she left the building and started up the rocky path through the olive grove and into the woods. She had finally gotten a map of the farm from Linda and kept if folded in her pocket. She withdrew it now and found her location. She wanted to get as far from the printed word as possible and set herself in the direction of the woods behind the villa, determined this time to find the pigs.

In the midst of the woods she encountered a clearing with a shed, silos, and a small tractor hitched to a wagon containing large bins. Scattered around the ground were bits of corn. Encouraged, she kept going, assuming that where there was pig food there soon would be pigs. She wasn't disappointed as she rounded a curve on the path and emerged out of the woods onto a large expanse of rising meadow. At the farthest edge, before the woods began again, she detected movement.

Her reward at the top of the hill was an enclosure inhabited by a sow sprawled on her side as a dozen tiny piglets scrambled for a teat, climbing over one another.

The sow adjusted her position and settled into the dirt of the enclosure, tolerating her hungry offspring with equanimity.

Izzy watched from the fence with rapt attention. Pam had been so right to encourage her to come up here. She wished she'd done it before Pam left, so that she could have let her know how wonderful she found it. Izzy's father had always been the one to call her attention to the creatures that inhabited the dunes and meadows of their island home. It was from him that she had learned to be still and watch. The practice of those childhood years had instilled in her both curiosity and wonder.

Once again, on a day filled with the usual challenges and discoveries, Izzy was finding release and safety in the present moment of contemplating the natural world. She didn't have to do anything up here but enjoy the frenetic scrambling of the piglets and the grunting acceptance of their mother. She envied the pigs in the enclosure adjacent to the sow, rolling around in the dust or stretched out in the shade.

Eventually, her fatigue overcoming her, she pulled herself reluctantly from the fence.

When she turned away from the pigs and retraced her steps to the villa, some of her anxiety had dissipated. Her upcoming meeting with Raffaello in the gallery loomed less as an oral exam. She'd already told him, hadn't she, that she knew nothing about the Etruscans? All he would expect of her would be to listen and observe. She could take notes, as she always did, but she wouldn't have to hide her notetaking, scrambling as she often did to find a quiet place to record a conversation or the bits of flotsam and jetsam that drifted across her day and demanded the attention of memory.

She realized that her interest in the Etruscans was quelling her disquiet about Raffaello's potential disappointment in her. She willed herself to focus on the spark of curiosity that she was trying to nurture with each new day at Portarello.

It was nearly time for dinner when she arrived back at the villa. After quickly washing off the dust of the trail, she joined the guests on the terrace. A couple of vacationing families had arrived, easy to identify apart from the scruffy, intense archeologists. Izzy introduced herself and initiated the patter she had practiced for newcomers.

CHAPTER SEVEN

MAY 1

After dinner that evening, Linda caught up with Izzy as she slipped away, eager to avoid another drinking party.

"Izzy," Linda called to her. "My grandfather revealed at dinner that he has finally welcomed you. I'm sorry he hadn't reached out to you sooner."

"It's fine, Linda. I wasn't expecting to be singled out, especially when he's so preoccupied with the dig."

"Still, I had to remind him that you are Maria's friend and not a stranger to us. Do you have a few minutes or are you rushing off with evening plans?"

"No plans. Of course I have time for you."

"Let's sit by the cypress trees. I've got some of our homemade limoncello and a couple of glasses. I've wanted to catch up with you, but I've been so engulfed by the needs of the dig. I'd forgotten how much a group of young men can eat when they've been excavating deeply buried artifacts all day."

Linda chose a wrought iron table and chairs at the far end of the lawn, away from the others. She poured them each a thimble full of the yellow liquid. Izzy's nose picked up the bright aroma of lemons.

"It's quite potent, so sip it," Linda warned. She waited for Izzy to taste the fragrant liqueur and smiled at Izzy's reaction.

"Oh, wow! This is unlike anything I've ever tasted."

"It's a secret family recipe from my zia Norma. We bring it out for special occasions."

"Is this a special occasion?" Izzy was puzzled.

"My grandfather would consider this entire summer worthy of celebration. It has been his life's dream, his obsession, to have the opportunity to plunge into the secrets held by Portarello's mountain. Izzy, I must ask you, are you happy here?"

The abrupt redirection of the conversation startled Izzy. A drop of the limoncello spilled on her hand.

"I ... of course, I'm happy," she stumbled over the words. Was this a conversation Linda had with all the interns, or was she being singled out? Whether it was because she was Maria's friend or because Linda had noticed something amiss, Izzy wasn't sure. But either scenario made her uneasy. Izzy stopped drinking the limoncello. She needed to be sober to navigate this conversation.

"Good, good. I ask this of all our interns after their first few weeks, but I'm especially interested in your acclimation. Not only because I feel a certain responsibility for you as Maria's friend, but also because I make it my business to observe my interns, and what I'm observing concerns me."

More than one troubling thought raised Izzy's anxiety. Had she forgotten an important assignment or not met Adelina's expectations in the garden? Izzy summoned her voice.

"Have I done something wrong?"

"Oh, Izzy! Not at all. My concern is your isolation. You don't seem to have formed any connections with the other interns. I don't expect the members of the team to become best friends, but by the end of a couple of weeks I usually see a cohesiveness developing. As far as I can tell, you are contributing fully to group efforts, like the day we got the villa ready for the arrival of the archaeologists. But you remain outside the group. You retreat. I often see you alone, either wandering in the early morning with your sketch pad or losing yourself in the solitude of the library after your chores. That's why I knew where to send Nonno this afternoon to find you."

Izzy felt both a sense of relief that she hadn't made a serious misstep in her responsibilities and a troubling warning signal that her efforts to avoid mistakes had only heightened Linda's perception that Izzy was "different."

"I remember you as much more vivacious when you visited with Maria. Full of questions, willing to massacre the language with your attempts to speak Italian, and delightfully open to new experiences. You tried every morsel of food offered to you and came back from every excursion full of wonder and excitement. Except for your morning walks, I don't think you've left the grounds since you arrived. You aren't the Izzy I remember."

Because I'm not! Izzy screamed silently to herself. A part of her longed to unburden herself to Linda and reveal her secret. Linda was offering her an opportunity to do so. But Izzy was aware that Linda thought she could fix whatever was holding Izzy back. She struggled to deflect Linda's concerns.

"You know, the rigors of my first year at Harvard really wore me out. Lots of burning the midnight oil in the library, hiding from people so I could do the demanding work. I guess I got out of the practice of relaxing with people socially. It's always taken me some time to get comfortable with new people. Growing up on an island, I didn't get much practice. I hope I'm not causing you unnecessary worry. I'm simply shy, and I'm better with a close-knit group I've known for a long time. It may take me longer, but I'll find friends here."

"That's a relief. And I do understand. I was very shy myself growing up. I want you to flourish here, and if there is anything I can do to help, please ask. I know with a community like Portarello, where we both work and live together, the dynamic can sometimes be stressful. I want to make sure that you don't feel shut out."

"Not at all! It's very kind of you to be watching out for me."

But Izzy was chafing under Linda's watchfulness, feeling like a child who needed coddling. Had Maria revealed more to Linda about Izzy's recent history than Izzy had wanted? She took another small sip of limoncello, hoping to dispel any sign that she was uncomfortable with the conversation. Getting up and stalking off, as she knew she wanted desperately to do, was not an option here.

"Adelina is delighted with you, if you haven't already realized. I know she can be a bit gruff and direct, but she thinks you are a natural in the garden. She says you have a gift, that your hands talk to the plants, communicating love."

Izzy laughed. "That's more words than Adelina has said to me since I knelt down beside her to learn the difference between a weed and an artichoke."

"Well, she definitely thinks you've learned that lesson well. She's actually lobbying me to allow her to keep you in the garden beyond your rotation. As much as I like to keep Adelina happy, I think it would be good for you to explore other roles on the farm."

"What will be my next assignment?"

"It's the pigs. At the end of next week you move up the hill. I expect those talented hands of yours will find lots of opportunities to exercise your skills."

"I can't wait! As much as I'm enjoying the garden, working with the pigs will be an adventure. I went to see them for the first time this afternoon. Even in that short visit, I could see personalities emerging."

"Now, that's the Izzy I remember—curious and open and observant! But I should let you go off to your own pursuits."

"Have a pleasant evening. And thanks for indulging me in my role as mother hen. I want all my chicks to be happy."

Izzy smiled as Linda gathered up the glasses and the bottle and sauntered off to the villa.

CHAPTER EIGHT

MAY 7

Izzy was carrying a basket of Swiss chard up to the kitchen when she heard her name called from an upper-story window. She nearly dropped the basket as Maria leaned out.

"I'll be right down. Wait for me."

Izzy had a moment of anxiety. Had Maria written her that she was coming and she'd forgotten? Wouldn't Linda or Raffaello have mentioned Maria's visit? She had no more time to mull over her confusion before Maria burst through the door and ran down the stone steps from the terrace.

Izzy managed to get the basket on the grass before Maria enveloped her in an embrace.

"It's so good to see you. Look at you! You're a Portarello natural from what I hear from my cousin. I knew this would be a good place for you!"

Izzy stepped back, overwhelmed by Maria's exuberance and assumptions.

"I didn't know you were coming," she admitted.

"It was a spur-of-the-moment decision. My summer job fell through, and word has spread in the family that this dig of my grandfather's could use a few more hands. But I want to hear about *you*. Are you busy now, or can you take some time to talk?"

"I've got to deliver the Swiss chard to the kitchen and then thin some lettuce. Why don't you come down to the garden with me. We can catch up while I show off my newly acquired agricultural skills."

Maria threw her arm around Izzy and accompanied her to the kitchen.

"It's so good to be here and to be with you."

After Annunziata, the cook, welcomed Maria with open arms and the offer of a taste of the sauce simmering on the stove, Izzy led her to the orderly rows of lettuce.

Kneeling side by side, they separated the tightly packed plants and slipped into the familiar intimacy bred by years living together as roommates.

"How are you finding life here? Was it the right decision? I feel responsible for suggesting it."

"It's been good. I love working on the farm in ways I hadn't anticipated. But it's also been harder than I expected."

"In what way?"

"I thought I'd be free of the burden I felt at home, with my parents hovering over me. At least I'm not carrying their worry on my shoulders. But what I haven't escaped is my own need to prove myself. I don't want to fail at this, this opportunity to find peace with who I am now."

"You always were a perfectionist," Maria grinned. "I hoped you'd find peace here as well. It's why I proposed it. You're still you, Izzy."

"No, Maria. I'm not. I'm not the 'brilliant scholar' even Linda and your grandfather seem to remember and constantly bring up. You know, I naively thought I could come here with no past to live up to. But apparently I made quite an impression on your family on that Easter visit years ago."

"One of these days you'll realize people love you not for your brain but for your spirit, Izzy. Whatever happened that day on Route 2 may have taken away some of your memories, but it didn't steal the core of who you are."

"But aren't our memories part of what defines us?"

"I don't think you've forgotten how to be kind or compassionate. That is who I know you to be."

"Thanks, Mar. I didn't know how much I missed your pep talks. I'm really glad you're here."

"I am too. Now let's get this lettuce done and then go for a swim. If I don't, my jet lag will catch up with me and I'll fall asleep right here."

The pool was protected from view by a thick hedge, and it was empty when they pulled open the gate. They swam laps, racing and egging each other on, just as they had when they'd studied together at Smith. Izzy finally gave in, splashing Maria and teasing her that she had actually won because she'd been swimming with only one good leg. Maria splashed back, and the two spent the next half hour laughing and doing cannonballs into the pool.

It was the first time Izzy had felt unguarded since she'd arrived at Portarello.

As they dried off, Maria invited her to have dinner with Raffaello. "I'm staying at Linda's house, but the family eats together every night at my grandfather's place."

Izzy shrugged. She'd enjoyed the afternoon with Maria—the comfort of friendship and the freedom from the strain of hiding her history. But the sting of Linda's observations about Izzy's isolation and the expectations of

Raffaello made Izzy wary of spending an extended amount of time with them in such a private setting.

"Won't your family want you all to themselves, to catch up?"

"Frankly, Izzy, I need a buffer. My grandfather is waiting for me to announce either my engagement to be married or an offer of a position at the Brookings Institute. I can do neither right now, and I need to distract him."

"Is either of those options likely? Have I been out of the loop so much since my retreat to the Vineyard this winter that I don't know this?"

"You're not out of the loop. There's nothing to know. I'm not even dating, but in Italian families hope springs eternal that I'll find someone in time to produce the requisite number of bambini."

"And the Brookings Institute? Have you not told me because you didn't want to hurt me?"

"Oh, God, no. I'm simply floundering, not sure what I want to do with my life. Raffaello, as enlightened as he is, would like to see me go into archaeology and carry on his legacy."

"But that's not what you want?"

"I spent my summers here as a kid digging up pottery shards, but it's not my passion. There is so much unrest in the world—the war in Vietnam, the Troubles in Northern Ireland, nearly every nation in the world with the bomb conducting nuclear tests. Hiding away in an ivory tower seems pointless to me."

"Is that what I'm doing, hiding away?"

"Not at all. Portarello is trying to save the world through farming. I'm not joking. It's Linda's cause, her philosophy."

"Well, it's saving me. Sure, I'll be your buffer at dinner tonight. I enjoy your grandfather. I just don't want to disappoint him."

"Neither do I. Come at six. It's early, but I'm not ready to have a one-on-one with Nonno yet. If you're there, he'll stay away from the hard questions."

The evening with Raffaello and Linda was as relaxed as Maria had promised. Raffaello got to regale his granddaughter with the progress of the dig, Linda was pleased to see Izzy enjoying Maria's company, and no hard questions for either Maria or Izzy surfaced to dispel the conviviality of the evening.

"Strength in numbers," Maria whispered to Izzy as they said good night.

"Tomorrow is your day off. Linda told me when I asked her if I could steal you for the day. I've got a little Fiat Cinquecento. Let's quit this joint and escape to Siena. What have you seen of Italy since you got here?"

"Nothing. I've pretty much stuck to the mountain."

"Well, let me be your guide. Seven o'clock sharp; I'll meet you in the outer courtyard."

Izzy left Maria, smiling.

The next morning, Maria navigated her tiny car down the mountain, passing the familiar landmarks Izzy had sketched on her walks. Once on the *Strada Provinciale* heading northeast, she watched the Tuscan landscape as Maria rambled in her conversation, touching on former classmates who were marrying or writing plays or going to law school, her volunteer work on the McGovern campaign, and a group of young activists who met for Sunday dinner at her mother's house.

"My mother is happy watching them devour her ravioli and chicken Francese. As long as they eat and then do the dishes, she doesn't care about their politics."

"I think my mother would do the same, although she'd probably agree with their activism. My brother's antiwar work after he came back from Vietnam made her a believer."

Maria slapped her forehead. "God, I'd forgotten that Jo is a Vietnam vet. Do you think he'd be interested in joining us?"

"I suppose you could ask him, but I think he's wary of working with folks who don't understand his experiences as a soldier."

"I hear you. I'll call him when I get back and test the waters. Maybe I'll even go out to see him again. I can never get enough of your mother's pies."

"They'd love to see you. But you have to promise me that you'll be selective in what you tell them about me. I don't want my father getting on a plane to come here and rescue me."

"What could I possibly tell them that would worry them? I told you yesterday, you are still Izzy. The fears you have about disappointing people are based on some myths you've created for yourself. I can assure you, given what Linda and Nonno said last night after you left, they adore you."

"Really? I guess I'm hiding my infirmity better than I thought."

"Izz, you don't have to hide!"

"How about we stop talking about this and just enjoy the day." Izzy tried hard to keep her tone light, but from the look on Maria's face, it was as if she had slapped her. She immediately backtracked.

"I'm sorry, Mar. I'm still trying to figure out who I am. Forgive me for not being able to believe you. The last thing I want is for us to be angry with each other. I'm so grateful that you are here. I really need you."

Maria reached over and grabbed Izzy's hand.

"I'm sorry, too, for being my usual know-it-all self. I can't fathom how hard this is for you. But I'm here for you."

"Thanks. I feel sometimes like a parent who has lost a child. I'm bereft."

"You're in mourning, and I'm telling you to get over it. What an insensitive clod I've been!"

"Stop beating up on yourself. Can we declare a truce? I'll stop whining about my lost intelligence if you'll lighten up on telling me I haven't lost anything. Deal?"

"Deal. And just in time. There's the tower of the Palazzo Pubblico. We're here."

They arrived back at Portarello late in the evening, sated with *acciughe sotto pesto* and *pappardelle con lepre* and laden with shopping bags filled with art books from the National Gallery, handmade shoes of butter-soft leather, and dresses knit from merino wool. The open-air market had been a revelation to Izzy, who listened, mesmerized, as Maria had haggled for their purchases.

As she was unpacking her discoveries, she thought with longing how perfect the dress and shoes would be for an English professor teaching at a university in Boston. She fingered the fine fabric and wondered where in her life now she might ever wear this outfit.

She folded the olive green dress, a color Maria had insisted enhanced her hazel eyes. Wrapping it up again in the tissue paper from the market stall, she tucked it away on a shelf behind the jeans and tee shirts that were now her daily uniform.

Despite the frenzied pace at which Maria had led her and the exhaustion that followed, Izzy struggled as usual to fall asleep. Her leg throbbed, and her brain fought to still the fragments of memories flitting in and out of her consciousness. At first she compared them to the fireflies she'd tried to catch as a child in the garden at Innisfree, their lights teasing her to come follow and then going dim as she got near. But the fireflies had been benign. These memories hovering close and then whipping away were more like wasps, threatening to sting. Swatting them away was useless, but trying to pull them close was fraught with potential pain.

Sleep finally came and churned with dreams, many set in her childhood home at Innisfree. The faces of her family moved in and out of the familiar rooms. Naomi, wordless, smiling at her and nodding approval as she sat knitting on the porch; Mae, rolling out pie dough and gesturing to her to fill a pail with blueberries; Tobias, his damaged but nevertheless strong hands rigging the Sunfish for her; Josiah, tugging at her arm, frustrated that she wanted to stay at the pond instead of going to the Boat House for lunch; and then, a child's face, deep in concentration, studying some tiny animal making its way across the clam flat. This little girl appeared to be in a trance, seeing something more than the physical world in front of her. Izzy heard herself in the dream asking the child, "What do you see?" but the girl didn't hear her. Izzy felt a desperate need for an answer, reaching out to shake the girl and shouting at her, "Tell me!"

Her own voice woke Izzy, forcing her body up from the pillow, trembling with rage. But she couldn't remember what had made her so angry. Frightened at her own vehemence, she threw back the covers and stumbled to the bathroom to wash her face and banish her unease.

It was too early to go for her usual morning walk, but the confines of her room were stifling. She grabbed a sweatshirt and her sandals and left, making her way down the stone steps and into the night.

Wary of leaving the grounds, she headed for the garden gate instead. She winced at the sound as she pulled it open, disturbed by the screech of metal against metal that she was sure she hadn't heard before in all the days she'd passed through on her way to her work. She looked up at the villa to see if the noise had awakened anyone, but all the windows were dark. It made her feel like the only person in the world with insomnia.

She descended the path. It was unlit, but her feet had travelled the route often enough not to trip her. She had no destination in mind, no plot of particular vegetables she thought might soothe her. Somehow, pouring out her worries to a zucchini vine didn't feel like a solution. She just wanted to keep moving, and the garden was a safe place to do that—not only because she knew the terrain, but also because it was the one place where she found peace. In the daytime she didn't have to think when she worked in the garden. Perhaps she could find that same escape from thought here in the dark.

She walked in and out of the orderly rows laid down by Adelina in the last few years, but she imagined that

her path had been trod for centuries by the peasants
who had once farmed this land. That comforted her, that
connection to the past. She could no longer hold onto her
own memories, but she found solace in sensing that this
earth itself was holding the memories of all those who had
toiled here and found sustenance in that toil.

She didn't know how long she walked. Her watch was
still next to the lamp in her room. But she sensed the
change in the light as the varying tones of grey around
her gave way to the greens of spinach and lettuce and
Swiss chard and the frothy tops of carrots. By the time she
climbed back up to the villa someone might have started
the coffee pot.

As she hoped, sounds emanated from the kitchen
when she entered the lower hall. A faucet running,
voices murmuring, crockery landing on the stainless steel
counter. She stuck her head in from the hall.

"Coffee ready yet?"

Annunziata, at the stove, raised an eyebrow at this very
early bird. She motioned with the spatula in her hand
toward a metal thermos on the table and gave Izzy a
puzzled look as her eyes swept over Izzy's attire.

Izzy looked down and saw that her sweatshirt was inside
out and her flower-sprigged L.L.Bean nightgown peeked
out from beneath the shirt. The hem of the nightgown was
damp and mud-spattered in places.

"I couldn't sleep," she explained, as she pulled a mug
from the cabinet in the hall and entered the kitchen to
pour some coffee. She thanked Annunziata and climbed
the stairs back to her room, her hand protectively shielding
the coffee from spilling en route.

Back in her room she gulped down the coffee, its strong flavor and caffeine-heavy dose offering her the jolt she needed to get through the day. A note she'd taped to her dresser mirror reminded her that this was the day she was to visit Raffaello's Etruscan gallery. Izzy admitted that she felt less anxious since her dinner with him, but she was still unable to free herself of the sense that every encounter with anyone at Portarello was a test.

It was Sunday, which meant she wouldn't have the calming work in the garden to dispel her anxieties.

She stood under the shower to amplify the work of her early-morning coffee in rousing her from the effects of her wakeful night. With water streaming down her face, she felt a pang of regret that she'd never embraced Naomi's deep faith. When she'd turned away from her grandmother's spiritual wisdom it hadn't been a sharp break but more a drifting carried by the tide of her intellectual life. Had she kept even the awe of a small child for Naomi's abiding belief in a power greater than herself, would she have found the peace she so desperately sought?

The water was beginning to cool, and she abruptly turned off both the faucet and her fruitless regret. Naomi's faith would never be Izzy's.

After a breakfast of yoghurt and fruit, Izzy took the path behind the villa to the old granary, where the gallery was housed. She pushed open the heavy oak door and found Raffaello bent over a work table filled with pottery fragments.

He looked up with a welcoming smile as Izzy entered the room.

"Isabella! Welcome. Just give me a moment to finish this task. Please, feel free to wander around the display."

Izzy was grateful for the few moments to herself, an opportunity to take the measure of her surroundings. In the weeks she'd been at Portarello she'd never ventured into the gallery, mainly because she'd forgotten, of course, that it was there. Too many other, more important places to remember in the vastness of the villa and its surroundings.

She first stood in the middle of the room and reminded herself to allow her senses to take in the space. The ceiling arched above her. At one time, there may have been two levels, but now it was one immense open room. The morning sun was cut into sharp angular panels of light by the two windows, one above the door and the other on the opposite wall. Three sides of the room were lined with shelves on which the ancient Etruscan pottery was displayed. Some were mere shards, and others were recognizable shapes of daily life—a bowl, a pitcher, something that appeared to be an oil lamp.

She turned to the table where Raffaello's deft fingers gently cleaned an amphora with a brush only a centimeter wide. His back was bent over the table. Izzy recognized intense concentration and knew he had already forgotten she was there.

She should leave, slip away. It would be a relief, or at least a postponement, from her fear of disappointing Raffaello. As much as she had been drawn to understanding the Etruscans, she was bitterly aware that whatever Raffaello could impart would disappear as quickly as the words reached her ears. Unexpected anger rather than sadness rose up within her at the thought of the longed-for knowledge just beyond her reach.

Fists clenched, she turned to leave.

"You're welcome to touch whatever speaks to you on the shelves. I find that holding a piece brings a connection that mere observing cannot give me."

So he was still aware of her presence. Had he also recognized her compelling need?

She relaxed her fingers and moved toward a bowl, surrounding it with her bare hands. She didn't lift it at first but felt the texture and shape fill the circle of her embrace.

"Why don't you bring that here and come sit beside me? That bowl is as good a piece as any to start your initiation into the mysteries that fill this room and this land."

Izzy took a grateful breath and brought the bowl to Raffaello, its heft familiar, as if she had filled it once before and taken nourishment from it, as she knew she was about to now.

She settled in on a stool next to the old man and hovered close as he began to speak.

When Izzy pulled out her notepad to record what Raffaello said, he stilled her hand.

"Wait," he said. "I've noticed you, always writing, anxious, it seems to me, to capture every word. Let it be this morning. Touch. Smell. Listen."

Izzy bit her lip to quiet her protest. How could she tell him she needed the notes without revealing her damaged self?

"Isabella, trust yourself. You have a gift. It may not be the brilliant mind that enabled you to become a scholar, but the brain is a mysterious organ. Yours is trying to forge a new path of knowing. Let it do its work."

Izzy tensed. "How did you know? Did Maria tell you?"

"No, Maria has said nothing. I'm a scientist, Isabella. I observe, I record, I draw conclusions. The fragments arrayed on the shelves here have given me glimpses into the lives of those who created these objects. Over the time you've been with us, I've caught fragments of your experience—mostly through Linda but also from seeing you occasionally in action, especially in the garden. Always, I see you scribbling in your notebook. At first, I thought you were a particularly disciplined writer, keeping a journal of your experiences here. Early one morning, on my way to the dig, I saw you sketching with intense concentration.

"When you came to dinner with Maria on Friday evening I began to piece together these fragments. Your focus during the conversation at the table, listening so carefully, sometimes repeating what one of us had said, as if to confirm what you had heard but actually an attempt to remember. I knew from Maria about your auto accident but not the extent of your injuries. I saw the scar on your forehead and made an educated guess that you'd sustained a head wound. You've lost some memory function, haven't you?"

Izzy nodded.

"Not just 'some.' My short-term memory."

She lifted her hands. "I probably won't retain anything I learn from you today."

"The Etruscans were lost to history, and yet we are now slowly excavating their secrets. Whatever you lost in the accident you may rediscover in another form. Don't give up on yourself."

CHAPTER NINE

MAY 17

"Come with me to Volterra tomorrow morning," Raffaello said to her one evening at dinner. "I want to show you something."

Once a week, Raffaello joined the archaeologists and interns for dinner under the pergola at the communal table. One of the archaeologists, holding a serving spoon over a platter of broccoli rabe, stopped midair for a fraction of a second when he heard Raffaello's invitation. A flicker of curiosity, or perhaps envy, animated his face. But then he put down the spoon, picked up the platter, and passed it to the person seated next to him.

Raffaello was waiting for Izzy's answer. She took a sip of water, not the wine at everyone else's place, her fingers nearly slipping on the condensation slicking the outside of the tumbler.

"What time are you planning to go?" She waved her fingers toward the hillside. "The pigs, they have to be fed."

Raffaello's lips thinned to a taut smile. "I'm sure Linda can find someone else for one day."

Izzy shrugged. Linda was her boss but Raffaello's granddaughter. Of course Linda would find someone else.

As soon as the meal was over, Izzy scraped back her chair and turned toward the house, trying not to move quickly but nearly tripping over her clumsy feet.

The next morning Izzy rose with her alarm. She saw the note she'd written to herself propped against the face of the illuminated travel clock, a gift from her parents before her departure. She had taken it gratefully as a sign of their acceptance of her decision.

"Volterra with Raffaello—8:30 a.m."

She stirred from beneath the sheets, pulled her towel from the rack, and marched to the bathroom as if it were the principal's office. The water coming out of the tap was tepid at the best of times, but this morning it was positively frigid. She hurried through her shower, which she needed more as a wake-up boost than a thorough scrubbing. She had sloughed off the dirt and sweat from her work with the pigs the afternoon before.

She chose a dress from her armoire rather than her usual jeans and tee shirt. Raffaello hadn't offered any details of their excursion, but Izzy assumed that a visit to the city would require more than her working attire. She braided her hair, slipped her notebook into her tote bag, and closed the door behind her.

The dining room was empty when she arrived. A relief, really. She didn't want to face either outright questions or minimally disguised hostility from the archaeologists. She'd sensed the tension at dinner—not only curiosity but resentment. Why had Raffaello singled her out when everyone at the table was anxious to have his attention?

She tossed a roll on her plate, carved a slab of butter from the rapidly softening stick on the table, and poured herself a large cup of very dark coffee, fortification for the unknown day ahead. She took her rapidly assembled breakfast out to the stone wall overlooking the vegetable garden, out of view of the pergola. She was in no mood for conversation, speculation, or even stilted small talk.

She stood sipping the steaming, bitter coffee and glanced down at the garden. In the distance she saw Raffaello doing what appeared to be calisthenics, his body moving smoothly and rhythmically through a series of motions. He was in his mid-seventies, but from what Izzy had observed, he was as strong and limber as the grad students in their twenties. She knew the work at the dig was strenuous, and Raffaello was not one to supervise from a distance.

His back had been turned from her when he was exercising, but when he finished and began the climb back up through the garden, she saw not the fit, age-defying man she expected but someone haggard, the color drained from his face and sweat stains forming on his shirt. She knew that face, recognizing in it her own struggles when she pushed herself through pain during physical therapy to strengthen her leg muscles.

Raffaello had clearly been driving himself close to his limit and Izzy wondered why. That kind of compulsive behavior didn't match what she'd learned of him in the last few weeks. To her, he was supremely confident, sure of himself, and calm. What she'd just witnessed seemed to have its roots in fear. Raffaello didn't strike her as a man afraid of old age or even death. He had surrounded himself with death his whole career, culminating now in this dig that could possibly reveal a tomb. Something else was hovering over him to evoke the transformation she saw as he left the garden.

She didn't think he would want her to see him in such disarray, so she slipped to the far side of a cypress tree. She doubted he would come in her direction, as there was a side gate to his terrace at the top of the garden.

She heard the click of the latch and the slap of the wood as the gate swung shut. When she was sure Raffaello was on his way to his house, Izzy picked up her cup and retreated to the kitchen through the door under the terrace. She could hear voices in the dining room as she moved down the hall. She ducked into the kitchen, rinsed her cup, and left again quickly. She had more time than she'd anticipated before she was supposed to meet Raffaello and decided to run up to the library.

It was a task she'd meant to do the night before but had forgotten. She knew Linda kept a stack of local brochures on one of the tables, guidebooks and pamphlets for the interns who wanted to explore the surrounding countryside. She rifled through them until she found one for Volterra and started flipping pages for a clue to where Raffaello was taking her. She found it, prominently displayed—the Guarnacci Etruscan Museum. The image illustrating the museum's extensive collection was a marriage bed depicting an older couple, their faces lined with wrinkles but with expressions of tenderness.

She tucked the brochure into her notebook and left the library. Raffaello was waiting for her in the upper courtyard beside his Land Rover.

"Ready for an adventure?"

Izzy smiled uncertainly and nodded. Perhaps she was wrong about the museum, which she'd hardly define as an adventure. She climbed into the passenger seat and they drove away, raising the usual cloud of dust along the driveway and then down the mountain.

When they reached the valley, Izzy found her curiosity overwhelming and turned to ask Raffaello where they were going.

"Cerveteri," he answered.

"But last night you said Volterra." Izzy was sure. She'd written it down.

"We'll eventually end up in Volterra, but first, I want you to experience an Etruscan necropolis. To understand what we are digging for at Portarello, you need a more immersive understanding of what we know about Etruscan burial practices."

"I felt awkward, being singled out at dinner."

"You mean the envious glances from the team that I hadn't invited them along?"

"So you noticed them too?"

"Oh, yes. It's why I told you we were going to Volterra. There's an Etruscan museum there. They all know it and have been there. It made it easier for them to dismiss the attention you were getting from me."

"Nevertheless, they crave your notice. As mundane as a trip to Volterra might have been for them, it would still have been time spent with you."

"You're quite observant of the eddies and currents swirling around Portarello right now."

"I have to be. You know that. I'm already isolated not only by not being an archaeologist but also because of my impairment. By appearing to be your favorite, I'm even further set apart."

"First, it is not simply appearance. You are my favorite, for reasons I hope to help you understand. But I thought you preferred your isolation. That it protected you."

"Yes," Izzy admitted. "I don't feel safe among the others. Except for Maria, you're the only one I've been honest with. Because you accept me as I am now, not because of your memory of who I was before. I haven't even been open with Linda."

"Linda cares about you."

"I know. She worries about my happiness, and I don't want to disappoint her. I'm very grateful to be here. For the work. For the refuge."

"I can assure you that you haven't disappointed her. In fact, there isn't a single member of the Portarello staff who has found you lacking."

Izzy shook her head. "*I* find me lacking."

"Isabella, I am going to ask you for a promise on this excursion today. A promise to be open to what you will see and learn and not to worry about what you'll be able to retain. I ask that you allow yourself simply to experience it. In the same way you picked up the bowl in the gallery and absorbed its meaning and its history."

"Will I be able to touch things?"

"Yes. I have some authority where we are going. Touch. Smell. Inhale the very atmosphere. Feel the stones under your feet. All of it. Do you promise?"

Izzy felt her scalp tingle and goosebumps rise on her arms as Raffaello spoke. His words stirred something in her that she hadn't felt in a long time. A hunger that had lain dormant since her realization that her short-term memory was gone.

"I promise," she whispered.

They drove for more than two hours, the roads becoming narrower and less traveled the farther they ventured into the Tuscan countryside. Their conversation subsided into a comfortable silence.

When the car came to a stop, Izzy stirred, realizing she'd dozed off.

"We've arrived," Raffaello announced. "The Banditaccia necropolis, one of the best examples of Etruscan funerary architecture."

Ahead of them was a gatehouse staffed by a single guard who came out as Raffaello and Izzy approached.

"Professore Richetelli! Welcome. We've been expecting you. It's good to see you again."

"Likewise, Arturo. May I introduce Isabella Monroe, an intern this summer at Portarello and an avid scholar, new to the world of the Etruscans."

Arturo shook her hand. "Welcome, Signorina. Please, may you discover our treasures here. There is much to learn."

He opened the gate and waved them in. Izzy was struck by the absence of tourists. "Why is no one else here?"

"It's a Monday. The necropolis is closed to the public, but open to you. I told you, I have some authority here. Now, remember your promise. I'm not here to guide you or lecture you. Just wander. Stop where you feel the need. You'll need this, however, once you descend." He handed her a headlight. "I'll wait for you over by the fountain." He indicated a stone bowl, gently burbling with falling water.

Izzy slipped the light over her head and began to traverse the path that led her to a series of mounds. As she explored, she saw what appeared to be small huts with doors. She glanced around, seeking Raffaello, as if to ask him for permission to open a door. But he was no longer at the fountain. Had she forgotten where he said he'd wait? She hesitated. She knew with certainty that he had told her to stop wherever she felt the need. She had permission. She took a deep breath and reached for a door handle.

Beyond the door was a set of stone steps overgrown with lichen descending into a pit. She reached up to turn on the headlight and took her first steps down into the tomb.

At the bottom of the steps she found a hard-packed earthen floor, damp close to the steps but farther in she could see puddles. She was assaulted by a rank odor—not quite raw sewage but close, as if she'd entered a cave where the inhabitants had relieved themselves and left it to rot.

Izzy found it difficult to believe that a site as famous as the Banditaccia necropolis was so poorly maintained. She couldn't imagine tourists being led down here by a guide and confronted with such filth.

Hesitant but not yet deterred by the smell, she took a step deeper into the chamber. She turned her head slowly, using the lamp to illuminate the boundaries of the room. She detected stone walls that appeared to be decorated and moved closer to examine them.

Her eyes tracked life-sized figures, either warriors in combat or athletes wrestling, she wasn't sure; but the grace and physicality of the drawings made them seem to move. Izzy shook her head to clear her sight. An illusion, she assured herself. A trick of a very sophisticated artist. But to what purpose in a tomb? To entertain the gods? To assure the dead of a life beyond?

She reached out her hand, reminded of Raffaello's encouragement to use all her senses. What did she think, that she could stop the movement on the wall with her touch? But as soon as her fingers reached the pigment, she pulled them back. The walls were as damp as the floor, the paint as tacky as if it had been laid down only a few hours before. Her brain sought a logical explanation. The room was probably being restored, she thought. Maybe that also accounted for the smell, some reconstruction of ancient pigments to mimic the original work.

She moved back from the wall and turned to explore the other corners. The odor was less intrusive away from the wall and had shifted subtly from urine to decay. *It's a tomb, Izzy. Of course it's going to smell like decay!* Farther into the tomb the ceiling sloped down, and Izzy had to crouch to avoid hitting her head. She found a stone platform—or rather, it found her, as she bumped her knees against the sharp edge. The platform ran around two sides of the chamber, reminding her of built-in furniture. They've constructed a home for the dead, Izzy thought, a recreation of the familiar and domestic to ease the transition to the next life. She discovered more wall paintings in the second chamber that appeared to be a family celebration: a table set lavishly with abundant food, dancers, musicians.

She took some comfort in the intentions of the space, despite its dank and unpleasant twentieth-century manifestations. She wasn't afraid down here, alone in the dark, and that surprised her. It had no resemblance to her own experience of death, which had been full of light and bliss, but she recognized it for another interpretation of the human hunger to know what lay beyond. She felt at home here. Welcome.

She shivered. She realized with sudden clarity that she didn't want to feel welcome. She turned abruptly and found her way back to the steps and the patch of light that revealed the opening of the tomb. She reached up to turn off her headlamp and slowly climbed the steps. The smell of death lingered on her clothes as she emerged into the sunshine.

Raffaello was waiting for her. Instead of questioning her, as she expected, he let her be. They wandered together for a short time and then left.

"You may want to write down what you experienced—for yourself, not for me."

On the ride back to Portarello, Izzy filled her notebook as quickly as she could get the images in her brain translated to words.

Daniel

CHAPTER TEN

JUNE 15 – 16

Daniel Richetelli, S.J., fastened his clerical collar, slipped on his black jacket, and picked up his gray Samsonite suitcase. Checking that his airline ticket and passport were in his pocket, he left his austere quarters on the Fordham University campus without a backward glance. The taxi was waiting below.

Once in the cab, he leaned his head back against the seat and closed his eyes. He hadn't slept well the night before. Hell, he hadn't had a decent night's sleep in the last six months. His last conversation with his spiritual advisor replayed in his brain as the cabbie negotiated the Bronx traffic toward the Whitestone Bridge.

"Daniel, the provincial's decision has come down. You're to take a leave of absence, effective immediately. I considered requesting a delay to allow you to teach the summer semester, but you and I both know you don't have the resources to get you through the next two months. I've already spoken to the dean about finding a replacement for your classes.

"Go to your family. Sleep. When you're ready, try to pray again. I'll be here, waiting. As God is."

The words, meant to be reassuring and full of hope, had only reinforced Daniel's sense of despair. The Jesuit spiritual practice of daily meditation and self-examination had failed him. The guidance of Francis Xavier Fallon, his advisor, although well-meaning and compassionate, had been inadequate to pierce the impenetrable prison of his grief. God was definitely not waiting for Daniel Richetelli.

A crisis of faith, the provincial had labelled it. Daniel wasn't alone in these troubled times to be questioning the basis of Jesuit ideology—to find God in all things. But most of the young men who had confronted their crises had worked through their demons—whether women, or addiction, or the attraction of the radical politics of that other Daniel, Berrigan. The provincial had given them a choice: obey or leave.

Daniel didn't know if he wanted to leave, and so he was, for the time being, obeying. He was going to his family. He wasn't sure about sleeping. Or praying. The provincial hadn't questioned the plane ticket to Italy, even though he must have known Daniel's parents lived thirty minutes from Fordham in the Westchester suburb of New Rochelle. They were not the family Daniel had chosen to seek refuge with. No, he was turning to his grandfather. Or rather, to his grandfather's isolated home on a mountain outside of Siena.

The old man hadn't questioned why Daniel was coming. He had long ago extended an open invitation to all his grandchildren. The villa would always be there for them, he had told them one Christmas. If you need a refuge, if you want to dig in the dirt with me, or if you simply need a few days to hike in the woods and eat well, come to Portarello. You don't even have to let me know in advance. Just show up at my door.

Daniel had sent a telegram. Despite his grandfather's magnanimous offer of perpetual hospitality, in his fragile state Daniel knew he didn't want to show up in the middle of one of Raffaello's archaeological symposia, with bearded academics pontificating about the meaning of the afterlife in Etruscan culture.

His grandfather's response had been immediate. "Come."

That was it. No "Why?" No "Have you told your parents?" No "Do you have the permission of the provincial?" Especially not that question. Raffaello was in possession of a characteristic more often associated with Southern Italians—a deep and abiding distrust of the Church.

When Daniel had announced his intention to enter the seminary ten years before, Raffaello had sat with him over a bottle of Scotch through a long and brutal night of questioning—pushing him to articulate and justify and make unassailable his reasons for wanting to become a priest.

"Not just a priest," Daniel had insisted. "A Jesuit."

In the end, he had told his grandfather that his decision couldn't be defined and explained with logic and a tightly built case. "It's a leap of faith," he said. "I only know I've been called. I don't know why—yet."

He wondered how Raffaello would react when he learned the reason for Daniel's visit. Exultant? Vindicated?

Daniel stared out the window at the congested highway, the graffiti on the walls, the blight of crumbling tenements and prison-like housing projects. Within those buildings a world of pain and hopelessness existed, and he had been unable to offer those living there any solace.

He put his hand up to his collar, the outward symbol of his identity that even in these tumultuous times still brought him a measure of respect. Once, it had given him satisfaction to wear. But now, in the confines of this cab hurtling toward the next stage in his life and within the isolation of his angry and despairing mind, the collar was choking him with the falsehood it represented. Given his fractured spirit, he didn't deserve to wear it. He especially didn't want to arrive in Rome proclaiming himself to be a priest.

He reached behind his neck and unbuttoned the stiff white band. He caught the eye of the cabbie in the rearview mirror.

"Takin' a vacation from the priesthood, eh, Father?"

Daniel shrugged and stuffed the collar in his pocket. He saw the cabbie's smirk and felt like a husband who slips off his wedding ring when he goes on a business trip. But Daniel knew that wearing the collar at this moment in his life was more of a betrayal of his vows than not keeping it on.

They rode on in silence until the cab pulled up at the Pan Am terminal.

"Have a good trip, Father." The cabbie handed him his suitcase. "Put in a good word for me with God."

God hasn't been listening to me lately, Daniel wanted to tell him. But out of instinct or habit, he made a quick blessing over the man after he paid him his fare. Then he turned toward the building.

After getting his boarding pass, he made a stop in the men's room to change his shirt, furthering the process of peeling away his priestly layers. If only it were this simple, putting off the garment as easily as it had been put on, as St. Paul had described in his epistle.

No one told you this would be uncomplicated and clear-cut, he reminded himself.

He ordered a Scotch as soon as the drinks service began on the flight and saluted his grandfather. Here's to another long night of conversation, Nonno.

The familiarity of Rome stung him with unexpected pain. He'd spent a year after seminary here, doing research in the Vatican Library for his doctoral thesis on the mystics. The cacophony of the streets, the majesty of the architecture, even the cats lounging on the tumbled columns of the Forum were mementos of another time, another Daniel. He'd been driven then, committed not only to his scholarship but also to a deep and empathetic understanding of the lives he was studying. He had envied their total abandonment of the self, their ability to place utter and complete trust in their God. The total isolation of the anchorite Julian of Norwich, the ravages of visions endured by Catherine of Siena, had been crucibles in which their profound understanding of the Divine had been formed. He'd been cautioned then by Francis Xavier not to descend too far into the dark nights of these gifted but tortured souls. Keep your intellectual distance, Francis Xavier had written him from the safety of a 20th-century college campus. Daniel had chafed under Francis Xavier's restrictions but had not defied him. He'd produced a masterful and dispassionate thesis that was both intellectually rigorous and emotionally empty.

He had left Rome without truly grasping the how and why of mystical experience, and he believed that was at the root of his current state of despair. He had stayed away from the edge of the chasm, absorbing Francis Xavier's fears, and instead had enveloped himself in the mantle of observer and analyst rather than engage in his own spiritual battle.

But now, the chasm was beckoning him, and Francis Xavier had relinquished his role by sending him away. To rest, to sleep, he said. But sleep for Daniel was elusive. And when it came, it brought nightmares.

Daniel shook away the regrets of his failed sojourn in the Holy City. The Roman traffic was as chaotic as it had been six years before, and what he needed in that moment was to focus on getting out of the airport and onto the A1 autostrada in an unfamiliar rental car that was entirely too small for his six-foot-two body.

By the time he arrived at the gates of Portarello, he had endured everything he remembered hating about Italian drivers and was questioning why he had ever imagined this place as a refuge.

He pulled into the courtyard and found it silent and empty. He hadn't called from Rome to let Raffaello know when he might arrive, so there was no reason for there to be a welcoming committee. But he nevertheless felt an overwhelming loneliness. What had he expected? That someone might have seen the car tooling up the mountain and run ahead to the villa to announce, "He's here! Danny is here!" It was siesta, for heaven's sake. No one was out in the vineyards or the olive grove where the road was visible.

Daniel turned off the motor and emerged from the car, stretching his cramped muscles and breathing in the mountain air. Behind him, he heard the rustle of the beads that hung in the open door of the Portarello farm office.

"Danny? Danny!" It was the voice of his sister Linda. It had been two years since they had seen each other at a family Christmas gathering in New Rochelle. She was five years older, the first-born among the four siblings. Although their father was Italian—Raffaello's son Dominic—their mother was an American from Charleston, South Carolina, who had come to New York to break into publishing. Clara Snowe had landed a job as an editorial assistant at Simon & Schuster and then landed a husband in Dominic Richetelli, a dashing photographer who had been hired to take portraits of the Simon & Schuster authors for their book jackets. They had been incredibly young and idealistic when they married, but four kids and World War II put their dreams on hold. Daniel imagined it was his mother's thwarted career that led her to encourage her daughters—both Linda and their younger sister, Anne Marie—to aim for something more than bambini and keeping house.

Linda Richetelli-Pepe had gone to college at Mt. St. Vincent's, living at home as most Italian Catholic girls did in the 1950s, if they went to college at all. She spent her junior year abroad in Italy—of course, under the watchful eyes of their grandparents, Raffaello and his wife, Lucia. Linda fell in love with her grandparents' country and with Benno Pepe, a jazz musician and teacher at the Liceo Musicale E. S. Piccolomini in Siena. After she graduated from college, she married Benno and returned to Siena. When Lucia passed away, she stepped into her grandmother's formidable role as mistress of Portarello.

Daniel watched as his sister approached. Like all his siblings, Linda had inherited their father's height and dark hair and their mother's eyes, a shade that was neither blue nor gray but hovered somewhere in the middle. She shaded those eyes with her dominant hand, left like Daniel's, and appraised him as thoroughly as he was assessing her.

"You look like shit. When was the last time you had a full night's sleep or a decent meal? Did the Jesuits obliterate any common sense when they trained you to be Christ's intellectual elite?"

"I love you too, Lin."

"Come here. I can see I have my work cut out for me." Linda extended her arms and Daniel willingly stepped into her embrace.

"I'm glad you decided to come here, little brother."

"Me too," mumbled Daniel into her shoulder.

After a long hug, Linda released him. "Do you want to stay at Nonno's or up here in the villa?"

"I have a choice?"

"I'm giving you a choice. I wasn't sure what you needed, so I—shall we say—managed Nonno's expectations. He'll want you to join us for dinner, but he's willing to forgo a slumber party at his house. At some point, he's going to want to ply you with Scotch and interrogate you, but I think I've persuaded him to let you get over your jet lag first."

"Thanks, Sis. I'll take a room at the inn, as long as there's a shower in the vicinity."

"That's what I assumed you'd want. I've got a room ready for you at the back of the house. It's quieter there in the evenings. The intern crew tends to congregate on the front lawn late into the night. Grab your bag and follow me."

After leading him to his room, Linda filled him in on the comings and goings of family currently at Portarello.

"Benno is on tour with his quintet and will be back in a couple of weeks. He's looking forward to seeing you. And Maria arrived from Boston to spend the summer, but she's off in Rome for some meeting of expatriate Democrats, trying to build support for McGovern. It will just be the three of us for dinner tonight—you, Nonno, and me."

She encouraged him to stop by the villa terrace later for a glass of wine before their family dinner if he felt like socializing with the archaeological team working on Raffaello's dig plus a small group of guests currently under Portarello's roof.

"It's the usual international crowd we attract: a couple of Médecins Sans Frontières docs on leave from Biafra, some minor French actor and his psychotherapist wife, and an Israeli sustainable agriculture scientist. They've all been out doing Siena today, and the archaeologists have been digging at the site down the mountain. No pressure to go, but you might enjoy the change of conversation from your impressionable ivory tower college students. Or has the world finally breached the walls of Fordham University?"

"That's a cynical comment from someone who actually lives in a tower."

"Touché, little brother. But the world does come to us up here. We aren't merely offering a refuge from the ills of society. We're trying to translate what we learn on the farm to solve those ills."

"That's all very noble, Lin. But you have no idea what kinds of ills I see every day outside Fordham's walls. Shattered families, unequal justice, thousands of body bags arriving from the war, decaying neighborhoods ... I could go on."

Linda held up her hands.

"Peace, Danny. I didn't mean to get you all riled up. I shouldn't have made that snide remark about ivory towers. I forgot that you're in the trenches, not just in the classroom. I know you've come here for a reason, and it's not because you lead a privileged life. I don't want us to fight, not on your first night here. I'm sorry."

"Apology accepted. I'm not angry with you. I don't want to fight either. I came here to sort out my life, not have it thrown in my face."

They parted in truce with Daniel not sure he could face the guests, even over small talk. Despite Linda's description of them as a departure from his students, they sounded a lot like his academic colleagues, doing "important" work and probably feeling pretty good about themselves for doing it. As someone who wasn't feeling good about himself, he wasn't sure he wanted to engage in the usual banter expected of strangers meeting over a glass of wine.

After Linda left, he unpacked his bag, sloughed off his traveler's grime under the ancient, groaning plumbing in the tiny bathroom adjacent to his room, and changed into a tee shirt, shorts, and hiking boots. After eight hours on a plane, two hours straightening out his car rental reservation, and another three hours on the autostrada from Rome, he was more than ready for a climb beyond the villa to stretch his legs and his lungs and remind himself why he continued to come back to Portarello.

It was when he reached the crest of the hill, just before the woods began, that he noticed the young woman engaged in filling the pig troughs with grain from a wagon at the edge of the pens. She moved with a rhythmic grace, dipping a large plastic container into the fodder, scooping it full, and turning to distribute the yellow kernels evenly along the trough. Then she unlatched the gate to let the complaining, hungry pigs climb over one another to reach their dinner. She moved along the pens, her gestures practiced and confident, until all the pigs were snorting with contentment and her wagon was empty.

She trundled it back to the small silo on the side of the track, wiped her hands on her jeans, and then returned to the first pen, where a sow and about a dozen piglets luxuriated in the late afternoon sun. The woman crouched down next to the nursing sow and watched them, transfixed and oblivious to anything, including him, beyond the small circle of scruffy meadow she shared with the pigs.

Her stillness and concentration elicited a memory for him, pulling him back to a childhood summer on his Grandmother Snowe's South Carolina farm. It had been a mare and her new-born foal, not pigs, that had drawn his attention and stopped him. He must have been—oh, about ten years old—banned from the house for the duration of his grandmother's afternoon nap and told to "amuse himself." He had scuffed his way through the gravel path to the paddock and leaned against the fence, bored with the isolation of a child in a house full of adults. His siblings—Linda, Anne Marie, and Robert—were off with his mother somewhere for the afternoon.

But his boredom had evaporated within a few moments of watching the foal move from stumbling to cavorting soon after birth within a perimeter closely guarded by its mother. He had stood at that fence for nearly an hour, so absorbed in the drama before him that his world contracted. All sound was shut out, except the whinny and clop of horses reveling in movement; and his field of vision was limited to the area in which the spindly foal and watchful mare moved.

He remembered this summer afternoon with a sharp intake of breath—the sense of awe and delight and total immersion in the present moment. Like the foal learning to stand, then walk, then run, Daniel had discovered that day the power of losing oneself in the contemplation of what he would later call the Divine.

That is what he believed he was witnessing as he observed the young woman and her pigs. Once recognizing what was taking place, he retraced his steps back to the villa, not willing to disturb her.

And now, she had disturbed him.

Instead of going to the terrace after his hike, he returned to his room. As delicious as Portarello's wines were, he needed something stronger. He'd had the foresight to visit the duty-free shop at JFK before boarding his flight and had picked up two bottles of Glenlivet, one for his grandfather and one he'd tucked away in the armoire in his room.

He retrieved it and poured himself enough to wind down from his conversation with Linda and prepare himself for dinner with his grandfather. He stood at the window, grateful that Linda had put him in a room at the back, overlooking the olive groves and the woods beyond instead of the chatter and tinkling glass of the wine hour. As he sipped his Scotch, he saw a figure emerge from the woods and recognized the girl he'd seen caring for the pigs. But now, rather than the tranquility that had filled him with such longing earlier, her face was troubled, anxious.

She was hurrying down the hill, her progress hampered by what he could now see was a serious limp. She seemed to be dragging her left leg, leaning heavily on a walking stick as if it were a crutch. As she got closer to the villa he saw her wiping away what must be tears with her free hand.

The change in the girl was extraordinary and made him question what he thought he'd seen up in the meadow with the pigs. By the time she reached the villa she appeared to have herself under control, although by no means as centered and whole as he had witnessed ... and envied. She disappeared around the corner after pausing to straighten her back and take a deep breath, as if girding herself.

Daniel glanced at the clock on his nightstand just as he heard a far-off tinkling of a bell. It was time to brace himself for dinner with his grandfather as firmly as the young woman he'd watched stand tall and lift her chin. He swallowed the last of his Scotch, grabbed the bottle he'd brought for Raffaello, and quietly left his room.

Raffaello's house was across the rear courtyard, set on a rise that commanded a sweeping view of the valley below and the mountains beyond. Daniel approached it slowly, forcing himself to measure his pace. As much as he was not relishing this first encounter with his grandfather, a part of him wanted to get it over with quickly. The conversation was sure to be explosive and draining.

Perhaps that is what he needed after months of caution and evasion in his spiritual sessions with Francis Xavier. A shouting match with his grandfather. Daniel ran his fingers through his hair, much longer than his usual Jesuit trim. But haircuts had been one of the first things to slide as he began his descent into doubt and depression. He hadn't bothered to shave after his shower, but it was barely noticeable. Unlike his father, whose five-o'clock shadow started appearing around noon, Daniel had inherited the facial-hair gene of his South Carolina relatives, among other characteristics.

"You are your mother's son," numerous family members had reminded him every time he had visited the Snowe farm. Unlike his siblings, he had inherited not only her coloring but her temperament, a tightly wound reserve cloaked in anxiety. It had suited him well until this disastrous year.

He lifted the latch on the gate in the front of the house and stepped into the garden, a lush enclosure brimming with flowers. He heard the murmur of voices and the tinkle of glass around the corner of the house and turned in that direction, toward the terrace with its commanding view.

His grandfather stood at the stone wall surveying the vast Richetelli forest, wine glass in hand. Linda was placing a platter on the glass-topped table—slices of a deep burgundy salame, a pungent cheese, and some olives. She looked up as Daniel came around the corner.

"Danny! You made it. I thought you might have crashed and fallen asleep."

"I resisted the urge to put my head down and went for a walk instead. *Buona sera*, Nonno."

Raffaello put down his wine glass and opened his arms.

"Come here and let me look at you."

Daniel placed the Scotch on the table as Raffaello welcomed him in an embrace that Daniel stiffly entered.

After the hug, Raffaello held Daniel by the arms and observed him.

"When was the last time you got a full night's sleep? You look like hell."

"Apparently my sister agrees with you. Is this the new greeting at Portarello? Part of a marketing campaign? You look like hell. Come to paradise and let us restore you to heavenly bliss?"

"If only we could, my boy. Your sister is on a mission to save the world through farming, but my guess is you will need more than planting a few acres to bring you back to health. Have a glass of wine and tell me why you're here. This isn't just Father Richetelli takes his annual vacation."

Linda, who had stood back during Raffaello's greeting, now handed Daniel a glass of red wine and picked up her own glass from the table.

"To family," she offered. "May we always find a home here."

The three stood for a moment in silence as Daniel sent a brief nod of gratitude to his sister for temporarily halting his grandfather's immediate launch into interrogation. He sipped the wine, readying himself to address Raffaello's question, when his grandfather spoke again.

"Have they kicked you out, or did you leave of your own accord?"

Daniel had expected his grandfather to be provocative and combative when he made the decision to come to Portarello. It may even have been his main reason for coming—knowing he'd be forced to confront and delve and gnaw through layers of muffled pain. He had understood that Portarello, for all its sunshine and abundant nourishment and deep family roots, would not be a safe haven where he could drift in haze of avoidance.

He had come because Raffaello would push him to find the answers he needed.

But not today. He knew enough not to plead jet lag for his inability to articulate a coherent answer to his grandfather's deliberate challenge. But he was too weary of spirit to spar with Raffaello. He put an end to the verbal battle before it had a chance to burst into words both would regret and neither would take back.

"Neither and both, Nonno. I'm on a leave of absence, not out. The provincial directed me to take it, but I had already acknowledged to myself that I wanted a break. I'm here because this is where I knew I could find the answers I need—with your help, Linda's love, and the peace that has always been waiting for me here at Portarello. But I'm not in any way ready to plunge into the hard work I know is ahead of me. Until I give myself up to Portarello's enveloping grace and get some rest, anything I say tonight will be meaningless. I'm here. I'm looking forward to long nights of conversation over this very fine Scotch I carried all the way from New York for you. But not tonight. Can we just enjoy the meal, the sunset, and the fact that we haven't seen each other in two years?"

Raffaello smiled and shrugged in resignation. "I can wait."

Linda, who had been watchful and protective of them both, visibly relaxed.

"Well, it looks like I can safely leave you two for a few minutes to finish dinner and be reasonably secure you'll still be civil when I return."

"Can I help with anything, Lin?"

"Stay put. Everything's ready except for a quick stir of the sauce. I'll be right back."

Daniel grabbed a slice of salame from the platter and joined his grandfather at the wall.

"Lin tells me you've got an archaeological team from BU on the site this summer."

"A group of young bucks all vying for the career-defining discovery that will put them on the fast track for glory and a tenured position."

"You sound as cynical as I remember," Daniel replied. "Weren't you as ambitious when you were their age?"

"Precisely. Which is why I recognize the signs, although I'm finding myself less tolerant than I was only a few years ago. The tension at the dig is hampering our progress. They're like schoolboys on the play yard, pushing and shoving."

"Literally? Isn't it a bit cramped in the pit?"

"Not physically pushing, no. I'm referring to the competition for my attention. I practically trip over them, as they attempt to accompany me on my way in or out of the site."

"I thought you enjoyed the adulation of the young." As soon as he said the words, Daniel regretted them. He was baiting his grandfather and knew he was provoking retaliation as only Raffaello knew how to give.

But Raffaello surprised him.

"What I've discovered in my old age is that what I truly enjoy is nurturing curiosity and imagination. These guys from Boston believe they have nothing to learn from me and everything to gain by impressing me with their prowess. I'd much rather spend an hour with Maria's young friend Isabella, whose curiosity is infectious. She comes to something new with an almost childlike awe. She reminds me of why I studied archaeology in the first place."

"Who is Isabella?"

Linda stood at the French doors to call them to the meal and overheard Daniel's question.

"She's Maria's college roommate, working here as an intern. Nonno has become captivated by her, and I think the captivation is mutual. Come, eat."

The rest of the evening was spent by candlelight over Linda's delicious pasta. The topic of the dig was left on the patio as Linda steered the conversation to catching up on family. Daniel suspected that she had decided to protect Raffaello and him from each other. He understood his own need for the buffer of his sister, but he had never seen his grandfather as vulnerable, especially to him. Something simmered beneath the surface, illness or diminishment, Daniel wasn't sure. But it troubled him. More than that, it frightened him. He had come to Raffaello because he had always been a bastion of strength, assured and very much his own man. Raffaello was a legend in their family—anti-Fascist, scholar, patriarch. Daniel struggled with how much he wanted to know of Linda's obvious concern for their grandfather. But the wine, the food, and the jet lag had successfully dulled his wits, and he knew he had to leave his questions for another day.

He offered to help Linda clean up after the meal but hoped she'd recognize his fatigue. She did, pushing him out the door in the direction of the villa.

"Go! You're about to collapse. You'll have other opportunities to help, believe me. I'll see you tomorrow."

Daniel gratefully made his way across the courtyard and into the villa. As he navigated the halls and stairs he heard snatches of conversation and music wafting through open windows. The interns and their late-night gathering, he surmised, and was glad once again that Linda had put him in a room in the back.

He fumbled with the ancient light switch and aimed himself in the direction of the bed, where he stretched out fully clothed and shut his eyes without uttering a single word of prayer.

He didn't know where he was when the thunder and lightning disrupted his dream—a welcome respite, he realized, as he woke drenched in sweat and disoriented from the panic of a nightmare. He pulled himself up and recognized the shadows of the ornately carved armoire and dresser across the room.

He rubbed his face, unwilling and unable to retreat into sleep again. He thought about having another shot of Scotch and reached for the bottle on the bedside table.

As he did so, his hand grazed his missal, its worn leather cover curling at the edges. It had been a gift from his parents when he had professed his vows, and he'd carried it everywhere with him.

With reluctance, he picked it up. He remembered he hadn't prayed when he'd crashed earlier. He stood and thought to kneel where he was, at the edge of the bed, but then changed his mind. He needed more than the missal.

With a sense that he was being pulled, his feet found their way to the family chapel. As he expected, a single votive burned on the altar and he used it to light several candles around the familiar room.

And then he prayed.

Izzy

CHAPTER ELEVEN

JUNE 16

Izzy discovered the chapel after a thunderstorm pierced the silence of the mountain, the strobing flashes of lightning blinding her briefly as she struggled to find sleep. When the rain began, its insistent, clattering rhythm against the ancient tiles of the roof became yet another impediment to her futile attempt to rest. She unwound herself from the twisted sheets, wrapped herself in a shawl against the chill driven by the rain through her unshuttered window, and quietly unlatched the door to the darkened corridor.

Her intention had been simply to walk the length of the villa, pacing off her agitation in utter surrender. But when she turned to enter the rear hall that paralleled the hard-packed dirt drive behind the building, she noticed a door ajar. A door that, since her arrival, had stood not only firmly closed but also locked.

A dim night light illuminated the shadowed hallway and she proceeded slowly across the tiles. When she reached the half-open door, she pushed it further and slipped into a small anteroom. At a right angle to the door a burgundy drape hung in an opening, shrouding what lay beyond.

Her nose detected the aromas of melting beeswax and stale air before she saw the glimmer of candlelight through a tear in the curtain. Someone else was seeking a respite from insomnia tonight. She hesitated. Perhaps it was someone's room, not a common space. And even if it were open to all, whoever was within might not welcome an intrusion in the middle of the night. She turned back to resume her pacing, when a voice called out gently.

"You are welcome here. The curtain isn't a barrier."

She stopped, surprised that she'd been found out. She didn't recognize the voice. Perhaps it was a newly arrived guest. Although she had difficulty remembering new names and faces, the cadence and tone of her fellow interns' speech had become familiar enough.

She reached up and drew aside the curtain. A man she definitely didn't know turned to face her, his features lit by the flickering candles on what she saw immediately was an altar. The shadows of pews and a few scattered chairs filled the room around the solitary man.

"It's a chapel! I'm so sorry to disturb you." She saw the book in his hand, his finger holding his place where he'd been interrupted by her furtive arrival. "You're at prayer."

"My own remedy for insomnia. I usually recite a psalm from memory, or the Beatitudes, but tonight memory as well as sleep failed me and I've turned to this."

He held up the black book with a soft leather cover embossed with a simple gold cross.

Izzy's Catholic mother had just such a book, a missal, containing the order of the Mass and the prayers associated with each day of the canonical year.

"We're in the chapel of St. Catherine of Siena. A perfect place to be reciting a petition to her." He swept his arm around the room, ending with the painting on the rear wall above a marble holy-water font. Another candle, in addition to the six on the altar, was nestled in the well of the font, illuminating the face of St. Catherine, serene and in a state of ineffable bliss. Even in the dim light, Izzy recognized eyes that saw a vision that was not of this world, and she shuddered with loss. She turned away from the painting and back to the stranger.

"I shouldn't have intruded on your solitude. I'll leave you to your prayers." She spoke the words without conviction, her sense of duty and courtesy overriding an inexplicable longing to remain.

"But on the contrary, you are the answer to my prayers. Please stay." His gaze, reflecting the flames on the altar, caught her with his own longing.

Something passed between them beneath the white-washed vaulted ceiling as the rain continued to beat its relentless cadence.

Izzy stepped into the room, a space that held at once repose, memory, and death.

CHAPTER TWELVE

JUNE 17

When Izzy woke the next morning, she wasn't in her bed. She was instead stretched out on a wooden bench and covered with a threadbare blanket that carried the faint odor of mothballs that had long since lost their power to deflect attack by hungry insects. She ran her fingers through her tangled hair, as she always did on awakening, a gesture that brought her at least a flitting moment of familiarity in this strange setting.

She sat up and stretched her arms, but her legs, especially her polio-weakened left one, were severely cramped. She managed to massage the stiffened muscles, but she had to lift her leg with her hands to move it off the unforgiving wood. She stood, tentatively, holding onto the back of the pew to support herself. Only then, her bare feet firmly planted on the stone floor, did she look around.

She was in a chapel. Sunlight coming in through a high window dispelled some of the gloom and illuminated a flotilla of dust mites that Izzy had disturbed in shaking off the moth-eaten blanket when she rose.

Ahead of her stood an altar draped in ancient lace. Wax puddled around several candles that had burned down to nubs. Two cut-glass vases held bouquets of withered flowers that had once been magnificent enormous blooms of peonies and roses and gardenias, now reduced to brittle, almost-colorless remnants. Behind her on the wall, the image of a saint, her face shining in the midst of a smoke-blackened background, elicited a sharp cry from Izzy.

"St. Catherine of Siena." The words formed in Izzy's brain, and she spoke the name out loud. She remembered! Not from the deep recesses of childhood and the CCD class she had attended at her Irish Catholic mother's insistence. No, this was a much more recent memory. A chill passed through her, not of fear but of excitement. And then Izzy tamped down the hope as if she were drawing that meager excuse for a blanket around her again.

Even if the memory was new, all she had was the saint's name. Nothing else. No understanding of why she had spent the night in this abandoned and forgotten place or how she had found it.

She looked at her feet. They were clean and showed no sign of tramping through the fields or the garden surrounding the villa. Amidst the jumbled rooms of the villa, added over the centuries and a constant torture to Izzy as she tried to find her way—to the kitchen, to the sitting room, to the library—must be where this chapel is located. But her need to place herself, to find the answer to why she was here, was gradually dissipating. She found herself, instead of seeking what lay on the other side of the door, studying the face of St. Catherine. She drew nearer to the portrait, as if pulled there.

Another glimmer of memory, perhaps, or was it something she was seeing for the first time? She bit the thought back in frustration. These doubts were keeping her from something, something that was right in front of her in Catherine's gaze.

"Let it be." A voice inside her? Or was it a memory from last night?

She took a deep breath, stopped berating herself, and gave herself up to the painting. She understood, suddenly, that it didn't matter when she had come to the chapel, or what had happened during the night. What mattered was that she was here now, and in the eyes of the saint she saw the peace and bliss of the moment when she, Izzy, had died those many months ago. She collapsed on the floor and wept.

The release of her tears was a balm, and after a few minutes she wiped her eyes with the back of her hand and pulled herself up again. With a last glance at St. Catherine, she turned toward a curtained opening in the wall that appeared to be the only way in or out of the chapel, except for a heavy barred door at the back of the room that Izzy could see, from the window above it, led outside.

She pulled the curtain aside, a burgundy velvet that kindled another sense memory. She must have touched it when she entered the chapel. The nap of the velvet was worn, almost as threadbare as the blanket covering her when she had awakened. Many hands had parted this curtain in the past.

Izzy moved beyond the curtain into a small vestibule and faced a closed door. A brief moment of panic surged as she reached out her hand to the doorknob. Was she locked in? But she felt the latch release as she turned the tarnished brass knob.

Beyond the door she found herself in a tiled corridor lit by one lamp. After a few steps, Izzy gained her bearings and recognized where she was—just a few turns from her own room. She picked up her hesitant pace and found her signpost, the desiccated basket of flowers on the windowsill outside her door.

After a quick stop in the bathroom, where a glance in the mirror revealed a face that looked moderately and, surprisingly, well rested, she returned to her room. Her watch on the bedside table indicated it was six a.m. The curtains at the window were damp when she pulled them open, and the glass panes were spattered with raindrops. A memory of the storm during the night tugged at her, its disturbance what must have prompted her to leave her bed and pace the empty halls of the villa until she stumbled upon the refuge of the chapel.

And a refuge was what it had been. Despite the stiffness of her limbs, when she woke, she knew she had slept there. Her sense of peace, awakened by the image of the serene St. Catherine, had stayed with her since leaving the chapel and returning to the familiar surroundings of her room.

Izzy sat on the bed and took up her notebook. A feeling of urgency overcame her, a need to record what she had experienced since awakening and her assumptions about why she had been in the chapel during the night. She wished she could recall what had happened before she slept, but she recognized the futility of focusing her brain to remember. She let go of the questions, the echo of what she had told herself in the chapel before she gave herself up to simply being there.

When she finished her notes, she shivered and dressed and then left for the kitchen and an early breakfast. By

seven a.m. she was on her way up the hill to feed the pigs
and check on the sow and her piglets.

She loved her early-morning hours with the pigs. Later
in the day guests would arrive, curious and chattering, and
part of her intern responsibilities would be to explain the
heritage and care of this special breed, answer questions
and keep any rambunctious children from climbing the
fence and disturbing the animals. But in the morning and
again in late afternoon, Izzy had the pigs to herself.

Like her work in the garden with Adelina, the sheer
physicality of the tasks kept her focused. It was muscle
memory, like practicing the piano, or the endless hours she
spent in physical therapy for her leg.

Once she'd loaded up her grain wagon, hauled it to the
enclosure and filled the troughs, she took up a position
on the fence to watch the pigs scramble over one another
for a place at the trough. She delighted in the individual
personalities of the pigs, but she was also watching out for
any signs of illness or injury. Marcantonio, who had picked
her up at the train station weeks before, was the animal
manager on the farm and had trained her when she started
her rotation with the pigs.

"You come recommended by Adelina," he had told her.
"Not easy to earn her praise."

Izzy had ducked her head but smiled at what she knew
must have been a very short but direct assessment of her
abilities.

After she finished the feeding, she checked on the
piglets, starting with a count. When she realized one was
missing, she vaulted the fence into the enclosure isolating
the sow from the rest of the drift. She began slowly to
walk the perimeter, heading toward a cluster of trees on

the northern edge that provided shade in the heat of the day. She quickened her pace as much as she could when she caught site of a lump of black and white against the exposed root of the tree.

With a pained gasp, Izzy knelt and gently lifted the piglet into her arms. Its body was limp and its breathing labored. She couldn't find any visible signs of injury but knew something had happened to cause such a significant change from the evening before, when all of the piglets had been energetically seeking a teat.

Cradling the weak animal with one arm, Izzy pushed the call button on her walkie-talkie and summoned Marcantonio in her halting Italian.

He understood enough of what she was saying to arrive at the enclosure with his truck within a few minutes. He took the piglet from Izzy's arms and examined it carefully.

"*Troppo piccolo. Troppo fragile.*" "Too small. Too weak." He shook his head. "Nothing we can do to save it."

Izzy struggled with his assessment. She knew the piglet was the runt of the litter, but it seemed to be overcoming its disadvantages in the scramble for nourishment. She couldn't believe Marcantonio would give up so easily. The piglet's limitations were too close to her own, its less than perfect body an impediment to its survival without help.

"Let me at least try," she pleaded with Marcantonio. "Tell me what I can do."

Marcantonio shrugged but told her she could try bottle feeding it, although he didn't hold out much hope.

She took the piglet from Marcantonio, and together they left in the truck for the barn. There, Marcantonio prepared a bottle for the ailing animal. Izzy found a seat on a stool in the yard and tried to coax the piglet to suck.

Marcantonio watched form the doorway, his face a mask withholding judgment.

Izzy was grateful he had acceded to her plea for help, but she understood his skepticism. She murmured to the piglet, rubbing the nipple with its droplets of milk along its lips, but it was unresponsive. Its tiny chest was barely rising. Izzy tried massaging the flaccid body, unwilling to accept such a drastic change since the previous night. Searching for anything that might elicit a response, she squeezed a few drops of the milk onto her finger and gently inserted it into the piglet's mouth. She was struck by how dry its gums were and added more milk to her finger.

"Come on, sweetie. Swallow!" she whispered, and kept her finger in the piglet's mouth, trying to generate any kind of response. Izzy looked up in despair at Marcantonio, who gently shook his head.

One more time Izzy dripped milk onto her finger to moisten the dehydrated piglet's mouth and was ready to withdraw her finger when she felt a feeble tug. Izzy held her breath as the sucking strengthened, and then she slipped the nipple of the bottle in as she pulled out her finger.

The piglet's eyes fluttered open for a few seconds and then closed again as it continued to suckle. Izzy let out her breath.

She felt Marcantonio's hand on her shoulder.

"*Bene.*"

Izzy smiled. "*Grazie.*"

Izzy held the piglet until it drained the bottle and fell asleep.

"What now?" she asked Marcantonio. "Do we return it to the litter?"

"No. We need to build its strength with the bottle feedings. I made a bed for it here in the barn. Come back in an hour."

Izzy handed the sleeping piglet to Marcantonio and watched him place it gently on a pile of empty hemp bags in a wooden box.

"It's not, how you say, 'out of the woods' yet," he warned her. Izzy nodded and left to return to the enclosure. She had to retrieve the grain wagon and check on the drift.

On her way back up the meadow she examined her hands, which were trembling. She recognized the signs of her adrenaline dropping after the intensity of the minutes she'd spent trying to save the piglet's life. She wasn't sure that she had saved it but only given it a few more hours, another chance. She understood Marcantonio's caution but shook off the doubts now assailing her. She had to believe that the piglet would live.

Lost in her thoughts, she didn't see the man at the edge of the enclosure until she was almost at the fence. Her initial reaction was annoyance. She didn't think she had the energy to engage a guest with her pig lecture, and she was sure it was still too early for the tour the villa offered. She was about to put him off and ask him to come back later when he turned to her and greeted her with warmth, as if he knew her.

"Good morning. Did you sleep well?"

Izzy looked at him in confusion. She was sure he wasn't an archeologist, and he didn't resemble any of the guests who'd been at dinner the night before. She'd developed a simple system of remembering newcomers, and he was not one of them. But something about him was disturbingly familiar. Her face must have registered her confusion.

Not only was her memory searching frantically for a key to who he was, but the intimacy with which he greeted her frightened her. How could she not know someone who seemed to know her well enough to be aware of her sleeplessness?

His own face reflected her dismay.

"I am sorry. You must feel like I am stalking you."

"Stalking? You mean you knew you would find me here?" Every cell in Izzy's brain was firing. Who is he? What does he want from me?

"You told me that you were the caretaker for the pigs and you invited me to come see them."

"When ...?" Then Izzy stopped herself.

The fear of discovery that had hovered over her since her arrival at Portarello had finally caught up with her. This man now must realize she had no memory of him. But instead of fumbling for an excuse, like having had too much to drink, she found herself ready to admit her impairment to this stranger—but not a stranger—standing before her with compassion rather than ridicule.

"I apologize for my rudeness. You seem familiar to me, and I sense that you know me. But I do not remember you. It's not that I have a poor memory. I have no short-term memory." She'd said it. After weeks of hiding, here she was speaking of her loss out loud.

"I suspected as much last night, although you compensate very well. It must take a great deal of psychic energy to navigate through daily life."

"Last night ...," Izzy whispered. The details escaped her but not the emotional experience of the chapel.

"You were in the chapel."

"Yes."

"Thank you. As I told you, I don't remember what happened. But I woke at peace this morning. I thought St. Catherine had smiled on me, but it must have been you."

"On the contrary, it was you who smiled on me. We were two insomniacs roaming the halls of the villa who sought refuge in the chapel. I'm grateful for your company and your conversation."

"I must have been very unguarded ...; I don't easily engage in conversation. I must have reason to trust you. As I do now, for reasons I cannot explain. I wish I remembered. I don't even know your name."

"Forgive me. I'm Daniel Richetelli."

"You're a member of the family?"

"I'm Raffaello's grandson and Linda's brother."

"And therefore, Maria's cousin."

"Yes. How do you know Maria?"

"So I didn't reveal that last night? We were roommates at Smith. We bonded over our naturally curly hair." Izzy smiled and pulled on one of the wisps escaping from her braid. She shook her head in amazement at her own playfulness and comfort in Daniel's presence. The tension she felt in all her interactions at Portarello simply wasn't an element in this conversation. "Did I at least tell you my name? If not, it's Izzy."

"You know, Linda told me a friend of Maria's was working at the farm this summer, but I was so jet-lagged at dinner last night I didn't make the connection."

"You just arrived yesterday? Well, that's a relief. I was afraid you've been here a while and my memory was worse than I realized." She smiled again.

"I can assure you, I've been here less than twenty-four hours."

"What brings you here? Are you an archeologist?"

"It has been my grandfather's fondest wish that at least one of his descendants would take up the profession, but I'm not one of them. No, I'm here on vacation. A bit of R and R and a chance to catch up with my sister. We don't see much of each other."

Izzy caught the momentary hesitation when Daniel described the reason for his visit. It was possible he had talked about it during the night, but in the bright sunshine of the meadow, he appeared to be deflecting what might be a deeper reason for his visit. I suppose we all have secrets, Izzy thought.

Daniel changed the subject before Izzy could ask what his profession was, since he wasn't an archeologist.

"You were quite passionate about your work here and sufficiently intrigued me about the pigs— something I wouldn't have anticipated in my life before encountering you. You promised me a tour and a lecture in the care and feeding of heritage pigs."

"I'm surprised you don't know much about them."

"I haven't been here since …; it must be a least five years. Linda introduced the pigs only in the late 1960s."

Izzy noted the hesitation again and let it pass. She looked at her watch.

"Come along then. We'll start at the barn where there's a piglet in great need of care and feeding."

When they reached the barn, Izzy hesitated. The piglet had been responsive and had finished the entire bottle before she'd left, but a sense of foreboding fell over her as she drew the door open. Marcantonio was gone, and all was quiet—too quiet for Izzy. She had expected to hear squeals of hunger or at least sounds of snuffling as the piglet rooted for a teat.

"Wait here a moment," she said to Daniel, holding up her hands. If she found the piglet dead in its box, she couldn't bear to have to explain to him. She knew she wouldn't be able to find the words and she would want to be alone in her grief.

Daniel didn't question her but stepped aside as she entered the barn. It smelled of grain and earth. She made her way past wagons and bins and tools to the corner where she'd left the piglet.

She knelt by the box, holding her breath as she scooped up the tiny animal and placed it against her chest. With her fingers she felt for a pulse, searching in different spots when she couldn't detect even a faint thrumming. The piglet hadn't moved or opened its eyes or its mouth. A small amount of milk had dried on its chin. Izzy began to massage its chest, murmuring to it, unwilling to stop even when she knew it was useless.

She sat back on her heels, cradling the piglet in her arms and rocking back and forth, losing sense of time passing.

A hand on her shoulder disrupted her.

"Izzy, are you alright?"

She looked up blankly into Daniel's face, not recognizing him or understanding why he was there at first. And then, in a burst of insight, his name formed on her lips.

"Daniel! I'm sorry. I lost track of time and of you."

"Is this the piglet?" He reached out his hand to stroke its head.

"It was the piglet. I can't seem to rouse it and can't feel a pulse."

"May I?" Daniel knelt beside her and reached out his hands. Another memory flitted across Izzy's brain of those same hands holding a book, with one long finger marking the place where he'd been interrupted.

Reluctantly, she passed the piglet to Daniel and watched him examine the animal closely, repeating the same futile gestures she had made, searching for a glimmer of life.

After a few moments, he shook his head.

"It's my fault. I should have recognized days ago it wasn't thriving. My efforts to save it today were too little and too late. I shouldn't have been trusted with the life of another living thing." Izzy scrambled to her feet, agitated, and raced for the door. She could barely breathe. When she reached the yard, she bent over, retching.

Daniel's shadow fell across the patch of dirt, alerting her to his presence, although he said nothing and didn't touch her, as he had in the barn. After a few moments, he simply handed her a handkerchief.

She straightened and wiped her mouth.

"I'm sorry," she whispered. She had revealed far too much to this man in the last twelve hours and couldn't understand why. She felt raw and frightened and vulnerable but, at the same time, a sense of freedom that she didn't have to hide or pretend she was something other than she was.

"I'm sorry, too. Not only for the loss of the piglet, but also for your loss of confidence in yourself. I have a confession to make. Last night in the chapel was not the first time I'd seen you."

Izzy interrupted him. "You mean I've met you twice before today?"

"No, no." He rushed to still the dismay in her voice. "I only saw you. We didn't speak then. It was late yesterday afternoon. I took a walk after arriving to stretch my cramped legs and shake off the jet lag. I went up to the meadow and saw you with the litter. I held back, not wanting to disturb you. I'm telling you this for two reasons. The most important is that what I saw was someone totally focused on her task. You were sitting on the ground by the sow—not interfering with the litter but clearly observing, watchful. If the piglet had been failing then, you would have seen it."

Izzy listened, shaking her head, wishing she could remember and wanting to believe him.

Daniel seemed to understand that immediately.

"Believe me, Izzy. I know what I saw."

"What was the other reason?" You said there were two."

Daniel hesitated and looked away. Then, apparently deciding to go on, he turned back.

"Seeing you in there, so completely absorbed in the piglets that you were oblivious to my presence, reminded me of an experience I'd had as a boy on my other grandfather's farm. I envied you." He said the last quietly.

Izzy couldn't imagine anyone envying her. Not at any time in her life and certainly not now.

"Why?"

"You were at peace. Sure. Knowing."

Izzy was about to deny that she was any of those things. Peace, surety, and knowledge had been elusive, always out of reach. Not just since the accident but throughout her life. But she was forced to acknowledge that since coming to Portarello, she had been experiencing moments just as Daniel described. These moments had always been associated with work, in the garden and now with the pigs. She had trained herself to shut out distractions so she could concentrate and, yes, remember.

Watching Daniel's face as he waited for her to respond, Izzy recognized both his vulnerability and his compassion. But she also experienced another fragment of memory from the night before. Not his finger marking his page in a book this time but his eyes. Filled with comfort but also longing.

"You're seeking your own peace, aren't you?" She asked with the sudden insight that comes from recognizing one's own need in someone else. "We've both come to Portarello looking for refuge."

"Somehow I knew you'd figure that out. This isn't just a vacation and a family visit for me."

Silence settled between them as the revelations sank in. They pulled their eyes away from each other only at the sound of Marcantonio's voice.

"Daniele! Linda told me you had arrived. How long will you stay with us?"

Daniel turned to greet Marcantonio and was immediately enveloped in a bear hug.

When they broke apart, Marcantonio gestured to Izzy. "I see you've met Isabella. Adelina claims Isabella has a gift with living things. I saw it myself when she revived a failing piglet this morning. I swear, some life force must emanate from her. ..."

"Izzy reached her hand to stop Marcantonio. When he saw the look on her face, "*Che cosa?*"

"The piglet is dead, Marcantonio. I didn't do enough. I'm sorry."

"No, no, Isabella. You did more than enough. It was a miracle that you revived her even for a few hours. She's inside?" He gestured toward the barn.

Izzy nodded.

"I'll take care of burying her."

"No, Marcantonio. Let me. Please."

He shrugged. "*Va bene.*"

"Where?"

"Up the hill, behind the stone shepherd's hut."

Izzy left both men outside the barn and went in to retrieve the piglet's body and a shovel.

When she returned to the yard, Marcantonio was gone, but Daniel had waited.

"May I help you?"

At another time, with anyone else, Izzy would have said no. But she was finding an unfamiliar sense of comfort with Daniel, as if she had known him—and he had known her—in another life.

She nodded her acceptance and handed him the shovel as she cradled the piglet, wrapped in a burlap grain bag, in her arms. Together, they began the trek to its burial place.

Digging a grave for a newborn piglet was not the same as preparing the garden for a hundred tomato plants. A month ago, Izzy had discovered both her strength and her joy in her ability to nurture life. Both Izzy and the garden had flourished under the lessons she had absorbed from Adelina. It had all been so easy: turning over the earth, planting the seedlings with care, nourishing them with manure and water and the help of the Tuscan sun. This, now, was not easy.

Izzy put the piglet on the ground and took the shovel from Daniel, who seemed to understand that she needed to dig the grave.

She shoved the blade into the dirt with her boot. The earth up here on the hill was baked into a crust and strewn with rocks. Wild thyme and straggly weeds were scattered across the narrow plot, enclosed by roughly laid stone walls. It was just past noon and the sun was blazing overhead. Far off below them, Izzy heard the bell at the villa calling guests and staff to the midday meal. Sweat began to trickle down her forehead, and she could feel her shirt dampen under her arms. She wiped her arm across her eyes, acknowledging that the sweat was now mingled with tears. She pushed again on the shovel.

Daniel stood back, stooping only to toss rocks out of the way as they emerged from Izzy's efforts. Finally, Izzy knelt by the deep hole she had dug and placed the wrapped piglet at the bottom. Daniel had gathered a few sprigs of thyme and tossed them into the grave, murmuring something that Izzy thought was Latin. They both scooped up a handful of dirt and scattered it over the grave.

Only then did Daniel take the shovel and fill in the hole. With her hands, Izzy smoothed the top of the grave and stacked the rocks she had unearthed into a mound over it, marking it as the other graves within the walls had been.

When she was done, she sat back on her heels, the energy that had driven her from the moment she had discovered the ailing piglet finally dissipating. It was over. Whatever she could do for the animal was now done. What she could do for herself, in her failure to care for it, she didn't know. All she knew now was her exhaustion. She was depleted and felt as limp as the piglet when she'd found it under the tree. She knew she had to move or her limbs would stiffen and cramp. But when she tried to get up, she stumbled and fell, scraping her hands on the rough terrain.

"Shit!" She was angry with herself, with her body that had betrayed her. She didn't want to look up at Daniel, expecting pity. She hated being perceived as needy or "less than" whole.

"Do you need to let the spasm stop before you stand, or can I give you a hand?" His voice was calm, offering her the choice. So many others in her life, some of her family included, rushed in to pick her up when she fell—either physically, like now, or mentally when her brain faltered. It was why she had fled to Portarello. She now did look at him.

"Thanks. If I wait, it could be minutes or it could be hours. What I need is fluids. I'm dehydrated. I think we'd better get me up and back to the villa."

With a nod, he held out his arms and Izzy grabbed them, pulling herself up. They stood together, facing each other. Once again, looking into Daniel's eyes, Izzy had a glimmer of recognition. But she also saw discomfort and even fear. She attributed it to his concern for her fragility.

"Don't worry," she sought to reassure him. "I won't break. But I will need your arm as we go down the hill."

She moved out of the circle of his arms to his side. "Ready?"

They started down the steep path, Izzy clutching his arm harder than she had anticipated. Her leg continued to spasm and she need to stop periodically.

Daniel said nothing as they walked. At first, Izzy was grateful for the silence. No questions, hence no need for her to explain. But she realized about five minutes into their descent that she wanted to tell him.

"It's the result of polio. The spasms. I contracted it as child. One of the rare cases that resulted after I received the vaccine. When I am stressed or dehydrated, both of which worked their magic on me today, I can pretty much predict I'll spasm. I should have brought my canteen with me when we started for the gravesite. I'm usually better at taking care of myself. I've been doing it for a long time."

"How old were you?"

"Seven."

"It has shaped you." He said it not as a judgment but as an insight.

"Not in the way most people think. My parents taught me to see polio as something I had but not who I was."

"I didn't mean what I said in that sense. In the short time I've known you, I've been awed by how centered you are, how focused on the present moment, in addition to your compassion and reverence for life."

Izzy laughed with an undertone of bitterness.

"I'm focused on the present moment because that is all I can possess."

They had reached the road behind the villa. Izzy felt Daniel stiffen as they approached the back door, almost as if he were wary of someone seeing them together. Not only together but literally arm in arm.

"I think I can make it on my own from here, now that we're on flat ground," Izzy spoke quickly as she detached herself and demonstrated she could stand alone.

"Are you sure?" His relief was barely disguised.

"Go on. I'm fine. I need to clean up from our grave digging before I make an appearance at lunch."

She wanted to ask him whether he'd be joining the other guests for the meal, but she held back. He was clearly uncomfortable now that they were no longer on the hillside, and she was both bewildered and hurt. Better to retreat and allow herself to forget whatever connection had bound them, both in the chapel and in the graveyard. She turned toward the villa, hoping he wouldn't see the tears welling up in her eyes.

She grabbed the railing and pulled herself up the shallow steps and into the villa. She didn't turn to see if he was still on the road or had walked away.

Izzy leaned against the cool stone wall a few steps into the hall. Getting up to her room was not going to be easy. She was already exhausted from the trek. Taking a deep breath, she put one foot in front of the other, using the wall as support until she got to the stairs and began her slow climb. By the time she reached her room she was near collapse and barely made it to the bed. She had to pull her leg up with both hands to settle herself and stretch out. What she really needed was a heating pad, but she didn't have the energy to hunt for one or the willingness to expose herself to questions if she encountered anyone during her search. Instead, she leaned back against the pillow and gave herself up to both her fatigue and her dismay.

She didn't know how long she'd lain there when she heard a knock at the door.

"Izzy, it's Linda. May I come in?"

Izzy called out to her as she pulled herself up to sit, her back against the headboard. At least the spasms had stopped.

"I missed you at lunch and thought you might need some nourishment." She placed a tray on the dresser and then sat on the edge of the bed.

"Marcantonio told me about your efforts with the piglet. It was brave of you to try to save her and even more courageous to bury her. I just wanted you to know you went above and beyond. So thank you."

"Thanks, Linda. I just wish I could have done more. I'm still learning, and it felt like a failure this morning."

"I understand, Izzy. But, as you'll realize the longer you are here, we can't control everything, as much as we prepare and plan. Nature has a way of thwarting us." She seemed about to say something else but hesitated.

Izzy thought about telling Linda she'd met her brother but reconsidered. If she'd read Daniel correctly, it was best kept to herself until she understood what, if anything, was going on there. She'd kept her own secrets from Josiah. Who knew what undercurrents were thrumming beneath Daniel's homecoming and his relationships with Linda and Raffaello.

"Will you be able to take care of the evening feed, or should I find someone to do it for you? Marcantonio told me he thought you were having trouble with your leg when he saw you coming down from the graveyard."

Well, so much for keeping Daniel's secrets. If Marcantonio saw her, he also saw Daniel holding her, which meant Linda knew very well Izzy had been with Daniel. Izzy was as perplexed by Linda's avoidance of mentioning Daniel as she was by Daniel's reluctance to be seen with her.

"I'll be fine, Linda. I just needed some rest and some fluids. It happens now and then if I push myself beyond my limits, as I did this morning. I know better. I'll get the pigs fed later, no worries. But thanks for the offer. I don't have any other duties this afternoon, so I'll lie low for a while."

"Do that," Linda said, as she squeezed Izzy's ankle and got up from her perch on the bed. She moved toward the door and then stopped and turned around.

"Izzy, I feel that I'm more than your boss. You're like a kid sister, so please forgive me if what I'm about to say seems intrusive. I know you met my brother this morning. He's in an extremely fragile state right now, and I'm hovering over him like a mother bird watching her fledgling trying to leave the nest. Be careful. With him and with yourself. I don't want either of you to get hurt."

Perhaps Linda expected Izzy to be surprised or insulted by her comment. But she was neither. Linda's caution only reaffirmed what Izzy herself had detected, and it certainly explained Daniel's behavior. He had expected Linda to react exactly as she had. Izzy couldn't begin to fathom why. She and Daniel were adults. Broken and hurting but definitely capable of both protecting themselves and revealing their vulnerabilities to each other—as they already had. But she wasn't going to disclose that to Linda. She was back to keeping Daniel's secrets. If he chose to tell Izzy what was going on, so be it. If he needed to retreat, she could bear that. Whatever light he'd brought to her, she'd attempt to hold onto. All she could do now was nod.

"Thanks, Linda. You're a good sister. To Daniel and to me."

DANIEL

CHAPTER THIRTEEN

JUNE 17

Daniel watched Izzy enter the building and then turned away—from his sense of guilt, from his lack of courage. What had compelled him to seek her out this morning? Compulsion was the right word. He had left her asleep in the chapel after covering her with the threadbare blanket he'd found on one of the pews. He'd stood in the doorway watching her, envying the peace he saw illuminating her face. She possessed a power that he sensed she was not aware she held—a power derived from experience he recognized as mystical. He'd immersed himself in the writings of Julian of Norwich and Catherine of Siena, and he had longed for what he had read and what he now saw on Izzy's face. The bliss of the Divine.

His guilt now lay in what he feared he was doing. Using her gifts to rescue him without thought of what it might do to her. He understood her raw vulnerability because he himself was vulnerable. In a rare moment of prayer as he walked away from Izzy he asked for forgiveness.

Later that day, without choosing where to go, his footsteps took him to the granary. The large double doors were open to the late afternoon sun, and he knew he'd find Raffaello within.

Daniel knocked on the door frame. "Nonno?"

Raffaello looked up from his workbench and waved him in with a smile.

"Are you still jet-lagged, or have you joined the living?"

"I'm awake enough. What are you working on?" Daniel wanted to turn the focus away from himself.

"I'm studying the newest artifacts this team from BU has extracted in the last week."

"Anything interesting?" *Keep him talking about pottery shards and away from the fragments of my shattered psyche.*

"The evidence is getting stronger that we may have found a burial site. I am holding my expectations in check though. I've been in this position before, only to have my hopes dashed. The young bucks, unfortunately, are unable to rein in their emotions. As a result, they're working too fast, eager to get down to the next layer."

"Is that a problem?"

"It is if the excavation collapses because of their impatience. Someone could get hurt."

Daniel was surprised by Raffaello's caution. In the past he had always thought of his grandfather as a risk taker. The same sense of premonition he'd felt at dinner the night before washed over him. Something was definitely off, but he wasn't going to bring it up. He imagined that, with his usual astuteness, Raffaello was very much aware that he was not acting with his usual driving energy.

"Can you show me what you have there?"

Daniel moved to Raffaello's elbow.

Raffaello glanced at his grandson with a skeptic eye.

"Since when did you develop an interest in archaeology?"

"Let's just say it's hard to avoid right now, with the place teeming with dust-covered academics. So tell me about this piece."

Raffaello spent the next twenty minutes describing in minute detail the vessel that had been unearthed only days before, its markings indicating that it had belonged to a higher caste than most of the pottery scattered across Portarello's fields and woods.

"What if you have found a grave? What does that mean for you?"

"It would be a capstone to my career. A fitting ending as I bequeath the profession to the next generation."

"Is this it for you? No more digs?"

"If you haven't noticed, Daniele, I'm an old man. Getting down in the dirt is a young man's task."

Raffaello wiped his hands on a rag.

Daniel did not want to hear his grandfather acknowledge what he had already begun to notice. But he didn't dispute Raffaello's pronouncement. They would have plenty of other topics on which to dispute each other.

"Let's go have a drink and watch the sunset."

Raffaello steered Daniel out the door and then locked it shut.

Together they crossed the courtyard to Raffaello's house and took the path through the garden to the patio.

Daniel took the lead.

"Scotch or wine, Nonno?"

"I think it's time we opened that bottle of Glenlivet, don't you?"

"Exactly what I was thinking. Sit. I'll go get it."

By the time Daniel had retrieved the Scotch and two glasses, Raffaello had settled into a chair and closed his eyes to the sun.

Daniel was struck once again by how haggard Raffaello looked.

"Here's your drink, Nonno."

Raffaello looked up and took the glass.

"To the Etruscans," Daniel said, raising the amber liquid in the direction of the dig.

"I detect you've been expressing so much interest in my life's work to avoid a discussion of your own. Are you ready to talk, or should I listen to your sister and give you a few days' respite before you do battle with your favorite devil's advocate?"

"I wouldn't have come here if I didn't want to talk with you."

"Did you come because you knew I'd support your leaving the priesthood? Do you want my blessing or my absolution for a decision you won't make on your own?"

Well, despite the ragged state of his appearance, there was nothing ragged about Raffaello's bite.

"I didn't seek your approval when I entered the Jesuits, so why do you think I want it now?"

"What do you want from me, Daniele?"

"I want your sharp mind to help me dissect my life, your sharp tongue to keep me from dissolving into self-pity. Whether you believe me or not, your intellectual honesty and no-bullshit approach to everything you encounter have guided me since I was a kid. Help me to tear down the façade my life has become and rebuild myself. I'm a mess, Nonno."

Raffaello was silent, his eyes closed again, and for a moment Daniel thought he had fallen asleep, oblivious to the painful confession Daniel had just uttered.

Then he stirred and turned toward Daniel.

"Thank the god I no longer believe in that you are willing to admit your anguish. Most men would have refused to acknowledge their doubts and buried themselves in a life of numbing despair. Be grateful for the pain, Daniele. It will lead you to where you need to be. It is only the brave who venture beyond the point where there be dragons. Who are your dragons, Daniele?"

"The provincial and my advisor asked me that question, expecting it to be the usual: women—or men—alcohol, gambling, or drugs. It's as if they have a standard checklist for faltering priests. But when I didn't fit into any of their neat boxes, they threw up their hands and sent me packing to pray."

"And have you been praying?"

Daniel looked at his grandfather. "The words, yes, as if their repetition, like an incantation, will lead me to the enlightenment I need. But the words are hollow, meaningless to me. Like my life. I've lost purpose. I don't know why I'm here—not here at Portarello but here in this life, in this body."

Daniel took a gulp of the Scotch and drained his glass.

"I'm going to make a suggestion. You can take my advice, which I will assume you are willing to do, since you came here. Or you can dismiss it as the absurd idea of an old man. Forget about praying and contemplating your navel. Throw yourself into the work of the farm. Stop thinking. Stop agonizing. Simply do. Embrace the physical here. Pay attention to the information that bombards your senses.

Live the life of the body instead of the life of the mind. Then come back to me to talk again. But give it at least a month. Can you do that?"

"You make it sound so easy. Dig some holes, build some fences, chop down some trees. Exhaust myself so I don't have to think."

"Are you sleeping?"

"How did you know?"

"Look at yourself in a mirror. If you do as I say, you'll start to sleep. That's a prerequisite if you're going to figure out who you are and what you want."

"I'm an academic, not a farmer."

"Neither was your sister. Neither was I."

"That's it? No bristling arguments thrown at me until I throw up my hands in defeat?"

"I don't want to defeat you, Daniele. You're doing a fine job of that yourself. I want you to flourish."

"I came prepared to do battle."

"The battle isn't with me, Daniele. So what's your answer? Are you going to follow Dr. Richetelli's prescription?"

"Where do I start?"

"You can go down in the garden and harvest some lettuce and peas, to begin with. You do know what a pea looks like in its natural habitat, don't you?"

"Now, that's the Nonno I remember." Daniel got up and was on his way out the gate when Raffaello called him back.

"You might want to take a basket with you," and he pointed to a wicker container on the stone wall.

Daniel grabbed the basked and followed his grandfather's orders.

When he reached the garden he surveyed the rows of vegetables before locating Raffaello's requests. He knelt in the earth and began plucking the dangling pea pods.

He soon achieved a rhythm that soothed him, stopping only when his basket seemed full enough to feed his grandfather and him. He moved on to the lettuce and was astonished to see five different varieties. He took a few leaves from each type.

With a smile on his face, he climbed back up to Raffaello's terrace, where he found the old man dozing.

Slipping past him into the house, he took the basket to the kitchen and began foraging in the refrigerator and cabinets to turn his hoard into a meal. He couldn't remember the last time he'd cooked a meal from scratch. Most of the time he ate lunch in the faculty dining room, and in the evening he put a TV dinner in the oven and ate it while he watched the news or read *The New York Times* or *Commonweal*.

He found a chunk of prosciutto in the fridge and a package of fettuccini in the cupboard. On the windowsill were a couple of ripening tomatoes.

He shelled the peas, popping a few raw ones into his mouth, put a pot of water on to boil for the pasta, and rinsed the lettuce for the salad. After dicing the prosciutto and chopping a couple of cloves of garlic, he heated a cast iron frying pan with a film of olive oil.

His mother had not loved to cook. She had a few Southern dishes in her repertoire—cheese grits, smothered pork chops, Smithfield ham, and sweet potato pie. It was Dominic, his father, who had approached cooking with the gusto he brought to everything he did and who had taught the Richetelli children how to cook. And

Daniel found, as he made his way around his grandfather's kitchen, that cooking was like riding a bicycle—a skill that was muscle memory. You didn't forget it, no matter how long you'd been away from a stove.

He sautéed the prosciutto, threw the fettuccini into the salted boiling water, and added the peas in the last few minutes before the pasta was perfectly al dente. He found a pair of tongs and lifted the pasta into the pan with the prosciutto and garlic, then scooped up the peas with a slotted spoon and tossed everything together with a few handfuls of grated parmesan.

He turned to call his grandfather to the table and saw him standing in the doorway, arms folded and a look of satisfaction on his face.

"I could smell it from the terrace. Your grandmother used to make this dish when there was little left in the house except a rind of prosciutto and a can of peas."

"Dad taught me how to make it. *La cucina povera*, he called it. Are you ready to eat?"

"All we need is to open a bottle of red. I'll get the wine glasses, you get the corkscrew."

The two men sat for the simple meal and put aside the tension of the earlier discussion.

After the salad, Daniel cut up a few figs and put them out with some cheese.

"Let's sit back out on the terrace," Raffaello suggested. "It's still light."

Settling again with refilled glasses of wine, they spoke little until Raffaello broke the silence.

"*Grazie*, Daniele."

"You don't usually speak Italian to me, Nonno, even though you know I understand it."

"I am speaking from my heart right now, and it is easier for me to express in my native tongue. *Te amo.*"

"*Io so. Anche io.*" I know. I love you too.

Raffaello reached across the space between them and grasped Daniel's hand.

"You will make it through this, my boy."

Daniel wanted to believe him.

At that moment, Raffaello released his hand and pointed down the hill toward a figure moving up a path that led from the woods.

"There she is."

"Who, Nonno?" Daniel leaned over to follow where his grandfather was pointing.

"La bella Isabella, the young woman I was telling you about. Maria's friend. Full of wonder and curiosity."

Daniel saw Izzy wandering slowly up the hill, unaware that she was being observed.

The warmth in his grandfather's voice startled Daniel, and he found himself bristling inside. He was dismayed by his reaction, by the voice that said, *No, she's mine!* Trying to modulate his tone to one of mild interest, he asked Raffaello, "What do you know about her?"

"She's a gem. Everybody on the farm adores her. Adelina, who doles out compliments like Scrooge before he saw the ghosts, sings her praises to anyone who will listen. Marcantonio says she has a gift with the animals."

"And you?" Daniel struggled to keep his voice under control.

"I've taken her under my wing, to the great consternation of the archaeologists."

"Does she want to be an archaeologist?"

"Not at all. But she's curious and open to new things. I took her to Cerveteri. It was as if she was communing with the dead. There is something extraordinary about the girl."

"It sounds like you spend a lot of time with her." Daniel could not believe how painful he was finding his grandfather's fondness for Izzy. But at the same time, he was struck by how oblivious Raffaello appeared to be of Izzy's own struggles. For reasons he did not want to admit, he was relieved that Izzy had not shared her secrets with Raffaello.

"She's not one to mix with the other young people. Linda was concerned about her solitude, so I found her one day in the library—hiding, I think—and invited her to the granary for a tour and a lesson in the Etruscans. She seems to enjoy my company. I'm familiar to her, after all. Whenever I was in Boston for a symposium, I took the girls out for dinner. When you're a student, a meal out in a nice restaurant, even with a grandfather, is appreciated. She was at Harvard after she and Maria graduated from Smith. A brilliant girl with a lot of promise, until tragedy struck."

So Raffaello did know.

If he stayed, Daniel knew his resentment would bubble to the surface, not only destroying the current rapprochement he'd achieved with his grandfather, but also providing Raffaello with another way to wound him. Daniel didn't know what his feelings for Izzy were, and the last thing he wanted was for Raffaello to be aware of them. As far as Raffaello knew, Daniel hadn't met Izzy yet, and Daniel preferred to keep that knowledge to himself right now. It was already unsettling without Raffaello knowing the turmoil Izzy had caused in Daniel's troubled spirit.

"I'm fading, Nonno. I'm going to try to get some sleep. Who knows, maybe your miracle cure has already had an impact."

Daniel got up, kissed his grandfather goodnight on both cheeks, and left the terrace.

He had no intention of going to bed, a place that still held only nightmares and restlessness, despite his hopeful comment to Raffaello. Instead, he walked across the courtyard and down the driveway in the direction he'd seen Izzy go. As soon as he was out of sight of Raffaello's house, he quickened his pace to catch up with Izzy.

As he walked, he questioned what he thought he was doing. Unable to answer, he accepted that he was caught up in what he could only describe as longing. The only experience he could liken this to was his failed desire to truly understand—and experience—the visions of the mystics. What he had observed of Izzy over the last two days churned within him. He felt like the bleeding woman in the Gospel of St. Matthew who wanted only to touch the hem of Christ's tunic, believing that touch could heal her. Is that what compelled him about Izzy? The possibility that she could heal him? That she could offer him a glimpse of what she, in her broken state, seemed to know with such certainty? Once again a wave of guilt engulfed him, accusing him of selfishness. He almost stopped to turn back when he heard his name called.

"Daniel?" Izzy had stopped up ahead at the back entrance to the villa and must have seen him in the deepening twilight. She was waiting on the steps, where he had left her earlier in the day.

Daniel caught up with her, glad for the dim light hiding what he was sure were reddening cheeks.

"Were you out for a walk? I didn't see you on the path or I would have stopped and waited for you."

"No, I've just come from supper with my grandfather."

He thought about making up a reason for being on the driveway but plunged ahead with the truth.

"I saw you as I was heading back to the villa and decided to catch up with you. I want to apologize."

He thought Izzy would ask, Apologize for what? But instead, she nodded.

"You mean for your discomfort in being with me so close to the villa. You aren't very practiced at disguising your emotions, are you?"

"I'm sorry. I should explain."

"You don't have to. I of all people understand the need for secrets. Keep yours."

Daniel struggled with revealing to Izzy the turmoil he felt—his overwhelming need to be with her and his guilt for that need. Even now, she was giving him a way out, not asking anything of him.

"I can't talk about it. Not now. Please just know I'm sorry." He sank back into his cowardice, both relieved that she hadn't demanded more of him and bereft that he hadn't the courage to be honest with her.

"Sure. But you should know that I'm grateful you were by my side today. You helped perhaps more that you know."

Izzy turned to go in.

"Wait! Please."

She was still, her hand on the doorknob. She didn't make a move to face him again.

"Do you have time to walk a bit more? St. Augustine has said that walking is a form of prayer, and I could use some prayers right now."

She finally turned back to him.

"I don't think my legs could take another step, especially in the dark. But if it's prayer you're in need of, I'm happy to sit with you in the chapel for a while."

Daniel smiled and let out a breath of relief. "Thank you."

Together they climbed the stone steps to the second floor and entered the chapel. Instead of turning on the lights, Daniel lit the altar candles and the candle in front of St. Catherine. The aroma of beeswax and a faint remnant of incense permeated the enclosed space. For several minutes, neither spoke. Daniel knelt at a prie-dieu, and Izzy settled onto the pew where she'd slept the night before.

Daniel felt calmed by the familiar gestures of prayer, his knees pressed against the cushion of the prie-dieu, his hands forming the sign of the cross. But no words of either entreaty or praise passed his lips. He simply breathed, at a loss for what to say to the God who had been so silent these last several months.

Izzy spoke.

"This place has an extraordinary effect on my state of mind. Do you feel it too?"

Daniel got up from his knees and joined her on the pew. "What do you feel?" He truly wanted to know.

"Peace. And memory, which is astonishing. I had never been here before last night, and yet, it all seems familiar. Embracing. Something held me in its arms last night.

When I woke, I thought it had been St. Catherine. Is that weird?"

Daniel was stunned by her description. It echoed what more than one mystic had described of their encounter with the divine—the experience of comfort that eluded him.

"No, I don't think it's weird at all. It's a gift, a part of you that remains open to feeling such profound connection."

"As much as I've been consoled by this place, I'm reluctant to define it as anything more than a confluence of sensory impressions—the candlelight, the fragrance of the herbs, even the pattern of sound made by the storm. It reminds me of my grandmother's rituals, carried down from her ancestors. Rituals that I've grown apart from, that lost their meaning for me. I've resisted them in the past, but I feel like I'm being dragged back. Still not believing but intrigued."

"Who were your ancestors?"

"I thought you knew. The Chappaquiddick Wampanoag. I'm one-half Native American."

"And yet, you don't believe?"

"I'm very far from my roots—which, by the way, are also Irish Catholic. Not just because I'm here in Italy, although coming to Portarello was indeed to put space between me and my family. I left Chappaquiddick behind a long time ago. First Smith and then Harvard."

"What did you do at Harvard?"

Isabella was silent, a pained look crossing her face.

"I didn't mean to let that little piece of my history escape from my mouth. You seem to have the ability to elicit more from me than anyone I've ever met."

Daniel acknowledged to himself that her remark suffused him with what he could only describe as pleasure. Was it only a notch above what his grandfather believed he had with Izzy, or was he truly a man capable of instilling trust?

"You can trust me with that history."

"I know that. I'm still surprised by my willingness to confide in you. Have you entranced me, Daniel Richetelli, like this room and the saint who appears to inhabit it?" She had a smile on her face, a moment of lightness in what was turning into more than Daniel had bargained for.

"And yet," she said, "you do not trust me."

He started to protest and then held back. He shook his head.

"Years of containing my secrets are difficult to undo in only a few hours. Give me time."

"How much time do we have? We are fools if we try to hold onto more than the present." She waited, her eyebrow lifted, as if daring him to speak.

Instead, he deflected.

"Tell me more about your reluctance to accept the power of your grandmother's rituals."

"I am ... no, I *was* an intellectual, an academic. If I had spoken out loud about the moments of transcendence my grandmother witnessed or was part of, I would have been told to go study anthropology and document Native culture. My childhood was devalued in the eyes of my erudite professors, and so I learned, with practice, to dismiss it. I lost touch with a part of myself at that time. It is ironic to me that what I've lost now is everything I honed at Smith and Harvard. The joke is on the girl who put aside her heritage in order to assimilate and now has nothing. I think Italo Calvino found a folk tale that echoes that story."

"But aren't you rediscovering those ancient skills? You said yourself that this room is enveloping you in a solace you haven't experienced in a very long time."

"I think perhaps my experience here has more to do with you than any mystical visions attempting to break through my skepticism."

"I'm honored that you see me as a conduit. But I've heard you describe a state of bliss, Izzy. A bliss that I ache for." Daniel whispered the last sentence.

Izzy looked at him, stunned.

"So, you finally reveal something to me. I am the one who is honored, Daniel. That is a profound longing. And the word you use is exactly what I feel here. I know, I actually remember—which in itself is extraordinary—that I felt bliss when I woke up here this morning. And I expect that was also my experience last night, although those memories are more diffuse. A cloud, as opposed to something substantive that I can grasp and turn and examine. But you were here. You witnessed my bliss, which is why you want it too. Are you ashamed of that? Is that why you've held your longing back from me?"

"I'm in awe of you, Izzy. Your generosity. Your perceptiveness. Your empathy. I have been tortured by the fear that I am using you to realize my own longing. That is what I am asking forgiveness for."

"Oh, Daniel, this bliss isn't something to be hoarded! If I knew how, I would share it with you. But it's also ephemeral. I can't hold onto it. It escaped me today—you saw how devastated I was by the loss of the piglet. But you were there for me. As you are now. I was being only slightly facetious earlier when I said it was you and not the chapel that is my comfort. Who are you? Are you some illusion, a vision that appears when I am most in need?"

"I am very real, Izzy. And as much in need as you are."

Daniel reached out for her and she leaned toward him. Without thought, he embraced her and she responded, encircling him with her arms.

They held each other in silence, only their heartbeats resounding, blending. And then he kissed her. Not the chaste kiss he had bestowed upon his grandfather earlier but a kiss expressive of the overwhelming need he felt for the woman in his arms.

And then he drew back, not to cut off the intimacy but to hold Isabella's face in his hands and look into her eyes, filling now with tears.

"What do you want, Daniel?"

Daniel was silent, unable to answer. He pulled her close again and whispered in her ear. She smelled of verbena and Ivory soap and fresh hay.

"I don't know, Izzy. That is why I'm here at Portarello. To figure out my life. But instead of clarity, I am finding only more complexity."

"Am I one of the complications?"

"No. If anything, you are placing in stark relief one of the choices I have before me. An unanticipated choice. Not an unwelcome choice."

Izzy moved gently out of his arms and stood up.

For a moment he felt bereft, about to be abandoned for his recklessness. And then she reached out her hand.

"Come with me."

She led him out of the chapel and down a dim, unfamiliar corridor. No one locked doors at Portarello, and Izzy eased open a door at the end of the hall. It was dark inside the room, but Izzy made no motion to turn on a light.

She took him to her bed and pulled down the covers, and then she knelt to take off his shoes.

"We both need to sleep. This is more comfortable than the pews in the chapel, and I know I will find some rest and peace if you hold me."

"Are you sure? No regrets in the morning?"

"Right now, I am sure. You exhaust me. I have no idea what tomorrow will bring or if I will remember that I took you into my bed or why. But in this moment, I want nothing else."

Daniel sat on the bed and put his arms around her waist as she stood in front of him. She stroked the hair back from his forehead and he gave himself up to her touch. He pushed out of his consciousness and his conscience the sheer recklessness of what they were doing. In all the years he'd been a priest, he had never been tempted to be with a woman, never fought a desire for intimacy. Until this moment, a moment he had invited by the kiss.

"Trust me, Daniel."

And so he did.

Izzy

CHAPTER FOURTEEN

JUNE 18 – JUNE 21

Once again, Izzy woke from a blessed slumber. This time she wasn't on a narrow pew but in her own bed. She stretched her arms above her head and shifted to glance at her alarm clock. As she did, she saw her clothes on the floor, where she had apparently dropped them the night before. But she saw something else in the pile that wasn't hers. A faded blue plaid handkerchief.

What have I done? Did I drink last night? The contentment with which she had awoken quickly dissipated, draining out of her like the water in the claw-footed tub when she soaked her aching muscles.

She was alone now in her bed, but she knew she had not been—not from a specific memory but from her nakedness and from the scent wafting up from her sheets. The scent of sex and Old Spice and faint traces of Scotch. The other side of the bed was still warm; the pillow still held the imprint of his head. Daniel's head, of that she was sure.

Shaking off the doubts and questions that cluttered her thinking, she rose from the bed, found her robe, and made for the shower. Under the stream of water she grasped for answers. One thing was perfectly clear. They had fucked.

She surprised herself with the explicitness of that word. Synonyms had not presented themselves to soften what had taken place in her bed. It had been a long time since her body had felt like this, and it had definitely been a fuck. Maybe several. As the water rippled over her skin, she could not suppress a smile.

But the reality of what had happened still left unanswered questions. How had they ended up in her bed? Who had initiated it? Why had he left before she awakened?

She toweled dry and dressed. The answers could come only from Daniel. Until she found him, she had work to do.

She made the early trek to the pigs and tried to focus on her chores but found she was distracted by her heightened senses. Every breeze, every birdsong, every ray of sunshine that warmed her face reminded her that she inhabited a body, a body that had given her pleasure—and that she hoped had also given Daniel pleasure.

When she returned to the villa shortly before the midday meal, she considered looking for Daniel, although she didn't know where to begin. She had no idea if he was even staying in the villa. After a futile search of the common rooms, she retreated to her own room. The bed was still unmade, its tangle of sheets a testament to what had taken place there during the night. She sat on the edge and picked up the pillow on Daniel's side, holding it as if to extract from it the memories she could not retrieve.

Again, her intensified awareness of her surroundings picked up the sound and light enveloping her. Her window was open to the front lawn, a desultory breeze wafting the curtains. Voices rose up from below, and it took her only a few seconds to recognize Linda and Daniel in heated conversation.

Izzy moved to the window. She couldn't see them, but the words were distinct, angry, impassioned.

"How could you not tell her!" Linda's tone was one of outrage and disbelief. "What were you thinking, to spend the night with her? I don't know you anymore, Danny. Maybe I never did."

"Since when have you become my keeper? And why were you in my room? I'm not a teenager who has stayed out past curfew."

"I was in your room waiting to talk to you about Nonno. Who, if you haven't noticed, is failing. When you didn't turn up by midnight, I left. I wasn't spying on you. But I happened to be in the corridor by the chapel this morning because someone left several candles burning there. It was only then that I saw you coming around the corner from Izzy's room with your shoes in your hand and you half-dressed."

"What happened last night is none of your business, Lin. Stay out of my life."

Izzy watched in dismay as Daniel came into view, his face contorted in pain and his fists clenched as he stalked away from the villa and out the gate.

Izzy shook her head in bewilderment. Her earlier impression of Daniel had not yet slipped from memory. She didn't remember the words they had spoken to each other, but she definitely still held within her the powerful sense of calm his presence conveyed to her. A glimmer of one conversation pushed its way up into her consciousness—an acknowledgment that they had both come to Portarello to seek refuge.

Up until this moment, Izzy would have been hard pressed to believe that Daniel was struggling with demons. Something stirred within her. In all the time she'd been at Portarello, she'd remained in the background, reluctant to get close to anyone, an observer—just as she had been now, listening and watching from her window. But what had been happening between Daniel and her had precipitated a change in Izzy. She continued to feel it—a loosening of restraint, a willingness to come out of hiding.

She got up from the window and made a decision. She dug her cane out of the bottom of the armoire. She didn't know how far she was about to walk, but she was unwilling to venture without support. She didn't want to be hampered by the possibility her leg would fail her.

She closed her door firmly and moved as quickly as she could out of the building. Once outside, she followed the trajectory she had watched from her window and left the grounds to find Daniel.

Her path was familiar, the route of her early-morning walks. But she had no time to notice the shape of a branch or the fragrance of cypress. She was determined to catch up with Daniel and gave no thought to how ridiculous that might be—he, pummeling through the heat of the afternoon and his own heated response to the conversation, and she, still somewhat stiff and not completely recovered from burying the piglet the day before. But something was driving her, propelling her down the mountain in pursuit. At first, there was no sign of him on the road ahead and she despaired that he had turned off into the woods. But the road at this point was bounded by deep ravines, and she dismissed the worry that she had lost him. Finally, as she rounded a curve, she saw him below her, still striding furiously. Izzy quickened her pace as much as she could without risking a fall. She considered calling out to him but suspected that would be disastrous. Izzy knew she was at the heart of Daniel's angry response to Linda, but she also knew Daniel's rage wasn't directed at her.

As she moved forward she kept Daniel in her sight. He finally stopped and turned off the road onto a narrow path where the forest had levelled off. Within a few minutes, Izzy arrived at the same point and pushed ahead into the trees.

It was cooler within the woods, the large overhanging limbs providing a dappled shade. Up ahead, Izzy saw a clearing and more sunlight. When she reached the edge of the clearing, she stopped to catch her breath.

Daniel was in the middle of the field on his knees, his back to her. His hands, now unclenched, were outstretched, and his head was bent.

It was a position of prayer, of supplication. Izzy felt a familiar twinge, a sense that she was intruding and the feeling she had been in this situation before with Daniel. He must have been praying in the chapel the night I interrupted him, she thought.

The impulse to follow Daniel and the burst of energy that had enabled her to do so ebbed slowly as she stood watching him. She did not move, afraid that even the slightest rustle of the decaying leaves on the path would disturb him.

She was torn. She ached to confront him, to question why he and Linda had been arguing so passionately about her. But she was also both awed and frightened by what she was witnessing. Daniel was praying in Latin, the ancient words an incantation in the midst of this very ancient land. The rhythm of the language awakened in Izzy a resonance with another form of incantation. Her father's drumming and singing during the summer PowWow. Although the meaning of Daniel's words was unknown to Izzy, they elicited a piercing recognition—of anguish and confusion and despair.

Izzy had suspected Daniel's vulnerability, and now she was witnessing it. How damaged was he to take himself to this hidden place and bare his soul to the trees and the sky?

Izzy closed her eyes and listened, drawn so deeply into her own place within that she didn't notice at first when Daniel's voice finally fell silent. When she did realize he had stopped, her eyes flew open, pulling her back to the meadow.

Daniel was no longer upright on his knees but had collapsed, bent over with his head touching the ground.

Without thinking, Izzy went to him. She said nothing but sat next to him and waited.

He didn't move at first but then lifted his head.

"How long have you been here?" He didn't look at her as he spoke.

"Long enough. I overheard you arguing with Linda and saw you leave in anger. I didn't think. I just came."

"So you know the argument was about you."

"Yes. But I don't know why. We've known each other for barely two days. Days that have exhausted me emotionally and physically but also exhilarated me. I've never met anyone like you, never felt so safe, never felt so free. And yet, now I doubt that any of the goodness I felt in your presence is true."

"Do you think I lied to you?"

"I don't know what to think. You were upset that Linda knew you'd been with me. You were ashamed."

"No! I'm not ashamed. I wanted only to protect you from Linda's prying."

"Well, it sounds like Linda wants to protect you from me. Am I dangerous to you, Daniel?"

Daniel sighed and rubbed his face roughly.

"Linda thinks you're a distraction."

"What do you think?"

He finally turned to look at Izzy. "No. Which is why Linda and I were arguing."

"Then why did you run away? Why were you praying?"

"I left to calm down. Praying is like breathing to me. It focuses me. I have a question for you. Why did you follow me?"

"It disturbed me to hear your harsh words with Linda. And it confused me. I told you. I don't remember well. I thought I had misinterpreted what I was feeling. I thought I had made a friend. I shouldn't have followed you. I've violated your trust and also caused a rift between you and your sister. I'm sorry. I'll let you be."

Izzy rose, brushing off the leaves clinging to her jeans.

"Please don't leave me."

Izzy stopped. He hadn't said, "Don't leave." He'd said, "Don't leave *me*."

"We found each other in the chapel the other night for a reason, Izzy. We both have holes that need to be filled, hurts that need to be healed. I thought I'd made a friend also. The goodness is real, not a lie. I don't know how much I can give, but I know you offered me a gift I desperately need. But I ask you to understand that I'm limited in what I can offer you in return."

"That seems to be Linda's concern. That I may expect more from you than you are able to give."

A revelation struck Izzy, and she slapped her forehead.

"Oh, jeez. You're married. And you're here trying to sort yourself out so that you can get back with your wife."

She saw Daniel flinch and realized she'd flung away all the excuses and uncovered the source of her uncertainty and discomfort.

"You should have told me before I ..." Izzy choked back the words that stunned her as they rose up unbidden. *Before I fell in love with you.*

"I'm not married, Izzy. I'm a priest. A Catholic priest."

Izzy leaned into her cane to steady herself. Her body, as it often did, reacted to her emotions as if she'd been physically struck. When the sensation of reeling subsided, she took a deep breath.

"Of course. The chapel, the missal, your prayers here in the meadow. I should have recognized. ... No wonder Linda is so agitated. I was brought up Catholic, Daniel, in my mother's faith. I was an occasion of sin for you. I caused you to break your vow of celibacy."

"No! Don't place that responsibility on your shoulders. I didn't introduce myself to you as Father Richetelli. I deliberately kept that from you."

"Why?" Izzy's voice was barely above a whisper.

"Honestly? I think I was trying out how it felt not to be immediately slapped with a label—a label that I am no longer sure defines me."

"So I was your guinea pig? Talk to the girl in the chapel and see how it feels not to be constrained by a Roman collar? You know, your being a priest feels like more of a betrayal than if you were married. Figure out who you are without me, Daniel."

Izzy turned away, feeding her outrage in order to suppress how hurt she felt.

Daniel didn't call her back, and he certainly didn't reach out to touch her.

She made her slow way through the woods and out to the road, where she began the arduous climb back up the mountain. Out of sight of Daniel she allowed her tears to flow. She couldn't get her thoughts around all that she had experienced in such a short span of time, especially how unprotected she had allowed herself to be.

How could she have been so stupid, so vulnerable?

Izzy spent the next few days in a fog, burying her grief in a frenzy of activity. Another sow was about to give birth, and she left the pens every evening extracting a promise from Marcantonio that he would call her, even if it were the middle of the night. She kept the walkie-talkie by her bedside, eager to hear the squawk summoning her. She wasn't sleeping anyway.

She hadn't seen Daniel since she'd left him in the meadow, and she'd made no attempt to seek him out. The few times she'd seen Linda, their exchanges had been brief and without warmth, but also without accusation. If Linda blamed her for what had happened between Izzy and Daniel, she was keeping it to herself.

Raffaello was also among the missing from Izzy's daily life, but she heard from the buzz around the dinner table that he was spending most of his time at the dig. Excitement had been building over the last month as more and more was uncovered at the site. The anticipation of a major discovery was palpable. Izzy wished she could share in the energy crackling throughout the farm, but Daniel's absence and his betrayal of her trust had carved a hole in her heart. She remained on the periphery. Her only solace was the pigs and the garden, where she often went to help Adelina weed when she had a few hours to spare.

She was startled by the buzz of the walkie-talkie around two in the morning. "It's time," she heard from Marcantonio, and hurriedly dressed and climbed to the barn. Marcantonio had moved the sow there as her time grew closer.

Marcantonio welcomed her, and she knelt beside the sow, who was struggling. It was her first litter, and she was agitated, getting up and down.

"Talk to her," Marcantonio whispered. And so Izzy did, murmuring encouragement, stroking her, comforting her. About thirty minutes after Izzy arrived, the first piglet was born and Izzy was ready to towel it dry and place it under the heat lamp Marcantonio had set up away from the sow. Over the next six hours, the remaining seven piglets were born. The sow stood, peed, and then settled on her side for the piglets to find their mother's teats and suckle. Izzy watched in awe as the sow grunted softly to her babies and they fell asleep.

She helped Marcantonio clean up the pen and spread fresh short straw. "We keep it short so that the piglets don't get hidden and at risk of being squashed by the mother because she doesn't see them."

It was late morning when Izzy returned to the villa, the exhilaration of witnessing the birth outweighing her exhaustion. She was filthy and stripped off her clothes as she entered the bathroom and turned on the shower. After lathering, scrubbing, and rinsing, she emerged clean and still on her adrenaline high from the birth. Back in her room she rummaged through her dresser for clean clothes and was reminded that she needed to do laundry. After pulling on a tee shirt and jeans, she heard a knock on her door. Her pulse quickened, and for a brief moment she wished that it was Daniel on the other side of the door. But it was a woman's voice that called her name.

"Izzy, it's Linda. Are you there?"

"Yes, come in."

Izzy braced herself, wary of what would bring Linda here in the middle of the day.

"I heard the sow's litter arrived, healthy and robust."

"All present and accounted for, and Mom seems to be adapting with patience." Surely this was not why Linda had come. Marcantonio would have given her a full report.

"Good. And good for you for making it through the entire farrowing. Marcantonio once again says you have a gift."

Izzy's own patience after the long night had reached a limit. Emboldened by the remnants of adrenaline still coursing through her, she made the decision not to wait Linda out. She wanted to know why she was here.

"Apparently I have other gifts that seem to have been mistaken for temptations. I did not seduce Daniel, if that is why you are here."

Linda flinched.

"I'm not here to make accusations, Izzy. If anything, I need to apologize."

"There seem to be a number of Richetelli apologies directed at me. It is not only Daniel who is vulnerable." Izzy held on to her defiance, unsure how long she could sustain her outrage before collapsing into despair.

"I don't blame you at all, Izzy. Please believe me. I was furious with Danny for putting both of you at risk."

"I'm responsible too. I should have been more sensitive to the signals."

"Can we call a truce? I didn't come to accuse you. I came for your help."

"What do you need from me?" Izzy took a deep breath.

"Danny has disappeared."

Now it was Izzy's turn to flinch.

"Why do you think I can help? I haven't seen or spoken to him since the day. ..."

"Since the day he and I argued about you. I know you followed him after he left me. I saw you. But you came back alone."

"Didn't he come back?"

"At some point. I don't know when. He cleared out his room and left in his car."

"Without saying goodbye? Not even to Raffaello?"

Linda shook her head.

"Linda, that was days ago. Why are you coming to me only now?"

"I wanted to give him some time to cool down. But when we didn't hear from him, I thought he might have said something to you or called or written. ..."

"You distribute the mail. You know I haven't heard a word from him."

"I was holding out hope that somehow he or you would come to your senses."

"There is no sense at all in what happened between Daniel and me. I can't help you, Linda. He doesn't want anything to do with me."

Izzy wanted to scream, to berate, to accuse Linda. If she hadn't argued with Daniel and laid such a guilt trip on him, he might not have collapsed into remorse, hating himself. He might not have left. But "might not" was useless now.

"Aren't you worried about him?" Linda asked.

"Until this moment I had no idea he was gone. I thought he was staying away from me. I was furious with him. I felt betrayed. I don't know what to feel now. If I had a clue about where he might be I'd tell you, but as you know, he wasn't terribly forthcoming about himself. He kept his secrets, Linda."

Linda ran her fingers through her hair, which Izzy could see was not twisted into the usual sophisticated chignon she usually wore, but was loose and tangled.

"You're worried. Do you think he might harm himself?"

A chill ran up Izzy's spine as she realized what she'd said.

"God forbid," Linda whispered, making the sign of the cross. "I'm a wreck. My grandfather doesn't know about the fight we had. He's my baby brother, Izzy. I can't bear the thought that I've pushed him over the edge."

DANIEL

CHAPTER FIFTEEN

JUNE 18 – 19

Daniel watched Izzy stalk away from the meadow, her cane striking the grass with fury and scattering the butterflies and insects in great clouds of disarray. How had he managed to destroy the one good thing he'd found in the months of anguish and uncertainty his life had become?

We have only this moment, Izzy had reminded him as they fell into each other's arms. He had lost his virginity during his seventeenth summer with Lisa Fitzgerald at her family's beach house at the Jersey shore. He hadn't yet been called to the priesthood, and although he'd felt a shiver of guilt, he'd easily resolved it in confession. He had wondered then why we call it "losing," when his experience with Lisa had been one of gain. Because of that summer, he thought he understood what he was giving up when he took his vow of celibacy. Until last night.

The sex with Izzy had been a revelation to him. She had known with such clarity what they both needed when she'd taken him by the hand from the chapel to her bed. Everything that had gone on between them—finding each other in the chapel during the storm, recognizing their kindred spirits, even burying the piglet—seemed to come

together in the moment when their bodies joined. And
yet, he saw now why Izzy felt betrayed. The revelations in
their relationship had been one-sided. He had withheld.
No, he had lied. He knew, as any Jesuit would, that a sin of
omission is still a sin. The breaking of his vow of celibacy,
in his eyes, was less sinful than keeping his priesthood a
secret.

He had damaged further an already damaged, fragile
spirit. He remembered the look of bliss on her face when
they made love. And he knew his own face mirrored her
joy. Its loss, in the light of day and his final admission to
Izzy that he was a priest, was all the more painful. Their
bodies had met in a moment of searing recognition, only
to have them torn apart by his lie.

He didn't know how long he remained in the meadow.
The tranquility of the place, its calling to him as another
chapel, a sanctuary where he could empty himself of his
pain, was now disturbed. The flattened grass where he had
knelt and the imprint of Izzy's cane and limping leg, were
as vivid an image of disorder as the twisted sheets in Izzy's
bed when he had slipped out of it earlier in the morning.

Why hadn't he stayed? He had awoken at dawn,
disoriented both by the unfamiliar room and his own
nakedness. And then he had become aware of Izzy, her
back to him and her honey-colored hair a riot of curls
tumbling over the pillow. He propped himself on his
elbow and watched her face in repose. A slight smile parted
her lips and her breathing was mesmerizing. Awe and
wonder were the operative words in finding himself in her
bed. A part of him wanted only to wrap his arms around
her, press himself against her back, and sleep again. To lose
himself in the memories of their lovemaking. And when

she awakened to love her again and then recreate in words the memories she would have lost.

But he didn't. He crept from the bed, retrieved his clothes from the floor, and quickly pulled on his jeans and thrust his arms into his shirt without buttoning it. He recognized that he was at war with himself, and the coward had won out over the pilgrim. He was afraid, plain and simple. Afraid that he had truly messed up not only what had been growing between him and Izzy, but also the hard work that still lay ahead of him in discerning what God wanted of him. Was Izzy a detour, or was she the true path?

Daniel pulled himself out of his reverie. He had no answers, neither for himself nor for Izzy.

Slowly, he made his way out of the meadow and climbed back to the villa. He was drenched in sweat, not only from the walk but also from his despair and remorse. He'd been on the mountain only two days and had already abandoned the discipline and good intentions he thought he'd carried with him along with those bottles of Scotch.

When he reached the gates he saw that people were already gathering on the terrace for the wine hour. The tinkle and sparkle of glass; the murmur of cheerful, relaxed voices; and the glow of the setting sun were exactly what defined Portarello. His father should have been there with his camera. He was relieved to see that neither Linda nor Izzy were on the terrace. He avoided the gate and took the driveway to the back entrance. By the time reached the door he knew what he had to do.

Back in his room he pulled his suitcase onto the bed and began throwing his clothes into it, not taking the time to fold or organize in his usual meticulous, ordered way. He wanted only to fill the bag as quickly as possible. He went into the bathroom and scooped up his toothbrush and shaving things into his dopp kit, zipped it, and scanned the shower for anything he'd missed.

He opened the door to his room slowly and checked the hall before venturing out and down the back stairs. Outside at the landing he left the suitcase under a widespread tree and walked up the driveway toward the rear courtyard where his car was parked. He tried to stroll casually, aware that he was in view of any of the windows facing the courtyard. To an unaware eye, he wanted to appear as if he was taking the car for an afternoon drive—an errand or a short sightseeing trip. He climbed into the Fiat and drove it around to where he'd left the suitcase, hopped out, and stowed it in the trunk.

And then he was on his way down the mountain.

It was nearly eight in the evening when he arrived in Florence and pounded on the gate of his Zia Letitia's villa in the hills of the Oltrarno. Daniel could hear the old caretaker fumbling with the keys as he demanded to know who was outside the walls.

Daniel identified himself, and the old man, grumbling, swung open the heavy, dark-green gate.

"Your zia, she's not here. Gone to Ischia for the sulphur baths. She has the rheumatism, you know?"

"I know, Enzo. I need to spend a few days in Firenze. You know my great-aunt has always welcomed any of the family to stay here when we are in town."

"*Si, si. Va bene*. You're not the first."

"Is anyone else here?"

"Not this week. Your cousin, the playboy, had a party two weeks ago. They stayed outside at the pool but it was a *bacchanalia*. I kept my granddaughter away. Do you need dinner? My wife can bring something up to the house."

"Thank you, Enzo. How is Carmela?"

"Getting old. Like all of us. You haven't been here in a long time. What brings you to Firenze?"

Daniel shrugged. He didn't want to explain, and he didn't want to lie. "I just want to spend some time in a beautiful city."

"The professor, your grandfather, he is well?"

"Yes, thank you for asking." Daniel was becoming uncomfortable. He had hoped for some anonymity by coming here, but Enzo had recognized him even after five years. Please don't have him ask for a blessing, Daniel silently prayed.

"I can take the key and settle myself in the house alone," Daniel told him. "If Carmela puts together something simple to eat, you can just leave the basket on the steps tonight. I'll go to the market tomorrow. She won't have to cook for me again."

Enzo handed him the keys through the car window, and Daniel drove past the caretaker's cottage along a cypress-lined gravel road. He parked on the side of the villa, a building older than Portarello's villa and definitely showing signs of its age. Crumbling stucco, rust stains from the gutters streaking the façade, and the Madonna in the alcove above the front door pocked from centuries of weather and the roosting birds in her hair.

He opened the ancient door and fumbled for the light switch. The hall smelled musty and airless, a layer of dust filming every flat surface. No wonder his cousin had held his party outside. Daniel retrieved his suitcase from the car and dragged it up the stone staircase inside to one of the bedrooms overlooking the garden, and beyond the stone wall of the garden, the Duomo. He threw open the shutters to the night air. The bed wasn't made, but he didn't care. He kicked off his shoes and stretched out on top of the mattress.

He didn't know how long he'd slept. It was still dark when he woke abruptly, chilled by the lack of a blanket and hunger pangs. In his stockinged feet he padded downstairs and opened the door, hoping to find Carmela's food basket on the stoop. He wasn't disappointed. He lifted it, grateful for its heft and the clink of glass. Under a red-and-white striped cloth was a bottle of Chianti in addition to some cold chicken, half a loaf of bread, a hunk of cheese, and some peaches.

In the kitchen he hunted for silverware and a glass. Success achieved, he pulled up a stool at the enameled work table and ate ravenously, washing down the meal with two glasses of wine. He'd gnawed the chicken down to the bone, but a remnant of the cheese and bread remained. He wrapped them back in the cloth and put them in a fridge that was probably fifty years old. The villa still had its grandeur, but clearly Zia Letitia preferred to spend her money on her own pleasures instead of the house's upkeep.

Too restless to go back to bed, Daniel wandered through the villa with the wine bottle in his hand, throwing on lights to illuminate the pre-dawn shadows.

Enzo was correct, it had been five years since Daniel had been here. Letitia had been in residence and happy to entertain her Jesuit grandnephew then. She was Raffaello's younger sister, widowed twice—first by the war and then by cancer. Each marriage had enhanced her wealth, which she used to throw lavish parties. Her grandson, the playboy cousin Enzo had no love for, had apparently followed in his grandmother's footsteps.

Daniel walked down a hallway lined with family photographs. Some, sepia-toned and spotted with age, portrayed Daniel's ancestors—the great- and great-great-grandparents whose villa this had been originally. He took swigs from the wine bottle as he moved from generation to generation, observing the transformation of his family. He found two family portraits of Raffaello and his siblings—one when they were children in starched pinafores and knickers, and a later one, where Raffaello appeared to be in his twenties. Daniel hadn't remembered seeing the later photo the last time he'd been here. It sent a chill looking into his grandfather's eyes and seeing himself staring back.

By the time he finished his wandering through the house, the pink light of dawn had begun to limn the marble walls of the Duomo. He clambered down the stone steps of the garden, past the algae-covered swimming pool to the wall overlooking the city. The hill on which Letitia's house was perched was called Bellosguardo. Beautiful view. He sat on the wall and emptied the wine bottle as the city came alive across the Arno. From his vantage point, everything was the size of toys, the cars and trucks like the Matchbox vehicles he'd played with as a boy. But in addition to watching the city like a puppet master, he recognized his isolation, his separateness. Life was surging in the streets of Florence. Grocers were raising their shutters and arranging oranges and tomatoes and zucchini and artichokes in carts under awnings; artisans were repairing a fountain drained of water, the mosaics at the bottom glinting with the coins of those who had cast their hopes into the water; the bells of Santa Maria dei Fiori and a hundred other churches tolled in celebration of a feast day or in somber recognition of a funeral. But Daniel sat above the living, pulling himself away from the cacophony and confusion and vibrancy, and he retreated into himself.

He would encounter no one here. Linda would not be lurking in the corridor, ready to cast her judgment and berate him for his failures. Raffaello would not be sitting on the sun-warmed stones of the loggia nursing a tumbler of Scotch and waiting to play devil's advocate to Daniel's ill-conceived plans. And Izzy would not be haunting the chapel, her grief palpable and her bliss shattered by his senseless and selfish lies. He could stay here at Bellosguardo, hidden and safe from their questions. And with enough booze, hidden from his own.

The issue of booze reminded him that he needed to stock up if he wanted to be left alone. He took one last sip, draining the final drops of the Chianti, and went back to the house to grab his keys and go shopping.

He stayed on the Oltrarno, not crossing the river into the center of the city. His head was too fuzzy and his hands too jittery to navigate the narrow, crowded streets. He found a neighborhood cluster of markets at the bottom of the hill and filled his basket with provisions—cheese, bread, figs, prosciutto, eggs—and more wine. Once he returned to the villa he didn't want to venture out again. He reassured himself that he was holding it together. Engaging in a normal activity, planning ahead, making practical choices. He didn't notice the constrast between the meager amount of food and the case of wine he loaded into the trunk at the end of his excursion. He knew only that he wanted to get back to the house as quickly as he could and close the gates.

Once inside the villa, he deposited the food on the table and immediately opened a bottle of wine. It was nine in the morning.

He took the bottle to the loggia and collapsed into a rattan chair. An empty bird cage hung in the corner and Daniel vaguely remembered an exotic bird with gaudy plumage that had once inhabited it. He imagined the bird had died of Letitia's neglect, as much of the house and the surrounding gardens reflected that same abandonment.

Daniel drank for the rest of the day. It kept him from thinking, from remembering. At one point, unable to focus on how he had gotten here or even why he had chosen this place, he was still sober enough to reflect that his present state of mind, with immediate memories lost to him, must be how Izzy felt all the time.

The fact that he was still thinking of Izzy meant that he was failing at what he'd set out to do in coming here. He wanted to obliterate thought, emotion, pain. He reached for another bottle of wine.

Izzy

CHAPTER SIXTEEN

JUNE 26

Maria was back from Rome, and after a few days of helping Raffaello bag and label artifacts from the dig, she suggested another excursion to Izzy. "You cannot spend the summer in Tuscany and not visit Florence," she insisted.

Izzy was glad to get away from Portarello. Daniel had not returned, and as far as she knew, no one had heard from him. Although the daily pace of life at Portarello continued with its familiar rhythms, Izzy was aware of tensions below the surface. Work at the dig was accelerating. From the buzz at the dinner table every evening, she detected a barely contained excitement as more evidence was uncovered that the excavation indeed held a tomb. In addition to the archaeologists, more guests were in residence, and Linda seemed to be everywhere, anticipating needs and putting out fires, all the while clearly still distracted by Daniel's absence. Izzy had felt the need to pull back from Linda after their conversation, too aware of Linda's judgment and unable to distance herself emotionally when she encountered her. She continued to feel that Linda saw her as responsible for Daniel's disappearance. So yes, when Maria suggested a day trip to Florence, Izzy jumped at the chance.

They took off early in the morning and arrived on the outskirts of the city within ninety minutes.

Maria deftly navigated the narrow streets of the Oltrarno.

"There's a spot I want to take you first, with a spectacular view of the city. It's called Bellosguardo because of the view."

The car labored up a serpentine hill and passed by trucks laden with vegetables and tan young men wearing aviator glasses and riding powder-blue Vespas. They finally arrived at a faded green wooden gate, propped open with a painted white stone. Beyond the gate, a long drive led to an ancient villa. Maria pulled in and parked along the drive. "It's odd that the gate is open. Normally I have to ring for the caretaker. Maybe he's expecting some workmen and left it open for them. Let me tell you about this place. The villa is older than Portarello—twelfth century. Rumor has it that it's where Dante met Beatrice. It's definitely where Elizabeth Barret and Robert Browning lived."

She grabbed Izzy's hand and pulled her away from the villa and across a sloping lawn toward a stone wall. "This is what I brought you to see."

Below them lay the city of Florence across the Arno. The Duomo rose majestically in its midst, and Maria began pointing out landmarks surrounding it.

As much as she found interesting the living map spread out beneath them, Izzy was more intrigued by Maria's description of the history of the property on which they stood. *Dante walked here*. His eyes saw what she now saw; his skin felt the breeze and the early-morning sun warming her bare arms. She moved away from the wall and wandered through a tangled and unkempt garden. She had to stop herself from getting down on her knees to pull weeds. The flowers hidden among the dense foliage gave off a rich scent that was on the edge of rot. She wondered how much of this greenery had been here to inspire Dante. The grass was badly in need of mowing, still wet from the morning dew and soaking her sandaled feet. A cat, its fur matted, slithered under the bushes, apparently on the hunt. Her sense of the place was one of contradictions—an aging grace in the crumbling stucco of the villa, where a stone Madonna looked out with vacant eyes from an alcove; an algae-covered pool flanked by once-elegant tiles that were now slick with moss; a tarnished silver tray holding cloudy etched-glass goblets left by the side of the pool.

The place felt abandoned, as if the inhabitants had left hurriedly, fleeing some unknown danger, like the inhabitants of Pompeii.

"Does anyone live here?"

"It belongs to my great-aunt Letitia, Nonno's sister, but ..." she inclined her head toward the silver tray, "I don't know when she was last here. Her grandson, my cousin Gino, sometimes uses the place. Letitia herself spends a lot of time traveling."

"As beautiful as Bellosguardo is, something sinister and decayed emanates from it. I find it hard to believe your aunt finds peace here. No wonder Dante wrote so evocatively of hell. He was probably channeling this place."

Maria looked at her and shook her head.

"You amaze me sometimes. If we weren't planning on diving into the treasures of Florence, you probably would stay here having a lengthy conversation with Dante about the meaning of life and death."

Izzy flinched at how perceptive Maria was. She had been very close to what Izzy had been experiencing in Bellosguardo's contradictions: Beauty and death. A lush, vibrant garden overtaken by choking weeds. Loss and abandonment. Maybe she hadn't heard Dante's voice, but she certainly had heard her own obsession with death.

"Time for a cappuccino. Then on to art, shopping, and vino."

As Izzy and Maria climbed out of the garden and back to the car, Izzy stopped abruptly, her thoughts interrupted by a flash of metal around the far corner of the villa.

"There's a car parked on the side of the building. Could your aunt be home?"

"I doubt it. She's in Ischia soaking in the sulfur baths. Nonno told me last night."

They moved closer to where Izzy had seen the car, a small Fiat.

"I think there was a car like this in the courtyard at Portarello last week."

"These Fiats are ubiquitous. You see them everywhere." Maria dismissed the idea that it could be the same car.

"Does this mean someone is here, even though your aunt is away?"

"Maybe a cleaning lady."

"Or your cousin? Shouldn't we at least say hello?" Something tugged at Izzy, a foreboding similar to what she'd felt in the garden. She knew only that they had to go inside the house.

Maria reluctantly agreed. "I don't want to get caught up in a family visit, complete with pastries and espresso. I have so much to show you in the city—artwork, shopping, architecture, shopping. ..."

"OK, we'll decline the refreshments. I'd just love to see the inside. If it's anything like the garden, it must be both spectacular and neglected." Izzy didn't want to alarm Maria with her premonition.

"Come on then. Maybe Dante's ghost is wandering around inside and you can finish your conversation."

They banged on the door with its massive knocker. No one answered.

"Whoever owns the car must have gone for a walk." Maria was ready to give up.

Izzy wanted to persist. Something continued to prickle in her brain, warning or pleading with her to stay. She picked up the knocker and with renewed force swung it against the door.

This time, the energy from the knocker—although it didn't summon anyone to answer the door—was forceful enough to loosen the latch. The door swung open.

After the bright sunshine of the Florentine morning, the house inside was cloaked in shadow and reeked of stale air and rotting food.

"Hello! Buon giorno!" Maria called out as Izzy felt herself pulled to a passageway that led from the living room.

"Where does this go?" she asked Maria, who continued to call out.

"That takes you to the loggia. I'll check the kitchen."

Izzy felt a sense of urgency the closer she got to the loggia and increased her pace. Her cane clattered to the floor as a surge of adrenaline pushed her and kept her steady.

French doors faced her at the end of the corridor, and she thrust her arms out to open them. When she stepped into the loggia, the smell of vomit and sweat assaulted her. She saw his legs stretched out on the stones, the rest of his body hidden by a rattan chair. She recognized those legs immediately—legs that had strode confidently next to her climbing the hill to the graveyard; legs that had steadied her own on the downhill return; legs that had wrapped themselves around her after lovemaking; legs that had knelt in a meadow in anguished prayer.

She ran to his side, forgetting her own damaged leg and lowered herself. He was still breathing. She felt for his pulse and it was strong.

"Thank you, God," she whispered.

All around him were empty wine bottles.

She gently turned his head away from the puddle of vomit but realized she couldn't move him alone.

"Maria! Maria! Come to the loggia!"

She looked for something to wipe Daniel's face and saw a pile of cocktail napkins decorated with fleur-di-lis on a cart near the window. She grabbed a handful, and with Daniel's head cradled in her lap, she began to gently clean him up.

Maria arrived and stood in the doorway.

"Who is it?" Her nose wrinkled in disgust at the smell.

"Daniel."

"Holy shit! So this is where he's been. Is he alive?"

"He's breathing and he has a pulse, but we have to wake him up. Can you help me get him to a tub or a shower?"

"There's one on this level near the kitchen. But maybe we should get him outside and douse him with the garden hose. I don't think we can carry him as far as the bathroom."

Maria strode across the loggia to doors that led outside to a small enclosed garden and flung them open. Although tiny, Maria was strong and moved to join Izzy.

"I'll take his legs if you can grab him under his arms. Will your leg be able to bear the extra weight?"

"I'll make sure it does. Nothing is going to stop me." Izzy spoke with a force of will that stunned Maria.

"Something is going on here that I do not understand. ..."

"Later," said Izzy through gritted teeth. "Let's get him outside."

Together they lifted and dragged him across the stone floor and out onto the grass without a flicker of response from him.

Izzy continued to hold him in her arms as Maria found a hose.

"Are you sure you don't want to move? You're going to get soaked."

"It's fine. I don't care. Turn on the water."

Maria directed a stream of water at Daniel's head, and after a few seconds his body jerked and he groaned and coughed. He turned his head away from Izzy and retched.

Maria shut off the water and joined Izzy on the grass beside Daniel. She was furious.

"Danny! What the hell? You're not the cousin I'm supposed to find in a drunken stupor. Gino is the one we have to worry about, not you! What were you thinking?"

Daniel looked up at Maria in a daze. As far as Izzy could tell, he was still coming into consciousness and unaware that she was there. She didn't speak, letting Maria read him the riot act as a family member.

Izzy herself was coming down from the terror she'd experienced when she thought Daniel was dead. Tears welled up in her eyes and she began to sob uncontrollably. It was then that Daniel became aware of her presence. He turned, saw her, buried his face against her breast and cried with her.

Maria shut up and stepped back with the hose, returning it to its coiled position by the faucet. She hesitated, watching them, and then left to clean up the mess she'd found in the kitchen.

Izzy and Daniel were unaware of anyone except each other. For Izzy, finding Daniel here in this house of mystery and contradictions reinforced her own ambivalence. Since his disappearance, she had protected herself by denying that his leaving had any effect on her. She had deliberately told Linda that she didn't care where he was and had tried to believe that. But in that moment when she thought he was truly gone, she knew that her denial had been a lie. Too many lies were swirling around them, tangling them, choking them. This had to stop.

When she had no more tears left, she spoke to Daniel. "Let's get you cleaned up and then talk. I'll send Maria away. This is just between us."

Daniel sat up. "I'm a mess," he said, pointing to his soaked, reeking clothes. "So are you."

He slowly climbed to his feet, but Izzy could see him wavering. She scrambled up and put her arm around his shoulder.

"Lean on me this time," she ordered him.

Together they went back into the loggia and down the corridor toward the kitchen, where they heard water running and pottery clattering. From the doorway Izzy could see Maria at the sink, a dishtowel around her waist.

"Maria, I'm going to get Daniel into the shower, and then I'm going to stay here with him until he sobers up and we talk.

"I'm sorry all the plans you had to show me the wonders of Florence have been ruined. I promise we'll do it another time. But I'm not leaving him alone."

Maria faced them with her hands on her hips. "After I finish fumigating this kitchen I'm assuming you want me to disappear. I will only do that if you promise me that one—you and my idiot cousin are going to be OK, and two—you tell me what the hell is going on when you get back to Portarello." She had enumerated her points with fingers thrust at them.

"I promise. I'll even call you this evening, if this house has a phone. When you get back, let Linda and your grandfather know we found him. But please don't tell them the condition we found him in. That will only send them racing up here. Believe me, that is the last thing he—or I—need. Can you promise me that?"

"Agreed. But I'm worried about both of you. I love you both and something powerful and possibly dangerous is going on. You said it yourself when we were out in the garden. This house is a place of both beauty and death. You've already died once, Izzy. Don't do it again any time soon."

"I'll do my best."

Daniel remained silent throughout the exchange between Izzy and Maria. It appeared he was barely aware of the words or their meaning.

His weight was beginning to tire Izzy.

"I need to be pointed in the direction of the shower."

"I'll lead the way and turn on the water for you."

When they reached the bathroom and the water was flowing, Maria turned to leave them.

"I'm going to make a leap, as unbelievable as it is for me to think of my cousin, the priest, in this way. I assume you've already seen him naked and getting him undressed is not going to destroy either his or your innocence."

"Thank you, Maria."

"It's been a strange day, full of revelations, not any of which I understand. But I do know that your premonition or whatever it was that made you insist we come inside has saved his life. Everything else I learn I can absorb. I'll let myself out, and I'll keep Linda and Raffaello away. Take care of him, Izzy. And take care of yourself."

"I love you, Mar."

"I love you too. And apparently, so does he."

CHAPTER
SEVENTEEN

JUNE 26 – JULY 5

Left alone with Daniel, Izzy got into the shower with him, stripping off first his clothes and then hers. Gradually, as the last remnants of his week-long journey of destruction washed down the drain, he began to speak.

"You saved my life."

"Are you disappointed?"

"I wasn't trying to kill myself."

"I'm sure the Catholic Church and your entire family will be happy to hear that. Just exactly what were you trying to do?"

"Finally be able to answer the question you asked me in the chapel."

"You mean the question, 'what do you want'?"

"That's the one."

"And you thought you'd find the answer in a dozen bottles of Chianti?"

"I came here with good intentions. I thought if I stayed away from you I'd be able to sort it out. But I lost faith, lost courage. I cannot do this alone."

"I think we've both learned that. None of us can do it alone, Daniel. Will you let me help you? I mean more than revive you from a self-destructive stupor and clean up your vomit? I mean truly help you? Body and soul? Your leaving helped me clarify some of this also."

The water streaming over them was turning cold. Daniel put his arms around her and whispered, "Yes."

The first thing Izzy did after they left the shower was find some dry clothes for both of them. Daniel led her to the bedroom where he'd left his suitcase, and she rummaged amidst the hastily packed bag for some underwear, pants, and a shirt for him.

"Do you think your aunt would mind if I borrow something to wear until I do a load of laundry?"

"Take your pick. Letitia converted an entire room into her closet. It's down the hall."

Izzy found the room, filled with racks of dresses, shelves containing shoes and handbags, and built-in drawers filled with elegant silk lingerie. She sorted through the hangers until she found a brightly flowered sundress she thought might fit. She realized quickly that the bras in the drawers were designed for a woman much more well-endowed that she was. Rather than stuff the cups with some of the monogrammed handkerchiefs scented with lavender in one of the drawers, Izzy went without.

She came back to Daniel. "Can you please zip me up in back" She turned away from him, and he deftly pulled the tab from below her waist to between her shoulder blades. Then he kissed the back of her neck.

"I haven't seen you in a dress before. You look beautiful."

"My normal attire is a pair of overalls." Izzy twirled, and the skirt billowed out. She fingered the material, letting it slip through her fingers like water tumbling over a mountain stream. The feel of the silk was calming, a sensual moment in what had been a horrific, jarring morning.

"It feels strange to be reveling in an article of elegant clothing after what we've just been through."

"Sometimes we need to seek solace in ordinary things."

"Like clean clothes and food. I'm famished. Do you think your aunt has a washing machine? I'll also see if there's anything in the kitchen I can turn into a meal."

"I'll go on the hunt for the washing machine." Daniel picked up their dirty clothes and carried them out of the room.

Izzy's focus on the practical was deliberate. She knew they still had long hours of discussion ahead of them, conversations that probably would not be complete before they returned to Portarello. But order was essential to her. It was her lifeline to making sense of her world. Chaos in her physical surroundings amplified the chaos in her brain.

Izzy was wary of the intensity that had vibrated between them in the shower. They had to talk before they made love again—if they were going to make love again. It was too easy to fall back into each other's arms, each other's needs.

Before she left the bedroom, however, she found the linen closet and made the bed.

In the kitchen she found eggs and parmesan in the fridge. Randomly opening cabinet doors, she located a pantry stocked with dry pasta and a few canned vegetables. Zia Letitia's priorities clearly led to fashion and not food.

Izzy took the dish towel Maria had used as a makeshift apron and tied it around the floral dress. As she set a pot of water on the stove and beat the eggs, Daniel joined her in the kitchen.

"I found the laundry room and started the wash."

He sat on a stool to watch her.

"Do you like to cook?"

"I can improvise. My mother was—is—an amazing cook. She had a restaurant when we were kids."

"Tell me about it. ..."

"We lived on a remote part of Chappaquiddick Island. Maria's been there. The only way to reach the café was by boat. Mom served simple fare—clam chowder, chicken salad sandwiches, and pies. She was famous for her pies. My brother and I helped out in the garden and also did the clamming for the chowder."

A shadow flitted across Izzy's consciousness, a fragment of a dream that had been triggered by the mention of clams. She shook her head to clear it.

"Are you OK?"

"I'm fine."

"Izzy, if we are going to help each other, that means we have to be honest, yes?"

"Do you think I'm not being honest when I tell you I'm fine?" She put down the fork she was using to whisk the eggs.

"I don't believe either of us is fine right now. Not after this morning. Not after the ten days since we met, and certainly not after the hell we have lived through individually in the last year."

"Fair enough. I'm not fine. But I'm ... hopeful. For the first time since I arrived in Italy. That little disturbance you just witnessed, that seems to have alarmed you, was a fragment of memory. A memory, Daniel, from a recent dream. That came back to me. So believe me, even if it wasn't a particularly good memory, I'm fine." She turned back to the eggs.

Daniel held up his hands. "Peace. I'm not trying to provoke you."

"Why don't you do something useful like set the table?"

"Where do you want to eat?"

"Not the loggia. After I'm fortified I'll clean up out there, but not yet."

"I'll help you clean up."

"You bet you will." Izzy smiled.

"There's a wrought-iron table in the garden, under a pergola. Shall we eat there?"

"I'd like that."

Daniel gathered dishes, cutlery, a tablecloth, and napkins on a tray and left for the garden while Izzy made the pasta. On a hunch, she went outside the kitchen door and found what she expected—an herb garden spilling onto the flagstones. She plucked some parsley and brought it inside to chop.

While the spaghetti cooked, she grated the chunk of parmesan she'd found. And then, with the swift, confident motions one needed for a dish like spaghetti carbonara, she drained the pasta, turned it into a bowl, and poured the eggs, cheese, and parsley over it, blending with vigor. The heat from the pasta cooked the eggs, and then Izzy stirred in a small amount of pasta water she'd saved to thicken the sauce. She'd watched the Portarello cook use that method and marveled at how silky it made the sauce. As smooth as her dress.

Izzy lifted the bowl in both her hands and pushed the kitchen door open with her hip. Her bare feet moved over the grass, taking pleasure in the gentle feathering of the blades against her skin.

She found Daniel under the pergola putting the finishing touches on the table. In the center was an ancient clay pot with deep pink begonias cascading over the edge.

"I think I saw some bottled water on the floor of one of the cabinets. ..." Izzy placed the bowl on the table.

"I'll get it."

"Bring the cheese and the grater I left on the counter," she called after him.

When he returned, Izzy served, using two forks to lift the pasta, glistening with pale yellow filaments of egg and punctuated with the sharp green flecks of parsley. The sun dappled the table under the slats of the pergola. Grape leaves climbed and twined around the structure. Neither Izzy nor Daniel spoke. They were both apparently ravenous and savored the improvised meal.

The warmth of the sun, the satisfaction of the food, and the beauty of their borrowed surroundings lulled them into a sense of domestic contentment. Izzy recognized it first. The al fresco meal had enclosed them in a bubble, transparent and fragile, but nevertheless protective. For half an hour they could pretend that all was well. They were an ordinary couple sharing a simple meal as if this were what they did every day. Even cooking for Daniel had cast a spell of normalcy on this most abnormal day. Izzy divided her life into before and after the accident. This meal, this moment, was a recreation of before.

The realization caught Izzy by surprise, and without warning, she began to cry. She grabbed her napkin to catch the tears and was about to deflect what was happening by gesturing to the pollen in the air. But then she stopped herself. The tears were real, were honest. And she need not hide them from Daniel.

"What has made you sad?"

"These aren't tears of sadness. I think they are tears of confusion. Bear with me as I think this out loud. I was caught up in the moment of contentment this meal has brought me. Cooking—especially cooking for you; sitting here in this beautiful garden—with you. It struck me as so wonderfully ordinary. Not fraught. Not tense with the hard work ahead of us. Just a dish of pasta filling a very basic need. And I was struck by how moments like this used to be a regular part of my life. The life I call "before." To be transported to "before" was a gift. And why I'm crying. They are tears of joy, but also tears of awareness that this contentment may be fleeting. Does that make sense?"

"Perfectly. Raffaello often talks about the importance of what happens across the table. We celebrate. We bless. We come together. Sometimes we argue and the table shakes. Sometimes we get up from the table unsatisfied. But we always come back. Life happens here."

"Too soon there will be others at the table. This bubble here will burst."

"Then let's make the most of it." Daniel reached across the damask tablecloth and took her hand. "I think we'd better begin in the loggia. The scene of my despair."

They gathered up the remains of the meal and carried them to the kitchen. Izzy saw that the washing machine had completed its cycle and pulled their damp clothes into a wicker basket. Beyond the herb garden she'd seen a clothesline.

"Do you want to wash up or hang laundry?"

"You cooked. I'll wash up. Do you need help with the basket?"

"Thanks, no. I can handle it. I'll meet you in fifteen minutes in the loggia."

Izzy carried the laundry outside and began pinning clothes to the line. A slight breeze lifted them, and she was hopeful they'd dry quickly. Like souls absolved of sin in confession, Daniel's shirt and her dress no longer carried the stains of Daniel's fall from grace. She didn't recognize the fragrance of Letitia's laundry detergent, but she knew this was one of those sense memories she'd be able to retain. It would represent for her the first step in starting anew, associated with the sparkling cleanliness of their clothing and the heat of the Tuscan sun baking away the remaining dampness.

She pushed her hair back from her face and lifted it off her neck. It was good to feel the sweat dribbling down her back, a reflection of the physical work that kept her centered. She strode back into the house ready to do battle with the mess in the loggia and the turmoil in both Daniel's and her life.

The kitchen was empty and gleaming when she returned to the house. In the distance, in the direction of the loggia, she could hear the clank of glass on glass. When she reached the loggia, she saw that Daniel had collected the empty wine bottles in a slatted wooden box. In a corner, a mop was propped up in a bucket.

"You've started without me."

"This is my mess. My responsibility. Besides, I don't want you to ruin your dress. It's really too delicate to wear mopping floors."

"I can go find something more practical."

"Don't. Stay with me. This is better penance than a whole novena of rosaries. It's forcing me to confront the consequences of my cowardice."

While Daniel swabbed the stones, Izzy surveyed the space. It looked out upon a small walled garden through floor-to-ceiling windows. Rolled shades of bamboo kept the sun from turning the loggia into an oven. It was decorated with objects Izzy recognized as Indian—statues, fabric on the walls and the cushions on the rattan chairs scattered around the room, a sitar leaning in the corner.

"Did your aunt travel?"

"She was an anthropologist, a complement to Raffaello's archaeology. After the war, when she was first widowed, she began to explore the Indian subcontinent, which is why you see so much from there in this room."

"What about you? Have you traveled much?"

"Summers here in Italy or at my other grandparents' farm in South Carolina when I was a kid. I spent a year in Rome after seminary to do the research for my dissertation."

Izzy felt a stirring of intellectual curiosity that she hadn't experienced in a long time. Another "before" moment inserting itself into this day. "What was your topic?"

"The mysticism of St. Catherine of Siena—her search for perfection and truth." Daniel offered his answer without enthusiasm.

"She had visions?" Izzy asked quietly. Her curiosity was more than intellectual, she realized. Daniel's answer hit her in her gut.

"She did. And then she wrote about them."

"You seem unwilling to expand on what you learned. Is she no longer interesting to you? Were you disappointed in her?"

"I am disappointed in myself."

"Why? Did you fail?" Izzy winced at her own bluntness. This conversation was probably not going to end well.

"On the contrary. My work was praised with high honors. My dissertation was published and is often used as a text in courses on the mystics. I taught one myself at Fordham."

"So why the reluctance? Why your disappointment in yourself?"

"Because I held back from truly understanding Catherine's tortured experience with her visions. I remained detached, an observer."

"And what you wanted was something more visceral? To be inside her, absorbing what she saw and heard, rather than simply watching and analyzing?"

"Exactly."

"It isn't easy being green."

"The Kermit song?"

"Yes. It isn't easy being at the center of a maelstrom. Doubting what you've seen and heard. Exhausted by the visitation that is often unwelcome and sometimes frightening. Someone who isn't religious may be tortured by the thought she's going mad."

"My superiors thought I might go mad if I descended too deeply into Catherine's experience, and so I held back."

"You have regrets." It wasn't a question.

"Yes. It's part of why I'm here. Trying to sort out if I have failed to understand the depth of Catherine's mysticism because I obeyed the constraints placed on me by the Jesuits."

"You said it's only part of the reason. What else is driving you on this quest? Are you now looking for perfection and truth somewhere else because you didn't find them in your scholarship?"

"I hold back. You've already suffered at my hands because of the constraints with which I bind myself."

Daniel was mopping as he spoke, a rhythmic, almost contemplative repetition that was also extremely thorough.

"You appear to be seeking perfection in your mopping," Izzy noted with a smile.

"Maybe that should be my next calling. Seeking nirvana through cleaning up."

"You sound like you want to do something entirely different from the scholarly life."

"The truth, Izzy, is that I am paralyzed."

Izzy stiffened. "You have no idea what it means to be paralyzed, either physically or mentally."

Daniel stopped, suddenly aware of Izzy's pointed and valid criticism.

"Forgive me."

"Words matter, Daniel. Am I supposed to give you a pass because you were using it metaphorically? There is nothing metaphorical about my paralysis. You know, I was going to be gentle with you today, give you some time to recuperate from your binge. We both needed a respite. But I'm not so sure that's a good idea anymore. To use your phrase, Daniel, the truth is that I am infuriated with your wallowing in despair. I want to shake you. I want to scream at you. I understand where you are because I am in the same place and I'm exhausted. I'm treading water, buffeted by currents and getting nowhere in my search for who Izzy Monroe is now. You almost went under today, Daniel, weighted down by your blindness. You are a good man. You may no longer be a good priest, but you are being called to something new. Be willing to listen instead of drinking yourself into oblivion."

"I'm stuck. You're right. I'm no longer a good priest. But I have no idea who I am if I'm not Father Richetelli. As unhappy and adrift as I am, my identity as a priest is still familiar."

"Your ambivalence is eating away at you. And at me. Let me ask you a question because even though I was there, I don't remember. Did making love to me bring you happiness in that moment? Don't think about your answer."

Daniel was surprised by Izzy's question, but he answered without hesitation.

"It was one of the most meaningful and joyful moments of my life."

"What then turned you away from that joy?"

Daniel started to protest.

"But. ..."

"Don't go wandering off into denial. You left me. I do remember waking up to an empty bed that still smelled like you. I have very strong sense memories, Daniel. I knew you had been there. But you left. And within hours you were on your knees trembling with rage and then shame. Your mea culpas were probably heard in the valley.

"What pulls you from joy to self-loathing?"

"I don't know, Izzy."

"Love yourself, Daniel. I love you."

"Your love is a gift."

"Then accept it." Izzy turned to leave the loggia. "I'm drained. I need to get some fresh air and go for a walk."

"Do you want company?"

"Not right now. I just want to be alone. Promise me you won't have another drink."

"I promise."

Izzy found her cane lying on the floor in the hall. She must have dropped it when she saw Daniel's legs stretched out motionless in the loggia. Too many times in the last two weeks she'd needed the cane. Earlier in the summer she didn't remember using it so much; her work with Adelina in the garden had strengthened her, given her confidence in her legs. Now, she clutched the carved handle like a talisman to keep her safe. Her father had found the sturdy branch on one of his hunting trips and brought it back with the eight-point buck he'd also found. Over the winter Tobias had shaped and oiled the stick and etched it with the animals and birds that inhabited the dunes and meadows of their land. When he gave it to her on her birthday, he told her it was not meant as a sign of her weakness but instead as a symbol of her power, an extension of herself to free her. And it had given her freedom—allowing her to forget about falling and focus on moving wherever she wanted to go.

Once outside she followed the flagstones through the overgrown shrubs, past the swimming pool, and down the sloping lawn to the stone wall overlooking the city. The sun was beginning its long descent behind the western hills, and the façade of the Duomo facing Bellosguardo was now in shadow. The Italian light on the Arno as it wended its way through the city was as entrancing as the play of sunlight and storm clouds over the mountains of Portarello.

Izzy sat in stillness, garnering energy for another conversation with Daniel. She was at a loss to know how to shake him out of his despair, but she knew she had to ready him before they returned to Portarello and the intensity and fears of his family.

Although she tried to keep herself focused on the present moment, her thoughts wandered to the coming evening and the uncertainty of their sleeping arrangements. She knew what she wanted—to be enfolded in his arms in his bed. But his ambivalence, his love/hate response to his own desires, left her wary. She knew she could not bear to be abandoned again, to face another empty bed. She also feared for Daniel's spirit if once again he descended into guilt after their lovemaking.

Izzy's head ached from all the unanswered questions. She felt inadequate in the role she had defiantly seized, keeping Daniel here with her instead of bringing him home to Portarello. Despite her fears, however, her instinct persisted in reassuring her that she had done the right thing. Daniel's family had very clear ideas about what was right for him. Especially Linda, whose conviction that "once a priest, always a priest" came across loud and clear in her warning to Izzy and her fury with Daniel. Although Izzy didn't know what Raffaello thought, she assumed he would also be playing a significant role in shaping Daniel's decisions about his future. Even Maria placed Daniel in a box in which he no longer belonged, despite her apparent acceptance that Izzy and Daniel were lovers.

Izzy stopped in her reverie at her choice of words. Words were important. That phrase reverberated in her brain.

Had she said it? The word Izzy had chosen to define her relationship with Daniel was "lovers." She and Daniel were lovers. And that would guide her for the rest of her life.

Reassured, Izzy returned to the house.

On the front doorstep she found a basket filled with tomatoes, zucchini, eggplant, and fresh figs. She carried it to the kitchen and called out for Daniel. When he didn't respond, she started searching, fear mounting with every unanswered summons. The loggia, although sparkling and smelling fresh with all the windows open, was empty, as was the walled garden.

Izzy climbed to the bedroom. It, too, was empty, but his suitcase still sat on the floor by the bed. That was mildly comforting. If he had decided to leave, wouldn't he have taken it? Izzy fought her sense of once again being abandoned. She would not believe that of him. She could not. She resumed her search, opening every door on the second level. Then she saw the staircase leading up. One end of the house had a tower, and these stairs must lead to it.

Slowly, her bad leg starting to spasm, Izzy climbed the steps, pulling herself up with the railing. This time she didn't call out Daniel's name.

When she reached the top, she saw a door that was slightly ajar. Holding her breath and whispering a prayer, she gently pushed the door open and looked out upon a flat roof with scattered planters holding fig and lemon trees, tomato plants, and roses.

The warm late afternoon sun was redolent with the fragrance of the greenery. Izzy saw Daniel on a wooden lounge chair, his long, lean body stretched out and his eyes closed. She whispered another prayer—this time of gratitude—and collapsed on the tiles of the roof to wait.

The sun was well below the roof when Daniel finally stirred. He saw Izzy immediately and called to her.

"Have you been here long?"

"Not sure. I didn't want to disturb you. Feeling any better?"

"Marginally."

"Someone dropped off a basket of vegetables. I could fix us a light supper."

"That would be Carmela, the caretaker's wife."

Daniel sat up and rose from the lounge chair, stretching his arms over his head.

"I think this is my favorite spot in all of Bellosguardo. When I was a kid and wanted to get away from the tumult of siblings and cousins, I would hide away up here."

"Did you sleep then too?"

"No. I brought a book." He reached down beside the chair and retrieved a well-thumbed paperback. "I found this in the library. It's mine. I must have left it here years ago."

Izzy approached Daniel with her hand outstretched.

"May I see it?"

Daniel handed her the book, *The Phenomenon of Man*.

"Teilhard de Chardin! I know this name." She flipped through the first few pages, smiling at the marginal notes and underlining but seeking some clue to memory, some aha phrase that would bring back the book's message to her in a flood of recognition. That is what she always did when she encountered a book she might have read before. But nothing resonated except for the fragment of insight she gleaned from Daniel's handwritten notes. She could see at a glance that almost every page was marked.

"I think I could learn a lot about you from this book."

She extended the book back to him.

"Why don't you keep it," he said. "Maybe you can decipher something from my scribblings."

Izzy was surprised but happily so. She hugged the book to her chest. "I'll guard it with my heart."

Together they descended to the kitchen, and Izzy began chopping vegetables while Daniel brought in the laundry. He folded it on the kitchen table as Izzy cooked.

"We're being domestic again," he observed.

"I could get used to this," Izzy smiled, "if I ignored reality. Which isn't so hard for me to do after all. I suppose I'd not thought about that before—that I lose the bad memories as well as the good ones. I could remain in a state of ignorance, pretending that all is well. Little Suzy Homemaker, content in her kitchen, busy cooking dinner for her husband."

Izzy stopped, conscious of what she had just said. Daniel was not her husband. How had that come out of her mouth? She kept her head down, focusing on the zucchini in front of her and hoping that Daniel had not heard the last words out of her mouth.

But he had.

He moved behind her and put his arms around her waist. Izzy put the knife down.

"Is that what you want, Izzy?" he whispered in her ear.

"I'm sorry. I was making light of our playing house, Daniel. Because that is what we're doing. We're pretending. We eventually have to go back to the farm and resume our roles there."

"You didn't answer my question. Let me ask it a different way. Do you want to be my wife?"

Izzy stiffened in his arms.

"I can tell you what I don't want. I don't want you to give up the priesthood for me. I don't want to be the symbol of everything that will change in your life—because I'm afraid I'm not enough. You didn't know me, Daniel, before you came to Portarello. You came because you had work to do, to sort out who you are and what you want. But it feels to me that you want to take a shortcut on your journey. Choose a life with Izzy and all is solved. I don't think it works that way."

"You sound like my superior."

"And Linda and Raffaello and even Maria," Izzy added.

"Are you siding with them?"

"No! Would it make it easier for you to untangle your life if I do answer your question? I will tell you what I want, but you need to figure out what you want."

Izzy turned around to face Daniel and took his hands in hers.

"I may have been teasing about our domesticity, but the words that came out of my mouth were unfiltered. The answer is yes, Daniel Richetelli. I want to be your wife. I want to spend the rest of my life loving you. But I also want you to choose a life with me because that is what you want. Not to please me or defy your family and the Jesuits. I love you. Let that knowledge give you strength in coming to your decision, but don't let it be the only reason."

Izzy stopped speaking and waited. Had she ever said the words "I love you" to anyone else? Had she taken the leap of faith before, only to be hurt? What had possessed her to reveal the longing to be his wife? Was it because she'd given up hope in her shattered state that she'd ever be someone's wife? The magic of Bellosguardo had enveloped them today. Their seclusion had made them oblivious to the world beyond the gates. Is that why she had slipped so effortlessly into the goddess of the house, complete with the silk dress and pasta? There were shadows in this place. She had sensed them earlier when she'd wandered in the garden with Maria. But she wanted to ignore them, stay away from the dark corners and the decay lurking under the lush and vivid foliage. She wanted to give herself up to the passion she felt for this man standing before her, uncertain and questioning but now knowing the depth of her love for him.

"Come to bed." He still held her hand and gently pulled her away from the counter.

They climbed the stairs hand in hand and entered the bedroom. Daniel swept the covers off the bed and reached behind Izzy to unzip the dress. It fell in a ripple to her ankles, and she stepped out of it.

Daniel's hands slid over her bare hips and then he knelt and kissed the scars on her leg from the multiple surgeries that had allowed her to walk without braces. She had worn pants most of her adult life to cover them and the shape that didn't match her healthy leg—that didn't match the world's expectations of "normal."

Then he picked her up and laid her on the bed. She watched him unbutton his shirt and slip off his pants. As she studied him, she realized the clothes she had pulled out of the suitcase earlier for him were the black uniform of the priesthood. He was removing them with deliberation, keeping his eyes locked with hers, and she nodded, understanding what he was doing.

"I'm yours now, not the Church's, not my family's. Yours," he said as he lay with her and took her in his arms.

Within his embrace she felt no limits. Experienced no moments of anxiety, only moments of gratitude, pleasure, intensity, loving. Her hand guided his with gentle dexterity and the unspoken. This is what I want. This is where I want you. To have you. To let you have me. Not to take. To have. Bliss. Honesty. Joy. Opening the window on each other's souls. Understanding that their lovemaking was a kind of prayer. A prayer of awe and gratitude. Not a prayer of need.

They slept. Fully, peacefully, his body wrapped around hers.

Around midnight, they awakened and faced each other with grins on their faces.

"Are you hungry? I believe we left dinner preparations unfinished."

"I could use a bite to eat."

He pulled on his pants and she took his shirt, and they made their way barefoot to the kitchen.

Izzy fried the zucchini and onions she'd chopped earlier, beat some eggs, and whipped together a frittata. They ate sitting at the counter, washed up, and went back to bed.

When they woke in the morning, he was still with her, and they made love again.

"If I make love to you every day, we can recreate the days before so you will never feel the loss of memory," he whispered.

But she was remembering. Not the murmured words, or the sequence of events, but the sense of his touch, his lips, his body moving within hers. She remembered the slickness of their sweat, a layer between them; she remembered his fragrance, mingled with her own. Sex, it appeared, was something the brain did not forget.

"I want to show you Florence," Daniel told her after breakfast.

"That sounds like you're in no rush to return to Portarello."

"I'm not ready. Why, are you?"

"Not at all. They know where we are and that you're safe. I think we could both use time away. I promised Maria I would call, and I'll ask her to take my chores."

Izzy went to the phone in the hall. She managed to convince the intern who answered the villa phone to find Maria and was relieved that it wasn't Linda who had picked up.

"Are you OK? Has Danny recovered?"

"We're fine. But we're going to stay here in Florence for a while. Do you mind caring for the pigs while we're gone? Marcantonio can show you what you need. If you would let Linda know, I think Daniel would rather not talk to her right now."

"Happy to do it but only on the condition that you tell me everything when you get back. How long do you think you'll stay?"

"As long as we need. But realistically, probably about a week. Do you think you can hold off the cavalry for that long?"

"Leave it to me. They were relieved to hear that Danny is at Zia Letitia's and hadn't taken off for parts unknown. I did not describe the condition in which we found him."

"I knew you would be circumspect."

"I also explained your absence by telling them he was going to show you a bit of Florence."

"Which he is. Always better to keep as close to the truth as possible when you're trying to keep family from knowing what you're really up to."

"I mean it, Izzy. You need to tell me all when you return."

"Thanks, Maria. I promise."

After the call, they departed from Bellosguardo and crossed the Arno armed with both a list of churches and museums (Daniel's) and a grocery list (Izzy's). They left the car near the train station and spent the morning wandering on foot from the Duomo to Orsanmichele and the Piazza della Signoria. After lunch at a trattoria, they spent the afternoon at the Uffizi. It was a day to put aside the questions that were bombarding them and allow the beauty and magic of the city to transport them into another world.

"I find it incomprehensible that you've been in Italy since April and haven't once ventured into Florence. Of all the cities in Italy where I've spent time, this is my favorite."

"Your enthusiasm is infectious," Izzy smiled. "I didn't feel confident enough to navigate the trip on my own, and I don't hang out with the other interns socially, so anytime they planned a day here, I would have been an awkward appendage. I'm glad I'm seeing it for the first time with you."

"I want to show you what I love so that you'll know me as more than a tortured soul."

"Like your underlined passages in *The Phenomenon of Man*? How can I reciprocate? What do you want to know about me, beyond my constant need to take notes?"

They had stopped for coffee at a café on the Piazza di Santa Croce. "What are some of your favorite things? For example, what did you bring with you from home?"

"Ah, that's an easy question. Beach stones. I collect stones on my beach walks. Stones that have been worn smooth by the ocean. I always take a handful with me when I'm away from home. Whenever I'm agitated or distracted, I hold them in my hand and rub them, like worry beads or a rosary. I keep them in a small basket by my bed."

"Did you bring the basket, too?"

"Yes. My grandmother wove it for me when I was four or five to keep my treasures in. It's pretty ragged now from being dragged along wherever I've lived."

"You've mentioned her before. Tell me more about her."

"She's fiercely protective of the family, deeply spiritual, an herbalist with a gift for healing. I wish I were more like her."

"In what way?"

"When I left the island to go to Smith, as St. Paul wrote, I put aside what I considered to be childish things. I think I mentioned to you once that, in my pursuit of an intellectual life, I became severed from my grandmother's connection to the natural world and her belief in God. Since that night in the chapel, I find myself longing to reclaim that grounding, that rock-solid certainty she has. May I ask you something?"

He looked at her across the table. "Anything."

"What do you believe in?"

He shook his head and smiled. "I guess I wasn't expecting that one. I believe in the Resurrection. That new life is possible."

"New life," Izzy whispered. "I like that."

For the next ten days, their lives took on a rhythm of exploration not only of Florence and its surroundings, but also of each other. They climbed the towers of San Gimignano and Pisa; admired the sculpture of Michelangelo and the paintings of Botticelli, Fra Angelico, and Filippo Lippi; and wandered through the Boboli Gardens and the Convent of San Marco. They ate their midday meal out and dinner in, cooked by Izzy from whatever they found in the market that day. And throughout their explorations, they talked.

Each night, in bed, they learned more about each other.

One evening, as they sat on the wall at Bellosguardo watching the sunset, Daniel reflected on the time they had spent together. "This has been a honeymoon. Apart from the world, just the two of us, beginning to understand and know each other. It would not have been possible at the farm."

"I'm glad we stayed." Izzy leaned against him in contentment. "But I know the time is coming when we'll have to return."

"Are we ready?"

Izzy was struck by the note of uncertainty in Daniel's voice. She wasn't sure what it would mean for both of them to be thrust back into the turmoil of family expectations and the stress of Raffaello's dig. She shook off her own doubts. Whatever awaited them, they would face it together, wouldn't they?

CHAPTER EIGHTEEN

JULY 7

The next day they languished, watching the sun move across the walls, in no hurry to rise and move closer to the inevitable, the return to Portarello. But the knowledge that they would have to leave began to creep into the bed with them. Izzy's restlessness emerged first as she scanned the room for a clock.

Daniel pulled her back.

"What is it?"

"Just wondering what time it is."

He reached over her to the night table and lifted his watch.

"Almost noon."

"They must be getting anxious on the mountain. I don't know how long Maria can placate them. I'm surprised they haven't called."

"Do you want to go back? You seem ready to leave my arms."

"I don't want to go yet. I do want you to have more time to sort yourself out before they corral you with their questions and their needs."

"I can handle them."

"That's not what I saw and heard when you had your argument with Linda."

"That was before you came to Bellosguardo. Before you told me you loved me. Knowing that gives me courage."

"I am here for you."

"I know."

"Let's go for one more walk before we leave the bubble of Florence."

"Why are you so eager to leave this bed?"

"Real life, Daniel. It's waiting for us, especially at Portarello. And we need to be prepared."

He kissed her one more time and then released her.

She started the water in the tub and was not surprised when he joined her. The warmth of the water, the fragrance of Zia Letitia's bubble bath, and the gentle massaging of Daniel's hands lulled her once again into a state of contentment that blotted out her earlier disquiet about returning to Siena.

"Turn around," she told him. "Your turn."

She lathered Letitia's washcloth and soaped Daniel's back and neck and behind his ears.

"I feel like one of Jane Goodall's chimpanzees, grooming the alpha male in the clan."

"Am I the alpha male?"

"You are to me."

"Wait till we get back to Portarello."

"You mean Raffaello."

"The epitome of the alpha male, wouldn't you say?"

"My guess is he has been grooming you—in a different sense of the word. He's preparing you to replace him as head of the family."

"I think Linda was planning to step into that role. Besides, as I'm sure he'd tell us, he's not dead yet."

Izzy was silent for a moment. Something niggled at her memory, something about Raffaello and—not death—but something. She gave up. She'd learned that trying too hard to retrieve a fragment often only sent it farther back.

She only said, "Appearances can deceive. He may be trying to hide something."

"Do you know something?" Daniel shifted to face her.

"I can't remember. An observation, maybe, that was slightly off or unexpected. I'm sorry. Whatever I saw is gone."

"Linda said something to me the other morning when we had our fight. She was worried about Nonno, but we didn't get far because everything then exploded between us."

"Now you're restless. I was right. Living in the present and not being bombarded with memory does have some advantages." She splashed him to bring him back to the moment.

They were laughing and playful when they heard banging below and then a voice.

"Danny? Danny? Are you here?"

It was Linda's voice.

Daniel ceased his laughter, closed his eyes, and muttered, "Oh, shit," as he heaved himself from the tub.

He wrapped himself in one of the—thankfully—voluminous towels hanging on a warmer and strode out of the bathroom to do battle with his sister.

Izzy stared at her wrinkled fingers and toes and then leaned back to slide completely under the water.

Daniel stood at the top of the stairs and called to Linda. She came around the corner from the kitchen and looked up at him.

"You're alive."

"Why wouldn't I be?" His voice was tense. How much had Maria told her?

"You disappear without a word, in a state of *agita* like I've never seen before. That's why."

"But Maria told you I was here, didn't she? Why did you come?"

"Because I'm your sister. Because Maria, bless her heart, knows nothing of what you're going through. Can you get dressed so we can talk? Standing looking up at you there half-naked, as magnificent as your body is, is giving me a crick in the neck. I brought some food from the farm. I'll make us something to eat. Meet me in the kitchen."

She didn't ask "Where's Izzy?" Perhaps it suited her to believe Izzy had left him, or perhaps she didn't want to know. Either possibility infuriated him. He went back to the bedroom to dress. Izzy was still in the bathroom.

"Are you OK?" he called to her.

Izzy was toweling herself dry. Her hair was wrapped in another towel.

"The more important question is, are you?" she said, concern and tenderness written across her face.

"I'll be fine."

"At least she didn't arrive an hour ago," Izzy smiled. "Do you want me to stay out of sight?"

"No!" His voice was emphatic. "She has to know you are here and needs to be aware that you're not going away."

"I've got your back, Daniel. But I'm not going down there with just a towel wrapped around me. My clean clothes are in the laundry basket in the kitchen. I'll be down the hall in Letitia's closet and will be ready in a few minutes."

"We should go down together."

"Agreed."

As Izzy promised, she dressed quickly and emerged from the closet in a pair of turquoise slacks and a sleeveless white blouse. He saw that she had covered her legs this time. No floaty dresses like she'd been wearing all week.

Her hair was loose and tumbled in damp ringlets down her back. She looked beautiful and rested. She looked like a woman who had been lovingly pleasured and had given pleasure in return. Without saying a word, she'd send a powerful message to Linda.

Together they descended the stairs hand in hand, just as they'd been doing every day.

Linda was sautéing vegetables at the stove. A large pot of water was boiling on a back burner, and a bag of tagliatelle sat on the counter.

"I'm making pasta with salsa ortolana—" She stopped mid-sentence as she turned and saw Izzy.

"Izzy." Linda nodded. "Maria told us you decided to stay with Daniel. She thought it was a good idea not to leave him alone, although I would have expected Maria, as his cousin, to be the one to stay. But thank you. It was serendipitous that Maria brought you here for the view. I should have realized this would be the first place Danny would choose if he needed to get away."

Linda continued to babble, her back turned away from the stove.

"Lin, the vegetables. ..." Daniel pointed out that they were starting to burn.

Linda grabbed the handle of the cast iron pan with her bare hand and moved it off the burner.

"Shit!" she cried out, and ran to the sink to run cold water over her hand.

Izzy approached her. "Did you burn your hand? Can I take a look?"

Linda pulled her hand away from Izzy. "It's fine."

Izzy stepped back.

"I'll finish the pasta. Daniel, why don't you take Linda out to the pergola? I'll bring the food when it's ready." She directed Daniel with her eyes and hand gestures. He didn't want to go but reluctantly agreed. Sooner or later he'd have to confront Linda, and he guessed it was going to be much sooner than he would have liked.

Izzy handed him a clean towel and some ice for Linda's hand and practically pushed them out the door.

Once outside, he took long strides to lead Linda away from the house and out of earshot. Izzy had already been hurt enough by his earlier argument with Linda, and he didn't intend to compound the pain with whatever was about to come out of Linda's mouth.

"You didn't have to come. We were planning to return later today."

"I wanted time to talk with you alone, without Nonno and Maria hovering."

"And also without Izzy? Surely you knew she was here."

"Why did she stay? If you still needed time away from the farm you could have asked her to go back with Maria."

"I wanted her here."

"Daniel, you know how I feel. How can you make a reasoned, thoughtful decision if you are in the throes of whatever with the first woman who has ever tempted you?"

"You sound like some fire-and-brimstone preacher, Lin. She's not a temptress."

"Did you sleep with her again?"

"That is none of your business."

"Which means yes. She was raised a Catholic, Danny. She should know better."

"She didn't know I was a priest the first time."

"But you did. What are you doing, Danny? Sowing the wild oats you should have before you went into seminary? Did the provincial give you carte blanche, all sins forgiven, to cast out your demons?"

"I didn't know I would fall in love. I don't think the provincial was expecting this outcome."

"Is this an outcome or simply a stopping point on your way back into the fold?"

"Why is it so important to you that I remain a priest?"

"You *are* a priest. A wonderful priest. It breaks my heart to see you throw away a calling that I thought brought you peace and joy."

"That's the point, Lin. It no longer brings me peace and joy. I'm adrift, in search of a life raft to get me to shore."

"And so you grasp the first thing that comes floating by and hold on for dear life. Izzy is a beautiful person, inside and out. She's sensitive and thoughtful and cares about people. I'm not surprised that you've been pulled into her orbit. Even Nonno, under that crusty shell, is gaga over her."

At the mention of Raffaello's infatuation with Izzy, Daniel stiffened.

"If everyone thinks she's so wonderful, why are you so opposed to her being in my life?"

"Because you are so vulnerable. I don't know what is causing your malaise with the Jesuits, but your unhappiness is palpable. I've worried about you since you arrived on our doorstep. And your vulnerability makes you susceptible to someone who is offering you comfort and understanding."

"I'm a grown man, Lin. I know I'm vulnerable, but accepting Izzy's love isn't going to destroy me. It is healing me. She's a good woman."

"I don't doubt that, Danny. But is a woman what you truly need?"

"Think about your own need, Lin. Does celibacy make sense for you? I don't think so. As far as I know, you have a loving and physically fulfilling life with your husband. I had no idea what was missing from my life until I met Izzy. And I'm not talking about the sex, although that is a beautiful part of it. I'm talking about being seen and heard and understood by another human being who shares herself with me in extraordinary ways. She's a gift."

"You're like a kid in a candy shop, Danny, let loose for the first time in your life and stuffing everything in your mouth while the grownups aren't looking. Do you remember my friend Tina, who went into the Sisters of St. Joseph when we graduated from high school? She did not stop at go but took off her cap and gown and put on a novice's habit two weeks after we got our diplomas."

"I didn't do that."

"Hear me out. Tina lasted ten years and then left. I had visited her out in Chicago at the convent, and I could sense something was changing but I didn't want to believe that Tina, who had such certainty and commitment to her vocation, was giving it up. But she did. I found out later why. She fell in love with a priest at Loyola. They had an affair. But after she made the decision to leave the order—to leave for love—her relationship fell apart. She's now alone, without community and as burned by her dreams and her naiveté as my hand is right now."

"I'm sorry for Tina. Truly. But I wasn't an innocent when I entered the seminary, Lin. I was twenty-two. I'd finished Georgetown and had lived enough in the world to know what I was giving up. I wasn't a virgin, if you're thinking that what I'm going through right now is all about sex. It's not. The one thing I had not done before I became a priest was to experience love. I thought I would find the transcendence I was seeking in Christ's love. But I didn't. In the last year, I've felt abandoned by God. That, if you want to know, is why I left."

Daniel was drained. He hadn't intended to reveal so much to Linda, although he knew enough to hold back the devastating experience of his binge. He wanted to shout to Linda, Izzy saved my life! But, wisely, he kept that to himself.

Izzy appeared at that moment carrying a tray laden with the pasta, dishes, cutlery, glasses, and water.

Daniel leapt to take the tray, and she spread the cloth draped over her arm across the table. It caught a breeze and billowed like a sail. Izzy held a brief image in her head of an actual sail on a boat that took them away from all the tension shimmering between Linda and Daniel.

The tablecloth settled, and Izzy came back to the moment, pulling items from the tray and setting the table. When all was ready she gestured to Linda.

"Please sit."

As they took their places, Linda looked at her brother.

"Danny, would you please say grace."

Izzy understood what she was doing and made a decision.

"I'd like to say grace, Linda. It's one I learned as a child from my Wampanoag grandmother. It's in our native language, but I'll translate it when I'm done."

Izzy held her hands out over the food while Linda and Daniel folded theirs and bowed their heads. Izzy intoned the ritual prayer and then spoke it again in English.

"Bless these fruits of the land you have bestowed upon us as we give thanks for the sun and the waters and the earth that have nourished them and us. Amen."

Izzy looked up at Linda, whose face remained rigid.

"That was very nice, Izzy. Thank you."

"My pleasure. The bounty of the earth and the sea are gifts my people accept with gratitude. Would you like to serve?" Izzy handed her an elegant silver serving fork engraved with Letitia's monogram.

They ate in silence, without a toast. Izzy had brought out only a bottle of water. She was not inclined to break the tension with small talk and so waited for whatever the siblings were going to do. Her only role was to protect Daniel.

By the time they finished the figs and cheese, it appeared that Linda was ready to open the flood gates.

"I want you both to know I'm not the enemy. In fact, I care deeply about both of you. I'll admit, I'm old-fashioned, and it's hard for me to see my brother the priest as a man. I don't want him hurt, first of all. And I don't want him to make a decision he'll regret. The time you two have spent here alone may have been idyllic, but it's not the real world."

"We know that. That is why we're coming back. We're not hiding—although I will admit that was what I was doing when I first got here. I needed to be alone, away from the loving but opinionated voices of my family."

"Linda, we both know how challenging Daniel's decision is—for him and for your family. I love him. Please know that. And I want him to make the choice that will bring him peace and happiness. Even if that means he remains a priest."

"What has happened between you is hard for me to grasp. It was so fast, which is why I distrust it. You are two vulnerable souls."

"Our vulnerability is what binds us. We are honest with each other now because we understand the cost of withholding how we feel."

"Linda, please give Daniel some space and time. He still has a lot to sort out. And he needs to know you'll accept whatever he decides."

"Of course I will." She reached across the table and squeezed his hand. "I should go. Nonno is anxious. He blames himself for your disappearance, although he won't admit it. He expresses his concern with the usual anger and dismissive comments."

"He thinks I ran away from his questioning. He thinks I'm a coward."

"He loves you. More than the rest of us. You know that. It's why he gives you such a hard time. You are him, Danny.

He sees in you everything he hoped to become. Did you know he was going to be a priest?"

Daniel's head shot up.

"What? No! Why didn't he ever tell me? How do you know?"

"I don't think he knows that I know. I was looking in some boxes in the tower where we store the villa's archives. I want to write a history of the farm and use it for marketing. Buried in a file from the 1920s I found some documents accepting him into the Benedictine seminary at Monte Oliveto Maggiore."

"But you didn't show them to him? Or ask him about them?"

"No. You know how he is about his past. What's done is done. We move forward."

"That puts my relationship with him in a different perspective."

"Don't throw it in his face, Danny."

"I won't. I promise."

"Linda, is Raffaello all right? Daniel said you had some worries. ..."

"We never got to talk about it," Danny interjected.

"That's because you left."

"Can we talk about it now?"

"I think it's his heart. He won't say anything, of course, but I see him pushing himself and then collapsing in exhaustion. This dig has become an obsession. I've never seen him so driven, so concerned about finishing this summer. It's as if this is his last opportunity. That he won't be here next year to witness the culmination of his life's work."

"That is the memory that was eluding me!" Izzy exclaimed. "It was early morning, and I was drinking my coffee above the garden. He was exercising vigorously, but when he finished and began climbing the hill, he looked to be in pain, his face ashen. He took something out of his pocket and swallowed it."

"Nitroglycerin. I saw it on the bathroom sink."

"What can we do?" Daniel asked.

"Keep watch. Try to get him to ease off. When you come back, offer to work at the dig."

"I will. I promise."

"I'll go now. Make sure you write a note to Zia Letitia to thank her, and leave a tip for Enzo and Carmela."

"Yes, big sister." Daniel smiled and gave her a hug.

"I can't help myself," she shrugged and turned to hug Izzy. "Take care of my baby brother," she whispered in her ear.

Izzy and Daniel cleaned up the kitchen, laundered the sheets and Letitia's clothes, and scrubbed the bathroom, even though they knew Carmela would do it all again as soon as they pulled away from the gate.

"Italian families love to gossip. All Carmela needs to see is that we slept in one bed and the Tuscan telegraph will be buzzing with disapproval and novenas for the fallen priest."

"You especially don't want word to get back to Raffaello, do you?" Izzy asked as they folded the sheets and stored them in the linen closet.

"I think that's a lost cause. Maria may slip up, and given Raffaello's sharp radar, I don't think we're going to fool anyone for very long."

"Does that bother you?"

"That people on the farm will wonder why morose Danny is smiling? Let them wonder."

"I mean Raffaello. His opinion is important to you. Is he going to disapprove?"

"He may express it as disapproval, but my guess is that the underlying emotion is jealousy."

"Jealousy?"

"The last time I spoke with my grandfather, he filled the conversation with you—how much he'd enjoyed your company in Boston with Maria, how he'd found you in the library and took you under his wing, how fragile you were. It was a brilliant display of male plumage, marking his territory—you."

"That's ridiculous! He's a 75-year-old man!"

"If there is one thing Raffaello is not, it's ridiculous. And he won't be happy, or be made a fool of, when he realizes we are lovers."

"Do you honestly believe he wants me as a lover?"

"Not physically. But he wants you for himself. A protégé. That's what he described, and how taken he was with your gifts."

"I'm gobsmacked, Daniel. He's been kind to me. Given me a glimmer of confidence. But I never felt possessed by him. A favorite, yes, much to the consternation of the archaeologists."

Daniel shoved the last of the linens onto the shelf.

"Are you anticipating his jealousy because you are jealous of his relationship with me? I'm not a contest to be won, Daniel."

"I'm sorry. I sound like a jerk, don't I? I have such a fraught relationship with my grandfather that any disturbance in the delicate balance sends us to our corners ready to come out fighting."

"What do you want me to do? Pretend we're not lovers? You said yourself, everyone on the farm will see it, even if Maria and Linda keep mum. And I am finished pretending, hiding. You've given me the freedom to be who I am in this moment, not some shell of the Izzy who used to be."

"I'm not asking you to change or hide. I'm just warning you that Raffaello will be on alert and will take every opportunity to push my buttons once he realizes you and I are lovers."

"Then don't let him. Look at me." She took his face in her hands, a practice she found helpful to focus his attention. Her touch, her eyes, held him while she spoke. "I love you. When Raffaello twists the knife and tries to make you doubt, remember that. I love you."

She kissed him.

He threw his arms around her. "I am an idiot."

"Then so am I. What has happened to us, what we have discovered, is either idiocy or a miracle. Whatever it is, Raffaello is not going to take it away from us. Let's get going. It's time to face reality."

They packed the car and drove to the caretaker's cottage. Daniel hopped out and knocked on the door. A smiling woman in an apron, her cheek smudged with flour, greeted him with a hug.

"Daniele! So long since we've seen you here. La signora will be pleased that you accepted her hospitality, but next time you must come when she is here." Carmela looked over his shoulder at Izzy in the car.

"A friend of my cousin Maria. She's working at the farm and came to see Florence."

Carmela shrugged. "*Va bene*." But they both knew that Carmela had seen Daniel and Izzy leave together every day and return in the evening to the house. Daniel understood how the world was going to perceive him from now on. He had disappointed Carmela, as he would disappoint many.

He slipped an envelope into Carmela's hand. "*Grazie mille*," he told her. "*Per tutto*."

She touched his cheek.

"You were always such a good boy," she said to him in Italian.

Daniel climbed back into the car, put it in gear, and drove out through the gate. Carmela closed it with a wave as they descended the hill.

CHAPTER NINETEEN

JULY 7 – 8

The traffic heading south was heavy, and it was dark when they began the climb up the mountain to Portarello. As they approached, the villa's windows glowed with a warm light from within.

The rear courtyard was empty when they arrived. Someone had a radio on, and a plaintive jazz tune wafted out an open window. The door to the villa was unlocked, so they didn't have to rouse anyone from their evening pursuits to let them in.

Without words, they climbed the rear stairs and separated to go to their own rooms. Of all the conversations they'd had on the ride down, they hadn't discussed whether they would sleep together.

"I need to wash up and then raid the kitchen. I'm famished," Izzy said, breaking the silence and giving them both some time to decide what would be best. She didn't know. "Meet you there?"

By the time she arrived in the kitchen, Daniel was already there making them prosciutto and mozzarella sandwiches. They carried their plates to the dining room and sat in a corner away from the door.

"We should let Linda know we're back."

"She's probably at Nonno's. Do you want to come over with me?"

Izzy couldn't decide if that was a good idea. "I will if it will help. But perhaps it's best if it's just you, tonight, with your family. Maria is sure to be there as well. I don't want to be a provocation to Raffaello."

Daniel hesitated, studying Izzy's face and her own uncertainty, and then made a decision.

"We should go together. If we wait, we're only postponing a difficult conversation. It could be tomorrow evening before Raffaello is back from the dig."

He reached for her hand, and they left the villa for Raffaello's house. They could hear conversation and the tinkling of glasses on the back terrace. As they came around the corner, conversation stopped and four faces looked up expectantly. Daniel saw that Linda's husband was there, apparently back from the gig he had with his jazz quintet. Daniel seized upon Benno's presence to welcome him and deflect, at least for a few minutes, the descent into discomfort the evening was sure to bring.

"Hey, Benno! *Come stai*? How was the tour?"

Benno got up from the table to hug Daniel and meet Izzy.

"I've heard so much about you from Maria and Raffaello and Linda. You've made quite an impression on the Richetellis."

"It's been mutual. I love Portarello." Izzy smiled.

Linda offered them some limoncello, and more chairs were brought to the table.

"Have you eaten? There's still some wild boar in the kitchen. Marcantonio had to kill an intruder before he messed with our sows."

Daniel and Izzy waved away the offer of food. "We just made some sandwiches in the villa kitchen."

"I thought I heard a car drive in earlier. That must have been you. How was the trip?"

"The usual. Too many cars, too little road, and too little patience."

The stilted small talk frustrated Daniel. He'd come ready to do battle, and, instead, everyone was sipping Linda's limoncello as if they were the farm's guests basking in Portarello's ambience.

Throughout the chatter, though, Daniel noticed that Raffaello was silent. He didn't seem to be following the conversation, his eyes staring out at the dark sky.

"Nonno, how goes the dig?" Daniel wanted to pull his grandfather back into the group.

Raffaello startled to hear his name and turned to Daniel.

"We've made major progress since you disappeared, Daniele. Getting closer to understanding what is buried there. I trust your time away brought you closer to excavating the depths of your dilemma."

"Bellosguardo is a good place to think."

"It was never a place of solitude when Letitia was in residence. My sister knows how to entertain, but I don't think she ever imagined Bellosguardo as a place of contemplation. What did you think of it, Isabella?"

"I found it to be a place of contradictions," Izzy answered. "Beauty and decay. Light and shadows."

"Izzy was communing with Dante as soon as we were in the garden," Maria added.

"What did he impart to you?" Raffaello quizzed her.

Izzy couldn't remember. Vague impressions of darkness and rot flitted across her brain, but nothing coherent, and nothing she wished to share with the people around the table.

"I imagined him walking in the garden. That's all. Its history pulled me in."

Raffaello looked at her for a long minute, assessing. Izzy felt that he knew she was holding back, but thankfully he didn't push. Instead, he shifted to Daniel.

"Did you come to any conclusions during your sojourn, Daniele?"

Daniel looked around at the waiting faces. Benno was merely curious. Daniel knew his brother-in-law had a particularly laissez-faire attitude toward the Church and probably couldn't care less whether Daniel remained a priest. Maria still seemed confused and ambivalent about what she'd witnessed at Bellosguardo and more than likely was waiting for him or Izzy to explain it all to her. Linda bit her lip, waiting for the explosion now that Raffaello had lit the fuse.

"Like your excavation, I've gotten closer, Nonno. Clarified what I still need to discover. But I'm no longer floundering. It would help me if you and I could talk, just the two of us. It feels like an inquisition here tonight—no offense to you all," he waved his hands at his family. "But one of the reasons I came to Portarello was so that I could hash out my decision with my favorite devil's advocate. I'd rather not have an audience."

"Fair enough, Daniele," Raffaello responded. "But not tonight. I need to be at the dig by dawn, and a late night would set me back."

"Understood. May I join you at the dig? Not to talk but to work."

Raffaello studied him. "I'd appreciate that, my boy. Very much. Now, if you will all excuse me, I'm off to bed. Enjoy yourselves. Close up, will you, Linda, when you're done?"

"Of course, Nonno. *Buona notte.*"

Raffaello placed his limoncello glass, half full, on the table, and went inside.

A collective sigh rose up from the group.

"That was a good move, Danny, to postpone." Linda said.

"I did it for myself. I'm exhausted. I thought I wanted to get it over with tonight. But what I saw in Nonno held me back. He's not the same. Still the bite, the edge, but it felt as if he was only going through the motions, not really engaged."

"I told you, he's consumed with the dig. When was the last time he left before the end of the evening? He always prided himself on being the last man standing."

"He's changed. I saw it as soon as I got back," Benno offered. He massaged Linda's back. "You're worried, aren't you?"

Linda nodded, rubbing her eyes. "This is not the summer I anticipated. Nonno, Danny. It's all too much."

"I'm sorry I've added to your worries, Lin."

"Will someone tell me what's going on?" Maria's plaintive voice broke through. "I'm a member of this family too."

"I'm leaving the priesthood, Maria."

Suddenly, the only sound was the wind rustling the leaves of the chestnut trees.

"You've made your decision?" Linda's voice was half whisper, half cry of pain.

Izzy reached out her hand under the table and squeezed Daniel's.

Maria shook her head. "I didn't want to believe what I saw last week. But it all makes sense now. You're very brave, cousin. Follow your heart."

"Thanks, Maria. I am. If you all don't mind, I'm done. I need some sleep."

Izzy rose with Daniel, said goodnight, and walked with him across the courtyard in silence.

When they reached the villa and climbed the stairs, Daniel finally spoke.

"I'm going to say goodnight to you here. I need to spend some time alone in the chapel."

Izzy froze, confused and overcome with a sense of abandonment that was all too familiar. She might not remember whole conversations, but emotions, like her sense memories, were becoming stronger. She started to ask why but cut her voice off as she saw the pain in Daniel's face.

"I understand," she managed to utter, understanding too well that the bubble in which they had lived alone at Bellosguardo was no longer protecting them. How long had they been back at Portarello? An hour?

She turned away from Daniel toward her room, struggling to silence her sobs until she closed the door. Exhausted, she lay on top of the bed covers still dressed, hoping sleep would overtake her and allow her a few hours' respite from the tumult of the past few days. But after her tears were spent, she couldn't sleep and gave up trying. She went to the bathroom, splashed some water on her face, and left the building.

Her intention was not to wander in the dark but simply to make a circuit of the garden. She pushed open the gate and followed her nose, breathing in the aromas of basil and oregano as she made her way down the path. A half-moon partially lit the way, but Izzy's feet were familiar enough with the uneven surface and she didn't need much illumination.

She knew she had been here before in this emotional state, the searing sense of loss obliterating rational thought. She tried to assure herself that Daniel's need for solitude, and most likely prayer, was not a threat to her. But it was too late. She had ripped away every defense, made herself vulnerable, offered him her love. She had saved his life.

And he had turned away from her again. Was this to be the pattern of their relationship? Intense, fierce connections that brought them both as close to bliss as she had ever thought possible, followed immediately by Daniel's overwhelming guilt?

She wanted to scream. And then she did. Howling, shrieking. She didn't care if anyone heard her. She sank to her knees, knowing how difficult it would be to get up again and wanting only to curl into a fetal position and be swallowed up by the garden. She had an image of the garden at Bellosguardo and envisioned the vines growing over her, hiding her, until she eventually became one with the mulberry trees and hibiscus and lilies.

She was jarred from her bizarre vision by the sound of her name being called from what felt like a great distance.

"Izzy? Izzy, are you OK? Did you fall? I heard you scream."

It took Izzy a few seconds to recognize the face across from hers.

"Maria, I'm sorry. I don't really know how I got here—wherever I am." She pushed herself up to a sitting position and looked around. A garden. She had been in a garden ... but not this one.

"Oh, honey," Maria whispered, and then put her arms around her and rocked her.

Izzy's tears came again, released by the safety of Maria's embrace. When her weeping subsided, Maria spoke again.

"Do you want to talk about it?"

Izzy didn't give herself time to think. "I have to, or I'm going to slip back to the strange place I was when you found me."

"Do you want to stay here or go back to the villa?"

Izzy looked around.

"This has always been a refuge for me, a place apart where I feel safe. But I went somewhere else in my mind. To the garden at Bellosguardo."

"Definitely not a safe place," Maria shuddered in agreement.

"With you here now, I feel better. Anchored. I can talk here. At the villa someone might hear us."

"Someone like Danny?"

Izzy nodded.

"I love him, Maria."

"I know, honey. I saw it. I felt it. But now what? Did something happen after you two left Nonno's?"

"We didn't speak until we were inside the villa. And then he left me. To go to the chapel. I remember feeling abandoned. That's all. And somehow I ended up here. Thank you for finding me."

"It wasn't hard, Iz. You were screaming like my aunts over an open casket at a wake."

"It felt like that. A loss like death, only I was the one being left behind, not the one dying."

"You think he's left you permanently? That he's decided to stay in the priesthood?"

"I don't know if that is what he wants. What I do know is that he can't reconcile loving me with who he has always believed himself to be."

"A good priest."

"Who a good priest is supposed to be."

"Are you sure? It sounds like he just wanted to be alone for a while. I often feel that way after enduring a heated discussion with my family. Linda was fairly brutal tonight, and I gathered that she drove up to Bellosguardo to confront him."

"It was more than that. This is not the first time he has left me. I seem to incite a crushing episode of guilt after we. ..."

"You are lovers."

"Is it obvious?"

"Oh, Izzy, not just lovers. Soulmates. It was emanating from both of you like a force field."

"That is what I felt. But somehow he keeps ripping himself away from me. That's why he left three weeks ago to go to Bellosguardo."

"He's only gone to the chapel this time, Izzy. That's an improvement."

"I'm the one who wants to run away now, Maria. I can't keep doing this if every time we come together he's consumed with guilt. It hurts too much."

"And you feel you've endured enough pain in your life."

"Is that wrong?"

"No. I get that you're trying to protect yourself. Look, I'm only an observer here, but what I've witnessed between you and Danny is extraordinary. You are two very special people who've found each other at a time when you were both at a crossroads. Admit it, Izzy. You were adrift when I saw you out at Cove Meadow. Not only adrift, but miserable and numb. You are none of those things now. You are feeling something powerful right now. And as painful as it appears to be, I envy you. You have found the love of your life in Danny. Don't run away from this. Struggle through it with him. Yell at him instead of at the moon."

"Tonight I almost went over the edge with grief. I was wishing for death again. Freedom from all this mess. Daniel disappointed with himself; Linda disappointed with me for being the temptress leading him astray; Raffaello apparently jealous of Daniel for stealing me away from his orbit. I just want to go take care of the pigs, except even there I'm a failure. Argh! Life is so hard!"

"Yeah, sometimes it really sucks. But you're not alone in this, Izzy. I'm here, and I won't let you slip away into macabre visions. Look, I see a faint rim of light just beyond the mountain. It's a new day. Let's make a pot of coffee and take it to the roof of the villa and greet the day."

Maria hooked her arms under Izzy's shoulders and pulled her to her feet.

"I remember when you used to do that for me in the dorm. Thanks for lifting me up."

Together, they trudged up the hill to the villa. They stopped in the kitchen to make the coffee and then Izzy followed Maria up the spiral stone staircase to the roof of the villa, one hand braced against the wall to support herself. Maria carried both mugs.

At the top they could see a sliver of daylight just emerging over the eastern hills.

"Oh, my." Maria surveyed the condition of the terrace. "I don't think anyone's been up here in a while."

Broken tiles, scattered debris from animal nests, and a carpet of dead pine needles greeted them. In a corner they found some overturned and rusted wrought-iron chairs.

"Are you OK staying here, or do you want to go back down?"

"I've been taking care of pigs for weeks. A little bit of dirt isn't going to distress me. Besides, if it's this abandoned, no one else is going to disturb us. I really don't want to see or speak to anyone else right now."

Together they righted the chairs and placed them in the sunlight starting to creep across the roof. They sat in silence for a short time, sipping their caffeine and basking in the warmth. Izzy stretched out her legs and bent to massage her calf.

"Let me." Maria shifted her chair and took Izzy's leg across her knees, gently working out its stiffness.

"Thanks, Mar." Izzy leaned back and closed her eyes.

"If only I could smooth out the tightness in your heart as well."

"It's enough that you're here, ready to catch me when I fall."

"Do you want to talk? I promise I won't go beat up my cousin, although that is what he deserves."

"What am I going to do, Maria?"

"What do you want? Truly. Not what do you want for or from Daniel, but what do you want for yourself?"

Izzy smiled. "That's the question I asked Daniel." Then the smile vanished.

"For so long after the accident, I was torn between two competing desires. I wanted my life back, the life I'd imagined of teaching and writing. A life of the mind. If I couldn't regain that dream, I wanted the oblivion and peace I was thrust into, enveloped by, when I died."

She stopped to gauge Maria's reaction and only continued after the reassurance of Maria's silent nod.

"You were right, back in the garden earlier. When you came to Cove Meadow I was numb. And now I'm not. You were also right to suggest that I come to Portarello."

"If I remember, I think I did more than suggest."

"So much of what has happened to me in the last several months is because of Portarello: letting go of my despair at the loss of my memory and my "life of the mind," and immersing myself in the life of ... you know, I was about to say the life of the body, but it has, instead, been the life of the soul. The physical work, the connection to the land and the animals, and becoming part of this community all have nourished me. They've made me stronger. And encountering Daniel. ..."

Izzy took a deep breath and shook her head.

"I have never loved anyone with the intensity and sheer abandon that I love Daniel. And what astounds me is that I don't think the old Izzy, the Izzy I was before, could have experienced this love. So, yay, new Izzy. Living in the present moment has its gifts.

"But what I now do with this love has me caught again between two desires. I no longer long for death. Maybe it was the awe-inspiring hours I spent watching a young sow labor through the night to give birth—the pain, the blood, the fear. It reminded me of the mess, the chaos of life, interspersed with moments of bliss. That is what my relationship with Daniel feels like."

"Chaos and bliss?"

"Does that make sense?"

"From your perspective, yes. But my experience with Daniel—at least the Daniel before Izzy—was someone whose life was ordered and under restraint. Neither chaotic nor blissful. My girlfriends used to pine over him and refer to him as "Father What-a-Waste," so not available for the love of a woman. He was a rock in his commitment to his vocation. That is why I was so stunned when I saw what you meant to each other at Bellosguardo. You've transformed him."

"He's transformed me. It's curious, and I don't even know if I should speak this out loud for fear of losing it. But the deeper our connection, the more I've been remembering. Glimmers, mostly sense memories, emotions, that sort of thing. It's as if, because I'm not trying, but simply open to the present moment, my brain is holding on to what is important."

"So that's the bliss. But the chaos—his apparent ambivalence about you—that is what you are questioning."

"Yeah. When does the chaos completely engulf the bliss? That was where I was when you found me in the garden. How many times can I endure his turning away from me before I lose everything that his presence in my life has given me? Am I being selfish to say I can't do this anymore? I feel like all the understanding about myself that I've gained by being here is in danger of being shattered into fragments like Raffaello's pottery shards. But I'm also afraid that turning away from Daniel short-circuits this growing sense of the new Izzy."

"From what you're telling me, I'm going to make an observation. It appears that Daniel's guilt arises out of your lovemaking. Which seems to me to be a perfectly understandable response from someone who's been living a vow of chastity for several years. He is probably feeling as shattered as you are. I don't think there's any doubt about his love for you, Izzy. I saw it immediately. But I think he needs time to accept his desire for physical love.

"Maybe what you need is not a permanent break but simply a break from sex. Can you keep your hands off each other, go back to sleeping in your own rooms, so that this deepening relationship with you is less of a threat to his sense of himself as a priest? If you ask me, he also needs to take a step back. Linda isn't the only one who sees his decision to leave the priesthood as precipitous."

"I told him I don't want to be the reason he gives up his vocation. He's not the only one overcome by guilt. I was innocent at the beginning because I didn't know he was a priest. But I didn't stop—I couldn't stop—loving him after I did know."

Izzy looked down at her empty mug and then stood up.

"Enough agonizing. Thanks for listening to me and helping me to sort out what I need to do. I'm going to go feed the pigs, check on the piglets, and clean out the barn. What are you doing today?"

"Nonno asked me to do some cataloging in the granary while he's at the dig. He's behind in the paperwork that's going to need to go to the Ministry of Antiquities, and I'm much better at administrative detail than sifting through piles of dirt. Shall we meet for lunch?"

"Sure. Noon under the pergola? We could go for a swim after while my laundry is in the wash. I found a pile of dirty clothes in the bottom of my armoire that I'd forgotten about when we went to Florence."

They descended together and headed off in different directions. Izzy grabbed an apple in the kitchen when she dropped off their mugs and then went to her room to change into her jeans. She was still wearing the clothes she had worn coming back from Florence.

When she entered her room, she saw immediately the rumpled sheets and bedspread hanging nearly to the floor. She thought that she hadn't even gotten into bed the night before and was confused. If she'd gone to bed, she would have undressed, not still be wearing the same outfit. She sat on the bed and bent her head to the pillow. She didn't know what prompted her to do so, but as soon as she detected the scent wafting up, she knew that it had been Daniel who had slept in her bed. She took the pillow in her arms and curled around it, both soothed and troubled. What would have happened if she'd stayed and not gone to the garden, been in her room when he arrived? Would her turmoil and fear of abandonment been allayed? Would they have fallen into each other's arms and recreated what they'd experienced at Bellosguardo? So many *what ifs-*. She tried to identify what she was feeling, knowing he had come to her. Regret? Loss at a missed opportunity? Or relief that the cycle had not begun again, with yet another experience that would trigger Daniel's guilt and abandonment and her sense of loss?

She must have drifted off to sleep, despite the coffee, and woke in the midst of a dream. She glanced at her bedside clock and saw that nearly an hour had passed. She roused herself, made the bed, and changed into her work overalls and boots.

Once out of the villa, she trudged up the hill to the pigs. It was still early, and she was the only one there when she arrived at the silo to fill the feed wagon. She quickly peeked in the barn at the sow and her litter. She pulled her notebook from her pocket and found the date the litter had been born and the number of piglets at the birth. A quick count assured her that all the piglets were present and flourishing.

Climbing into the feed wagon, she put it in gear and bumped up the dirt road to the pens where the rest of the drift wandered from field to woods. At the sound of the motor, at least fifty pigs converged on the troughs.

As she filled each trough, she smiled and spoke to the scrambling pigs, comfortable in her familiar surroundings and glad to be back meeting their simple and straightforward needs.

DANIEL

CHAPTER TWENTY

JULY 7– 8

After leaving his grandfather's and returning to the villa with Izzy, he had left her on the stairs without looking back, knowing that she would perceive his abrupt departure as abandonment but barely able to breathe for the crushing weight of his guilt. He needed to be alone, and he needed to pray.

He lit the candles on the altar and threw himself onto the cushion of the prie-dieu embroidered by his great-grandmother and now worn to faded threads by the countless knees of the supplicants who had come before him.

He was beyond the point of thinking, beyond forming words to express his anguish to a God he doubted was listening. He focused on the unsteady flame of the candle directly in front of him and tried to breathe.

This must be what Christ felt like, resisting the temptations of Satan in the desert, he thought, as memories of the last several days unspooled in his brain: the despair and anesthesia of alcohol; the degradation of vomiting and passing out in a stupor that had finally obliterated the pain; the shock and shame of being discovered by Izzy and Maria; and Izzy's strength and absolute devotion in pulling him back from the ledge he had deliberately crawled out on, wishing to be finally free of anguish and hard decisions.

His inability or unwillingness to accept Izzy's love gnawed at him. He knew he was causing her pain again by hiding in the chapel instead of cradling her in his arms, and he was bereft. The joy of their time at Bellosguardo—a gift, a blessing—was wafting away like the smoke rising from the candles to the whitewashed, vaulted ceiling of the chapel.

He wanted to scream, to cry out, to wake himself from the nightmare he knew he had created. He had come to the chapel to avoid his room where he knew the bottle of Scotch was still lurking in the bottom of the armoire.

He heaved himself up, acknowledging the wildly shifting emotions of desire and regret, and sought another refuge because the silence of the chapel had given him no answers. He found himself at Izzy's door, hesitating but recognizing that she was the safety he needed. He knocked and was answered by silence. He couldn't blame her for shutting him out, but rapped again, calling her name. He tried the door and it opened. No one locked their doors at Portarello.

He whispered her name as he moved toward the bed, hitting his knee against the carved frame. Even his cry of annoyance didn't wake her, and then he realized the bed was empty.

It was then that he heard an anguished scream from outside, below in the garden. An owl had probably snatched his prey. The mountain at night often echoed with the sounds of wild things on the hunt.

Daniel resisted the urge once again to unearth the Scotch and instead collapsed on Izzy's bed and fell asleep.

An unfamiliar clanging awakened him, and he groaned as he turned over to an alarm clock. He fumbled for the off switch and was about to roll over again when he remembered he'd promised to join his grandfather at the dig. He silently thanked Izzy for setting her alarm before disappearing during the night.

He had no time to shower or change. Instead, he grabbed a pair of clean socks and his hiking boots from his room and hustled out to the courtyard, where his grandfather was striding out of his house, keys to the Land Rover in hand.

"You made it. I must admit, I had my doubts I'd see you this morning. Did you sleep?"

"I did, thanks. Are we heading out right now:"

Raffaello nodded and held out the keys. "Would you like to drive?"

When Daniel broke into a broad smile, Raffaello tossed him the keys and Daniel caught them.

As they settled in the car, Raffaello reminisced. "I remember the first time I let you drive this already ancient and battered machine."

"I was fifteen. We went up the trail where a wild boar was threatening the pigs. You had your shotgun and wore a beret. My grandfather, looking like a Hemingway hero about to take on Franco's Nationalists."

"Your timing is off, Daniele. I became a grandfather during the Spanish Civil War. No, my war was the Great War."

"Why do you never talk about it?"

Daniel was relaxing into the familiar rhythm of driving the old car and relieved to have his grandfather's history be the topic of conversation as they lurched down the mountain.

"Take a right up ahead where the road flattens. You'll have to stop to open the gate and close it again after we're through."

After they were past the gate and headed deeper into the forest, Daniel repeated his question.

"It was a dark time, Daniele. One learns things about oneself that one would rather bury."

"And do they remain buried?"

"For some men, yes."

"And for you?"

"Lately my past has been pushing itself into my consciousness, demanding a reexamination, perhaps, much as your Jesuit discipline requires of you."

Of course Raffaello would direct the conversation back to Daniel. But he wasn't ready to go there yet.

"Do you have regrets? A road not taken?"

Raffaello was silent, and then he shifted in his seat to face Daniel, signaling a decision made.

"Do you know that I had planned to enter the priesthood?"

Daniel thought about feigning surprise but reconsidered. Raffaello's radar would pick up the lie immediately.

"Linda told me when she came to Bellosguardo. Is that why you argued so strongly with me when I told you I had been called to the priesthood?"

"Don't you want to know why I didn't enter the seminary?"

"Of course. *Mi dispiace*. I'm sorry for jumping ahead and making this conversation about me."

"Oh, it is about you, Daniele. But let me tell my story first. I had been accepted by the Benedictines. Your great-grandmother, God rest her soul, was ecstatic. Your great-grandfather, not so much. But a few weeks before I was to leave, Italy entered the war and I was conscripted. Even those promised to the Church were called up, and I went. For two years I endured, fighting for a cause few of us soldiers understood or believed in, suffering disastrous losses under incompetent leadership. The senseless violence and futility of fighting that I witnessed during those years turned me away from God as well as the corrupt government that had plunged Italy into the war out of greed for extending its borders. I held too many of my comrades in my arms as they succumbed to poison gas or starvation or freezing mountain temperatures and could no longer offer them the solace of a loving deity who promised them an afterlife. I came home, found your grandmother on this mountain, and decided to create my heaven here. Holding your father in my arms the morning he was born brought me more joy than I had believed possible."

"Why are you telling me now?"

"Because you're at a crossroads in your life, as I was. What did you witness that made you question the foundation of your life?"

"Thank you for recognizing that my decision is based on more than a rejection of my vow of chastity."

"But your relationship with Isabella is accelerating your decision."

Daniel's hands tightened on the steering wheel as he pressed his lips together to prevent himself from lashing out at his grandfather. He spoke quietly after taking a deep breath.

"Izzy has nothing to do with the despair that drove me to question my vocation. If anything, she has lifted me out of the depths that have prevented me from seeing my way forward."

Daniel struggled with whether to reveal how far he had fallen. Would the knowledge only be another weapon in Raffaello's arsenal? He decided.

"Izzy saved my life, Nonno. Literally. If she hadn't arrived when she did and recognized my condition, I don't think I would have survived."

Raffaello was incredulous. "Were you trying to kill yourself?"

"Not intentionally. Just stupidly trying to drink myself into numbness to stop the pain."

"You haven't yet answered my question. I understand that Isabella wasn't the source, but what was? What sent you—my brilliant, perceptive, thoughtful grandson—into such a downward spiral?"

"The suffering of others that I couldn't alleviate—the sterility of my academic calling teaching entitled young men who didn't give a shit about the poor, the disenfranchised, their less privileged friends dying in Vietnam or overdosing on heroin. There are some priests, mostly working in Latin America, practicing what they are calling Liberation Theology, applying their faith to actually effect change for the poor and oppressed."

"I've heard of them. So why can't you take up work such as that, as a priest?"

"Because the provincial laid down an edict: obey and don't engage in Liberation Theology, or leave the Jesuits."

"And so you left."

"Not at first. When I walked away from Fordham, I hadn't yet decided. I loved being a Jesuit. I was proud to be a Jesuit, a member of an intellectual elite."

"But you discovered they weren't a moral elite."

"That is the crux of the issue."

"What now? I imagine Isabella has complicated any plans to fly off to Peru."

"I don't know what I'm going to do beyond resigning from the Society of Jesus."

"There are other avenues for fighting for social justice beyond pissing off the Vatican and taking up arms against oppressive governments. Consider what any decision will cost you.

"As I mentioned, I'm looking back at my life, Daniele, and for a reason. I am telling you this first and ask you to hold it in confidence until I'm ready to tell the others. I am dying."

"Nonno. ..."

"It's my heart. I've refused surgery, which would prevent me from finishing the dig. I don't know how much time I have left, but I intend to make the most of it. Having you here, as challenging as it has been for you, is a gift, Daniele. I love you, my boy, no matter what you decide to do with your life. I hope you know that."

"I do, Nonno, I do."

Daniel parked the Land Rover in a clearing and hugged his grandfather.

Up ahead, staked quadrants and mounds of excavated earth emerged from the morning mist.

By the time they exited the car, Raffaello was no longer Nonno but Professor Richetelli, unlocking the gate to the dig and striding to the tent that protected the artifacts already unearthed. Daniel followed his grandfather, attempting to shift from the emotional revelations of the last minutes to the work awaiting him. He didn't know if they would continue the conversation, but certainly not while they were on the site, which was surprisingly empty of the team from BU that had been assisting Raffaello for the last two months.

"Where's your team?"

"They'll be here in about an hour. I wanted time alone with you before they arrived."

Inside the tent, long wooden trestle tables held a variety of tagged items, some merely shards but others whole pieces of elegantly shaped vessels with elaborate designs.

"May I?" Daniel asked, gesturing to a bowl.

Raffaello nodded and started to caution him but then pulled back.

"It's an exciting find," Raffaello explained.

"It's beautiful!"

"Not just beautiful. It's a funerary urn, an indication that below us may be a significant tomb."

"How close are you to confirming your expectations?"

"Come, I'll show you."

Raffaello led Daniel around the perimeter to a quadrant covered with a bright blue tarp. He knelt to release the fastenings, and Daniel moved around to loosen the other side. Then Raffaello stood back and awaited Daniel's reaction.

With a sharp intake of breath, Daniel took in the scope of the excavation. An underground room lay at his feet, at least ten feet below the surface. Daniel knelt to peer down at a wall vividly painted with human figures. A family.

"You've found it. Your capstone," he whispered across the divide to his grandfather.

Raffaello smiled.

"Why have you kept this a secret?"

"I want to get as much as possible uncovered before the Ministry of Antiquities arrives. The tombs were houses, Daniele. There are probably several more rooms beyond this one. This must be the resting place of a prominent family. That urn in the tent was my first clue. What you see below may be the middle or an anteroom. We need now to dig in both directions. I want to find the sarcophagus."

"How can I help?"

"Dig."

Although Daniel jogged and played pickup basketball at Fordham, his life as an academic had not prepared him for the arduous and meticulous work of an archaeological dig. He'd barely made a dent when the BU team arrived in their van and dispersed to their various tasks. By watching and pacing himself, he soon developed a rhythm. After a few hours down in the pit, he switched with a man at the top hauling up buckets of soil and spreading the contents over fine mesh screens, where another member of the team searched for fragments.

When he thought he couldn't lift another bucket, he heard a horn and the sound of a motor in the direction of the gate.

"Lunch!" announced the archaeologist at the screens.

All activity ceased as everyone clambered from below ground or other locations on the site. Daniel hadn't noticed a second tent under a cluster of trees.

"The mess tent," one of the archaeologists pointed out to him.

Two members of the villa's kitchen staff were unloading chafing dishes and carafes from the van. Outside the tent, a trough and a hose were the gathering point for team members, streaked with the clay of the mountain, to wash off before the meal. Someone, probably Linda, had put a great deal of thought into organizing the site for the needs of the crew.

A buzz of conversation greeted Daniel when he entered the tent, reflecting the energy that the exacting but exciting work of the dig was generating. Being members of the team that helped Raffaello make this discovery was probably going to make the careers of these guys. No wonder they were bounding as if they were hyped up on amphetamines. Daniel realized immediately that some of them probably were. This was grueling physical work, and they'd been doing it for months.

He found a place at a table after loading up his plate with caprese salad and pasta in a pesto sauce with peas and ham. The meal was delicious, which was no surprise given Portarello's attention to all things culinary. But it also gave Daniel an opportunity to observe and listen. He was curious to see how his grandfather interacted with the team and how they perceived him.

"You're new to the site," commented one of the men at the table who hadn't been working with Daniel in the morning. "Are you from the Ministry of Antiquities?"

Daniel understood the wariness that had greeted him when he'd sat down at the table. He smiled.

"I'm Raff—Dr. Richetelli's grandson, here to lend a hand under the watchful eye of my grandfather. As kids, my siblings and cousins and I spent many a summer sifting the Portarello earth for my grandfather."

"You've arrived at a propitious moment. Extra hands are always welcome, especially since Professor Richetelli is in a great rush to uncover the rest of the tomb."

Daniel kept his facial expression neutral despite the flash of pain elicited by the comment. He questioned how long he could keep the secret of Raffaello's illness, especially around the family. Did Raffaello not realize that his grandchildren had already noticed the changes in him? He pulled himself back to the present and chatted amiably with the men at the table before they all dispersed to their tasks as if a bell had chimed. The "bell" was the appearance of Raffaello at the entrance to the tent. He hadn't said a word, but all heads had turned and, within minutes, plates were gathered up and deposited in a bin and the team was on its way back to the excavation.

Daniel took up his position below again and saw his grandfather on his knees in a corner with a lantern scanning a newly exposed fragment of a wall.

Daniel didn't interrupt him. He didn't have time to, as the bucket clanged down from above, waiting to be filled.

They worked until sunset. Daniel found Raffaello in the tent, bent with a magnifying glass over a large fragment, his notebook open on the table.

"Another piece of evidence?" Daniel asked as he approached.

"I am willing myself to restraint. Too often I've reached this point in a dig only to be disappointed, so I am trying to temper my excitement with a harsh dose of reality. The early-morning trip out here is also catching up with me. I

say it's time we close up and go avail ourselves of whatever
Linda has conjured for dinner."

The team, obviously well trained in Raffaello's exacting
process, had already covered the excavation and delivered
the day's fragments to the tent for cataloging. Daniel and
Raffaello were the only ones left at the site, as they had
been at the start of the day.

Daniel watched Raffaello climb into the Land Rover, his
face rigid with pain.

"Nonno, I know you won't rest until you finish, so
I won't ask you to, but what more can I do to lighten
your load?" Daniel stopped himself from uttering the
words that were ready to spill from his tongue, words that
every member of the family would recognize. You're killing
yourself with this obsession. Because, of course, he was.
Refusing care out of his profound sense of mission.

"You are doing exactly what I need, Daniele. Carrying
out the physical work that now defeats me and leaving me
the energy I need to concentrate and document what lies
beneath us. *Grazie tante.*"

"Are you at least taking medication?"

Raffaello shook his head. "I can't risk the brain fog that
the most effective painkillers provoke. I'd rather be sharp.
Sleep helps. Let's go home."

It was full dark by the time Daniel parked the car in the
courtyard and escorted Raffaello into the house.

Linda was waiting with dinner simmering on the stove.
She kissed her grandfather on both cheeks and then took a
step back to assess.

"Do you want to shower and then eat, or shall I put the
food on the table?"

Daniel admired the skill with which Linda managed Raffaello. Give him choices. Don't tell him what to do.

"I'm famished, as I'm sure everyone waiting for us is. Let's eat. I assume you've set up on the terrace?"

Raffaello moved purposefully out to the garden, and Daniel stayed behind to help Linda carry out the food.

"How did it go today?"

"The dig or my conversation with Nonno?"

"Either. Both. You two look drained, and I wasn't sure what had caused it."

"The work is grueling, especially now that the pace is accelerating."

"Nonno isn't digging himself, is he?"

"No, no. He's conserving his strength for examining and identifying what we've uncovered. The strain of anticipation, trying to keep his expectations in check, appears to be what is depleting him. So much is riding on this dig for him, and I think he's terrified."

"I've never known Nonno to be terrified, Danny. That's a strong word."

"This dig is different, Lin. It's not like what I remember from our childhoods, when a dig was an adventure and a teaching moment for Nonno. This is the real deal. Something extraordinary lies beneath the mountain. It's palpable. And Nonno knows it too."

"But his superstition, or whatever you call it—that ancient Italian respect for the Fates—is keeping him tightly bound. He's not going to let go until he finds what he knows in his heart is waiting for him."

"You've got it. Nobody says the word out loud at the site. He's got us all rubbing charms and reading entrails."

"We should go outside with the food. He'll suspect you of giving me a report, and he'll hate it."

Arms laden with pasta and a platter of lamb chops, Linda and Daniel pushed open the French doors to the terrace and presented the meal to the assembled family.

Although Raffaello had arrived home slumped in exhaustion, the presence of an audience on the terrace apparently had revived him. He was sitting with Benno and Maria, who were listening raptly to his description of the day's finds.

Daniel took a seat at the table with Benno next to him and Maria across from him scowling at him as he sat down. He felt like an adolescent in junior high, being frozen out by the cool kids. Did everyone at the table know that he'd deserted Izzy once again? That is what he'd done, and he suspected that Izzy had shared her abandonment with Maria, given the icy chill emanating from his cousin.

"Danny, are you asleep with your eyes open? I just asked you to pass the parmesan." Linda disrupted his silent mea culpas and brought him back to the meal. At least she gave him some cover by attributing his silence to exhaustion. As soon as he'd finished eating, he got up.

"Sorry, I guess the life of the mind has not prepared me for the life of the dig. I'm wiped. If you'll all excuse me, I'm going to bed. Nonno, I'll be ready to go whenever you want tomorrow."

"Same time, my boy. I'm heading up to bed myself very soon."

Daniel bent to kiss his grandfather goodnight and left without another word.

Izzy

CHAPTER TWENTY-ONE

JULY 8

The rest of Izzy's morning rushed by, and she was famished by noon after having eaten only the apple she had hastily snatched earlier. When she arrived at the pergola, she saw a parade of kitchen staff hauling chafing dishes and giant pots to a van waiting in the driveway. She pitched in to help. After the van pulled away, she spoke to the cook.

"So much food! You must have started cooking before dawn!"

"Si, Isabella. Those boys on the dig are working up quite an appetite now that the pace has accelerated. The professor is there now all day, which keeps them on their toes. We're all waiting for the announcement."

"The announcement?"

"Word on the farm is that this is something big and it's coming soon. Any day, any day." She went back into the kitchen and returned with the lunch platters for those working at the villa and the guests gathering under the pergola.

Izzy found Maria and sat with her at the end of one of the long dining tables.

"Have you picked up on the excitement buzzing around that your grandfather is on the cusp of his discovery?"

"How can I miss it? I only hope it's soon. He's working relentlessly in the field instead of leaving the heavy lifting to his 'young bucks.' Linda's a wreck that he's digging his own grave as he unearths this Etruscan one. You saw how tired he was last night. He's been like that all week. Won't listen to anyone about slowing down."

"Have you been to the site?"

"Two days' ago, while you were still at Bellosguardo."

"What's it like?"

"A huge field marked off in quadrants, some only partially excavated and then abandoned when they yielded nothing. One major hole that's been identified as a room in the tomb. My grandfather has been working this site for over three years, which is why everyone is so excited."

"It feels like all this has happened since I left—or was I so busy with my pigs that I was completely oblivious to the progress being made?"

"I think Nonno was keeping a lid on the discovery, especially with guests around. He's superstitious, but he's also wary of interference from the bureaucrats in Rome. He doesn't want them swarming down here and taking control away from him."

"Enough about ancient civilizations. How are you feeling? Any more thoughts about my suggestion?"

"You mean for a time out? Yeah. I sat on a bench in the barn when my chores were done and watched the sow and her litter. I took a life lesson from her acceptance of all those squirming, scrambling piglets determined to find nourishment. I can't wave a magic wand over Daniel's dilemma and solve it for him. I can't absolve him of the guilt that's haunting him. I can only control my own choices. I hate thinking that I have to protect myself, but the pain is real and raw. I need, and I want, time to heal. So yes, a time out."

"When do you plan to tell him?"

"Tonight."

"Do you want to have dinner with us when Nonno and Daniel get back from the dig?"

"You know, I think not. I'd rather not be on display with your family again. Who knows what Daniel's thinking today, as opposed to last night? I'd rather be alone with him, without an audience."

"You can come get me afterwards if you need me. Throw some pebbles at my window."

"Thanks, Mar. I've got to put a load of wash in and then let's go for a swim."

After Izzy hung her wet clothes on the line outside the laundry house next to the pool, she left Maria to do her afternoon chores. When she was finished, she made her final check on the sow and headed down the hill with time to shower before dinner.

At the meal, Izzy sat with some of the new guests, a group of artists attending a workshop on ancient techniques. They had arrived only the day before, so Izzy was free from the pressure of remembering who they were. She listed to their exclamations of amazement and delight in Portarello and felt a sense of pride in being a part of it.

Across the dining terrace, the archaeologists, all looking gritty and rumpled, had descended on the table directly from their van. They'd been missing from the wine hour, and word had been passed to the staff that they'd been delayed because of Raffaello's decision to work another hour.

Izzy did her best to focus on the artists, but the murmurs from the archaeologists were distracting. Although Daniel wasn't among them, she expected that his mood would reflect the same suppressed tension she felt emanating from the table in the corner. She began to second guess her decision to seek out Daniel later in the evening. Would he be as exhausted and agitated as the others? Would the excitement at the dig overtake any emotional room Daniel might have for her?

When she realized she'd missed questions from her tablemates, she apologized and abruptly rose to excuse herself, mumbling something inane about needing to check on the pigs.

She retreated to the library to pass the time until she thought Daniel would be back in his room. She spent a restless hour flipping through a magazine. When she couldn't wait any longer, she steeled herself and made her way to Daniel's room. Let's get this over with, she told herself, as if she were facing one of the surgeries she'd endured as a child. She rapped on his door and when she didn't hear a response started to turn away. But she reconsidered when the image of Daniel on the floor in the loggia at Bellosguardo flashed through her brain. She turned the knob and called his name softly. The room was dim as dusk had settled on the mountain, but she could see it was empty. The bed, of course, hadn't been slept in. She was about to retreat, when Daniel appeared in the bathroom doorway.

DANIEL

CHAPTER TWENTY-TWO

JULY 8

Daniel barely had the energy to shower when he got back to his room, but forced himself to endure the almost warm water as an alternative to the bottle of Scotch that still whispered its siren call.

He watched the clay slough off his body and whirl down the drain. He'd felt the dirt burrow into his skin as he'd scraped away at the walls of the tomb, sometimes with his hands. He acknowledged that he'd absorbed some of his grandfather's obsession as the day had worn on, not only to support Raffaello in his dying wish, but also because he'd found himself enraptured by the tomb itself. At first, he'd merely been intrigued—by the evocative painting on the wall and the expansiveness of the "house" some ancient family had built to celebrate and be united in death. But after only a few hours, his intrigue had evolved into a fascination and a longing. He wanted to understand what the place and its objects meant to this unknown family.

Daniel's reverie was interrupted by a knock and the sound of his door opening. He dried himself and wrapped his towel around his waist before opening the bathroom door.

Izzy stood there, her hands on her hips.

How many days had passed since they'd first encountered each other in the chapel? How much had changed since that first extraordinary night? The tentative, sleep-deprived, cautious young woman who had entered his life at that moment was a long way from the fierce warrior facing him now.

In the space of a few seconds, he experienced both relief and dismay in seeing her. He hadn't spoken to her since leaving her the night before to retreat to the chapel. She wouldn't know that he'd gone to her room to find her. To sleep with her. He could barely nod hello to her. He knew his exhaustion was preventing him from acting normally. All he wanted to do was blurt out an apology to her, but she spoke first.

"I felt like one of the three bears this morning when I returned to my room."

So she did know. "You mean the observation that someone had slept in your bed."

"I would have preferred to find you there, rather than the rumpled sheets and the faint aroma of Zia Letitia's expensive hand-milled soap. In fact, I would have preferred not to have left my bed at all and, instead, had you holding me all night long."

"Why did you leave?"

"I couldn't sleep and went to the garden. It's a refuge for my insomnia. When did you come to my room? No, that's not what I really want to know. Why did you come to my room?"

"I couldn't pray. You are my refuge."

Izzy lifted her arms in frustration.

"Daniel, I don't know what to say to you. I spent the night howling at the moon, as bereft as if you had died."

"That was you? I heard the screams and thought it was an animal in pain, snatched by a bird of prey."

"I was in pain. And I understand that you left me to go to the chapel because you were in pain. Is this what our relationship has become? An endless round of inflicting pain on each other? In so many ways you have filled me up—with joy and hope and moments of absolute bliss. But right now I only feel depleted, drained. I am pulled in so many directions by the opinions of your family. Linda still sees me as a temptress, leading you away from your calling. Maria believes I've been awakened from an emotional coma and should rejoice that I can feel again, even when it hurts. And for all I know, Raffaello may feel I've turned away from him because I'm avoiding all of you."

"My family inserts itself into everyone's life. I've learned how to defend and protect myself from their self-righteousness, but I'm sorry you've had to endure their interference."

"We were still in a bubble at Bellosguardo, protected from the eyes and tongues of everyone here who matters to you. But now that we are back, we are confronted everywhere by their questioning and disapproval. I knew as soon as we left Bellosguardo we'd be challenged. I just hadn't anticipated how quickly you'd collapse under the weight of your guilt. I can't keep doing this, Daniel. I can't be both the source of your happiness and the cause of your grief.

"I love you. I want you to accept that and know that you are a good man. But if you can't love and forgive yourself, I cannot do it for you. I cannot bear what your guilt is doing to me and to us. And on top of that, I'm also finding it unbearable that our lives and emotions are on display to your family. I come from a family that acts with restraint. I'm not comfortable with so much drama.

"You've awakened me, Daniel. Given me glimmers of memories and the hope that the lost part of me might return. But the cost is becoming too high. It hurts so damn much! I love you so much, but I don't know that I can keep it together when you withdraw. I can't do that anymore!

"My grandmother once told me something about my mother that stunned me but I now understand. She loved—still loves—my father deeply. But she recognized that he had a mission to fulfill when my grandfather died—a duty to lead the tribe. My mother believed that she was standing in the way of my father's destiny. That's what Granny called it. His destiny. And so my mother stepped aside. Sacrificed her own happiness for the good of those who weren't even her people. You have a destiny, Daniel. It may not be the priesthood. But I feel I am standing in your way, blocking your path from finding it, just as my mother was thirty years ago."

"Izzy, so much of my anguish stems from knowing I am hurting you with my lack of courage. I am overwhelmed by what you've given me and yet incapable of accepting your love. I'm afraid."

"I am, too, Daniel. When I first came to Portarello it was to escape. I've told you how emotionally paralyzed I was, shutting out the love of my family because I no longer knew myself and couldn't bear the pity and the loss everyone tried to hide from me. I thought Portarello would be a place where I could start anew, reinvent myself because

I was among strangers. I was grieving—for my lost self and for the glimpse of peace and joy dying had given me. I was adrift. Until I met you.

"You have touched me, opened me to possibilities that I thought were closed to me. I have to follow those possibilities even though I am so frightened of failing, of losing these fragments that are starting to fall into place. I told you at Bellosguardo that I want to spend the rest of my life loving you. Not only loving you, but making love to you. And that is what I think is the source of the crushing guilt that causes you to leave my bed after what I know has brought us both happiness. It's the sex. As wonderful as it is, I think it's keeping you from sorting out your life. I don't think you can continue being whiplashed by your emotions any more than I can."

Daniel was reeling from Izzy's raw honesty. She had zeroed in on exactly what clawed at him. They had promised each other at Bellosguardo not to hide from the truth, and he needed to honor that promise now.

"I know you are right. I came here to escape too. To hide. Meeting you has cracked me open. And I need to put myself back together before I can offer you what you deserve. But every moment I spend with you, even now, in the midst of this painful conversation, fills me up. Nurtures me. Your love is a source of incredible power. Even as I bask in it, I envy your ability to give so much of yourself. I have a long way to go before I can love like that."

"But you have loved! That's what I'm trying to tell you. Maybe because we both came here broken, with missing pieces, our jagged edges fit together."

"What do you want, Izzy?"

Izzy held up her hands perpendicular to one another to form a "T," like a referee at a ball game.

"I'm proposing a time out. From the sex. Not a permanent withdrawal, I hope. But I think if we take a step back from the intensity, we'll both feel safer. I won't always be wondering when you're going to abandon me again, and you won't be consumed with guilt.

"But I also want us to continue challenging each other, talking, probing. We've both made some tentative steps toward our new lives, and I don't want to lose that. Do you think we can manage to be friends without also being lovers?"

Daniel rubbed at his forehead, as if he could massage away the pain he felt at Izzy's revelation. Pain that he had caused. He wanted desperately to reach out to her, but he sensed from her rigid posture that his touch would not be welcome. What a selfish fool he'd been.

"I know I'm hurting you, Daniel, but I don't know any other way to stop my own hurt. Believe me, it is taking every fiber in my body to restrain myself from crossing the space between us and taking you in my arms. But I cannot do that again, knowing that in what—a few hours, maybe a few days—you'll have left my embrace once again."

"Forgive me."

"Isn't that what sinners say to you in the confessional? Shall I assign you ten Hail Marys and ten Our Fathers, absolve you, and send you on your way free of your burden? I'm sorry. That was unfair. I don't mean to be flip or cynical. And I don't mean to place all the responsibility for this mess we're in on you. I didn't pull away after I knew you were a priest. And I should have understood the guilt that would consume you. I thought ... well, I thought that you loved me, and that love would overcome guilt."

"I do love you, Izzy," he whispered.

"Don't. Please don't." Izzy held up her hands as if to ward off a threat. "I can't bear knowing you love me and still find it necessary to leave me."

Daniel could see she was fighting to hold back her tears.

"I don't think I can stay here any longer. The resolve I entered with is seeping away and I can't afford—we can't afford—for me to give in to my aching heart."

"I know you're right, Izzy. I can't love you the way I long to until I confront all my demons."

"Overcome them, Daniel. And then come back to my bed. I'll be waiting for you." And then she turned and left.

He went to the armoire and retrieved the bottle of Scotch. He held if for a long time, staring into the amber liquid that beckoned him like a flame, promising warmth. Then he pried open the cap, walked back to the bathroom, and poured the source of his temptation down the drain. He tossed the bottle into the bin and went to bed.

When the alarm clanged the next morning, he was surprised and grateful that he was clear-headed. To guard against any backsliding, he grabbed the bin on his way out, determined to remove even the empty bottle from his room.

He dumped it without ceremony in the trash container in the courtyard just as Raffaello emerged from his house.

Raffaello raised his eyebrows in a wordless question—or was it a comment—at the sound of shattering glass.

Daniel wanted to defend himself against Raffaello's clear assumption that Daniel had already finished the whole bottle of Scotch. But he held his tongue. He wasn't sure what message his grandfather would take from the revelation that he'd poured the whiskey down the drain. A waste of good Scotch? An admission that alcohol had become one of Daniel's demons? Instead, he caught the keys and drove his grandfather to the dig.

The following days were an object lesson in archaeological excavation: slow, painstaking digging followed by meticulous screening and logging of every fragment uncovered as the team made its way from the initial room deeper into the tomb. Daniel's presence was accepted by the team, especially as he became more acclimated and held his own in both his ability to do the physical work and his careful recording of context and description when he encountered an artifact. He was also successful in getting Raffaello to pace himself during the day, especially during the more grueling excavation in search of the next room. As Raffaello developed more confidence in Daniel's ability to recognize something important, he was willing to stay above working in his tent until Daniel alerted him that his advice or direction was needed.

Their days took on a familiar pattern. On the early-morning drive to the site, they discussed the work of the previous day—the frustrations of reaching a dead end or the excitement of a possible breakthrough. Daniel's shared enthusiasm for the work was palpable, building a rapport with Raffaello that neither had believed possible at the beginning of the summer. They lunched together, sometimes in the mess tent and occasionally alone in Raffaello's tent when Daniel recognized Raffaello's need for both solitude and his grandson's companionship. In the evening, they repeated the process on the drive back. They joined the family for dinner and then each retreated in exhaustion to bed.

Although not unexpected, the probing conversations about Daniel's decision to leave the priesthood abated as the work at the dig became more intense and Raffaello's focus was entirely on the possible discovery of a sarcophagus. Despite the lack of discussion, however, Daniel found the work at the dig a form of meditation and reflection on his life.

His immersion in his grandfather's obsession also kept Daniel away from the farm and consequently away from Izzy. She hadn't joined the family for dinner since their first night back from Bellosguardo. Any opportunity they might have had for encountering each other in the evening was lost, given the hours Daniel kept in order to sustain the arduous schedule established by Raffaello's urgent need to finish the dig this summer.

Daniel missed her. Despite his physical exhaustion from the long days at the dig, his sleep had been fitful. The only nights he'd actually slept well since his arrival in Italy had been when he'd held Izzy in his arms.

CHAPTER TWENTY-THREE

JULY 22 – 23

Two weeks after Daniel had begun working at the dig, the team reached the inner chamber of the tomb and Raffaello began the hunt for what he hoped was the sarcophagus. He and Daniel arrived early at the site, removed the tarp, and descended to the tomb, lanterns in hand. Raffaello moved slowly around the perimeter of the newly excavated room, probing gently with a metal rod. He stopped his tapping and knelt carefully, scraping away a layer of loose soil with his bare hands.

Daniel watched as Raffaello grew more focused and intense. He lifted his head and ordered Daniel to bring him a trowel. Returning with the tool, Daniel knelt beside his grandfather and joined him in digging with his fingers. Raffaello was breathing heavily and, even in the damp chill of the tomb, was sweating.

Finally, Raffaello stopped and pointed to an edge of carved stone he'd uncovered.

"Is it a fragment or something more substantial?" Daniel asked, leaning in to see the design gouged into the stone.

Raffaello shook his head. "I don't know yet, but its position in this room gives me hope. Let's continue to unearth it, but gently."

Together they worked with exacting care to extend the amount visible. By the time the rest of the team had arrived, they had uncovered more than a foot of a stone rim.

Daniel resumed his usual task, removing the accumulated earth from Raffaello's painstaking excavation to the buckets waiting to be hauled up to the field. He watched his grandfather with both awe and concern. Raffaello was pushing himself beyond what Daniel recognized were his limits, but he knew he would not be able to pull Raffaello away to rest. The hum of excitement among the crew that Daniel had observed the day before, when they'd broken through to the inner chamber, was now reaching a crescendo as the intensity emanating from Raffaello spread in waves from the men in the tomb to those above. No one spoke. It felt to Daniel as if a collective breath was being held, and he found himself caught up in the excruciating tension of anticipation.

He moved back and forth between the buckets and the unknown stone slowly being stripped of layers that had accumulated over the centuries. Each time he approached the stone, he could see more of it exposed, revealing a solidity and massiveness that heightened the likelihood that this was no mere fragment.

Hours passed. When the bell tolled announcing the arrival of the food truck, Daniel was able to pry Raffaello away from the tomb.

"Come eat something, Nonno. You'll need your strength for the rest of the work today."

Daniel expected protest, and was surprised when
Raffaello agreed without complaint. But rising from his
kneeling position, he stumbled and grabbed Daniel for
support.

Daniel was shocked at how light Raffaello was as he bent
to help him. He wrapped Raffaello's arm over his shoulder
and with his other arm lifted him and practically carried
him to the ladder.

"Can you climb? I'll be right behind you."

Raffaello nodded, grabbed hold of the vertical supports
of the ladder, and hauled himself up to the surface.

After the meal, Daniel hoped Raffaello would take a
break—if not a nap on the cot in the tent then at least a
brief interlude above examining what fragments had been
found.

But Raffaello had no intention of remaining up above.

"We're too close, Daniele. I have to be there. My
mind would be too distracted waiting for the shout, the
confirmation. I want to feel it come alive under my hands."

"*Va bene*, Nonno. But the instant you feel unwell, I need
your promise that you'll take a break."

They descended again, and this time Daniel stayed by
Raffaello's side, following his lead as he meticulously
removed layer after layer of soil. As the afternoon wore on,
Daniel saw his grandfather's relentless concentration as it
became clear that something extraordinary lay just below
his fingertips.

"You're not going to stop today, are you?"

"No. Not now. I'd never sleep if I walked away. Best
to let the crew know we'll work through the night. Send
someone up to let Linda know that we'll need an evening

meal and a couple more generators. I want lights down here, as many as possible."

Daniel did as his grandfather instructed, knowing that Linda herself would return with the food and the supplies. He was not mistaken; an hour later, his sister entered the chamber.

"I brought reinforcements as well as food, Nonno. What do you need us to do?"

"Who's here?"

"Benno, Marcantonio, and Maria."

Daniel's head went up at the missing name. He wasn't going to ask Linda if she'd deliberately not asked Izzy to help or if Izzy had stayed away to avoid him. He turned back to his work, forcing himself to focus. The work was slow and deliberate, with painstaking care taken not to damage whatever lay below.

Raffaello gave Linda tasks for the new arrivals, stretching from the crouched position he'd been in most of the day.

At dusk he agreed to come above and eat, and then he resumed his work.

As the hours passed, Linda went back and forth, offering him water, a sweater, a plea to take a break. He kept at it.

Daniel refused to leave his side, moving past the fatigue to an almost trance-like state. And then he heard his grandfather gasp. He watched him brush away a final, fine layer of grit as a face emerged. It was entirely intact, not even a chip marring the incredible artistry and emotion chiseled out of the ancient stone.

Raffaello knelt as if in worship, tears streaming down his face. All around the chamber, the others stopped and a hush spread. Even the clanking of the bucket against the ladder was stilled as gestures conveyed the arrival of the moment all had been anticipating. Daniel put his hand on Raffaello's shoulder and squeezed.

"A camera," Raffaello finally whispered to Daniel. "Get me a camera." And then the spell was broken. Word was shouted up above, and a Nikon was lowered in the bucket. Faces crowded at the opening to the excavation, but everyone knew to stay above.

Raffaello moved from side to side, capturing the face from every angle. He handed the camera to Daniel.

"Now we rest. He will still be here tomorrow, waiting for us to learn his story."

When they emerged above, they were surrounded, the excitement palpable. Linda approached Raffaello and hugged him.

"*Tanti auguri*, Nonno."

After accepting the congratulations of the team, he conferred with the lead archaeologist to secure the excavation and set guards from this night going forward. He knew word would seep down into the valley before he even reached the villa, and the risk of vandals was real.

When he was assured that his orders would be carried out, he finally agreed to climb into the Land Rover and allow Daniel to drive him home.

When they reached Raffaello's house, Daniel accompanied him inside and to his bedroom despite his protests.

"Let me do this for you, Nonno. Lie down and I'll pull off your boots."

"That's all. I can undress myself. But before you go, grab that bottle of Glenlivet and pour us both a shot."

Daniel was happy to comply and brought back the two glasses.

Raffaello lifted his glass to Daniel's. "*Grazie, il mio ragazzo, per tutte.*"

Daniel felt the Scotch sear his throat as he finished the shot in one gulp.

"*Prego, Nonno. Buona notte.*"

He kissed Raffaello on both cheeks and left the room. On his way out of the house he met Linda and Benno.

"How is he?"

"Grateful. Satisfied. Himself. Didn't want any help, so I imagine he'll sleep in his clothes. I'm going to bed as I anticipate he'll want to be back on the site early. Thank you both for coming tonight."

"As soon as I heard he planned to work through, I knew I had to be there. Thank you for staying at his side."

"I wanted to be there. I'm off. See you tomorrow."

Daniel walked back to the villa. He could see that Izzy's window was dark. He ached to go to her and made it halfway down her corridor before turning back. He knew if he saw her now, he would want only to take her in his arms and pour out all that had happened in these last two weeks with his grandfather and within his own head. But he did not know if doing so would precipitate another descent into guilt. And so he retreated.

The next morning, Daniel woke abruptly to the sound of his alarm and resisted the urge to roll over and go back to sleep. He rubbed his face and launched himself from the bed. He'd managed to shower the night before, sloughing off the grit and clay of the excavation, so he needed only to dress to be ready to meet Raffaello for their drive to the site.

When he reached the courtyard, he was surprised to find it empty. The Land Rover was still parked in front of Raffaello's house, and no lights illuminated the windows in the pre-dawn darkness.

Quickening his pace, he crossed the yard and entered the house through the kitchen with the hope he'd find his grandfather filling his coffee thermos. But the stove was unlit and there was no sign Raffaello had been there.

Daniel climbed the steps two at a time, calling out for his grandfather. When he got no reply, he thrust open the bedroom door without knocking. Raffaello lay in bed, his back to the door. Daniel quietly entered the room and approached the bed, circling around to where he could see his grandfather's chest. With relief, he watched it rise and fall and listened to the gentle snoring he'd often heard when Raffaello sometimes fell asleep in the living room watching the late news on television.

Daniel debated waking him but then slipped down to the kitchen and started the coffee. He hoped Raffaello would forgive both Daniel for not waking him and himself for needing the sleep after the grueling hours spent uncovering the face on the sarcophagus the day before.

As Daniel puttered in the kitchen, he was listening for sounds of Raffaello and so was startled when the door to the terrace opened. He nearly dropped the bottle of milk in his hand as he heard his name.

"Danny, where's Nonno?"

"Lin! What are you doing here?" He set the milk on the counter.

"I was heading over to the villa to talk with Annunziata about increasing the food for the site now that more of us will be working there. I saw the Land Rover still parked in the courtyard. So where is he?"

"Still asleep. I decided to let him be because I'm sure he'll stay long into the night again. Did he tell you he wants you all there again today?"

"Before I left the site last night he told me to pull together a handful of the interns I trust to assist with the work above so all the archaeologists could be below in the tomb."

"Who are you planning to bring?"

Linda looked at him sharply. "You want to know if I've asked Izzy. You didn't see her yesterday, did you? Unless you went to her late last night."

"I went to bed. Alone. Why am I even answering you?"

"To answer your unspoken question, yes, I did ask Izzy. I didn't bring her yesterday because she was away helping another farm inoculate their pigs. But Nonno, despite his total absorption in the sarcophagus, noticed and specifically asked for her to help today."

"But you don't want her there."

"There's enough tension right now at the site without the additional complication of whatever is simmering between you two. The last time I saw Izzy she looked exhausted and distracted—dark shadows under her eyes and barely communicating. My big sister radar may be off, but I've had the sense that you two haven't spent much time together recently—that you're both lost in your own worlds. What did you say to her that, frankly, has turned her back into the recluse she was when she arrived here back in April? I know I should somehow be relieved that you're not sleeping with her, but this isn't what I intended when I expressed my dismay about your relationship."

"Our words often have unintended consequences, Lin. Both yours and mine." Daniel turned back to the stove and turned off the coffee.

"You're not going to tell me."

"No."

"Then do us all a favor, especially Nonno, and keep whatever is going on between you and Izzy off the site."

"Fine. I'm going up to bring Nonno his coffee before he charges out of here in a fury."

"I'll see you later."

Daniel took a deep breath before approaching his grandfather. Linda's observations about Izzy had crushed him with the additional weight of his cowardly behavior. Izzy had been so strong for him at Bellosguardo that he hadn't imagined she'd be as devastated as Linda described. That was not the Izzy he knew.

He knocked on Raffaello's door and heard a muffled response, so he stepped into the room.

Raffaello turned and lifted his head from the pillow and then glanced at the window, where the sky was already light.

"What time is it?" He rubbed his face and then pushed up into a sitting position, leaning back against the headboard.

Daniel handed the coffee mug to him as he answered. "It's seven o'clock."

Raffaello grimaced. "Not when I wanted to start the day. Why didn't you wake me?"

Daniel knew the question was coming, and he'd thought about how to answer without upsetting his grandfather.

Because I thought you were dead was not a good choice. But neither was *I thought you needed the rest after the exertion and excitement of last night.* Instead, he placed the lateness of the hour on his own shoulders.

"I overslept and thought to appease you by making the coffee first."

Raffaello raised the mug in his direction. "You did a good job." Then he added, "Not only with the coffee, Daniele. You did a good job yesterday as well. I cannot express to you how pleased I was to have you at my side at the moment when the stone came alive under my brush."

"It was a special moment for me as well, Nonno. These last two weeks with you have filled me with awe—not just for the discovery but for this glimpse into your life. Thank you."

Raffaello took another gulp of coffee, handed the mug to Daniel, and swung his legs over the side of the bed with vigor. Apparently the coffee had done its job. The ashen, exhausted face Daniel had seen only an hour before was now bright, the body formerly collapsed under the covers now springing into action.

"I'll meet you downstairs in fifteen. Meanwhile, find out from Linda if anyone else she's recruited from the staff needs to ride with us."

Daniel retreated to the kitchen and called Linda at her office in the villa. As he expected, she had two interns ready to ride with them, neither of them Izzy.

Daniel filled a thermos with more coffee, grabbed the keys, and waited in the Land Rover for everyone to assemble, drumming his fingers on the dashboard to the tune on the scratchy radio.

He put his head down to fiddle with the tuning, and when he looked up again, he was startled to see Izzy emerging from the laundry house across the courtyard, one arm toting a canvas bag and the other leaning on her cane. She slipped inside the villa without noticing him. He wanted to go after her. He wanted to ease the pain that had tightened around his heart as soon as he saw her.

He was almost out of the car when Raffaello slipped into the passenger seat. Close behind him were two of the interns Linda had corralled.

"Let's get going," Raffaello ordered.

Daniel turned on the ignition and put the car in gear.

IZZY

CHAPTER
TWENTY-FOUR

JULY 22 – 23

M arcantonio approached Izzy at breakfast, his hands lifted in apology.

"Isabella, I need a favor."

"Anything, Marcantonio—within reason." She smiled.

"I was supposed to help the Camerata farm today to inoculate their pigs. They're shorthanded. But my mother-in-law needs to go to Firenze for the doctor and the baby is sick, so my wife can't take her…"

"No worries. I can do it. How do I get there?"

"Grazie, Isabella! Angelo Camerata will pick you up in an hour. It may take most of the day."

"What about our own pigs?"

"I've already fed them. I'll check on them when I return from Firenze. *Grazie mille*."

Izzy welcomed the distraction of being away from Portarello. In the two weeks since she'd confronted Daniel, she found herself more agitated than relieved. His ability to keep his distance from her—even though she knew he was spending most of the time at the dig, even though it had been she who had initiated the break in their lovemaking—felt like a slap in the face. A repudiation of everything that had gone on between them. She felt too exposed to go near any of the Richetellis, who surely were aware that Daniel was avoiding her, as aware as they had been earlier that she and Daniel had become lovers.

The rear courtyard was empty when she arrived to wait for her ride. The BU van, Raffaello's Land Rover, and Linda's car were all gone. Izzy kept herself busy deadheading flowers along the fence near the pool, a spontaneous task that kept her mind from circling yet again through her unease.

A horn disrupted her, and the driver of a dusty pickup truck leaned across the seat to the open window. In Italian, he asked her where he could find Isabella.

"*Sono Isabella*." She smiled, grabbed the knapsack she'd left on the verge, and climbed into the truck.

Angelo Camerata was a talkative chauffeur, filling her in on his pigs, his farm, his friendship with Marcantonio, and his admiration for Raffaello and, especially, Linda.

"What she is accomplishing here helps all of us," he explained. "She's bringing back the Cinta Senese, the ancient breed of pigs, combining the best of the old ways with her new ideas. My father was skeptical when she started—suspicious, you know, of the Americana who thought she knew more than the farmers who've been working this land for generations. But then he saw the prices she was getting for her prosciutto and salame." Angelo rubbed his fingers together. "This is the language my father understands."

Izzy smiled at the voluble young man behind the wheel and decided she liked him. She was going to enjoy working with him.

They arrived at his farm about thirty minutes later, and Angelo introduced her to the others: a couple in their sixties who were his parents, a brother, a sister-in-law, and a couple of teenage cousins. Except for Angelo's parents, the others appeared to have been called in to help just as she had been. The experience of the two boys with their uncle's pigs was probably limited to eating pork.

Angelo's father nodded to her in greeting but said nothing. Based on Angelo's description of him in the car, Izzy assumed he was reserving judgment on how helpful she'd turn out to be. Her arrival seemed to be the signal that they would begin. No one else was coming. Angelo led the way to the pens, and Izzy got her first impression of how challenging the day would be. The drift was twice the size of Portarello's, and a good portion were very young pigs. She dug a bandana out of her knapsack and tied it over her hair. She'd wound her braid around her head earlier, rather than have it hang down her back. She was going to be in close contact with heaving, squirming, and, most likely, unhappy animals and didn't want to take any chances of one of them yanking on her hair. She pulled on a pair of gloves and was ready to go.

She was interested to see that the old man deferred to Angelo, who had set up the inoculation station and was assigning people to specific roles. It was clear that Marcantonio had briefed Angelo on Izzy's experience because he put her in charge of the injections. Although she'd never done anything like this before, she drew on her experience with the birthing sow. Calm the fears, use soothing touch, talk to the pigs. She found herself developing a rhythm as more pigs fell under her spell, and she became absorbed in her task. Once, she looked up as she released a particularly agitated pig that had settled under her touch, and she discovered the old man watching her. She nodded to him and he nodded back. No "*bene*," but it was enough. They each turned back to their work.

The day was interrupted by lunch, served at a table under a tree near the house. Simple, fresh food. Izzy voiced her gratitude to Angelo's mother, who responded by heaping more on her plate.

At the end of the day, Izzy helped clean syringes and collect used needles for disposal. Her fingers were cramped and her back ached. It had taken more out of her physically than she had realized in the midst of the work. But it had also protected her emotionally. Concentrating on keeping the pigs calm and still had actually imbued her with stillness. Thoughts of Daniel had been blessedly absent all day.

Angelo invited her to stay for dinner, but she declined. As much as the appeal of a few more hours away from the realities awaiting her at Portarello beckoned, she could sense her impatience building. *Enough, Izzy.*

But Angelo prevailed upon her to at least have a glass of wine. Instead of drinking it on the veranda, where the bustle of the family preparing dinner was a distraction, Angelo took their glasses and a bottle beyond the house to a stone wall overlooking a valley filled with the vivid yellow of rapeseed.

"Marcantonio told me you had experience with pigs, but I didn't expect what I saw you do today. You truly have a gift."

Izzy shrugged. "It's not something I consciously learned how to do, but I must have absorbed some lessons from my grandmother as I was growing up."

"Ah, I understand now. In Italy, too, the nonnas pass on their knowledge to the granddaughters. The mysteries of the evil eye, the incantations, and the amulets." He pulled a chain out from under his shirt and showed her the gold horn that hung from it. "The priest baptized me as an infant, but it was my nonna who spoke the words of the protective spell over this and pinned it to my shirt."

"Do you believe in the spells?"

It was Angelo's turn to shrug. "It's the twentieth century, not the fourteenth. I vaccinate my pigs. But when I see someone like you, I understand that there are forces we do not see, powers that cannot be explained. Thank you for helping us today."

Angelo was then silent, something that surprised Izzy after the animated conversation with which they'd started the day. She sipped her wine and felt the sun on her face, enjoying the quiet and peace after the raucous complaints of the pigs earlier.

When she'd emptied her glass, she put her hand over it as Angelo held up the bottle.

"*Grazie*, no. I should get back to Portarello."

"Of course." He rose and walked with her back to the house, where she bid farewell to his family. His mother kissed her on both cheeks and invited her back—to eat, not to work.

On the ride back to Portarello Izzy tried not to fall asleep. She felt her head drop a couple of times and jolted upright, apologizing. Angelo smiled. "You are human, not some spirit from another world."

Izzy chose not to tell him she'd been to that other world.

When they arrived at Portarello, Izzy shook his hand and climbed out of the truck. She waited and waved as he drove away. She was struck by the emptiness of the courtyard. Although it was dusk, when everyone should have returned from the dig, none of the vehicles was there.

She made her way through the villa to the kitchen, hoping she hadn't missed dinner. Glancing out at the patio under the pergola she saw only the artists at one of the tables. No archaeologists, no other interns.

She stuck her head in the kitchen.

"Annunziata, where is everyone?"

"Eh, the professor is working through the night. Linda brought them dinner and more helpers a few hours ago. You hungry? Did you eat at the Cameratas'?"

When Izzy told her no, Annunziata pulled a plate from the cabinet above her head and filled it with spinach risotto and a piece of grilled chicken.

"Take this. You look worn out. Food will revive you."

"*Grazie*, Annunziata."

The thought of joining the artists and having to feign interest in their conversation defeated her. Instead, she grabbed some silverware and took her meal back to her room. On her bed was a folded note with her name on it, and a sharp pain coursed through her heart. Had she missed Daniel again?

She put the plate on the dresser and picked up the note. She recognized the handwriting immediately as Maria's. *Linda rounded up everyone this afternoon to pull all hands on deck for the dig. Nonno is on the cusp of his discovery and won't leave tonight until it's revealed. Hope to see you tomorrow morning. Love, M.*

With a sigh, Izzy put the note down. She wasn't hungry but attempted to eat. As Annunziata had noticed, she was drained from the rigorous work at the Camerata farm.

After finishing about half of the risotto, she began to feel better and continued with the rest of the meal. She rinsed her plate in the bathroom sink but decided against returning it to the kitchen. By then, that end of the villa would be deserted, and she didn't relish navigating the darkened corridors. Instead, she took a long, hot shower, grateful for the abundant water pressure with no one else competing for Portarello's ancient plumbing. Sleep came more easily than she expected, thanks to her long day wrestling with piglets.

It was still dark when a knock on her door awakened her. It was Maria.

"Hey, sleepy head. Time to rise and shine. I'm here as a lieutenant of my cousin the commander. Nonno needs as many hands as possible on the site today, and Linda asked me to recruit you to the cause. I think my grandfather specifically asked for you last night when you weren't among the evening crew that arrived to spell the real archaeologists. Where were you all day? Nobody knew. Marcantonio was off to Florence with his mother-in-law, and the pigs were no help at all when asked about you."

"Marcantonio had asked me to help another farmer vaccinate his pigs. It took all day. When I got back, Portarello was a ghost town. Annunziata told me everyone had been called to the site. What happened?"

"Nonno achieved his triumph. At least the first evidence of it. It's an intact sarcophagus, from what's been revealed so far. Nonno himself did the painstaking work of exposing the face. He finally put his brush down around one a.m., and Daniel was able to pry him out of the tomb and get him home to bed."

"This is what he hoped for."

"And thank God. I don't think he would be able to bear another failure."

"What now? Why so many of us?"

"The rest of the sarcophagus has to be uncovered, images have to be drawn, and everything has to be photographed and documented. I think the urgency is twofold. Nonno's health and the risk of the news spreading down the mountain. The site needs to be protected now from both the merely curious and the looters—literally grave robbers. So hustle, my friend. You and I are driving down with Linda in about thirty minutes."

Izzy stretched and then swung her legs over the side of the bed, where she saw the pile of clothes she'd worn with the pigs, dropped on the floor when she'd undressed and climbed, exhausted, into bed.

"Ugh! I left my clean clothes at the washhouse. I totally forgot them yesterday. I've got to go down to get them because I've got nothing else clean. I don't think anyone wants to be near me if I'm wearing these." She toed the grimy overalls.

She pulled on a dress from her armoire, rebraided her hair, and left for the washhouse while Maria promised to grab them some breakfast from the kitchen.

When she crossed the courtyard she saw that all the cars missing the evening before were now in their usual spots. The late night must have pushed today's departure for the site forward another hour. Despite that, she did as Maria had urged her and hustled.

On the lines outside the washhouse she quickly unpinned her hanging clothes and stuffed them haphazardly into her canvas laundry bag. She retraced her steps across the courtyard, careful to balance the bag in one hand and her cane in the other. To fall now would be stupid, she warned herself, and so she didn't turn when she heard the engine of one of the previously empty cars come to life. By the time Izzy had deposited her laundry in her room and changed into clean clothes, Maria was back with a thermos and a cloth-wrapped bundle of brioche and hard-boiled eggs. They descended once again and met Linda in the courtyard.

On the way down the mountain to the site, Izzy listened to Linda's recounting of the night before and instructions for the two of them for the day ahead. They turned off the mountain road to a pasture gate guarded by two men Izzy didn't recognize. They waved the car through when they saw Linda.

"Who are they?"

"Friends of Marcantonio's from the village. We can't spare the archaeologists for guard duty."

As they drove deeper into the woods, Linda was concentrating on the uneven terrain and had stopped the running commentary that had marked the earlier part of the trip. But just before the clearing, she stopped the car and turned to Izzy in the back seat.

"I'm going to say something now that you may take offense with, but know that I gave essentially the same message to my brother. Whatever has been going on between you and Daniel since you returned from

Bellosguardo, I am asking you to keep it off the site. This is my grandfather's hallowed ground and he does not need to be distracted or disturbed by your drama."

Once again, Izzy felt like she'd been slapped in the face—this time by Linda's rebuke rather than Daniel's silence.

"Lin!" It was Maria who voiced indignation for both of them.

But Izzy didn't need Maria to speak for her.

"I'm here to work, Linda. I have no intention of disrupting what I know is Raffaello's life mission." Izzy called on every internal resource to remain calm and surprised herself with the ice in her voice. Linda seemed taken aback by Izzy's response. *What did she expect, that I would crumple into tears and curl up on the back seat like a wounded animal?*

"Fine," Linda grunted and parked the car on the outskirts of the site.

Maria rolled her eyes as Linda stalked away to Raffaello's tent.

"I haven't had time to reflect on the fact that, of course, Daniel is here. Since our confrontation two weeks ago, I haven't seen or spoken to him," Izzy admitted.

"I haven't talked to Daniel myself." Maria shrugged. "He never left Nonno's side down in the tomb except to eat something when the second shift arrived last night. He and Nonno ate in Nonno's tent, and I was busy in the mess tent dishing out risotto and then cleaning up.

"What's going on, Izzy? I'm sorry I didn't see you yesterday. I would have gone with you to help with the pigs if I'd known."

"Thanks. It was actually a relief to be away from all this." Izzy waved her hand at the commotion around the site—tarps being lifted, ladders and screens hauled from a shed, trestle tables set up adjacent to the screens. In all the activity, there was no sign of Daniel.

Maria took her by the hand. "Come on, Linda gave me a list of what she needs done. You and I are a team. We can talk while we work, if you need a sounding board."

Izzy followed Maria, who had a thick binder tucked under her arm, to the line of tables.

"There's a crate of shards that were brought up yesterday evening that haven't been tagged and listed yet. We'll get started on those before more start arriving."

"I thought the sarcophagus was intact?"

"Oh, it is. These are from the anteroom that was excavated first."

Maria ducked into Raffaello's tent and emerged with a wooden crate, a camera slung around her neck, and two pairs of cotton gloves stuffed into her jeans' pocket.

"Put these on. Do you want to shoot pictures or write up the descriptions? We can switch up later."

Izzy chose to start out taking the photos, and they developed a rhythm, cataloging the fragments and placing them in bags with tags that matched the list they were creating. It was meticulous work, but a task that Izzy found kept her focused. The churning anxiety she'd experienced earlier in the morning about encountering Daniel receded as she worked in tandem with Maria recording the artifacts that had emerged from the dig.

"Do you want to talk?" Maria asked, once they'd established a flow to the cataloging.

Izzy shrugged. "Nothing to report other than my solitude for the last two weeks. It's been harder than I anticipated, not being with him, even though I know I made the right decision."

"Well, if last night was a preview of how today will progress, you may not encounter Daniel at all. If he and Raffaello do emerge at lunch, I'll be your buffer. Better yet, we can take our lunch back to Linda's station wagon and tailgate instead of eating with the hordes."

"I like that plan."

When the van with the food arrived, Maria and Izzy helped Annunziata set up the mess tent and then slipped away with their meals before the bell rang calling the others to eat.

As she mopped up the remnants of pasta sauce from her plate, Izzy sighed. "I could curl up on the back seat right now and sleep. Between my anxiety and the pigs, I am seriously depleted of energy. No wonder I don't want to talk to Daniel. I don't have the physical or emotional stamina."

"I think everyone is running on empty, especially my grandfather. If you really are exhausted, I could get the keys from Linda and run you back to the villa."

"As appealing as that is, I'd feel that I was letting everyone down, especially Raffaello. Let's get back to work before I succumb."

When they walked back, Izzy was happy to see that the meal was well over and everyone appeared to be settled into their tasks. She and Maria switched roles from the morning, and Izzy took over the paperwork. They had only cataloged one item when she saw that she'd filled the last line of the blank grids they were using to record.

"Are there any more of these sheets?"

"Sure. In Raffaello's tent. There's a box on the shelf above the work table. Do you want me to get them?"

"No, I've got this. I'll be right back."

Izzy skirted the perimeter of the site and entered Raffaello's tent. After the brilliant Tuscan sunshine, it took her eyes a short time to adjust to the dim environment of the tent. She didn't see that someone else was there until she heard her name and jumped.

"Daniel!" He was standing at the workbench, his clothing rumpled and mud-stained and a fine layer of clay dust coating his dark hair. His skin, under the dirt, was pallid, as if he'd been in the tomb far longer than the two weeks since their return to Portarello.

The sadness that had engulfed Izzy in Daniel's absence flooded her, and she struggled to hold her emotions in check. Neither of them moved.

"I've missed you. ..." They both spoke at the same time.

"You first," Daniel offered.

"I didn't intend for us not to have any contact at all. I thought I wouldn't be a threat to your sense of who you were if we were no longer lovers."

"And I haven't meant to avoid you. I could claim it's because of the dig, but the truth is I don't want to risk hurting you again with my guilt. We should talk. But not here and not now."

"I assume Linda laid down the rules to you too."

Daniel nodded. "I need to get back to the tomb. Linda is adamant that from now on we quit before dinner and drag Raffaello home. No more all-nighters. Will you have dinner with us?"

"No." Izzy shook her head. "I can't—I won't—do that again. Can you meet me later? In the chapel? Ten o'clock?"

"I'll be there." He gathered up a handful of brushes from a jar on the table and started to move toward the entrance of the tent.

Izzy stepped back to let him pass, stifling the overwhelming longing to reach out to him. Her physical reaction to him startled her. She was intensely aware of the mingled aromas of earth and sweat emanating from him, as well as the barely contained tension simmering just below the surface. A vein in Daniel's neck pulsed visibly, and she wanted to stroke it. She knew that vein. She'd first witnessed it during their lovemaking but had also seen it emerge when he'd fought with Linda at Bellosguardo. That it manifested itself now, knowing that she was the cause, only reinforced her assessment of what was happening between them. She was the source of both longing and anger for Daniel, and in this moment, she wasn't sure which of those emotions was ascendant as he moved past her and returned to the tomb.

She took a deep breath after he left and had to reorient herself. Why was she here in Raffaello's tent? She hadn't come to seek out Daniel. And then her eyes scanned the workbench and the shelves and her lapsed memory clicked into place. The box of catalog forms.

She grabbed the box and returned to Maria, who was waiting with impatience.

"What took you so long?"

Izzy deposited the box on the table with more force than she intended, and several sheets flew out.

"Daniel."

Maria glanced at the scattered forms. "That bad?"

"Not really. I mean, we agreed we needed to talk, but not here. He promised to meet me in the chapel tonight."

"So why the *agita*?"

"Because my resolve, my intentions, go flying out the window—or in this case, the tent—when I'm actually with him. I swear, if he had asked me, I would have been in his arms immediately and made love to him in that tent in the midst of everything going on around us."

"But he didn't."

Izzy looked up sharply at Maria's bluntness.

"No," she whispered. "He didn't."

Over the next three weeks, as the lid of the sarcophagus slowly emerged under Raffaello's careful brush, Daniel and Izzy were also careful with each other, meeting in the chapel in the evening to talk but not to touch. It wasn't every night. They tried to balance the need to be with one another with their physical exhaustion from the work on the dig and the ever-present tension that could easily slip from emotional intimacy into sexual intimacy.

They talked about Daniel's reaction to the tomb, his growing understanding of the power of the Etruscan view of the afterlife, his deep appreciation for his grandfather's passion, and his acceptance of the spiritual work he still needed to do.

"I'm grateful to you, Izzy, for forcing me to step back from the bliss and the guilt and making me do the work of figuring out my life."

Izzy was also using her quiet nights. Her insomnia had returned, but instead of wandering in the moonlit garden when she couldn't sleep, she was writing or sketching in her notebook, recording their conversations or capturing images.

DANIEL

CHAPTER
TWENTY-FIVE

AUGUST 10

Daniel was at his grandfather's side as Raffaello brushed away the final layer of soil from the last element on the lid of the sarcophagus and stood up. They were alone in the tomb in the early morning, before the clamor of arriving vehicles, generators, and voices shouting across the field disturbed the stillness.

"It's done." Raffaello bowed his head and placed his hand gently on the carved arms of the embracing lovers whose bones lay beneath the stone cover. It was a gesture of both tenderness and gratitude.

Then he moved toward the outer room and began the ascent to the surface, ready to issue assignments and organize the remaining tasks to bring the dig to its completion. Daniel remained with him, attuned to both his grandfather's fragile health and mercurial moods.

Raffaello remained above after the team arrived and dispersed to their tasks, and he beckoned Daniel into the tent. He dug around in his knapsack and pulled out a flask.

"It may only be an hour past sunrise, but I think today we've earned the privilege of celebrating." He took a swig and passed the flask to Daniel.

"It's the Glenlivet," Daniel grinned. "To the Etruscans!"

The rest of the day was taken up with the mundane tasks of the dig. The sides of the sarcophagus still needed to be excavated, a rigorous job for the men younger than Raffaello, but the reveal of the entire lid was the confirmation and validation Raffaello had sought throughout his career.

They returned to the villa in the late afternoon to find tables set up on the lawn, firewood piled in a pyramid, and the kitchen staff bustling under the direction of Annunziata, who beamed when she saw Raffaello.

"Professore! What a propitious day for the final uncovering of the sarcophagus! *La Notte di San Lorenzo!* We had already planned a feast to commemorate the saint, and now we can celebrate your discovery as well. Will you do the honors to light the bonfire tonight?"

Later that evening, Daniel watched his grandfather transform from a tired, bone-weary old man to the master of ceremonies, leading the acknowledgment of the work of the archaeologists gathered around the tables, bowing to the toasts offered in his direction, thanking the staff who had stepped up to help at the site. When darkness descended, he rose from the table and took a torch handed to him by Marcantonio as the others gathered around the piled wood stacked midway between the villa and the stone wall overlooking the garden. He moved clockwise slowly around the circle, igniting the tinder at the base of the pile. Sparks flew upward in the night breeze, scattering above the trees and the crenellated tower of the villa, towards the August sky and the shooting stars that were the highlight of the *La Notte di San Lorenzo*.

Bottles of Portarello wine and Zia Norma's limoncello were set on the stone wall, and the drinking that had begun with the toasts at dinner continued into the night. Someone brought out an accordion and a violin. The tension and exhaustion of the summer floated up with the sparks as everyone basked in the collective glow of Raffaello's crowning achievement.

Daniel found Izzy on the periphery of the circle, her body swaying to the music drifting across the lawn and her face lit by the fire.

"This is how I imagine the Etruscans might have celebrated a communal feast, especially one tied to the stars, as this night is."

"I agree. With wine, and music, and dancing."

He watched as Izzy closed her eyes, slipped off her sandals, and began to dance around the circle. The dancing seemed to release her from the tension they both carried as the end of summer was fast approaching and whatever time they had left—for decisions and direction—was encroaching upon them.

The fire was burning down to coals, and people were beginning to drift away, some in pairs. Izzy returned to where Daniel had waited and retrieved her sandals.

"Do you have time for a visit to the chapel, or are you heading to bed?" She looked up at him, more relaxed than he'd seen her in weeks.

He shook his head. "I'm on guard duty at midnight."

"You're going to the tomb tonight?"

Daniel heard a plaintive note in her voice—a need, not simply curiosity. In a moment of recklessness, he reached out, not with his touch but with an offer that acknowledged that unspoken need.

"Would you like to come with me?" He held his breath as he waited for her answer. Given the caution they'd taken with each other, he wasn't sure she'd accept. But he saw the struggle work its way across her face. The time they had spent together in the chapel had provided them an element of safety; to accompany him to the isolation of the dig in the middle of the night was a risk. But he understood that something called to her from the tomb. Raffaello would surely allow her to go down in the coming days, but he could understand the pull to go now, in the middle of the night, with none of the frenzy of the others to distract her.

He waited, unwilling to influence her, but praying—yes, praying—that she would trust him.

"Yes. Thank you."

"No, thank *you* for allowing me to do this for you. You should change into warmer clothes and sturdier shoes."

She nodded.

"Meet me in the courtyard. We'll take the Land Rover."

"I'll be there in ten minutes."

They parted on the lawn, and once again Daniel prayed that she wouldn't change her mind.

IZZY

CHAPTER TWENTY-SIX

AUGUST 10 – 11

When Izzy reached the courtyard, Daniel had the Land Rover ready and they took off in the darkness, the high beams sweeping across the road as he steered into the turns. When they reached the pasture gate, the guards waved them through and he drove on. When he parked the car, he handed Izzy a hard hat with a headlight he'd retrieved from the trunk.

He strode toward the fence surrounding the dig and Izzy followed. An owl, its wings a startling five-foot span, flew above them. The adrenaline propelling her overrode the limitations of her leg. She wasn't conscious of her limbs at all, only the sense of her body moving across the field at a breathless pace.

When they reached the gate, Daniel spoke to the two archaeologists they were relieving. Although they cast a glance at Izzy, they had seen her at the site during the day and didn't seem to question her presence.

Izzy was aware of an urgency that had begun to build inside her that she didn't quite understand. But since dancing around the fire, she felt called to this place, called to look upon the faces carved in stone. To look at the faces of death and see if she recognized them.

As the archaeologists left the field, Daniel took her by the hand and led her around the edge of the grid to the tarp.

"Are you OK going down a ladder?"

"I'll be fine."

Daniel went first and waited for her at the bottom. About halfway down her leg cramped. She leaned her forehead against the rung of the ladder and breathed through it.

"Are you dizzy?" he shouted up at her. "The air down here is not the best."

It was her turn to signal with her hand.

"I'm OK. Just a cramp. I'm on my way down."

He was right about the air. A dank, suffocating smell rose up into her nostrils as she descended.

"This way," he directed her when she reached the bottom, and he led her a short distance. Underfoot was raw earth, damp and uneven. But the walls of the excavation were stone. They were inside the tomb.

Daniel took a large lantern from the floor and held it overhead as he led her into the next chamber.

"There," he pointed to a partially visible tablet about six feet long and a few feet wide. Around it the archeologists had dug a trench, the beginning of the intense process of revealing the entire sarcophagus. Only the cover was visible.

Izzy knelt close to the edge of the trench, wincing as she lowered herself. It took all her will power not to reach out and stroke the faces carved in the stone. A couple, their arms entwined, lay facing each other with gazes of utter and complete tenderness.

What she saw mirrored what she had felt that day when she had drifted between life and death. It was an enigma to her that the memory of those moments had left such an indelible mark on her, when everything else—the accident itself and any new encounters since that rain-slicked day—had had no staying power.

She studied the faces, in awe of what the ancient Etruscan stone carver had wrought. How could the artist have captured such bliss if it was not rooted in some passionate longing for what she saw in those lovers' faces?

She cast one more glance at the lovers, her longing heightened by her limitations. As soon as she climbed out of the pit, the memory of their faces would be lost to her. With a ferocity she didn't recognize in herself, she grappled in her back pocket for her notebook and pen. With a few spare strokes she drew the outstretched lovers. Her sketches on her early-morning walks had trained her eye and her hand to capture what her brain could not remember.

When they emerged from the tomb, Izzy moved away from Daniel and sat by herself in the shadows beyond the range of the lights. She needed the fresh night air after the dank atmosphere below. She needed time alone to absorb what had happened to her when she'd encountered those transcendent faces offering her a glimpse of what she had lost.

Daniel seemed to understand her need for solitude—not only because of the profound experience she knew he had witnessed, but also for the boundaries they'd observed over the last several weeks. She ached as she drew in breath.

She was exhausted. As if she'd traveled a great distance at a rapid pace. How long had they been below? Was Daniel aware as he'd watched her that she'd been somewhere else? Physically kneeling at his side, but mentally—no, spiritually—in a place apart?

She fought with the desire to unburden herself with him. She trusted no one else with these frightening yet exhilarating visions. There, she'd said it. Visions.

When her breathing had become more even, she glanced up at the entrance of the tomb. Daniel had replaced the tarpaulin and the plywood and sat on an overturned bucket, alert for anyone approaching. The transcendence of her experience in the tomb began to slip away as the sounds of the night surrounded her. Her notebook was still in her hand, and she flipped it open, turning the pages with relief as she saw that she had captured the images of the lovers on the sarcophagus. She stroked the paper, her fingers reimagining how she had desperately longed to touch the carved stone, absorb it through her skin. She had a fleeting memory of Raffaello encouraging her to pick up a piece of pottery in the gallery.

"Izzy?" She heard her name, pulling her back to the present, and jerked her head toward the sound.

"Are you OK?"

Daniel had risen from his perch by the excavation and was kneeling before her. Despite the shadows, she could see concern and compassion etched in the tired lines of his face. He didn't touch her but simply waited. Whatever restraint or resistance she'd attempted to gather within herself could not withstand her need for his understanding in this moment. Tears she'd withheld in the tomb finally spilled over, and her body was wracked with sobs. She felt physical pain as grief once again descended upon her. She wanted what she had seen, and knowing it was beyond her grasp caused her to convulse in tears.

She wasn't sure who made the first move—she reaching out to him or Daniel leaning in and taking her in his arms. He rocked her as she cried, the strength of his arms barricading them against the darkness and the edges of madness that she feared her visions had awakened.

When she could catch her breath, she sensed a shift in his posture as he turned his head to murmur in her ear. "Do you want to talk about what happened down there?"

She leaned away from him to wipe her eyes, and her notebook fell into his lap, open to her last sketch. He picked it up.

"These are the sketches you made below. May I look at them?"

Izzy nodded. The images conveyed what she'd experienced better than the words she couldn't find right now.

Daniel pulled his lantern closer and bent his head over the pages, keeping one arm around Izzy.

"These are extraordinary! You've captured not just the likeness of the stone faces, but also the emotion that emanates from them."

"Bliss," Izzy was able to whisper.

"Like your vision in the chapel," Daniel acknowledged with understanding.

"It happened at Cerveteri, too, but not as powerfully as tonight. Tonight was ... frightening and exhilarating."

Izzy felt Daniel stiffen. He put down the notebook and turned her face toward his.

"Death called to you from the other side." He wasn't asking. He understood. He wasn't telling her she was crazy to feel that way. He wasn't terrified, as her family had been, by her longing for those precious moments when she'd slipped through the "thin place" her Irish aunt Mo had recognized when she'd prayed at Izzy's bedside.

"It's very seductive, isn't it? To let go of the pain here."

"Last fall, when I was released from the hospital and went home to Chappy, my grief was unbearable. But I don't feel that despair now. These glimpses I've had this summer are a gift, not a tease of something that has been snatched away from me. I don't fear death. But I don't long for it anymore."

"Do you think those carved faces were a way the Etruscans expressed their own belief that death was a pathway to joy?"

"How could they not be? What a blessing to offer those left behind. To offer me."

Daniel kissed her forehead. "You are a blessing."

"Thank you. And thank you for helping me to talk out what happened in the tomb. You are the only one I trust to understand."

"Years of experience sitting in the confessional booth listening," Daniel shrugged and looked away.

"Don't minimize your own gifts, Daniel. No priest I ever talked to was willing to accept my fears and my grief with such compassion."

It was Izzy who now turned Daniel's face toward her, forcing him to look at her. She said nothing, but held his eyes with hers, pouring her belief in his goodness into her glance.

She knew it was a reckless thing to do. Had they not been charged with guarding the tomb, they would surely have found their way to the cot in Raffaello's tent and once again begun the cycle of lovemaking and abandonment that tormented them.

But they didn't.

Daniel got up abruptly, and the thread that had held them snapped.

"I'm going to check the perimeter." He picked up the lantern and moved toward the fence that enclosed the site.

Izzy watched him go and pulled her jacket tight against the pre-dawn chill. How was she going to do this? How much resistance would she need to keep away from him, when encounters like tonight pulled them ever closer? This time, he'd had the will to break away, and as he left she acknowledged that she felt both relieved and bereft.

She was also exhausted.

Somewhere around the site they had put down a thermos of coffee, and Izzy rose to find it, stretching her limbs and massaging her stiffened calf. She limped over to the entrance to the tomb, the tarp now secure and a barrier to what she'd experienced earlier. She felt reflexively for her notebook and patted it, and the toe of her boot bumped up against the thermos. She bent to pick it up and nearly fell over, she was so light-headed. She steadied herself and unscrewed the cap of the thermos with fumbling fingers. Gulping the lukewarm coffee, she looked out over the site. When she'd been here during the day working with Maria, it had been swarming with people—the archaeologists, the crew from the farm, all hands on deck. Now, observing the empty field, she was struck by its order and precision, like a huge chess board, with scattered trenches marking earlier attempts to unearth the secrets buried beneath the soil.

"It's remarkable, isn't it?" Daniel had returned. "I feel like I'm looking at a blueprint, all straight lines. Except that instead of building up, we're delving down. I never appreciated or understood my grandfather's obsession until working with him this summer. Everything about this project speaks volumes about who my grandfather is."

Izzy passed him the thermos.

"Has it helped your relationship with your grandfather, being with him this summer?"

"We've reached a détente, I think. I have no new wounds, although I've discovered muscles I never knew I had after spending hours crouched in the trench with a trowel and a brush." He smiled. "Nonno encouraged me, when I first arrived, to forget the life of the mind and immerse myself in the life of the senses." He paused and looked away. "I don't think he imagined quite all the ways I'd wind up following his advice."

Despite her efforts to restrain herself, Izzy couldn't stop a glimmer of a smile from escaping her lips. At that moment, Daniel nudged her.

"Look up!"

A shooting star flew across the sky.

After it passed, they continued to share the coffee, sitting vigil by the tomb, until the sounds of the returning crew alerted them that their watch was over.

Izzy got a ride back to the villa with Linda when she dropped off Raffaello. Neither she nor Raffaello commented on Izzy's presence on the site with Daniel. Izzy supposed Raffaello was too preoccupied with completing the excavation of the sarcophagus, but it surprised her that Linda didn't launch into another lecture. She seemed resigned.

"All was quiet during the night?"

"Only the owls. Is vandalism a big problem?"

"Now and then. It depends on what motivates the thieves—greed, poverty, national pride. I'm frankly surprised we haven't had trouble with looters, but it may simply be that word hasn't spread beyond the valley. My grandfather is both respected and beloved. The people around here share his pride and wonder about what lies beneath their land."

"What happens next, after the tomb is completely excavated?"

"The sarcophagus will go to the museum. The tomb itself may be closed."

"The site won't become open to the public, like Cerveteri?"

"It's too remote, and there aren't public funds to support it. I also can't imagine Nonno relishing his farm becoming a tourist destination."

"Have you been down into the tomb?"

"Not yet. Nonno has been limiting the people allowed below. It's a tight space. But I picked up the latest photos developed from the film he shot a few days ago. It's a remarkable find. A dream fulfilled for my grandfather. Here we are. After your chores with the pigs, can you come back to the site? You can catch a lift with the van bringing lunch at midday."

"Of course. It's an honor to be part of Raffaello's work."

Izzy left Linda in the courtyard and decided to go straight to the pigs while the coffee was still keeping her alert. She was afraid to go back to her room and the temptation of her bed.

Somehow, she made it through the day, returning to the site with Annunziata and the food for the crew. Izzy and Maria continued their cataloging. Maria had seen her at the bonfire with Daniel and quizzed her on what was happening between them, but Izzy deflected her questions.

"I can't talk about it now, especially here. And if I don't focus, I'll mess up the cataloging. I was up all night."

Maria paused, her hands stilled on the pottery shard they were tagging. She started to say something, but Izzy shook her head.

"Don't push, Maria. I'm not ready."

"You know I care about you."

"Of course I know. I'm just too raw right now, and I don't want to dissolve into a puddle of misery with all these people around."

"I'd give you a hug, but I suspect even that is too much."

"Thanks, Mar. Let's just do our work. It will help keep the sadness at bay."

They spent the rest of the afternoon finishing the fragments. Everything was bagged, labelled, and packed in straw in wooden boxes, ready for transport to the granary and eventually the museum.

Izzy hadn't seen Daniel all day, which was helpful, she had to admit. No wild swings of emotion, no opportunities for regret or hope.

When she returned to the villa, she stood under the shower until the water turned cold. She skipped the wine hour on the terrace and slipped into a place at the end of a table at dinner, smiling at the guests already engaged in conversation. They were busy enjoying their antipasto, and Izzy was grateful they had no need of her attention.

It was only nine o'clock when she returned to her room and fell exhausted into bed. She slept until dawn.

DANIEL

CHAPTER
TWENTY-SEVEN

AUGUST 11 – 12

Daniel knew he could not beg off joining the family for dinner when he returned to the house with Raffaello, but he managed to slip away to his room for a shower before they all gathered. He knew he needed to think, to absorb all that had happened with Izzy the night before. But he pushed his unease aside. Later, after the meal, which could range from banter and excitement for his grandfather or something more charged. He didn't know what to expect. Linda had been unusually subdued at the site, her concern for Raffaello evident in her watchfulness. She seemed resigned to his resistance to any suggestion that he should rest or leave the final excavation to the younger men. But she seemed always on the alert, ready to whisk Raffaello away if he showed the slightest sign of pain or weakness.

When Daniel returned to Raffaello's, he found Maria and Benno on the terrace setting the table. He could hear Linda on the phone inside the house.

"Where's Nonno?" He took glasses from a tray on the stone ledge and set them around the table.

"Going over some notes in his study. He just learned that someone from the ministry is coming tomorrow."

"Is he concerned?"

Linda answered as she came out of the house, wine bottle in hand.

"I think he's satisfied that the dig has progressed far enough under his control that he can allow the bureaucrats in now."

Daniel raised his eyebrows. "Do you really believe that? Nonno relinquishing control?"

"I don't know, but he's remarkably sanguine tonight."

"I imagine the fact that we were able to uncover the base of the sarcophagus today without any damage has given him a sense of relief. But until it's out of the tomb and in the museum, I can't see him letting go."

Linda sighed. "I know. Wishful thinking."

"Who was on the phone?"

"Robert."

Daniel looked up sharply. It was unusual for their brother to call.

"Everything OK?"

"With him? Yes. He'd heard from Dad about the find and Nonno's health. He wants to come over."

Inwardly, Daniel groaned. One more family member to insert into the already tangled relationships of this complicated summer. One more voice to add to the chorus reacting to his decision.

"Is he coming alone or with Janine and the kids?"

"Just him, and only for a few days. Could you pick him up at the airport?"

"When?"

"Wednesday. I wrote down his flight. It's on the pad by the phone."

Raffaello emerged from the house, rubbing his hands. "I'm starving. When's dinner?"

They settled at the table for a relatively quiet meal for the Richetellis. The drama and exhilaration of the uncovering of the sarcophagus was now a memory, and the conversation reflected the exhaustion each of them felt after the intensity of the last few weeks.

No one suggested lingering on the terrace with Linda's limoncello after they'd cleared the dishes and washed up. Daniel was able to depart before ten and make his way across the courtyard to the villa. He climbed the steps slowly, the hours spent crouched on the floor of the tomb now making their presence known in his aching muscles. His grandfather's stamina amazed him, but he understood that it was Raffaello's passion and obsession that sustained him—not only through this summer, but also throughout the years of failed attempts. If only, Daniel thought, I had such an abiding passion. He found himself at the chapel. It was empty. He considered turning away, retreating to his bed. But if he didn't begin now to examine the complicated and painful decision facing him, Robert's arrival in a few days would push it farther off.

He parted the curtain, lit only one candle, and knelt. It was the anticipation of Robert's presence that triggered his recognition of his need for solitude. Not just tonight, he realized, but going forward. Remaining at Portarello was impossible. The pull of the vortex of his family, especially with the addition of Robert, would only drag him back to old patterns, old expectations. And Izzy. Even if they were not lovers, she was still an emotional force that he could not ignore. A need he was unable to extinguish.

He buried his head in his hands and took a deep breath. He had not been back from the site since midnight. His entire day had been spent once again at Raffaello's side, either handing him tools like an operating room nurse to a surgeon or carefully wielding his own brush or trowel under Raffaello's watchful eye. But Daniel had also been watchful, alert for any signs of distress or discomfort in his grandfather that might presage a heart attack. Despite Daniel's concern, the old man had defied the God he didn't believe in and the gods worshipped and honored in the tomb. Daniel had not had even a moment to himself to reflect on his witness of Izzy's extraordinary experience in the tomb or his own need to find direction. He didn't know which to tackle first. He remembered reading once that some philosopher or psychologist had suggested that flipping a coin when faced with a difficult choice can actually clarify what you truly want. The key is to pay attention to what you wish the outcome to be while the coin is still in the air. He dug in his pocket and was surprised to pull out an Etruscan coin. He remembered finding it and thinking he needed to make a note of it. In the intense activity of the day's excavation, he'd forgotten the coin. He turned it over, rubbing off some caked dirt, and identified a head. Then, feeling slightly ridiculous, he tossed the coin in the air. As it fell into his palm he knew that he needed to sort out what had happened in the tomb first.

Izzy had slipped into a kind of trance, her entire body in a state of repose. The expression on her face had softened, erasing the taut, constrained façade she'd worn over the last several weeks. A smile had lit up her face, and although her eyes were open, he knew she wasn't seeing him. It took his breath away—with awe and agony. He had read about "thin places," folklore passed down from ancients and dismissed by the modern world. Izzy had referred to them afterward, when they were out of the tomb. Spaces where the passage between life and death, between the physical world and the world of the spirit, opens up and allows a glimpse of the other side. Izzy had seen through the veil. He had witnessed it once before on the night they'd first met in the chapel, but last night had been far more profound. The encounter had awakened in him the acknowledgment of the loss, the cavernous void that had robbed him of his faith and his conviction that his life as a priest had meaning.

A stillness had filled the tomb last night, far more than simply the absence of the archaeological team. Izzy had been able to shut out everything—even him—when she saw the faces on the sarcophagus and recognized what passed between them.

With insight born of honesty, Daniel knew that he had to find that silence in order to hear the still voice of God he so desperately longed for. He could not stay here amidst the loving, interfering cacophony of his family. He had to go. The relief of that decision flooded his spirit, released him from the fear he had that he'd remain stuck, repeating endlessly the same mistakes.

Izzy had recognized far sooner the solution to their—no, his—painful ambivalence. Her courage in confronting him, challenging him, astounded him. But he knew she was right. Neither of them could begin to heal if they remained caught in the web of his guilt.

He wanted to find his way back to her, if that was where the unknown path before him would lead. But he couldn't do that if he didn't first step away.

Without warning, he began to engage in the Spiritual Exercises of St. Ignatius, the contemplative practice that had once been a daily part of his life as a Jesuit and that he'd abandoned in his despair. He stumbled occasionally, but like a toddler learning to walk, picked himself up and took another step.

The next morning, Daniel stopped at Linda's house before picking up Raffaello. It was early, but as expected she was up and making coffee.

"Now that the sarcophagus is excavated, I'd like to take a break from Nonno for a few hours. Is there someone else who can take him to the dig this morning and watch over him? I have an appointment I've put off. I'll only be gone a few hours."

"You know the people from the Ministry of Antiquities will be here today. Can't you wait another day?"

"When do they arrive?"

"Around one. We'll have lunch at the villa and then take them to the site."

"I promise I'll be back by then. It's not something I can postpone."

Daniel didn't want to explain the urgency to his sister. He was afraid that if he didn't go that morning to set in motion the decision he'd made in the chapel, he'd slip back into his despair.

Linda seemed ready to launch into her inquisitor role but must have sensed his resolve and held back. Her only question revealed the lingering tension between them.

"Is Izzy going with you?"

"Honestly, Lin. Let it go, will you. She's not coming. What did you think—that we were heading off to elope?"

"I only asked because if she's not going, I can ask her to accompany Nonno this morning."

She turned away from him. "Go do what you need to do."

Daniel left the house and tried to shake off his agitation. Linda's disappointment with him, which always seemed to manifest itself as anger, was one of the painful entanglements that prompted his decision to leave Portarello.

He climbed into his Fiat and navigated down the mountain. He'd made an early-morning call and set up an appointment. In his pocket was the tattered card he'd saved from his year studying in Rome. When he'd phoned and identified himself, he was greeted warmly by the monk on the other end of the line.

"Daniele! What a joy to hear your voice. Are you in Italy?"

"I'm in Siena. I'd like to do a retreat, Sandro, and I'm hoping you have room for me at the abbey."

"Of course. Can you stop by today for a chat about what you need?"

Brother Sandro, a Benedictine monk, had become a friend when they were both studying at the Vatican. He'd shared Daniel's interest in the mystics, and they'd spent many a night poring over *The Cloud of Unknowing* as they poured the wine. Although they'd sent Christmas cards to each other over the years, they'd lost touch. His warmth in welcoming Daniel eased his heart.

He found the abbey without difficulty near the hill town of Asciano, about forty minutes from the farm. He'd accompanied Sandro there one weekend when they'd been students and remembered that time as a peaceful respite in the midst of his intense scholarly pursuits. That memory was why he'd sought Sandro today.

The abbey, surrounded by rolling fields and vineyards, was reminiscent of Portarello and had probably originated around the same time. Within its meter-thick stone walls, the August heat, already stifling in midmorning, dissipated. Daniel waited in the vestibule for Sandro to be summoned, pacing the marble-flagged floor as he rehearsed how much he would tell him of his need to embark on a retreat. He had no idea how many fallen-away priests Sandro had encountered. It was the first time Daniel had used the term "fallen away" to describe himself. He had an image of Milton's Lucifer falling from heaven and felt once again the physical pain of loss. Except that Daniel, unlike Lucifer, had never experienced the bliss of paradise. His rambling thoughts were interrupted by the rustle of cloth and the soft cadence of rope-soled sandals. Sandro appeared before him in the cowled white robe worn by this congregation of Benedictines and stretched out his hand in welcome.

If Sandro noticed Daniel's haggard appearance, he didn't comment on it. Instead, after a warm handshake and brief pleasantries, he invited Daniel to walk with him in the cloister garden to talk more deeply about why he'd come.

"I'm on a leave of absence from my teaching post and have spent the summer working on an archaeological dig on my grandfather's farm. The excavation is almost complete, and I decided last night I was finally ready to explore what had precipitated my withdrawal from religious life."

"You sound as if you've already made the decision to leave."

"It's complicated, which is why I thought to come here. This," and he waved his arms around the cloister, "represents the removal of distractions. I've lost direction and purpose, Sandro. I thought if I could find a place of stillness, apart from the world, I could hear the voice of God again."

"I thought you Jesuits were trained to hear that voice in the *midst* of the world." Sandro smiled. They'd often sparred with each other about the differences between the Benedictine rule of monastic life—its order, communal fraternity, and rootedness in the seclusion of the monastery—and the practice of the Jesuits, focused on self-examination while literally on the road as missionaries of Christ. "How long would you like to stay?"

"I honestly don't know. A month? Six months? I can help with the work. My summer on the farm and at the dig has rescued me from the sedentary life of an academic."

"We could use the help. I wondered about your pallor, unexpected in someone living on a farm. But now I understand. You've been underground."

"I often emerged from the tomb at the end of the day looking like an unfinished statue in Michelangelo's garden."

"Will you want a spiritual advisor?"

"Eventually. But at first, I think I need to immerse myself in silence."

"Understood. If at any time you feel the need to talk, you know you can come to me. I've been out in the world, as you know, and I've encountered my own demons along the way. When would you like to start?"

"Perhaps by the weekend. My brother arrives tomorrow, and I'll need to spend a few days with him before I go into hiding."

Sandro stopped and faced him. "We don't hide here, Daniele. We throw open the windows to the light; we pull out of the shadows all we've hidden there. This isn't a place to wallow in fear and self-pity. It's a place to find joy amidst the anguish of our human lives."

Daniel bowed his head. "That's exactly what I'm seeking."

Izzy

CHAPTER TWENTY-EIGHT

AUGUST 12

Izzy was at breakfast, pouring her coffee, when Linda strode into the dining room. The fatigue Izzy had noted on the ride back to the villa the evening before had been replaced by Linda's more usual quiet authority. She ducked her head at the pass-through to the kitchen to offer Annunziata a lilting "*Buon giorno*," and then approached Izzy.

"Izzy, would you be willing to assist my grandfather at the site today?"

Izzy put down her coffee cup. "I'd be happy to, Linda. But I thought Daniel's been working at his side." Izzy was wary of spending hours in the tomb with Daniel.

"Daniel is away this morning—and don't bother asking me where because he didn't tell me. I'm sure either he or Maria shared with you our concerns about Raffaello's health."

"They both did. I'm sorry."

"Thanks. He needs to be gently reminded not to push himself. As you know, he doesn't want to be told what to do. But I think he'd be less resistant to your suggestions than he's been to any of us grandchildren."

"Understood. When do you want me to go?"

"As soon as you finish your breakfast. We've got members of the Ministry of Antiquities arriving at one today for lunch and then a tour of the site."

"What needs to be done before they arrive?"

"I'm sure Raffaello has a list. But the main thing will be to have the site in order and the reports up to date."

"Maria and I finished the cataloging and packing yesterday. Did the boxes get delivered to the granary?"

"Marcantonio brought them up yesterday evening. They're stacked just inside, by the workbench. Here are the keys to the Land Rover. Have you ever driven one?"

"If it's anything like a Jeep, I'll be fine. Most of the driving I did on Chappy was either on dirt roads or the beach."

"Thanks. I'll meet you at Raffaello's. I'm on my way now to check on him and let him know about the change. I'm sure he'll be pleased. He's missed you."

"I'm honored to help him." Izzy watched Linda leave through the patio door. She wasn't sure how to interpret Linda's last remark. Izzy hadn't set out to abandon Raffaello, but staying away from Daniel's family had been necessary for her own peace of mind. Daniel's absence this morning, mysterious though it was, would give Izzy an opportunity to reconnect with Raffaello. She looked forward to it.

When she arrived at the courtyard, Raffaello was already by the Land Rover, his backpack on the ground at his feet and his coffee mug in hand.

"I understand you are to be my amanuensis today. I'm delighted. I'm eager to show you the tomb and hear your impressions."

Izzy smiled. "I'm equally delighted, Raffaello." So he was unaware that she'd already been down in the trench. At least she wouldn't have to pretend she'd never seen it before, since her memories of that night were fragmented. But they weren't nonexistent. Not everything about her time in the tomb had been lost, she realized with sudden and stunning clarity.

"Linda has informed me I'm to allow you to maneuver this beast of a vehicle down the mountain. Are you ready?"

Izzy held up the keys and climbed into the driver's seat. She'd answered Linda so confidently about driving, hadn't she? She took a few deep breaths and turned the key. After a jerky shift from first into second, she smoothed out her shifting and guided the car down the drive and out to the road. She drove slowly, her knuckles white against the steering wheel. She was grateful that Raffaello seemed to understand her need to concentrate and didn't interrupt her with conversation.

"You'll need to direct me to the turnoff. I've always been a passenger in the back seat when riding to the site."

"Slow down just beyond the next curve. The pasture gate is on the right. One of the watchmen should be there to open it."

Izzy made the turn and drove through the gate. The track meandered through the woods to a clearing where the archaeologists' van was parked. Izzy remembered the footpath to the site, a memory that she attributed to the repetition of walking it several times in the past few weeks. The roughness of the ground underfoot, the heady fragrance of the vegetation, and the sensation of branches brushing against her arms were all familiar to her. When they reached the excavation, Raffaello led the way to his tent, where he put his backpack and the now empty coffee mug on the workbench. He withdrew a Nikon from the pack, checked the number of pictures still remaining on the film, and pulled two more film canisters from a shelf above the bench. Then he repacked the camera and the film, picked up the bag, and slipped it over his shoulders.

"Let's go!"

The team had already rolled back the tarp and removed the plywood cover protecting the excavation. Someone hauled a ladder over from the utility tent. With Raffaello in the lead—a situation Izzy wasn't quite comfortable with—she and two of the BU archaeologists descended into the tomb. At the bottom they lit lanterns and walked along the ledge of a trench into a second chamber. In the center of the room, its massive shape dominating the space, stood the sarcophagus. Izzy hesitated, her back pressed against the earthen wall that marked the extent of the room's excavation. One of the archaeologists quietly motioned to her to move away from the wall, holding up his hands with about four inches between them. She stepped forward, understanding. Don't touch anything.

Raffaello paced around the sarcophagus, the camera slung around his neck but not yet aimed. Then he motioned Izzy forward.

"Tell me what you see."

A few images from her previous visit floated into memory—the carved lid of the sarcophagus, Daniel's face as they talked into the night, even the overturned bucket he'd sat on. But the images drifted away, replaced by emotions. They engulfed her and she stumbled. Someone grabbed her arm to steady her—it was Raffaello.

"*Va bene*?" He rarely spoke Italian to her. The phrase must have been instinctive, an automatic response to his concern.

She nodded. But she wasn't OK. She felt exposed and vulnerable surrounded by the others in this cramped space. When she'd been here before she'd felt safe, protected. With Daniel.

She wasn't sure she could do this—look once again at the faces of the lovers. She had studied her drawings for a long time, searing not only the images but her experience of them, into her brain. She felt as if she'd willed them to stay where she could find them again.

Izzy closed her eyes and took a deep breath. Raffaello needed her. She couldn't turn away and climb back above, as desperately as she wanted to.

She took a step forward and then swept her eyes over the length of the carved lid. She started at the base, where the bare feet of the lovers peeked out of the sheet covering their bodies. The lovers were turned toward each other, arms entwined, knees bent and nearly touching. She had no memory of this. The intimacy of the pose, lovers facing each other in bed, sent a shard of longing through her. She could not let go of the emotion elicited by these bare feet. Another memory surfaced, not from her previous time in the tomb, but from a time more distant. Daniel's bare feet stretched out on a wooden deck chair. They were high up—on a roof? In the distance, the tiled roofs of a city. Daniel asleep. Tears stung her eyes. The humanity of the lovers was captured by those bare feet, no longer covered, but exposed and vulnerable. She wiped away the tears with her palm. Her eyes moved up to the faces of the lovers. In her mind she saw her sketches, now tucked into her back pocket, and looked again at the stone faces. What had she seen before that she wasn't seeing now? What was she seeing in this moment that she'd missed before? The lovers stared into each other's eyes, the stone capturing the piercing gaze.

She began to speak of her impressions. "I see hope, tenderness, reassurance. The woman, especially, is offering her strength, her conviction, that they will be together for eternity. She knows the joy of this marriage bed will continue beyond death. In the man, I see a different kind of strength—physical, powerful, protective. In them both, I see love."

She looked back at Raffaello. "It's what we all wish for, isn't it?"

Raffaello smiled and nodded. "You have a poet's way with language. You've recreated in words what the sculptor transmitted in stone."

"Except that the stone remains. My words hang in the air for a few moments and then are gone."

"Not this time." Raffaello held up a small cassette recorder. "I'd like you to listen to this later and transcribe it. For the rest of the morning, please take your own handwritten notes. Describe in detail everything you observe."

Izzy was stunned about the recording. In some ways it felt like a violation—Raffaello the puppet master manipulating her to reveal hidden thoughts. But she also was exhilarated to learn that her words hadn't been lost. The recorder was simply another memory device, like her notebook.

Raffaello seemed to recognize her discomfort. "I'm sorry I didn't tell you about the recorder. I use it all the time in my work to capture first impressions, the immediacy of my reactions to what I see. I thought it might inhibit you to know the recorder was on. I apologize."

Izzy didn't say anything at first. Then, "Please don't do it again without telling me. I wouldn't have held back. I'm actually honored that you value my opinion. I don't need to be tricked into giving it."

"Am I forgiven?" He sounded genuinely remorseful.

"Yes, Raffaello, I forgive you." In speaking the words, she wondered if Raffaello—and all the Richetellis—forgave her for falling in love with Daniel.

"Let's get to work, shall we?"

Izzy pulled out her notebook and began to circle the sarcophagus as Raffaello shot photographs and the two archaeologists worked in a corner of the chamber where another, shallower trench had been dug.

After an hour of intense observation, often crouching or holding herself in an awkward position to see a hidden detail, she was relieved to hear Raffaello say it was time for a break above.

She stretched and followed him up the ladder.

"Let's go to my tent. I have an idea I'd like to run by you."

In the tent he puttered with a small Bunsen burner and a kettle and made them each a cup of tea.

"Isabella, the next stage of my work involves writing. I want to turn this discovery into a book, and I want to hire you as my editor."

He held up his hand. "And before you protest that you can't do intellectual work, I want you to take a look at your notebook and listen to the tape."

Hearing Raffaello make assumptions about her abilities and anticipate her objections, Izzy felt blindsided. The hard-won freedom she'd achieved to make her own decisions about her life had suddenly been snatched away by Raffaello's arrogant attitude that he knew what was best for her. She was furious.

"No! Stop trying to rescue me and convince me I can be the brilliant girl you once knew. This dig wasn't your only project this summer, was it? I was another. That little exhibition with the recorder was part of your plan. I can't edit your book, Raffaello. I *won't* edit it."

She had to get out of the tent. To hell with her responsibility for minding Raffaello. She pulled back the flap of the tent and stomped across the field to the path through the woods. She'd walk back to the farm and resume her work with the pigs. She'd left her cane in her room, not expecting to be hiking this morning. She'd find a branch along the way if she needed support. At the moment, her anger was fueling her, and she thrust one leg after another, trying to put as much distance between Raffaello and her as quickly as possible. She kept her head down, watching for stones and roots in the path that might trip her.

"Izzy!"

She hadn't seen Daniel approaching from the other direction and had nearly walked into him. He put his arms out to stop her from falling.

"What's happened? Where are you going in such a rush?"

"Let me go, Daniel. I have to get back to the farm. Go take care of your grandfather."

"What's wrong? What's upset you? Is Raffaello all right?" Daniel looked up toward the dig.

"Raffaello is fine. He's more than fine. Full of ridiculous, magical plans that I want no part of. Please let me go." She wrenched herself away and Daniel released her.

"Let me at least drive you back to the farm."

"No, thank you. I'd rather walk."

Daniel watched her retreat through the woods. All the calm and peace that had enveloped Izzy after her night in the tomb had disappeared. Had she lost those memories of her vision so completely?

He turned toward the dig to seek out his grandfather and try to understand what had happened.

CHAPTER TWENTY-NINE

AUGUST 12 – 13

I zzy made it out of the woods to the clearing where the cars were parked, brushed away the twigs that had caught in her hair, and massaged her leg before heading for the pasture gate and the gravel road up the mountain. She caught her breath when she reached the road. It would be a long trek, and she probably would regret her decision to turn down Daniel's offer of a ride. But she knew she needed to calm down, and the monotonous trudge to the villa would help her focus on why she'd reacted so strongly to Raffaello's request. It frightened her that she'd flipped into rage as if a switch had been pulled. She had truly thought that these months at Portarello had helped her to come to terms with her new self. The work in the garden and with the pigs had given her a sense of accomplishment and possibilities. Even the emotional upheaval of her relationship with Daniel was something to be cherished, not regretted. And the visions—the visions had given her joy.

Damn Raffaello for causing a crack in her façade of acceptance! For challenging her to venture beyond the safe and protective walls of what she knew were her limitations.

Why did he have to record her and expose her language and imagery to judgment? All her doubts about herself exploded when confronted by Raffaello's request. It hurt so much!

By the time she was halfway up the mountain, the sweat was pouring down her back. She was still wearing the sweatshirt she'd put on in the morning to ward off the damp chill of the tomb. In the warmth of the late morning sun, it was an encumbrance, and she pulled it off over her head. It was her old Chappy sweatshirt, faded green and soft from hundreds of washings. She tied the arms around her waist and thought briefly of home—of the wind through the marshes, the rhythmic pounding of the waves on East Beach, the bustle of Edgartown in high season. She wasn't homesick. Letters on thin blue airmail paper passed regularly between her and her family, and she was up on all the news: her mother's continued remission of her lung cancer, baby Caleb's crawling and babbling, the completion of the house Josiah and Grace were building on a plot of land next to Mae and Tobias. Their lives were full and busy. She couldn't imagine what she'd be doing if she'd stayed. Sitting at the window staring at the bay? No, she wasn't homesick.

But … was her life here at Portarello what she wanted?

The strenuous walk up the mountain was calming her fury, as she knew it would. But it also was taking a physical toll. If she didn't stop to rest, she'd pay in spasms and pain later. She looked for a spot where she could take a break and found a small clearing with a tumbled-down stone wall near a brook. She pushed away the tall weeds growing by the side of the road and found a section of the wall where she could sit. Before she settled herself, she knelt to scoop up some water from the brook to splash on her face and quench her thirst. She considered sitting on the mossy bank by the water but knew she'd have a much harder time getting up if she stayed so low. She took one more drink and then heaved herself up and moved to the stones. The wall was in dappled shade, and she closed her eyes. It was her way of focusing her hearing and sense of smell. She had a good nose, her Granny Naomi had once told her. Not its shape, but its ability to detect scent. Since her injury, her sense of smell had become a powerful and sometimes unexpected tool of memory. Sitting now in this glade, she ticked off the smells she detected, scents that represented Portarello's wilderness to her. The pine and wild thyme and rosemary and saffron comforted her and soothed her agitation.

Her notebook was an uncomfortable lump in her back pocket. She pulled it out and held it in her hand. She was tempted to put it aside on the ground until she was ready to walk again. She stroked the cover with her thumb, torn between leaving the new pages until later, as she always did in the privacy of her room, and reading them now. She glanced up at the road. It was barely visible, which meant she was relatively hidden, especially from a passing vehicle. With some trepidation, she opened the notebook. She had a brief memory of Raffaello's voice—"Read your notes!"—and almost stopped. She didn't want to listen to him. Didn't want to ... what? Be disappointed? Was that at the root of her resistance to his idea? Was she pushing back because she was afraid she'd fail?

Courage, Izzy. Her mother's voice, when Izzy had cried through the pain of her multiple surgeries and post-operative physical therapy, wanting to give up. Courage is facing what we fear.

Izzy flipped open the notebook to the last pages she'd filled that morning and read them. Then she read them again, running her fingers under the lines, smiling. The words brought back not only what she had seen, but the pleasure she'd felt—a deep satisfaction in her ability to observe and describe. She remembered her fascination and her curiosity. She remembered wanting to know more.

She closed the notebook, stood and stretched her limbs, and tucked the book back into her pocket. She made the final portion of the trek back to the villa with energy not fueled by anger but by hope.

When she arrived, she saw the main gate was open and two cars with Rome license plates were parked by the terrace. The officials from the ministry had arrived, which meant Raffaello, if not already back from the dig, would be there soon. Rather than encounter him in the midst of such a crucial meeting, she avoided the gate and slipped down the back drive to the path leading to the pigs. She'd make herself busy and come back later, when the visitors were gone and she could talk with Raffaello alone. It would be her turn to apologize and, she hoped, salvage her relationship with him. She didn't remember all the words she'd shouted at him, but she did remember how enraged she'd felt. That alone was a message that she needed to dig deep into her fears and find a way to overcome them.

She spent the early afternoon among the adolescent pigs. It felt as if she'd been away from them too long because of the dig. She knew everything at the farm had been relegated to only the bare essentials. Now, she watched with concern for any signs of injury or illness among the rambunctious drift. After assuring herself that all was well, she sat among them, enjoying their energy.

She looked up in surprise when she heard her name. Marcantonio stood at the fence, the feed wagon parked nearby. Was it already late afternoon?

"Isabella! I should have known you'd be here. Raffaello is ready to send out a search party for you. No one knew what had become of you after you left the dig."

Izzy stood up and brushed off the dirt of the pasture.

"I wasn't hiding."

Marcantonio looked at her and shook his head. "But you needed to cool off away from everyone. I wasn't at the dig, but I heard about your argument. Anyone above ground heard the shouts, although not the words."

"How is Raffaello? How did the meeting go?"

"Come down and ask him yourself. He's worried about you. I'll give you a ride. Save time. The truck is at the barn."

He brought her to the courtyard, and Izzy went directly to Raffaello's house. Marcantonio had been unusually quiet on the ride down, and Izzy had built up a scenario in her head that all was not well with Raffaello and she was at fault.

She knocked at the terrace door, but no one answered. She opened it and called inside but still got no response. Giving up, she hurried across the courtyard to the steps leading down to the front of the villa. The cars from Rome were gone and all was quiet, just as it had been at Raffaello's house. She went to the kitchen, hoping to find Annunziata preparing the evening meal. Her stomach growled, reminding her she hadn't eaten since breakfast. The lilt of Annunziata's voice relieved her and she ducked her head into a room filled with steam from a boiling pot of pasta.

"Isabella! *Grazie a Dio sei al sicuro*!" Annunziata made the sign of the cross. She looked Izzy up and down. "You're OK?"

"I'm fine, Annunziata. Where is Raffaello?"

"They are all down the mountain, looking for you. Raffaello, Daniele, Benno, the boys from the university."

"I don't know if I have energy to go after them."

"Wait. Linda is in the office. Go to her. She'll get word to them that you are found."

"I wasn't lost, Annunziata."

"Are you sure? Maybe not lost in the woods, but lost in your heart, eh?"

Izzy pushed her palms against her eyes to hold back tears. "I'll go tell Linda I'm here." She rushed away.

The door to the office was open, and Izzy could hear Linda on the phone. She stepped inside, and Linda rose from her desk, ending the call. She approached Izzy with open arms.

"You're safe. Thank God!"

"I'm sorry I've caused such an uproar. I was with the pigs."

"Of course. We should have looked there first. But no one saw you return from the dig, and we thought you were hurt somewhere in the woods. Let me get on the two-way radio and let them know."

She turned to pick up the transceiver. "Danny, she's here. Safe. Let Nonno know and come back."

Izzy stood in the middle of the office, ready for Linda's questions or criticism. She must know about the argument and, given her concerns about Raffaello's health, had every right to be angry with her.

"Why don't we go up to the house and have a glass of wine while we wait for them?"

That wasn't what Izzy expected.

"I'm filthy, between the dig and the pigs."

"So are they. You can wash up at the house. I want an opportunity to talk with you before they get back." Linda put her arm around Izzy's shoulder as they walked through the villa to the courtyard.

At Raffaello's they sat on the terrace with a bottle of Portarello's red and a tray of salame and cheese.

"My grandfather can be a demanding son of a bitch. All of us at one time or another have been subject to his very well-defined ideas about what we should do with our lives."

"So you know what the argument was about?"

"He told me. After the Roman bureaucrats left, he wanted to talk with you. When we realized you were gone, he admitted to me why he thought you'd disappeared. It surprised me. ..."

"That I'd left in anger?"

"No, *that* I understood. What surprised me was Nonno's remorse. It wasn't just that he had misjudged how you'd react to his idea. He was ... lost. And truly worried that he'd driven you away permanently."

"I've been equally worried that I caused irreparable damage to our friendship. I was truly awful. I walked away because I couldn't stop the angry words spilling out of my mouth. I went up to the pigs when I got back because I needed to be alone, to sort out why I'd been so furious with him. I wasn't trying to upset anyone—especially Raffaello. I'm sorry my absence caused so much turmoil."

"We all care about you, Izzy."

At that moment, Raffaello, Daniel, Maria and Benno came around the house, each wearing a different expression. Benno, a calming smile reassuring her that now everything was going to be OK; Maria, impatient curiosity, eager to hear what Izzy had been up to in the missing hours; Daniel, sheer relief and freedom from his fears for her safety; and Raffaello, a deep sadness that accentuated how much he'd aged over the summer.

"I'd like to speak to Isabella alone," he said, waving the others into the house. "Go make yourselves useful putting dinner together."

Like dutiful children, they left Izzy and Raffaello to face each other.

"I'm sorry!" They both spoke at the same time.

Raffaello held up his hand. "No, I am the one at fault. I should have learned, after this summer with Daniele, that I don't have all the answers. I had no right to push you. It was selfish of me. It's not an excuse, but I know I don't have much time left. …"

Izzy put out her hand and took his.

"I spent the long walk back from the dig trying to tease apart what had enraged me. It was fear, Raffaello. I was afraid of failing. What if I attempted the work and discovered that it would be forever beyond my reach? It would crush me, and that's why I've stayed in my cocoon of working with my hands. I may lose a row of tomato plants to aphids or a piglet too weak to survive, but I wouldn't be destroying your life's work or my fragile sense of self. I faced that fear this afternoon. You were only nudging me to realize how stuck I am. Forgive me for blowing up at you for confronting me with the truth."

Izzy leaned in and kissed him on the cheek.

"I would be honored to work with you on the book."

"*Grazie, cara*. And if we disagree, as I'm sure we will, promise me you will not run away."

"I didn't run away, Raffaello. I walked away. We all need time alone to reflect. But I promise you that next time, I will tell you where I'm going."

"*Va bene*. Now, some delicious smells are emanating from the kitchen. We should rescue the others, who have probably been listening at the window."

Raffaello opened the terrace door and called inside. "It's safe to come out now; we haven't killed each other."

Everyone emerged carrying something—bowls of pasta and salad, plates, cutlery, and more wine. With Raffaello and Izzy at peace with each other, no one referred to the disruption that had sent them all in search of her. Only Daniel seemed to be still unsettled as Izzy caught him watching her from across the table with questioning looks. She wanted to share with him her revelations, but not here with the others. Instead, she listened raptly to Raffaello's description of the meeting with the state archaeologists from the ministry.

The sarcophagus was to be removed from the tomb and sent to Rome for analysis, along with the major objects found at the site. Much later, the ministry would announce the discovery and hold an exhibition.

"I am hoping for a recreation of the tomb itself in which to display the sarcophagus. The ministry is in agreement with me that it needs to be in a protected environment. The mountain is too remote, and the site too inaccessible for it to become another Cerveteri. I am willing to host small groups of academics who wish to see the tomb in situ, but not casual tourists."

The group talked late into the night. Izzy realized she had missed these meals and the barbed give-and-take of the cousins with each other and with their grandfather. Although she and Daniel hadn't had an opportunity to speak directly to each other, she was aware of everything he said. When Raffaello finally called an end to the evening, she hoped they might walk back to the villa together. But he disappeared into the house and she felt foolish hanging around waiting for him. She wished everyone *buona notte* and left.

The climb to her room was slow going. The combination of wine and her miles of walking had finally caught up with her. When she reached her room, she barely had the energy to undress before she collapsed into bed.

The next day, she wasn't needed at the dig, but Raffaello asked her to meet with him in the granary in the afternoon.

"You've read your notes?"

"Many times. Would you like to see them?"

"Eventually. I've asked Linda to find you a typewriter. We can set up a space for you to work here in the granary."

He handed her a stack of typed pages. "This is a draft of my earlier notes. Marcantonio's sister Anna typed them for me, but she's not fluent in English."

Izzy took the pages. "You're writing in English."

"Which is why I need you, not only to correct my grammar, but also to make my words flow."

"Do we have a timetable, a deadline?"

Raffaello looked at her. "We both know I may not have much time, Isabella. Once the sarcophagus is gone, we'll work every afternoon. In the mornings, you do what you need to on the farm. Stay in touch with the land, with what you've learned about yourself. Keep your hands in the earth as well as on the keys of the typewriter."

That evening, Izzy had dinner again with the family. Linda had mentioned that another sibling, Robert, was arriving. As Izzy rounded the corner to the terrace, she heard a booming laugh. A dark-haired man, shorter and more solidly built than Daniel, was regaling Maria with a story, a wine glass in one hand and a slice of rolled prosciutto in the other. He stopped and smiled at her.

"You must be Izzy. Maria's told me about you—Smithy, Vineyard native. I'm a Block Island enthusiast myself. I'd offer you my hand, but as you can see, they're both full. Robert Richetelli. Roberto to my grandfather."

"Nice to meet you. How long will you be staying?"

"Only a few days. Just jumped the pond to see my grandfather."

The others drifted onto the terrace one by one. Raffaello came down, apparently directly from the shower, his hair still damp. He embraced Robert and kissed him. Then he took him aside to speak to him alone.

Benno arrived next, his hands laden with shopping bags full of groceries.

"Dinner will be a little late this evening. The traffic was impossible. The week of *Ferragosto* arrives, and everyone hits the road to escape to the beach or the mountains. Is Linda in the kitchen?"

Maria came out of the house and shook her head. "Haven't seen her. Here, let me help." She took one of the bags and led the way back into the kitchen.

Izzy stood alone at the wall overlooking the vegetable garden and poured herself a glass of wine. Robert and Raffaello were deep in conversation. The love between Raffaello and his grandchildren reverberated in the murmured words and gestures. Raffaello's arm was draped over Robert's shoulder, and his head was bent as he listened to him.

The only grandparent Izzy knew was Naomi, her father's mother. All the others had died well before Izzy had entered the world. Her connection to Naomi, while different from what she observed of Raffaello, was intense. She had been a bulwark throughout Izzy's bout with polio. And Izzy knew the story of Naomi's role in blocking the court from removing Josiah from Mae and Tobias when Mae's sister Kathleen had sued for adoption, claiming Mae was unfit to care for him because of her cancer. "Over my dead body," was the often repeated phrase whenever the story was told of Naomi marshalling the forces of the community to keep her grandson with his parents and his tribe.

Despite what she knew of Raffaello's tendency to be a sometimes dominant force in his grandchildren's lives, she considered them fortunate to have him as their champion. As she was, she had come to realize.

"You're off somewhere in the clouds. May I interrupt you?"

Izzy had not heard Daniel arrive and turned to smile at him. "Just thinking about grandparents."

"You seem to have acquired another one in the last few days. Have you met my brother?" Daniel glanced over at Robert and Raffaello.

"Briefly. He's very different from you."

Daniel shook his head. "I used to think that, but now I'm not so sure."

"What do you mean?" Izzy was curious.

"We had a long talk on the way from the airport. He announced that he and his wife are divorcing. He's probably telling Nonno now. Both Richetelli boys are renouncing their vows. I can't imagine how my parents will take it, especially my mother."

"Have you told your parents? I thought ...well, I thought you were going to take more time to explore what you truly wanted to do."

"I haven't spoken to them yet, but will need to before Robert gets back to New York. I don't want them to hear it from him. He's too eager not to be the only bad son."

"You're not a bad son! You're not a bad man." Izzy's voice was firm. "But what about taking time to figure out where your life is headed? Or did you do that yesterday morning when you disappeared on your mysterious errand that even Linda hadn't managed to badger out of you?"

"That's what I want to talk to you about. Take a walk with me in the garden. From what I hear in the kitchen, dinner will be a while."

Daniel topped off their wine glasses, and they went through the gate down to the garden. They stopped by the zucchini, and Izzy couldn't prevent herself from bending down to pull out a few weeds.

"So where did you go, and why was it a secret?"

"The abbey of Monte Oliveto Maggiore in Asciano."

"You're going to become a monk?" Izzy was confused and incredulous.

"No, no. I'm far too much of the world and also too much of a loner to join a community of Benedictines. I have a friend from my days studying in Rome. He's the prior there. I visited him to ask if I can stay at the abbey for a while. It was you who gave me the idea. 'You need to go away,' you told me. Remove the distractions of you and my family. I've decided to do a retreat. I leave after the weekend."

"Like Jesus going off into the desert for forty days."

"Exactly."

"To face your demons."

"I think you are doing the same. ..."

"You mean the work I'm going to do with Raffaello."

"That's a huge step for you."

"I'm not exactly sticking my toe in the water, am I? It's more like diving in head first. I'm scared."

"I am too."

"*Coraggio*. We'll both need it."

A bell clanged from the terrace, calling them to dinner. Together they walked back up to the terrace. They didn't touch, but the connection between them was unbroken.

By the end of August, the BU archaeologists were gone and the Ministry of Antiquities had arranged for the transport of the sarcophagus to Rome in the first week of September.

Izzy was helping Raffaello plan a ceremony for the removal of the sarcophagus. Throughout the dig, he had reminded everyone that it was a coffin containing human remains, and he was firm about respecting the dead.

"The couple so lovingly portrayed in stone were once a living, breathing man and woman. Never forget that in your careers. The bits and pieces you sift out of the earth were once worn on a human body, touched by a human hand. No matter how many thousands of years ago a tool was hammered into shape or an amulet carved out of bone, it was human curiosity and ingenuity that created it."

He had a way of inspiring wonder in the details that marked every backbreaking, tedious day on the dig.

Maria was flying out the day after the ceremony. She and Izzy were in the greenhouse weaving flowers into wreaths fashioned from cypress branches.

"I never considered my grandfather to be so spiritual, but he seems really caught up in ancient rites."

"There's so little known about Etruscan worship, so I think he's creating his own ceremony. I was over in Volterra yesterday digging around the library for anything that might be useful. These wreaths are a result of that search."

"How did that go, being in a library again?" Maria stilled her hands to listen. It wasn't an idle question.

"A little overwhelming at first. I clutched my security blanket—my notebook—and took a deep breath. And the smell of old books immediately filled my nostrils. Touching the texture of the bindings and the rag paper, listening to the rustle of pages being turned, it all reassured me. I managed to find the books I wanted without a panic attack. I've discovered that if I work in small bites of time—fifteen or twenty minutes—I can concentrate and comprehend what I'm reading. A year ago, that was impossible." Izzy shook her head in wonder. "I really didn't believe I'd ever be able to pick up a book with pleasure again."

"I'm happy for you, Iz." Maria threw her arms around Izzy and hugged her.

"I wish you didn't have to leave. Having you here this summer has been a major part of my recovery."

"I'm sorry to be going, too. But real life, in the form of my parents, is asking me when I'm going to start making a living. I got a letter this morning from the McGovern campaign, and they want to interview me for a staff position. My masters in political science may actually have been a wise decision."

"I can see you, working those voter lists, putting together fact sheets, and writing campaign speeches. You'll be brilliant at it!"

"I'll send you postcards from the trenches. And you need to do the same."

"I promise."

CHAPTER THIRTY

SEPTEMBER 7 – OCTOBER 28

Maria's departure and the removal of the sarcophagus marked a shift in the daily rhythm of Izzy's life at Portarello. A handful of tourists filled the beds in the villa. The last of the summer interns were winding up their duties and flying back to universities around the world. Only Izzy would be staying through the winter.

Linda approached her after Maria left. "Izzy, let's talk about your living arrangements for the next several months. We close up the villa during the winter. There's no central heating and we shut down the water. I've got a couple of options for you. You're welcome to take over Maria's room in my house, or you can move into the cottage next door to Raffaello. It's one open space with a sleeping alcove and a kitchenette. Either option is fine with Benno and me. Come take a look at the cottage and then you can decide."

Izzy followed Linda across the courtyard and explored the cottage. It reminded Izzy of a fairy tale, with leaded windows and a deep hearth. A rag rug covered the stone floor, and the bed in the alcove was hidden by a beaded curtain that caught the sunlight.

Izzy had never lived alone before. She and Maria had been roommates all through Smith and then shared an apartment in Cambridge when they began their graduate work at Harvard—she in English and Maria at the John F. Kennedy School of Government. She knew Maria's room, light and airy and overlooking the mountains. It probably still smelled of her Shalimar perfume. Izzy liked Linda and she enjoyed Benno, whose light-hearted and relaxed attitude about life was a welcome antidote to the intensity of the Richetellis. Her relationship with Linda had also eased with Daniel's departure for his retreat.

She fingered the beads and made her decision to take the cottage.

Over the next two months, Izzy and Raffaello settled into a routine, working in his studio at the granary, where he had access not only to his notes and slides, but also to the artifacts that had not gone with the sarcophagus to Rome. As the weather cooled, Linda brought over a space heater for them and an electric kettle to keep them well supplied with hot tea and coffee. Izzy kept up her work with the pigs in the mornings and late afternoons. She and Raffaello debated about the wording of passages. Izzy, ever in need of lists to keep her life and her thoughts organized, developed a structure for the book. Despite lapses, when she drew a blank at some reference Raffaello made, she was starting to feel comfortable. She learned to stop and count to ten whenever Raffaello would say something like, "Remember that note I highlighted on the wall painting in the anteroom?" She wanted to scream, I don't remember! Why can't you remember that? But she didn't. Instead, she learned to ask him questions that helped her retrieve the nugget of information he was seeking.

One afternoon her notebook fell off her desk and flipped open to the sketches she'd made the first time she'd seen the sarcophagus. She bent to pick it up, but Raffaello reached for it first.

He held it, transfixed, turning the pages.

"These are extraordinary. I had no idea you had such artistic talent. Your insight into what the sculpture conveys to the human spirit! Isabella, these drawings give me an idea. ..."

Izzy smiled and waited. Raffaello's ideas invariably meant some challenging work for Izzy, extending yet again the boundaries of what she thought she was capable of doing. She'd gotten used to his projects and no longer reacted with anger.

"Can you render these sketches as paintings?"

"I can try. I've worked in watercolors before, but perhaps oil would be better. I'll experiment with both."

The next day they drove to an art supply shop in Siena. Izzy reveled in the shelves full of tubes of paint in every shade, the brushes of varying sizes and textures, the canvases, and the art paper. Marcantonio found an old easel, and Linda gave her a wooden box to hold her supplies. Her first attempts resulted in a dozen crumpled watercolor sheets tossed with increasing frustration into the corner of the granary. But her thirteenth painting hinted at the secrets she'd witnessed that night in the tomb.

Izzy took her paints and a stack of paper back to the cottage, and in the evening after the communal dinner she shared with Raffaello, Linda, and Benno, she continued to work on the images.

By the twentieth painting, her hand and her eye were working together not to copy the original sketch but to attempt to create instead the emotion she'd experienced. She tacked each sheet to the wall and paced in front of them, searching. She was beginning to feel it was futile, trying to capture a moment that had had such a profound impact on her but that had been so fleeting. A whisper of eternity. A cloud.

Maybe that was the key. She'd been painting something solid, the stone. But what she'd witnessed had been beyond the walls of the tomb. She pulled another sheet from the stack, taped it to the easel, and swirled her brush in a mix of gray and white and blue on her palette.

She didn't know how long she'd been working when she heard the knock on her door. The cottage didn't have a phone and she assumed it was Linda stopping by with some directive for the next day from Raffaello. No one else was at Portarello. She pulled open the door, her brush still in her hand.

Daniel stood on the step, his face lit by the small lantern above the door. Daniel, who had been gone since the middle of August and now it was the end of October. Well beyond forty days. She had not heard from him at all, which she told herself was to be expected. He was on a retreat, for heaven's sake. A retreat from her in particular. Although he'd not written, she had—every day. When she and Raffaello had gone to the art supply store, she'd also bought a notebook. Not one that fit into her back pocket for jotting down what she wanted to remember, but a full-sized journal with marbled endpapers and narrowly ruled lines. She had begun tentatively, writing a few lines of reflection or observation, as if she were writing a letter to Daniel or continuing the conversations they had shared in the chapel. She didn't want to intrude upon his solitude but needed a connection to him, if only in her mind. But like any practice, the more she wrote, the more comfortable she became with filling the page with her words, words that were a record of her doubts and bursts of insights. Even a few words about what she was reading. Reading!

"May I come in, or am I disturbing you?" He looked beyond her to the cottage, as if he expected someone else to be there.

"Of course you can come in! Forgive me for being momentarily stunned by your presence. I thought you were Linda." Izzy stood aside and waved him in.

"Linda? Are you expecting her?"

"No, no. It's simply that there are only a few possibilities of who might be at my door at eleven at night. You aren't one of them."

"I'm sorry to show up unannounced. I wanted to see you before I left."

"Left? You've only just come back, as far as I know. From your retreat. Is it over?"

"Yes. I left the abbey today."

"And ...?" Izzy hesitated. "You don't have to tell me if you don't want to." She was feeling incredibly unsure of herself, as if she had no right to know the outcome of his spiritual journey. But she did, dammit. Whatever decision he had made was going to seriously affect her.

"Do you want some coffee? Or are you here to make a brief announcement and then be on your way?" She couldn't keep the bitterness out of her voice. *Oh, Izzy, you are so scared of what he's going to say and you're pushing back already to protect yourself.*

"I have time for a coffee."

"Then come and sit. Put a log on the fire while I turn on the kettle." She relaxed her taut muscles, realizing she'd had a primitive response, ready to fight or flee.

While she puttered with the coffee, she watched him pacing in front of the sheets tacked to the wall exactly as she had earlier.

"You're turning your sketches of the sarcophagus into paintings." His voice was filled with awe.

"Trying to. I had a sudden insight just before you arrived—that instead of recreating the solidity of the stone, I need to capture the clouds of the visions I witnessed that night." She pointed to the easel.

He approached it and studied the swirls of paint she'd laid down.

"That's brilliant, Izzy. In just those few strokes, I feel a sense of wonder and mystery." He turned to her. "What a gift you have!"

Izzy couldn't help herself from smiling. Some of her anxiety was easing. This was still Daniel, who understood her, who didn't need explanations or a blueprint for how her brain worked.

She handed him the coffee mug.

"Come sit and tell me why you're really here."

They gathered by the fire. Daniel stretched out his legs toward the hearth and kicked off his shoes. Izzy was not surprised to see that his feet were bare, and she had to restrain herself from touching them.

"I came because I wanted to tell you what happened to me at the monastery—because you were there with me every day, entwined in my prayers, haunting my dreams."

Izzy waited, unsure of where this conversation was going, or even if she could bear hearing it. He had said he was leaving, hadn't he?

"The first week was rough. Total solitude. I was invited to join the Divine Office with the monks, but I declined. I didn't pray the Liturgy of the Hours as a Jesuit, and, as you know, prayer had no meaning for me. So I spent the time alone, often in long walks, sometimes reading in the library. When the church was empty, between the Hours, I sat and waited.

"Eventually I began to listen, pulling apart the threads of my life, isolating what had been grace and what had been empty and numbing."

He reached out and took her hand.

"You have been one of the graces in my life." He turned over her hand and kissed her palm.

"My friend Sandro, the prior, helped as time went by. I was losing weight and still not sleeping, and he stepped in. We talked every day. In the early days, I thought he'd be judgmental because we'd chosen such different paths in our vows. But he understood my conviction that I needed to leave the priesthood, and he simply guided me to find the next stage in my life's journey.

"It was only in the last few weeks that a way forward became clear to me. When my life began to collapse, it felt like a helicopter rotor that loses a linchpin and its blades fly apart, flung in every direction. I was grasping for something—anything—to give me purpose. I once had thought I wanted to go to Peru and become a priest warrior in the Liberation Theology movement. I even told Raffaello.

"I considered that path again in the monastery—to go not as a priest but nevertheless to work among the poor in South America. But one thing had changed my life since I considered renouncing my comfortable and numbing academic life. That one thing was you. I know I don't want to choose a life that renounces you."

Izzy remained still, sensing there was more.

"I knew I could not ask you to follow me to Peru. So I looked closer to home for the purpose that will give my life meaning. I found it in New York City, which is fitting. I go away to seek my path, and it takes me back to where I started. There's a woman, Dorothy Day, who founded the Catholic Worker movement. They have communities all over the world, serving the poor, the homeless, the exiled. I leave tomorrow to take up residence in one of their New York houses to work among those in need. Not as a priest.

"So that's it. I'm still on the journey, but no longer floundering in despair. I'm here tonight not only to tell you, but also to ask you something."

"What is that, Daniel?" Izzy whispered, trying to absorb everything she'd just heard.

"Will you follow me, when you are ready? Will you come to New York? You asked me this summer what I wanted. I want a life with you, Izzy."

Since their tumultuous time at Bellosguardo, when Izzy had acknowledged her love for Daniel, she had yearned to hear those words but had steeled herself against the possibility Daniel might never speak them. In the weeks since Daniel had left on his retreat, she had immersed herself in the work with Raffaello. At first, to protect herself from dwelling constantly on Daniel's absence and her very real fear that he might decide to remain a priest. But as her involvement in Raffaello's book deepened and her creativity had emerged, she began to imagine her own possibilities—and the potential for a life that might not include Daniel.

She did not answer Daniel's question at first, but squeezed his hand, still holding hers.

"Let me tell you what has happened to me while you've been away," she said. "The work on Raffaello's book—not just the paintings you see here—has given me purpose. I'm not only his assistant, helping him to complete his life's work, but I'm also participating fully in its creation. He's offered me a co-authorship. Because of my perspective—my visions—this book is not going to be a typical archaeological tome, and Raffaello has embraced that. It's not been easy, neither the collaboration with him—as I'm sure you can imagine—nor my own doubts. But I've discovered that with discipline and organization, I can overcome what I feared would define me for the rest of my life.

"I would not have been able to do this if you had not come into my life. That day in Florence, you told me that you believed in the Resurrection. New life. That memory came back to me, as others have in the last two months. Meeting you was the crack in my armor that let the light in.

"I need you to know I'm not the Izzy you left in August. But I am the woman who still loves you. So yes, as soon as the book is finished, I will come to you."

Izzy stood and reached out her hand. "And now, will you come with me?" She led him beyond the beaded curtain to her bed.

Later in the night, she awoke and saw his bare feet sticking out at the end of the bed beyond the edge of the quilt. She slipped down to cover them and then settled herself again within his arms.

EPILOGUE

NOVEMBER 15, 1972

Izzy descended from the Green Line trolley in front of Boston's Museum of Fine Arts and checked her watch as she climbed the steps into the museum. She wasn't late, which was a relief. She hated having to rush, which always put her at risk of stumbling, even with her cane. Inside the lobby she saw the poster announcing the opening of the exhibition. She didn't need a map to find her way to the Etruscan collection because she'd spent several days there already helping to mount the exhibition. Somehow, Raffaello had convinced the Italian government to loan the sarcophagus to the MFA because of the involvement of the Boston University team of archaeologists.

She slipped into the hall ahead of the crowd waiting for the doors to open, flashing the temporary ID the museum had issued her. She assessed the setting one last time, a recreation of the inner room of the tomb, with the sarcophagus in the center and facsimiles of the wall paintings mounted around the perimeter. In backlit alcoves, a few of the museum's own artifacts—urns and funerary jewelry—completed the replicated chamber.

Then she crossed the room to embrace Raffaello, waiting with the rest of the family.

"*Tanti auguri, Nonno.*"

Raffaello beamed. The pacemaker he'd received in January, when he'd finally agreed to the surgery once the book had gone to the publisher, enabled him to enjoy this moment surrounded by his children and grandchildren. After the opening and the reception, he and Izzy would be signing the book in the Museum's bookstore. Izzy herself had unpacked the books, a rush order that arrived only the day before.

Izzy moved to join the families gathered by Raffaello. Not only the Richetellis—Linda and Benno, Maria and her parents, Daniel and his parents with Anne Marie and Robert—but also the Monroes—Mae and Tobias, Naomi, Josiah and Grace with Caleb.

Daniel took her hand and kissed her. "Hi, hon. You managed to get out of Cambridge on time."

Izzy had resumed her graduate work at Harvard. Her co-authorship on the book had not only given her the confidence she could once again do scholarly work, but it had also convinced Harvard she could. She had started classes two months before.

In the year since Daniel had shown up on her cottage doorstep at Portarello, Izzy and Daniel had written to each other nearly every day—she from Italy over the winter as she and Raffaello completed the book, and Daniel from New York. When Izzy received her acceptance letter from Harvard, she returned to Chappaquiddick for the summer and Daniel transferred from the New York Catholic Worker house to the Boston house. In September, bound by the thousands of words that had passed between them, they had begun their new lives together.

The museum director approached Raffaello. "Ready?"

And then he opened the doors.

Acknowledgments

Writing this book has involved many stages, populated by individuals who played important roles in my story's creation.

A Place of Refuge was, first of all, inspired by a place. Tenuta di Spannocchia is a 13th-century agricultural estate in Tuscany where I had the pleasure of staying and absorbing both its beauty and its mission of preserving its history and promoting sustainable living. The magic and healing power of Portarello that I describe in *A Place of Refuge* are based on the real world of Spannocchia, created by the vision and perseverance of Francesca Cinelli and Randall Stratton.

Naming characters in my stories often happens in mysterious ways. More than once, especially in constructing the First Light series, names have come to me in a flash of insight and were later revealed to have powerful connections to actual people. This time, two of the characters in *A Place of Refuge* are intentionally named after actual people. Pam McGrath, the intern who takes

Izzy under her wing when she first arrives at Portarello, and Linda Richetelli-Pepe, Portarello's mistress of all things, are named after women who won the privilege in auctions conducted by the First Church of Christ in Longmeadow (Pam) and the National Organization of Italian-American Women (Linda).

Over the years and the books I've written I've been fortunate to have a circle of support for which I am truly grateful. My enthusiastic sounding boards, Julie Winberg and Brian Murphy, listened and reacted to my musings as I developed the story. Jean Barish generously offered me her house in the mountains as a writing retreat and was an eager audience each evening as I read aloud the words I'd created that day. Daisy Miller, my constant beta reader, asked the hard questions as the story unfolded. Laurie Wall copyedited my words with care and curiosity. Julie Winberg returned to the text with her sharp pencil and sharp eye as proofreader. And Christine Richardson put her wonderful technical and artistic skills to work in designing both the print and ebook interiors. To all of them, I say *Grazie mille*.

Finally, my loving thanks to my husband, whose eye for the beautiful and intriguing once again produced the cover photograph.

ABOUT THE AUTHOR

Linda Cardillo is an award-winning author who writes about the old country and the new, the tangle and embrace of family, and finding courage in the midst of loss. Hailed by *Publishers Weekly* as a "Fresh Face," Linda has built a loyal following with her works of fiction—the novels *Dancing on Sunday Afternoons, Across the Table, The Boat House Café, The Uneven Road, Island Legacy, A Place of Refuge,* and *Love That Moves the Sun*; the novellas *Catriona's Vow, True Harvest,* and *A Daughter's Journey*; the short story collection *Italian Tales (*an Amazon #1

New Release); and the illustrated children's book *The Smallest Christmas Tree*.

She is also co-founder of Bellastoria Press, an independent hybrid publisher partnering with authors to produce, distribute and promote compelling and beautiful stories.

When she isn't writing, Linda loves to cook and is happiest when the twelve chairs around her dining room table are filled with people enjoying her food. She speaks four languages, some better than others. She plays the piano every night—sometimes by herself and sometimes in an improvisational duet with her younger son. She does *The New York Times* Sunday crossword puzzle in ink, a practice she learned from her mother. From her mother she also absorbed a love of opera, especially those of Puccini and Verdi, whose music filled her home when she was a child. She once climbed Mt. Kenya and has very curly hair.

For news and upcoming events, previews of new work, and musings on the writing life, sign up for Linda's newsletter at lindacardillo.com.

Made in United States
North Haven, CT
09 August 2022

22323449R00246